Also by Christian H. Smith

The Black Monkey
Bloody Bloody Bakersfield

BLOODY BAKERSFIELD BOOK 3

NEW SALEM

BLOODY BAKERSFIELD BOOK 3

NEW SALEM

CHRISTIAN H. SMITH

PERMUTED
PRESS

A PERMUTED PRESS BOOK
ISBN: 978-1-68261-696-3
ISBN (eBook): 978-1-68261-033-6

Permuted Press, LLC
New York • Nashville
permutedpress.com

Published in the United States of America

TWO DAYS BEFORE
HALLOWEEN

CHAPTER 1

8:05 PM

THE SOUTHERN VILLAS Mobile Home Community was located way down on the dead end of Old Main Street, the entrance tucked away in the deep shade between two ancient maple trees, as if deliberately hidden from sight. Easy enough to miss in the daytime, at night it was nearly undetectable. Even with the myriad dark and tawdry secrets Bakersfield held, the town seemed especially ashamed of this place. Though she had been out here to consult with her client twice before, Michelle Blair-Delany drove right past the entrance once again.

"Damn it," she swore under her breath.

She turned around in the Bakersfield U-Store-It yard that marked the terminus of Old Main, her tires making popping sounds on the gravel lot. Back on the road, her headlights cut through the dust cloud she'd kicked up and found the faded, brush-shrouded sign marking the Southern Villas entrance. "A Nice Place to Live!" the sign promised, with what might have been deliberate irony.

She turned into the park and rolled slowly past several trailers. Most were reasonably well-maintained. The narrow patches of lawn were mowed and free of trash. The trailers themselves were clean, porches and doorways tastefully adorned with multi-colored hanging lanterns or Halloween decorations. Most of the residents here took at least a modicum of pride in their humble dwellings. The same could not be said for the woman who lived in Unit 42. Sandy Aswell's trailer was dirty and dilapidated, large swathes of siding peeling off like diseased skin. The single-wide rested on a weed-choked parcel, the little yard cluttered with trash. Michelle pulled into Sandy's short driveway, behind the girl's rusty Ford Taurus.

Nineteen years old and six months pregnant, Sandy was a dark-haired, almost pretty girl. Slender before the baby, she had gained almost twice as much weight as she should have by this stage. Despite the menus Michelle had drawn up for her, Sandy's diet consisted mostly of fast food and sweets, high-sodium snacks and microwave pizza. It was frustrating. Sandy didn't listen to any of Michelle's advice. Michelle would have even let the poor diet slide if Sandy would have, at least, quit smoking, but she refused even to cut back on her pack-a-day habit.

The evening air had a cold nip to it when Michelle stepped out of her car, a whiff of Halloween's breath. Scents of wood smoke and decaying leaves, of distant rotting apples and candle-scorched pumpkin, struck Michelle with dreadful pangs of memory. Each season in Bakersfield carried its own weight of bitter associations, but late October was by far the worst. This was the season of the Snowman's rising, and of the death of Michelle's childhood friend Jess. Still, Michelle inhaled deeply of the redolent night, bracing herself in anticipation of the trailer's interior.

She knocked on the rusty screen door and heard a pained cry of, "It ain't locked!" from inside. Taking two final breaths of fresh air, Michelle opened the door and stepped into an atmosphere thick with the pungent, double-barreled assault of feline waste and unaired cigarettes. At Sandy's place, the litter box and the ashtrays were always overflowing.

Sandy's cat Midnight, as pure black as her name, bolted out the door between Michelle's legs. The cat paused on the porch step, flashing her chartreuse eyes back at Michelle as if to say, "You sure you want to be part of this scene?" When Michelle did not immediately follow the creature in her escape, the cat seemed to give a little shrug of indifference. "Your funeral, sister." Then she disappeared into the night.

"God, what took you so long?" Sandy cried as Michelle stepped into the trailer.

Sandy was pacing about her small living room area. The television was on, playing some horror movie at top volume. A teenage kid sat in a movie theater next to a nightmarish man-sized rabbit. Michelle dimly recognized the film, it had been one of her ex-husband Mark's favorites, but she couldn't at the moment recall the title.

"I came as soon as I got your call." Michelle raised her voice to be heard over the television. "Now, what's going on?"

"I told you, I'm havin' contractions!" Sandy clutched her stomach.

"You're not due for another twelve weeks," Michelle said calmly. She spied the TV remote on the cluttered coffee table and used it to turn off the set. "Remember, we talked about Braxton-Hicks contractions?"

"These ain't fuckin' Braxton-Hicks!" Sandy snarled.

"Would you say they're more painful than menstrual cramps?"

"Fuck yeah!"

"Are they coming in regular intervals, or do they seem random?"

"I don't know." Sandy finally seemed to take a breath. She sat down on the ratty couch. "Regular, I guess."

"How far apart are they?"

"I don't have a fuckin' watch!"

"You're going to need to calm down, Sandy." Michelle put her hand on the woman's shoulder. "Are you having any vaginal bleeding?"

"I don't know," Sandy moaned. Her fear made her seem even younger than she was. "I'm afraid to look."

"It's okay," Michelle said. "Let's lie you down. On your left side."

"Am I losing the baby?"

"I don't think so." Michelle kept her voice level. "But you need to lie down and relax. Once you're calm, I'll have a look, okay?"

"Okay."

The girl curled up on her tiny couch, pulling a little throw pillow under her head. Michelle stroked her sweaty brow. Sandy pressed against Michelle's hand like a baby starved for a mother's touch.

When she'd lived in Denver, Michelle had been a Certified Professional Midwife, but her Colorado certification was not recognized in Illinois. Attending a home birth as a midwife without a doctor present was actually a felony in this state. So, instead, Michelle had been advertising her services as a private pregnancy coach. Her ads had been up on Craigslist and a few other sites for several months now, but so far Sandy was her only client. She was a challenge, to say the least.

Michelle had at first wondered why Sandy had even sought out her services, when she refused to heed Michelle's advice on her diet or the cigarettes or anything else. After two visits and several long phone conversations, though, it had become clear. The girl was lonely. She'd declined to name the baby's father. She was too far along to have conceived, as several young women in town had, during the Sickness, but in any case, the father was not in the picture. She'd mentioned to Michelle that her parents had died when she was young. She had a sister somewhere, but Michelle gathered they were estranged. Sandy was unemployed, so she didn't even have any casual work acquaintances. Michelle might have been the extent of Sandy's support network. Her role so far had consisted of listening to Sandy vent complaints.

Though she worried about the effects of Sandy's lifestyle choices on both mother and baby, Michelle contented herself with fulfilling her role as caregiver as defined by her client. She listened, gave the girl an open ear, and made gentle nudging suggestions that she hoped had at least some positive effect. Sandy paid her without hesitation for the service, four hundred dollars so far. For some reason, she kept her cash in a mason jar in her freezer.

It was good to be working again. Those cold bills pressed into Michelle's hand had paid for most of Ben's school supplies this year. After more than a year of living on Lana's teaching paychecks and Mark's dutiful but erratic child support payments, she was happy to be contributing financially. But Michelle couldn't help wondering where Sandy's freezer money came from. An inheritance from her dead parents, perhaps, or maybe some kind of financial arrangement with the otherwise absent father. It wasn't Michelle's place to ask.

"Oh shit, here comes another one!" Sandy gasped, grabbing her stomach.

She let out an anguished cry. Michelle took her hand. Sandy squeezed back, hard enough to be painful. At this contact, Michelle got her first flash that something was very wrong.

"Ah Jesus, no," the girl moaned. She sat up suddenly, looking down between her legs. A damp stain spread, soaking through her jeans.

There was a slight but distinctive smell. Clean and earthy, like wet straw beneath the sharp yellow notes of dead cigarettes and cat pee. Michelle remembered the scent clearly from her own labor with Ben. It was the smell of amniotic fluid.

Sandy's water had broken.

CHAPTER 2

8:14 PM

"WHEN'S THE LAST time you went on a date?" Ellie Tarwater asked, stabbing her sharp brown eyes across the table at Mark. She had a knack, by tone or posture or by some combination of the two, of making everything she said come out weirdly ambiguous. Mark could not tell if this question had been delivered with teasing flirtation or outright challenge. Maybe even innocent curiosity, though there didn't seem to be anything innocent about Ellie Tarwater.

Regardless of its intent, he gave the question serious thought, and was honestly surprised at his answer. "Never, I guess."

"You've never been on a date." Again, this could have been either playful or hostile. It was impossible to get a read on this woman.

"My ex, Missy, and I got together when we were in high school. Married right after graduation. We never really, you know, *dated* dated. We just..." Mark trailed off. He possessed an appalling lack of instinct for this, but he knew at least that starting to talk about Missy would not be a good idea. "Why? Am I doing that badly?"

"You're doing all right." Ellie nodded, sipped her rum and tonic. "I can tell you're a little nervous, though."

"Maybe a little," Mark allowed, though he would have characterized it more as disorientation than nervousness. He hadn't even been entirely sure this was a date until Ellie had declared it so.

She was a co-worker. They were both "interpreters" at Lincoln's New Salem State Historic Site, a meticulously reconstructed village where Abraham Lincoln had lived as a young man. Mark usually worked in the blacksmithing shop, hammering red-hot metal while tourists took his picture. He found this oddly fulfilling. With the obvious exception of the all-too brief period of his life when he'd been able to write full-time, it was the best job he'd ever held.

Ellie's job at New Salem was to give live butter churning demonstrations. Mark had noticed her, of course. Any woman who could churn her own butter was automatically interesting. Mark found her recreation to be unconvincing on some essential level, though. Even in her period costume—a drab-colored wool dress with apron and bonnet—some indefinably modern quality always shone through with her.

He found her attractive, if a bit aloof, but hadn't considered asking her out to be an option. He was so inexperienced at this that he wasn't sure asking a co-worker on a date was even something that was *done* anymore. And even if it was, Ellie had not shown any particular interest in him until earlier that afternoon, when she'd approached him out of the blue and said: "You want to meet me for drinks tonight."

There are people who make statements into questions by lifting their voice at the end, but here Ellie had made what sounded like it should have been a question into a statement of fact. And again, her tone was frighteningly ambiguous. She might have been stating that Mark wanted to meet her for drinks to discuss a dire medical diagnosis as likely as she was asking him out.

"It's okay," she said now. Her voice was a low, undeniably sexy, rasp. "I'm a little nervous, too. I don't usually go out with older guys."

"Older?" Mark said. He hadn't ever considered himself such. "Am I?"

"Well, yeah," Ellie said. "How old are you?"

"Thirty-one."

"Jesus." Ellie laughed and gulped down the rest of her drink. "Yeah, see, I've never gone out with anybody in their thirties before."

"I'm not *in* my thirties," Mark protested. "I'm *thirty-one*. I won't be *in* them for at least a couple years. Why, how old are you?"

"Twenty-two."

"That's about how old I feel," Mark said. "I still think I'm getting away with something when I order a drink without getting carded."

"Older guys always say stuff like that when they're trying to get a younger girl into bed."

"I'm not really trying to…"

"Anyway, it's not your age, necessarily," Ellie went on. "You're divorced, with a kid. That automatically makes you more mature."

Now it was Mark's turn to laugh and take a drink. "I wish."

"You know what I mean."

Ellie fingered the lime wedge from her depleted glass and sucked it between her lips, eyeing Mark with what might have been cautious desire or a predator's wariness. He'd given up on any hope of interpreting her looks.

Despite, or more likely because of, her protective layer of challenge, Mark was finding her more interesting by the moment. Ellie had an off-kilter beauty. Dark eyes, black hair and a slightly dusky complexion. Her prominent nose and eyebrows hinted at an exotic but unspecified ethnic heritage, like she had a measure of Gypsy blood running in her veins. Plus, there was the matter of how she was dressed.

Ellie wore a short black leather skirt over sheer black stockings, and a long-sleeved maroon top with a wide-open collar, cropped to bare her midriff. A black choker necklace needlessly drew attention to her lovely throat and all the flesh surrounding it. But, radiating further mixed signals, Ellie seemed to wear her revealing outfit grudgingly, as if someone had forced her to put it on. She had no make-up on and her hair was tousled, like she'd refused to brush it as a form of protest. Her near-constant eye contact issued an unspoken challenge: *Yeah, look at my body. I fuckin' dare ya.* So far Mark hadn't chanced more than a few peripheral glances. These had been undeniably rewarding.

Her scent was odd and intriguing, too. She had a slight herbal smell to her, as if instead of perfume or deodorant, she'd rubbed her skin with fresh mint or basil or some unidentifiable mix of old world spices. It was weirdly alluring.

Putting everything together, Mark found the entire Ellie Tarwater package baffling and captivating in equal proportions.

"So you said your wife left you for another woman?" Ellie said, chewing the pulp from her lime.

"Yeah."

"Were you so bad in bed you completely turned her off men?"

The levity of this statement, if that's what was intended, was lost in the bluntness of its delivery. Only after the words were well out of her mouth did Ellie attempt to temper their apparent hostility with a burst of nervous laughter.

"Ha-ha." Mark laughed along with her, though he also winced a little. "I hope not. It's just, you know how some people say gender doesn't matter as much as who a person is inside?"

"Yeah, I think that's bullshit, though."

"Most of the time, I'd agree with you. But I really think that's how Missy sees things."

"You're still in love with her, aren't you?"

"What? No. Why would you…"

"It's all right," Ellie said, her voice softening a little for the first time. "I'm so bad in bed, the last *two* guys I dated turned gay after we broke up."

"Really?"

"Yeah. So we're probably pretty well matched that way. Either that, or it'll be so bad, we'll turn each other gay." She lifted the glass to her lips and seemed genuinely angry to only taste melted ice.

"Bartender!" she barked. "Two more."

She glanced down at Mark's glass, still half full.

"You're going to have to a better job keeping up," she said. "At this rate, you'll never get drunk enough to let me take you home."

CHAPTER 3

8:19 PM

THE AIR IN the trailer was nearly unbreathable. Hot and thick and stifling, the oxygen choked out by the smells of cat and cigarette waste and the sharp, alarming scent coming off Sandy herself. Pungent terror-sweat and the rotten, meaty smell of vaginal blood and bacteria.

"...un...wha...ur...gen..."

The 911 dispatcher's voice came through Michelle's phone in staccato bursts, buried under an underwater sound of cascading static. The connection was bad. Michelle had experienced this before, on previous visits. The trailer park was a pit of spotty coverage, as if even the cell signal didn't want to be caught down here at night.

Michelle shouted the salient details, hoping at least some of it was getting through. "Southern Villas trailer park, Bakersfield. Unit forty-two. A woman is going into premature labor. Send an ambulance, please. Quickly." She tried to simultaneously convey the urgency of the situation to the operator while at the same time keeping her voice calm and even for Sandy's benefit.

"...ay...dru...ease...peat..." came the reply.

Michelle repeated her plea verbatim and then hung up. Either it had gotten through or it hadn't. Optimistically, best case scenario, the operator had either received her message or had at least been able to trace the signal, and help was on the way. Even if this was the case, though, the nearest ambulance service was in Lincoln, twenty minutes away. She was afraid they didn't have twenty minutes.

Michelle knew with every intuitive fiber of her being that this was going to end badly. The terror in Sandy's pained cries and the dark tinge to the fluid seeping from between her legs were alarming enough, but Michelle detected a deeper current of dread. A nightmare feeling. Still, she couldn't let the sense—the *knowledge*—of impending doom drag her under. Her place here was to minimize the disaster, to pull this poor girl through to the least terrible possible outcome. She had to be strong.

Michelle looked away and allowed herself a single moment to express her own panic with a silent scream. When she turned back to Sandy, she'd composed herself with a cool, professional poker face.

"Okay," she said with gentle good humor. "Let's have a look under that hood."

While Sandy attempted to get her jeans off, Michelle reached over and tried to open the tiny sliding glass window above the couch. The damn thing wouldn't budge. She so desperately longed for the cool, fresh night air outside that for one second she seriously considered breaking the glass.

"Shit," she cried.

"I'm so sorry," Sandy said. "That window's broke."

"That's okay." Michelle turned with regret from the jammed window and forced herself to speak in a calm voice again. "Do you need help getting those off?"

"They're too tight."

"Here, I'll help."

Sandy had somehow managed to cram her pregnant ass into her pre-pregnancy jeans. Peeling them off her was a real struggle. Sandy arched her back and pushed at the waistband while Michelle tugged at the pants legs. Their joint effort had an almost comical intimacy to it. To anyone observing, they would have looked like awkward teenage lovers frantic to get naked. The same association must have occurred to Sandy, because she let out an incongruous giggle.

Finally, the jeans slid from Sandy's hips with a slight ripping of the strained seams. Michelle stripped them from her legs.

As she tossed the jeans to the floor, Michelle saw a glint of yellow-green light from outside the jammed window. Midnight was perched upon the sill, peering through the dusty pane with glowing eyes. The cat observed her mistress's tribulations with a clinical detachment.

Michelle reached into her purse and pulled out a plastic bag containing a pair of sterile, non-latex gloves and a small tube of lubricating jelly. "I want to do a vaginal exam, to see if your cervix is dilated. Is that all right?"

"Will it hurt?"

"Some women find it uncomfortable, but I'll be as gentle as I can."

"Okay." Sandy nodded, her voice tight. "Go ahead."

Michelle strapped on the gloves. She squirted the lube on her palms and then rubbed her hands together so the jelly wouldn't be so cold.

A loud mewling came from the window. Outside, the cat made an urgent cry that sounded to Michelle's ears like a warning.

"Don't do it, sister," the cat seemed to be saying. "In fact, get your ass out of there while you still can."

Ignoring the pleading yowl, Michelle pressed her left hand upon Sandy's hairless pelvis and slid her right hand into the canal. Sandy gasped and tightened a little at the incursion, but then relaxed and opened herself up. Michelle felt for the cervical opening and was surprised to find something hard. She probed it with her finger. Whatever it was, it was razor-sharp. It cut her finger.

"Ow!" Michelle pulled her hand out. Tearing the glove off, she looked down at the little bead of blood pooling up on her index finger. Again, she was reminded of a rose. It felt like she'd pricked her finger on a thorn.

CHAPTER 4

8:24 PM

Mark and Ellie laughed together, hard. Halfway through his second drink, he was starting to relax. Maybe a little too much. He was sharing something with her that he perhaps would not have if his tongue had not been loosened by alcohol. Ironically, the story he was telling was about something else he shouldn't have said while drunk.

"So the three of us were hanging out," he said. "We finished the second bottle of wine around the time Ben went to bed."

"You do know that's really messed up, right?" Ellie interjected. "Being so chummy with your ex?"

"Well, ever since the Sickness… You heard about the Sickness, right?"

"Uh, yeah. Bloody fucking Bakersfield. How can anybody stand to live there?"

"That," Mark took another drink, "is a *great* question. Anyway, that was an intense couple of days for the three of us. We got kind of close afterwards."

"Don't you get jealous of this Lana chick?"

"Here's the thing about that. She's *way* cooler than I am."

"That's hard to imagine," Ellie laughed.

"Seriously," Mark said. "She's beautiful, first of all. Stunning. Super smart, too. Kind, generous, an all-around amazing human being. Plus, she's got her shit together in ways I never will. So I don't blame Missy for hooking up with her. *I* would have left me for her."

Ellie laughed even harder at that.

"So, anyway. We're all pretty buzzed and then they lay it on me. They say they've been talking about it for a while, but they've finally decided the time was right. They wanted to get Lana pregnant, to give Ben a little brother or sister."

"Oh boy."

"Yeah. So after all the congratulations and everything, I offer, graciously I thought, to be the, you know, donor."

"You didn't," Ellie gasped.

"Oh, I did. Honestly, I thought that was the whole reason they'd invited me over, so they could ask me that. But there was just dead silence. They wouldn't even look me in the eye. God, it was awkward."

"I bet." Ellie signaled the bartender again.

"So, digging my grave even deeper, I start reeling off all the reasons why this is such a good idea. You know, this would make the kid genetically Ben's half-sibling and all the money they'd save by not having to go through a service. The whole time I'm pleading this hopeless case, they have these horror-stricken expressions, like 'oh my God, won't this idiot shut up?' For some reason, though, I don't get the hint. I keep going until I'm practically *begging* them to take my sperm."

Ellie laughed hard, leaning her head against Mark's arm for one thrilling second.

"Wait, wait," she said. "Just to be clear. Did you really think you were going to have sex with Lana?"

"No," Mark said. "God, no. That would be...no. I assumed it would be a turkey baster kind of procedure."

"Turkey baster?"

"You know..." Mark performed an elaborate pantomime, the universally recognized series of signs for masturbating into a cup and implanting the resultant seed with a baster. Ellie was nearly in hysterics by the time he was done.

"So after my little spiel, they patiently explain to me how awkward that would be for everyone concerned, and that they've already made arrangements for a donor."

"How does that work? I've always wondered."

"They found this online service that hooks up gorgeous, brilliant gay men with lesbians who want to conceive. I saw a picture of the guy. He looks like Denzel Washington's younger, hotter brother. And he's got a PhD in physics. No way my pathetic albino tadpoles could compete with that."

"So did she end up getting pregnant?"

"Yeah. She's six weeks along, due next June."

"Wow." The bartender set down two fresh drinks and Ellie took a grateful slug. "I never want to get pregnant. All the horrible, gross things it does to your body, and then you've got this *thing* growing inside you." She gave a horrified shudder. "I don't think I could be a lesbian, either. In fact, a pregnant lesbian is the last thing I'd want to be."

"Really." Mark took a sip of his own drink.

"What does that mean?" Ellie said, sharply.

"What does what mean?"

"Saying 'really,' with that look on your face."

"Look?" Mark was baffled by the sharp turn. He'd thought it had been going well there for at least a couple minutes.

"Sorry." Ellie grimaced. "I know, that was the complete wrong thing to say. Guys don't want to hear on a first date that a girl never wants to get pregnant. They take it as a rejection. But then if a girl on a first date said she *did* want to get pregnant, she'd come off as a clinging psychopath. Jesus, I can't win with you."

"I didn't even..."

"And you've obviously got a thing for bisexual chicks, so you don't want to hear that I'm not into girls, either. I mean, why is that such a big deal for men?"

"It's not..."

"Okay, so I slept with my music professor. Once. But it was really awkward because she looked a lot like my dead mother and there were some complications because I was dating her son and I ended up dropping out of school a week later and it was an all-around horrible experience and I don't want to fucking talk about it, okay?"

"That's...fine."

Ellie's face, twisted with anger, relaxed all at once and then she laughed again. Mark just looked at her. He had no idea how he was supposed to react here.

"I'm *so* sorry." She shook her head. "God, I'm a psycho. I mean, really. I need treatment. Forget I said that stuff, okay? The jury will please disregard statements pertaining to pregnancy and past same-sex experiences." She drained her drink again. "You're looking at me like you're scared of me now. You better say something normal or I'm just going to go home."

"So..." Mark grasped. "You studied music?"

Ellie looked at him with terrifying blankness for a few seconds, and then laughed like that was the funniest thing she'd ever heard in her life.

CHAPTER 5

8:34 PM

T HE TURNOUT FOR the open forum water quality meeting of the Village Board of Trustees was huge, as these things went. More than a hundred people had crammed into the meeting hall at the municipal building. All the folding chairs were full. People were sitting on the floor in the aisles and standing in the back of the hall.

The crowd had joined in an enthusiastic reading of the Pledge of Allegiance, standing as one with their hands over their hearts, facing the flag in the corner of the room. But after that, they grew impatient with the roll call and the reading of the agenda. All the preliminary procedural business seemed to them like unnecessary stalling on the part of the board.

The close walls echoed with the agitated babble of the crowd. There was much rustling of paper, people poring with disbelief bordering on outrage at the just-released water quality report they'd picked up from the stacks on the card table out in the hall. The frankly unbelievable report was employed as a fan by several of the attendees, as the mass of bodies in the hall had raised the temperature to a near-stifling level.

Ten men and women sat behind the long, faux-mahogany table in the front of the room. Mayor Buck Sager occupied the center chair which, by his specific proclamation, sat no less than six inches higher than the surrounding seats. On either side of him were the seven members of the board of trustees, chaired by Diana Clayton and attended by Village Clerk Daniel Holder, who was recording the proceedings on his iPad for later transcription. The guest speaker chairs on the far ends of the table were taken tonight by Wayne Wilson, a water inspector from the state pollution control board, and Gillian Hudson, the community relations director for Malovo Agricultural Development.

The restless murmuring had risen steadily and now the roar was deafening. Mayor Sager, who had brought his own gavel from home, banged it repeatedly on the hardwood block.

"Order!" he cried. "God damn it, I'll have some order!"

The wooden concussions finally cut through the crowd noise. The people turned their heads to the front of the room.

"Thank you, Mr. Mayor," Ms. Clayton said, grabbing the mayor's sleeve to arrest his banging, which he could keep up for several minutes if left unchecked. "Moving along, the next section is public comment. Is there any public comment tonight?"

The response was thunderous, a few dozen people leaping to their feet at once, raising their hands and shouting.

"One at a time, damn it!" The mayor pounded his gavel furiously. "I'll clear this room!"

Diana Clayton scanned the room with dismay, looking at the faces of the citizens demanding to be heard. She debated whether it was best to start with the crazy ones, to get them out of the way, or to begin with the ones who were borderline rational, in the hope that the frothing-at-the-mouth types would cool off a bit if they were made to wait.

"The chair recognizes Mr. Bill Potter," she finally said. The retired schoolteacher was an ornery old crank, but he was at least an articulate one.

Several other clamoring residents re-took their seats. Bill Potter received an encouraging hand-squeeze and a smile from his ex-wife Mara (with whom he was rumored to be rekindling a relationship following her separation from Sheriff Bates). He stepped halfway up the aisle, the rolled-up water report clenched in one fist as if he was preparing to swat a cockroach with it. In his other hand, he carried a briefcase. Potter wore a suit and tie tonight, in contrast to the sweatshirt and jeans he could usually be seen around town in, and his white hair was neatly combed, for once. Diana had a sinking feeling, as if Potter was about to announce he would be running for her seat.

"Thank you, chairwoman," Potter said. He half-turned, addressing the crowd as much as he was the board. "I just want to say that, like most of my friends and neighbors here in this room, I haven't had a chance to fully review this water report. We only received it tonight, though we've been requesting it for months now. But, based on a cursory glance-through, and with all due respect to Mr. Wilson, who kindly prepared the report, I can only conclude that it's a load of malarkey."

Huge response to that, cheering affirmations of this position, which provoked another volley of gavel-pounding by the esteemed mayor. Diana, her meeting-night headache giving a twinge with every wooden hammer strike, had a brief, vivid fantasy of shoving the thing up the Mayor's backside. Business end first.

"Mr. Potter," she said. "I'll thank you to use polite language, please."

"Respectfully, Madame Chairwoman, 'malarkey' *is* the polite term for my opinion of this report." He started flipping through the pages. "See, we have analysis here of the levels of microbial and inorganic contaminants. Pesticides and herbicides. Organic chemicals and radioactive contaminants. All of which, if I'm reading this right, are well below the parts per million that would make the water undrinkable. But do you really expect us to believe this report over our own eyes and noses? Have you *seen* the water? It has a strange, reddish-greenish color I've never even seen before, like something out of that Lovecraft story. It leaves stains on the porcelain you can't get out no matter how hard you scrub. And it smells downright *weird*."

There was a hum of murmuring assent behind Potter, though Diana suspected the Lovecraft reference had been lost on most of them. He nodded to acknowledge it.

"But the true testament to how bad the water is has to be this," he said. "My *dog* won't drink it. Now, a dog is not an animal known to be discriminating about his water. Given a choice between a pristine font from the purest spring and a slightly mucky toilet bowl, the dog will go for the commode every time. And yet when I try to fill Ramone's water dish from the tap, he gives me this look like I've got to be kidding."

The crowd gave him a good laugh. Potter had them eating out of his hands.

"So I've been buying our drinking water by the gallon from the Shop 'n Save, like most folks in town. Which is all fine and good, except I still have to use the faucet water to shower in and to do my laundry. Now I'll say something out loud that most people are politely trying to ignore. Because we're all packed in here close together, though, it's pretty obvious. Take a deep breath. We *stink*, folks. You can smell this stuff, on our skin and on our clothes. The odor is kind of musty, kind of plastic-y, though neither of those words quite describe it. It's definitely a chemical smell, like nothing that exists in God's natural order. And there's plenty of folks who haven't been taking baths as much as they used to, because they'd rather smell like a human being than something out of a mad scientist's laboratory. No judgment there, I can't say I blame them, but again it gets pretty obvious whenever we gather together. I can tell you, they're really laying into the incense over at St. Joseph's Church."

"Thank you, Mr. Potter," Diana said. "Let's give someone else a chance to—"

"Hold on, Ms. Chairwoman," Potter said. "According to your by-laws, which make for thrilling bedtime reading by the way, every citizen is entitled to up to five minutes of floor time during the public comment section of the meeting. I've been keeping my eye on the clock behind you there, so I know I've got about another two minutes left. I'd like to use that time to address the pachyderm in our presence."

"I'm sorry, the what now?" Diana had limited tolerance for rhetorical flourishes.

"I'm willing, perhaps, to accept that our recent problems with the water are unrelated to the sleepwalking sickness that struck our town back in May, though that seems like a mighty steep coincidence. But one thing that can't be denied is that there are a lot of women in town with five month bellies as a *direct* result of that weekend's festivities. Again, no judgment. Folks can't be blamed for any hanky-panky they got up to while they were dreaming on their feet. But can you tell me with any certainty that this...liquid you insist on calling safe drinking water has nothing to do with the fact that I personally know of three women right here in town who've suffered miscarriages just in the past few months?"

The crowd's murmuring again reached the level that triggered the mayor's gavel-banging.

"Well, Mr. Potter," Ms. Clayton said, "to answer that question, I'll defer to the expert we've invited to join us tonight. This is Mr. Wayne Wilson, from the state pollution control board. He authored this report.

Mr. Wilson, could there be a link between our water issues and these miscarriages?"

Wayne Wilson was a balding, bespectacled man who looked every bit the part of a bureaucratic scientist. Driving home the point of his outsider status, he was the only black person in the room.

"Well, ah," he said, consulting his notes. "There is some evidence that substances present in municipal drinking water can contribute to elevated miscarriage rates within the serviced community. Heavy metals, such as lead or mercury or cadmium, have been linked. This is an agricultural area, so pesticide run-off is always a concern. Also, I've read several studies recently that suggest trihalomethanes, which are by-products of using chlorine for water purification, may be related to higher incidents of miscarriage. But I've tested for all those substances, and they're all well below safe levels. Now, you've attested to some anecdotal evidence, but I've read estimates that up to ten to twenty percent of all pregnancies end in miscarriage. It could be that what you're reporting is perfectly normal, statistically speaking."

Gasps of outrage filled the room at that. Behind his glasses, Mr. Wilson's eyes darted about, as if calculating escape routes.

Potter, who had not relinquished the floor despite his five minutes having clearly expired, nodded thoughtfully. "Could be," he agreed. "Could be. But tell me this, Mr. Wilson. I'm not doubting that your testing was comprehensive, but you couldn't possibly have tested for *everything*, right? I mean to say, you've tested for every substance *commonly* found in drinking water. But what if this is something new, some chemical or something unique to this area, which you wouldn't even think to test for?"

"Obviously, I can't test for *every* possible contaminating substance," Wilson said, "but I assure you that—"

The rest of his words were lost in the roar of the crowd.

"Thank you, Mr. Potter," Diana Clayton said, raising her voice to be heard over the tumult and the mayor's incessant gavel. Her mouth watered at the thought of the tube of Tylenol in her purse. "Now will you please yield the floor and let someone else—"

"One more thing," Potter said.

"Mr. Potter, your five minutes are—"

"I know, I know. Please bear with me for one more moment. I've brought something to share." He pulled a clear plastic bottle filled with cloudy-looking water from his briefcase. "I filled this from my tap right before leaving for this meeting. Now if anyone sitting up there who seriously claims this water is safe to drink will take one good swig from this bottle, I will sit down and shut my mouth. I promise you won't hear another peep from me all night. Are you thirsty at all, Ms. Chairwoman?"

Diana looked at the sludgy fluid with barely concealed horror. "Mr. Potter, this is outrageous. Please sit down."

"How about you, Mr. Wilson? Care to back up your research with a personal demonstration? No? How about you, Mr. Mayor?"

"I'll drink it."

Every head in the room craned towards Gillian Hudson, the Malovo spokesperson.

"Ms. Hudson, you don't need to do this," Diana said.

"No, it's fine," said Gillian. "If it gets this meeting moving forward. I'd like to get home at some point tonight. We at Malovo conducted our own independent assessment of the water. Our findings back up Mr. Wilson's one hundred percent. The water is perfectly safe."

She reached out her hand. Bill Potter, looking a bit uncertain now, stepped forward and handed her the water. Gillian uncapped the bottle and took several hearty gulps, downing about half the liquid inside without flinching. Her microphone picked up and amplified her satisfied "Ahhh," for all to hear.

CHAPTER 6

8:40 PM

Something woke Ben Davies up. A sound. For a few disoriented moments in the dark, he tried to reason out if he'd really heard the sound or only dreamed it. At first, he wasn't even sure which of his bedrooms he'd awoken into. Then he made out the faintly glowing star stickers on the ceiling and knew he was in his room at Mom and Lana's house. His bedroom at his dad's house had a *Star Wars* poster on the ceiling.

Ben couldn't quite remember what he'd been dreaming. He seemed to remember a campfire in the woods, but the fire had been a strange, greenish color, which to his fading memory reminded him of the color of the star stickers. There'd been something about his mother, too. Something bad and scary happening to his mom. Strange that what had been so urgent behind his eyelids only a moment before should dissolve so quickly when exposed to the bedroom air.

Ben had just about concluded the sound had been part of the forgotten dream and was on the verge of drifting back out, when he heard it again. A scratching at his window.

He sat up. Listened. Tried to puzzle out the riddle presented by the digits of his alarm clock. The house had the dark silence of the dead middle of the night and Ben felt like he'd been asleep for hours. If the clock was to be believed, he'd only gone to bed a little more than half an hour ago.

The scratching came again, followed by a whisper so quiet he couldn't be sure he wasn't imagining it.

"Let me in."

"Who's there?" he called out. Had he been fully awake, Ben might have been alarmed. But in this dreamy in-between state, whispering at his window was not so extraordinary.

"*A vampire*," the voice whispered. If this had been meant to frighten him, the girlish giggling following this statement ruined the effect.

"Emily?" Ben said.

He looked out the window and saw his friend Emily Grady's laughing face staring in at him through the glass. The thin moonlight gleamed blue on her skin; her long brown hair looked black in the night. Ben's bedroom was on the second floor, and Emily must have climbed up onto the ledge overhanging the porch to get to his window. She was like a monkey.

Ben slid out of bed and crossed the room. He strained to pull the old window open, well aware of how loudly the swollen wood groaned as it slid up the frame. Surely Lana would hear.

"What are you doing here?" he whispered to his friend.

Emily swooped into his room with a whoosh of cold air, smooth as a night owl.

"Nice PJs," she said.

Ben's Transformers pajamas suddenly seemed embarrassingly childish.

"Why are you in bed so early?" she asked. "Did you forget tomorrow's Sunday? But it's really like Saturday because we have Monday off too. Three-day weekend!"

Monday was a teachers' in-service day. Whatever that was, it coincided with Halloween this year, a rare concurrence that accidentally gave that sacred festival the holiday status Ben had always thought it deserved.

"I was tired," Ben said defensively.

"Well, get dressed. There's something I want to show you."

"I'm not supposed to leave the house at night."

"That's why it's called *sneaking out*, duh," she said. "Oh, and bring your ghost camera."

"Why?" Ben said, his apprehension growing. Before the Sickness, he'd liked doing "field research" with the Digital Paranormal Investigation Kit his father had given him for Christmas. But that was before he'd seen what a *real* haunted house was like. The ecto-spectrum camera had once contained several pictures taken at the Hansard farmhouse outside of town, but Ben's father had deleted them all. Since that day, ghostly investigations had lost their innocent thrill.

"Don't worry," Emily said. "We're not going to a spooky house or a graveyard or anything like that."

"What then?"

"A party," Emily said.

"Party?"

"Yeah. I was at Casey's General with my mom before and I overheard these high school girls talking about a party they were going to out in the woods tonight."

"So what?" Ben yawned.

"So," Emily said. "By some of the things they were saying, I think it's going to be a *monkey* party."

"Really?" Ben only knew a little bit about the monkey the kids were supposed to bury on Halloween, based on a few cryptic things his father had said on the subject. Emily, though, was obsessed with the monkey.

"That's why I want you to bring your camera," she said. "In case anything weird happens, I want to get a picture of it."

"I'll let you borrow it," Ben said. "But I don't think I should go out."

"You're going to make me go out there all by myself?" she challenged. "Come on, you know you can't say no to me. We're wasting time arguing about it."

She did have a point there. Ben had never been able to resist Emily's demands for long.

"I don't want to get in trouble," he protested lamely.

"So don't get caught," she said, presenting this as a perfectly reasonable solution.

Ben thought about it. His mom was out, talking to the pregnant lady she was helping, but Lana was asleep downstairs. She slept a lot, now that she was pregnant herself, and she was almost impossible to wake up. So getting out wouldn't be a problem. The only way he could get caught was if Mom checked in on his bedroom when she got home. He didn't think she really did that anymore, though, not since he was a little kid. Of course, he would have to sneak back in later, but Ben pushed this consideration aside for the moment.

"Anyway," Emily prodded. "When you're a grown-up, what are you going to remember? The wild night of adventure you had, or how you got grounded the next day?"

"Okay," Ben said. "*Fine.*"

Emily's face lit up. "Awesome. Get dressed."

Unsure of what a girl seeing him in his underwear might do to him at this stage in his development, Ben pulled his clothes on over his pajamas. He slipped on shoes and his jacket and grabbed his ghost-hunting kit. They could have snuck downstairs and out the front door, but Ben followed Emily out the way she came in. It seemed adventures of this sort always began with children flying out their bedroom windows at night.

CHAPTER 7

8:48 PM

"MOTHERFUCKIN' JESUS SHIT-*FUCKER!*" Sandy released a burst of blasphemy that might have been comical if not for its depth of anguish and terror.

Where the hell is that ambulance? Michelle thought for the thousandth time. The atmosphere in the trailer was hot with a red, musky reek like an orgy in a butcher's shop. To keep her own anguish and terror in check, Michelle forced herself to take measured, even breaths of the poisonous air. She'd made five increasingly incoherent calls to 911 in the past half hour. The sheer repetition should have been enough to raise some alarms somewhere, even if her appeals had been hopelessly garbled. Not to mention, every one of Sandy's neighbors had probably made calls of their own by now. Based on the screams alone, it must have sounded like someone was being murdered in here.

Michelle had also sent a few frantic text messages to Lana, apprising her of the situation and telling her to call 911 as well. She had no idea if the texts were going out, or if Lana was even awake to receive them. The main symptom of Lana's early pregnancy seemed to be constant exhaustion. In her desperation, Michelle had even sent a few texts to Mark, but her ex wasn't responding, either.

"God, help me," Sandy begged. Whether this cry was addressed towards Michelle or literally towards the Almighty was moot at this point. Both seemed equally helpless to assist this poor girl.

Sandy turned and vomited again, most of it slopping into the plastic iced tea pitcher Michelle had set beside the couch for this express purpose. The fresh acid bile scent cut sharply through the other smells in the room, and almost triggered Michelle to throw up as well. To force the nausea back, she closed her eyes and dug her fingernails into her palm.

The uncleanliness bothered her almost more than anything else. Sandy's housekeeping could be politely described as "lax." Not so politely, the woman lived in filth. The conditions in the trailer were dangerously unsanitary. Coats of dust and cat hair painted every surface in the room, bonded with a yellow nicotine resin. Litterbox waste was scattered across the kitchen floor. The bathroom was appalling. Even the supposedly clean towels Michelle had taken from the tiny linen closet had a strong musty smell. That, at least, could be blamed on the town's water problems. For weeks, the water in Bakersfield had been dark and cloudy and strange-smelling. It did not quench, it did not cool and it did not cleanse. Clean water was the most essential thing Michelle needed here, and she did not even have that.

"It's okay, Sandy," Michelle said. This was either a meaningless reassurance or an outright lie. The words were unconvincing even to her own ear.

Her finger still stung where it had been pricked. Or bitten. She thought of the old folk tales about vagina dentata. Had Michelle felt a sharp tooth in there? The idea was absurd, ridiculous. Those superstitious tales had been created by men with infantile fears of female sexuality, or else by wise old women in order to dissuade those same men from rape. They had zero basis in medical reality.

Something *had* bitten her, though. What if it had been the fetus itself? What if something monstrous was about to be born? Michelle was stricken with the terrible sense that whatever was coming through possessed a hideous awareness. A malevolent being, delighted by the destruction wrought by its passage.

Michelle recalled a vivid dream she'd had when she was pregnant with Ben, in which she'd given birth to a litter of kittens. All pregnant mothers, she supposed, fostered fears that something inhuman was growing inside them. But she was not the terrified mother here. Her mind was not clouded by pain or hormonal turbulence. She was a professional caregiver. She had to remain rational. Sandy was experiencing a late-term miscarriage. That was all. If the baby, the human baby, was not already dead, it would not live long outside Sandy's body without specialized medical treatment. The ambulance may or may not be arriving soon. Michelle's duty here, her function, was to see the mother through this nightmare.

"It's tearing me up!" Sandy cried from the depths. "Get it out of me!"

"You're going to be all right," Michelle lied. A blatant lie now. The tears pouring down her face told the truth. She wept with outrage that Sandy's body was, in the midst of this trial, no longer her own. The maternal body in this state was dehumanized, an abject vessel. A mere channel for delivering life into this world from some other, unknown place. Sandy was just a conduit now, and if the conduit was destroyed by what it conveyed, then this was deemed by the cold, indifferent universe to be an acceptable sacrifice.

The head was on the verge of crowning. Sandy was stretched past all natural bounds. Her body looked like it was about to tear apart, to reveal its innermost depths. She looked like she was about to be turned inside out.

Michelle had witnessed birth many times before. She'd attended eight home births as an apprentice and assistant to her mentor Kika Beaumont, the legendary pillar of the Denver midwife community. Later, starting to establish her own practice, she had presided over two births as the primary. There had been scary moments, and even a couple of last-ditch emergency runs to the hospital, but the outcomes had all been good for both mother and baby. Her own son's birth had been a hospital delivery, but was drug-free and as natural as possible under those circumstances, with the resultant heights of both pain and ecstatic joy. Whatever role she had played, doula or assistant or witness or delivering mother, Michelle had been left on each of these occasions with the sense that she'd been privy to the miraculous. Without exception, she'd felt a humbled awe at the goddess-like power of feminine creation. Not now, though. Watching Sandy pass this thing into existence, she felt only revulsion and terror.

There was the sound of tearing flesh, of Sandy's shuddering breath, a fresh burst of blood. The woman issued a soul-wrenching moan as the malignant growth descended towards its final expulsion.

"Breathe," Michelle begged. This entreaty was nonsensical, but something had to be said.

She grasped Sandy's sweat-drenched hand. Sandy returned the clasp with weakening desperation and then let out a final cry before merciful unconsciousness overtook her.

The black hole between her legs yawned open, presenting a bulging dome of blood-smeared hair. Two sharp protuberances on the baby's head tore free of her flesh. Michelle had supposed teeth, but her earlier assessment of thorns had been closer to the mark. The baby's crowning head wore two sharp, glistening, perfectly formed horns.

CHAPTER 8

8:57 PM

IF SHE HADN'T had to pull over to barf her guts out, Alice Kiernan would have driven right past the new shop downtown without even noticing it. The random puking had been happening more and more frequently of late. Low-grade background nausea was a constant in her life. Every so often it crested with a sudden, urgent need to yak. She grabbed one of the plastic grocery bags she kept in her car for such occasions. Pulled over to the curb beside the town square and let loose a mighty hurl. Dad's spaghetti was not quite as appealing in sight, smell, or taste thus recycled.

Alice knew she probably shouldn't even be driving anymore. The unpredictability of the vomit attacks was potentially both messy and dangerous. More than once she hadn't grabbed the bag in time, and yesterday she'd nearly been rear-ended by a pick-up truck during one of her sudden pull-overs. But being trapped at home with Dad was too depressing. Besides, she loved driving her little red Toyota. Especially at night. As much as she didn't want to admit it, the time was coming all too quickly when she'd never be able to drive again.

Back in May, Alice had, along with almost everybody else in town, been struck by the sleepwalking epidemic that had everyone acting out their craziest dreams. Alice had awoken from that strange weekend to find her cancer had gone into a startling remission. For a while, she'd felt almost human again. It was as if the Sickness had conversely acted as a temporary cure. For the first time since receiving her diagnosis two years ago, she'd allowed hope into her heart. But then, as soon as the weather cooled, the cancer came back with a roaring vengeance. She'd been granted an unspoken wish for one final summer, but now summertime was over, and she was faced with the final harvest.

The chemo wasn't even holding back the tide anymore. Alice only kept up with the treatments because her doctor had told her he wrote her marijuana prescription for the sole purpose of easing the chemo nausea. The pot was all that was making life bearable right now. She didn't even know if it was doing much for the nausea at this point, but it helped keep the despair at bay.

Most of the time, anyway.

Once her stomach was completely voided, Alice tied the bag shut. She got out and walked on shaky legs over to the trash can conveniently located on the sidewalk across the road from the square, glad she wouldn't have to drive around with the barf bag stinking up her car.

That's when she noticed the new shop, occupying the spot that had once been Coney Island Cones, way back when. Heavenly Treasures, the new place was called. Quaint, touristy little Christian gift shops like this opened in town every so often, but they never lasted long. People never seemed to learn that Bakersfield was in no way a tourist destination, and the locals had no money to spare for that kind of crap.

The place couldn't have been open long, Alice would have noticed it before. In fact, a plain white banner stretched across the store front announced GRAND OPENING. "Grand" might have been a bit of an overstatement.

Mildly curious, Alice stopped to regard the window display. It was a cluttered jumble of goods, but at least some attempt had been made to tie them together with an autumnal theme. Three bales of hay were set up before a fake wooden fence. On one, there was a kitschy Thanksgiving display. Angelic-looking porcelain pilgrims and Indians sat around a table laden with toy food. The second bale displayed little throw pillows and framed plaques printed in warm earth tones with bold-print "inspirational" words, like FAITH, LOVE, and PRAY.

Nothing in the window held the slightest interest for Alice, until she saw the center bale in the display. Several hardcover books were propped open around the feet of a tuxedoed mannequin. The books, with titles like *Fifty Shades of Grace, Unchained Grace,* and *Christian: Grace Fulfilled,* were obvious knock-offs. It was the mannequin that grabbed Alice's attention. Strapped to his face was the coolest eyepatch she'd ever seen. Black leather, with little metal studs to give the illusion the patch was actually bolted on over his eye. Alice knew she had to have it.

She dashed back over to her car and opened the glove box to fetch out her wig. Slipping it on over her head, she stepped into the shop.

Chiming electric bells announced her entrance. The shop was sparsely stocked with the expected books and cards, knick-knacks and stuffed animals and t-shirts with churchy slogans. The items were widely spaced on the racks and shelves, as if spreading them out would give the illusion that the store carried more stuff than it actually did.

A woman Alice didn't recognize looked up at her from behind the glass counter at the back of the shop. She seemed a bit suspicious, as if a customer was the last thing she'd expected to see.

"We're closing." The clerk was a stocky woman, probably in her thirties or forties, wearing glasses with thick, chunky frames that had the effect of making her face look fatter than it was. Her blonde hair was stringy and dull beneath the fluorescent lights. A nametag pinned to her drab, shapeless blue sweater, identified her as "Denise."

"Sorry," Alice said. "I'll be really quick. I just need one thing. That mannequin in the window has an eyepatch..."

"Oh." Denise brightened a little. "Are you a fan of that series?"

"I haven't actually read any of those books, no," Alice admitted. She'd tried to read *Fifty Shades of Gray*, but had given up after about the tenth repetition of the phrase "holy crap." Alice couldn't even get into the book as a source of fantasy stroke material. Not only was the writing terrible, she was totally put off by the whole dominant male thing. The guy came off as an overbearing asshole to her. She doubted the Christian parody would offer anything better in terms of prose style, and would almost certainly have even less in the way of hot sex. "But I have to have that eyepatch he's wearing. It's amazing."

"That's not for sale, sorry," Denise said. "Nobody would know the mannequin was supposed to be Christian Grace without the eyepatch."

"The character's name is actually Christian *Grace*?"

Denise beamed. "Clever, huh?"

"Yeah." Alice nodded, tamping down a chuckle. "I'm only asking because I'm sort of self-conscious about my glass eye. That patch would be perfect to cover it up."

Alice tapped her false eye with her fingernail, a gesture that creeped most people out. Denise, though, leaned forward, fascinated.

"Oh dear," she said. "How did you lose your eye?"

"Cancer," Alice said. She wiggled her wig to demonstrate her chemo baldness. Playing the Dying Girl sympathy card did not make her proud, but fuck it. She really wanted that patch.

"You poor *dear*," Denise said, her hand going to her mouth. "Is it..."

"Terminal," Alice nodded. "They tell me I just have a few months left."

"I am so *so* sorry," said Denise. "I'll pray for you. Every night."

"Thank you. I appreciate that."

"But I don't know if I can give you the eyepatch. The publishing company sent that for the promotional display. I doubt I could get another one."

"I'll give you fifty dollars for it," Alice said. One benefit of being so close to the end was that her college fund was wholly expendable. "A hundred."

"It's not about the money." Denise shook her head, frowning. "Let me ask you something. Where do you go to church?"

"I don't really...I'm not that religious, honestly."

"Oh, honey. What's your name?"

"Alice."

"I'm Denise, Alice. How old are you, dear?"

"I just turned eighteen."

"So young." Denise shook her head again. "With your time on earth being as short as it is, you simply must get right with the Lord. Jesus can give you *eternal* life."

"Yeah," Alice said, backing away. She had no patience for that kind of talk. She'd gladly trade vague promises of Heaven for twenty years of real life here on earth. Or even ten. Hell, she'd be happy to see her twenty-first birthday. If Jesus wasn't prepared to offer her that, she didn't see the point. "Thanks anyway."

"Wait." Denise closed her eyes and bowed her head for a moment. "I'll make you a deal. I will *give* you that eyepatch if you come with me to church tomorrow. Do you know the Church of the Shepherd?"

"I've heard of it, sure," Alice said. Of all the Bible thumpers out there, the Sheep Shackers were the thumpiest. "It's out on Highway 54, right?"

"That's right," Denise grinned. "Meet me there tomorrow at eight o'clock."

"Okay, sure," Alice said. "But could you maybe give me the eyepatch now? See, I'm going to this party tonight."

"Not a Halloween party?" Denise frowned, giving this phrase the same tone she might grant "drug-fueled orgy."

"It's nothing like that," Alice assured her. *Unfortunately*, she thought. "Just some girlfriends getting together. That patch would make me the belle of the ball."

Denise's frown tightened to a scowl and then loosened a bit.

"All right," she said. "But you need to promise me you'll be there tomorrow."

"I promise."

"Seriously, Alice. I want you to swear it."

"Okay, I swear."

"In *His* name."

"Sure, in his name."

"In whose name?"

"Uh, Jesus?"

"Wonderful." Denise smiled, as if she'd tricked Alice into uttering that name and had thus bound her by some arcane Christian magic. "Here. I want to show you something."

She leaned back and pointed at a large shadow-box hanging on the wall behind the cash register, in which a pair of crutches were framed.

"I was in a bad car accident when I was about your age," Denise said. "My knee was damaged, horribly. The doctors told me I'd probably never walk without those crutches. But Pastor Tuttle, God rest his soul, laid his hands upon my knee during a tent revival. He invoked Jesus' healing spirit. I tossed the crutches aside that evening and have not used them since. I framed them, though, to keep them always as a reminder of the power of the Lord's grace. I haven't seen Pastor Peters perform any miracles yet, but he is a good man. I can't promise he can heal you, Alice, but I can attest that miracles *do* happen."

"Wow," Alice said. "That's really..."

"I can tell you don't really believe me. That's okay. All I ask is that you come with an open mind."

"That I can do."

"Wonderful," Denise said again. "Follow me."

Alice followed Denise out to the front window. Denise pulled the eyepatch off the mannequin's head and handed it to her.

Alice slipped it on. "How do I look?"

"It looks even better on you than it does on Christian Grace."

Denise beamed at her with such intensity Alice started to feel a little weird about it.

"Thank you, so much," she said, backing out the door.

"You're very welcome, Alice," Denise said. "I'll see you tomorrow morning."

"You bet."

Alice grinned as she walked back over to her car, imagining herself as a bad-ass pirate, and wondering if keeping her fingers crossed had been enough to counteract the vow she'd made in Jesus' holy name.

CHAPTER 9

9:05 PM

"OH, JESUS. WE drank too much," Ellie laughed. "I hope I don't puke."

She fell against Mark, almost knocking him off his precarious barstool perch. They'd get kicked out of here for sure if they fell to the floor together. *It'd be worth it*, he thought. He liked the warmth and the softness of her body bumping against his. He also enjoyed the fumy, boozy adult smell she had gained on top of the mysterious spice scent.

Is that rosemary? he wondered again, *or thyme?*

"Are you really going to puke?" he asked.

"Would that be a total turn-off?"

"Nah." He shook his head, a gesture that seemed to slosh his brain around inside his skull like a whole peach in a can of syrup. "We can puke together. It'll be romantic."

Ellie laughed again. "I usually have a higher tolerance than this. I'm half Russian."

"That only helps if you're drinking vodka," Mark said. "See, I'm part Irish, which lets me knock back a lot of whiskey. But we were drinking rum."

"Who can drink rum?"

"Pirates," Mark said. "Arrgh."

They laughed together. Sweet, stupid drunken laughter that brought them close enough together they probably would have kissed had they not knocked their heads together instead.

"Ow!" Ellie rubbed her forehead. "You head-butted me!"

"Sorry."

Ellie looked up at Mark with her customary inscrutability. Her choker necklace had slipped a bit down her neck, revealing a patch of vivid color peeking out from underneath. He could only see the top half of the tattoo, but it appeared to be a nude woman astride a crescent man-in-the-moon.

"That's cool." He reached out and curiously touched his finger to the ink-stained flesh.

Ellie recoiled, like he'd pricked her with a needle. She adjusted her necklace, giving him a look as if touching her there had been a serious transgression.

"Sorry," he said again.

"It's all right." She looked away. "I'm sore there, where Malcolm Stone bit me."

"What did you say?"

"You know, Malcolm Stone, the leader of the vampire revolution."

"That's from my book," Mark said, astounded. "You read *Blood World*?"

"Actually, I downloaded all three of them."

"Really? What did you...did you like them?"

"I love it when a guy says, 'Enough about me. Let's talk about my vampire trilogy.'"

"That's not fair. You brought it up."

"Fine." Ellie rolled her eyes. "If you must know, I actually thought the first one was pretty good, once you get past the slow parts." She picked up her glass and brought it to her lips, though it was mostly melted ice by now. "The second one started out okay, but the ending sucked. Sorry, but the whole vampire epidemic turns out to be some stupid corporate conspiracy? Lame. I just started on the third one, but so far it's a little better. I like the Lillithites."

The Lillithites were a coven of vampire witches who figured heavily in the plot of *Blood World's End*. Mark doubted he had ever heard their name spoken aloud by another person. A beautiful woman invoking one of his creations is one of the most gratifying things a male writer can possibly hear. It was almost enough to make up for her blunt assessment of Book Two.

"How did you even know I had books published?" It wasn't something he'd ever mentioned at work.

"Seriously? Did you forget what century we live in?"

"You Googled me?"

"Well, yeah. You didn't Google me?"

"Do people really do that before a date? I didn't even think of that."

"That's a relief," Ellie said. "I have a *ton* of amateur porn out there."

"You, ah," Mark raised his own empty glass to his lips, "really?"

Ellie let loose another peal of laughter. "God, the look on your face. Jesus, don't get your hopes up. You really think I'd do something like that," she sucked an ice cube into her mouth, "under my own name?"

"Um..."

"Just please, don't do a search for 'Nikki Bushfire.'"

"Nikki, ah.... Do you spell that with one 'k' or two?"

More laughter. "Seriously, though," she slurred, putting her head on his shoulder. She leaned in close, her whisper hot and breathy in his ear. "Seriously. You seem like a good guy. Are you a good guy?"

"I try to be."

"'Cuz I've been with a lot of creeps. You're not a creep, are you?"

"I don't think so."

"You wouldn't say so if you were." She spoke this into his collar, all her weight leaning on to him now. There was a touch of recrimination in her voice, a slight retreat behind the protective layer of hostility he thought she'd shed two drinks ago. "Would you?"

Mark wasn't sure how to answer, so he put his arm around her. She tilted her head back and he leaned into her. The kiss when it happened was hot and rummy, a wet mash of lips and tongue. Mark was more than a little dazed when he finally came up to take a breath.

"Let's go do something we'll both regret," Ellie whispered.

"I won't regret it," said Mark.

Ellie's laughter had that hard edge to it again. "You're so stupid," she said. "I like that."

They stumbled together out of the bar, into the cool autumn night, leaning against each other in an unsteady stagger down the sidewalk. Less than half a block from the hotel bar, they came across one of the historical plaques that dotted downtown Springfield.

"On this site stood the Globe Tavern," Ellie read. "The first home of Abraham Lincoln and his wife Mary Todd, from the time of their marriage in November 1842 until May 1844. Here their first child, Robert, was born."

"Wow," Mark said. "Our first date was at the same place Abe and Mary hooked up. That's a good omen, right?"

"Yeah, worked out great for them," said Ellie. "He got shot, she went crazy and three of their kids died. Come on." She tugged on his sleeve.

"You know," Mark said, pulling back. "I'm probably too drunk to drive."

"I'll drive," Ellie said.

"You're as drunk as I am."

"Nuh-uh. I'm half Russian, remember? Here, I'll prove it. 'Ver isk moose unt squirrel?'"

"That's great, Natasha. But listen, there's a hotel right above the bar we were at. I'll get us a room."

"Rooms at that place are like two hundred bucks a night."

"That's cool with me." His drunken horniness had rendered him temporarily incapable of sound financial decision-making. At that moment, money was an entirely abstract concept.

"I hate hotels." Ellie shuddered. "God, you don't know who's been in those sheets. Let's go back to your place."

"That's..." Mark said. "Well, it's a *little* awkward. I live with my nephew."

"Nephew." Ellie laughed again, as if that had been the punchline to a long, involved joke. "Well, I got kicked out of my apartment, so I'm staying with a friend. She'll *probably* be cool with me bringing somebody home. God knows she sleeps around enough. You have to let me drive, though. I'm kind of a control freak like that."

"How about if I call us a cab?"

"No cab is going to go all the way out to Mason City at this time of night."

"Mason City?" Mark said, uncertainly. Mason City was as far north of Springfield as Bakersfield was northeast, more than thirty miles.

"Come on, trust me."

Ellie pulled him around the corner, to a little off-street parking lot.

"Guess which one's mine," she said.

Mark surveyed the dozen or so vehicles parked in the lot. "You look like a Nissan Sentra kind of girl."

"Really? That's what you think of me?" She went over to a little orange Suzuki motorcycle and pulled it back out of its narrow parking space.

"Very funny," Mark said. "Seriously, though. You shouldn't mess with someone's bike like that."

She looked at him like he was as stupid as he felt. "This is my bike."

"Wha…" Understanding finally penetrated Mark's pickled brain. "You want me to ride on the back of that?"

"I'll let you wear the helmet."

"No," he said, almost coming to his senses. "Ellie, you're great. I've had a lot of fun tonight, and I hope we can do this again. I really do. But I'm not going to ride thirty miles on the back of a motorcycle driven by a drunk girl. I'm not quite that suicidal."

Ellie frowned and set her bike back up on the kickstand. "Come here."

Helplessly obedient, Mark went to her.

"Give me your hand," she said.

Ellie pulled Mark's right hand up into her short skirt, pressing it into a place that was very hot and very damp. She gasped at the contact. Mark made a sound too, though his was more of an embarrassing little squeak.

"You told me you haven't been with anyone since your divorce. How long ago was that, two years?"

"Twenty-eight months," Mark answered. Not that he was counting. He tried to pull his hand away, but Ellie pressed it more firmly against her. He could have taken her pulse.

She kissed him again. "That's a long time," she whispered into his mouth, still clasping his hand between her legs. "It can end tonight, if you want it to. Do you want it to?"

"Jesus, yes."

"So how suicidal are you now?"

"Just suicidal enough."

She released his hand and smiled up at him. Without saying another word, she straddled the bike. Mark's pants had suddenly become so tight it was difficult to lift his leg. Still, he managed to climb on the bike behind her. He was still struggling with the helmet straps when she started the engine. His headgear dangerously loose, he slid his hands around Ellie's waist and held on for dear life as she roared out into the night.

CHAPTER 10

9:13 PM

THE BABY WAS dead. The tiny girl had been expelled all at once, with a final liquid spurt into Michelle's gloved hands. She was no bigger than a kitten. Milky-clouded eyes open and forever sightless, little limbs stiff, skin bluish-white. Her stillborn features were malformed, twisted into a shape just near enough to human to be recognizable as such, with two horny protruding growths on her forehead. Despite the infant's sinister aspect, Michelle no longer received that flashing sense of malicious awareness from the poor thing. That had been a momentary lapse into irrational panic. Looking at the doomed girl delivered into the world in this state no longer elicited fear in Michelle's heart, but rather a bone-chilling sadness that was even worse. No living creature should be subjected to such an existence, however fleeting.

Michelle had cut the umbilical cord with a steak knife from Sandy's kitchen. The blade was crusted with dried brown sauce of some kind, and she had to wash it in the sink with the odd-smelling water. The blade was so dull she actually had to saw through the tough gray cord, clamping it with a binder clip she'd found securing the freshness of a bag of potato chips. Then she rested the tiny corpse on Sandy's coffee table, upon a musty towel, the cleanest spot in this filthy room. Michelle covered the child with a dishrag and turned back to Sandy. The baby was dead, but the mother was alive, and in terrible distress.

A steady pulsation of blood coursed like a red tide from Sandy's vagina, pooling in a spreading stain on the towel Michelle had placed beneath the girl's body. She was hemorrhaging, badly. Michelle was grateful Sandy was unconscious. She doubted she could put on a brave face for the girl's benefit any longer.

The blood flowing from Sandy was bright red, not the rich brownish maroon of the normal and expected lochia discharge. There was far too much of it for Michelle to pretend this was in any way normal. *It was the horns*, she thought. The sharp growths on the baby's skull had raked and torn Sandy from the inside, lacerating her to ribbons. She needed immediate medical attention if she was to survive.

Michelle glanced for the hundredth time at the clock hanging in the wall above Sandy's television. For the hundredth time, she was frustrated that it was frozen at a few minutes past three. How long had it been since she'd made the 911 call? It had to have been more than an hour now. Where the hell was that ambulance? Was this girl going to bleed to death beneath Michelle's hands?

The placenta had to pass, in any case. Michelle gave a gentle pull on the cord. There was a surprising amount of resistance. It actually seemed to be retracting as if, having lost the baby, Sandy's body insisted on reclaiming the afterbirth.

Michelle unbuttoned Sandy's blouse. Sandy had a striking tattoo, just below her naval, in the same approximate place where both Michelle and Lana had theirs. Where Michelle and Lana shared a comparatively demure dolphin design, Sandy wore a lurid, vividly colored image of a woman with her legs wrapped around a crescent moon. By the look of ecstatic abandon on the woman's thrown-back head, and the hungry leer of the man-in-the-moon's face, this obviously depicted an act of lunar cunnilingus.

Michelle placed her hand on Sandy's belly and felt, as Kika had taught her, for the knotted mass of the uterus. Perhaps intentionally, the lewd tattoo marked the exact spot. Michelle sank her fingers into the ink-stained flesh of Sandy's deflated belly, and kneaded her abdomen like bread dough. With every squeeze of her hand, she prayed to whatever god or goddess might be in attendance for Sandy's womb to expel the stubborn placenta.

Michelle applied gentle downward pressure, urging the ephemeral organ to detach from the womb. When she was practicing in Colorado, she'd always had a vial of oxytocin in her kit. Overcoming her fear of giving an injection had to have been one of the hardest parts of her training, but she'd give anything to have a syringe now. The hormonal drug worked miracles in causing the uterus to contract.

"Come on," she whispered under her breath, goading the recalcitrant afterbirth downwards. "Come on." She had failed in the most essential function of her vocation. The baby was lost. But she would not fail in this.

Michelle had personally known a few women in the enthusiastic home-birthing community back in Colorado who had actually eaten their baby's placenta. Michelle could never have done that, the practice verged on auto-cannibalism in her mind. It seemed a shame to just discard the organ, though. So Michelle had buried Ben's placenta in the back yard of their house in Denver, beneath a transplanted peach tree Mark had brought home from a nursery. They sold that house after the divorce, though. The abandoned fruit tree seemed a sad, potent symbol of the failure of her first marriage. She wondered if the family who'd moved there after them ever ate the peaches that had been nourished by her son's afterbirth.

Why am I thinking about that now?

Her mind was wandering, trying to detach from the scene. Michelle dragged herself back into the present by force of will. She continued to massage Sandy's uterus through her tattooed belly. Was it growing harder, or was that her imagination? Did the umbilical cord yield a few precious centimeters when she tugged on it?

Michelle heard a scratching at the door. For half a second, she had hope that help had finally arrived. Then she looked over and saw the glowing yellow eyes of Midnight the cat, peering through the screen. The animal meowed loudly, clearly wanting to be let back in. Michelle ignored it, and continued her work.

The cord gave, almost an inch. The hard mass buried in the soft flesh clenched beneath Michelle's hands, tightening like a fist. It was working.

The cat meowed again, louder. Demanding now, clawing at the screen. Michelle looked over at the creature and locked eyes with her for a moment. Midnight licked her lips. Communication clear as telepathy passed between them. The cat was hungry.

Sandy's womb tightened a bit more. Michelle pulled up the resultant slack on the cord, careful not to tug too hard. The tissue connecting the umbilical to the placenta was strong, but could still tear and separate. Even, gentle pressure was needed.

Sandy stirred a bit, her eyelids fluttering. She moaned. Michelle did not want her to wake. It was better she was senseless for now.

The cat squeezed her head through the hole she had clawed in the screen, her furry face stretching tight, letting out an agitated yowl as she wormed her way inside. She managed to get one front paw into the hole in the screen, and with it tore the opening wide enough to fit in her other front paw as well. She wriggled through, getting hung up for a second half-in and half-out. The cat snarled with frustration as she flailed, hanging from the screen.

Michelle felt pressure give beneath her right hand. Her left, tugging the cord, pulled looser. The placenta was definitely emerging. Unable to resist anymore, Michelle reached a gloved, cupped hand inside. She grabbed the bluish fleshy mass and, with a gentle twisting motion, pulled it free.

It was like unstopping a cork. The bloody flow became a torrent, gushing forth from inside Sandy Aswell. Michelle cried out, wishing she could awake from this nightmare.

Still, she had to make sure the placenta was intact. If any pieces had detached and remained inside Sandy's body, they could cause even more complications. With her right hand, Michelle pressed a wadded-up towel against Sandy's rupturing vagina, applying as much pressure as she could. With her left, she set the dripping placenta on the towel-covered coffee table, beside the still-born child, inverting it so the thick membranes were on the bottom and the dark maroon-colored maternal surface was exposed. The fleshy mass resembled a small, dark-colored brain, with multiple lobes. The structure appeared complete, as far as Michelle could tell at a glance.

Midnight finally forced her way through the slit in the screen. She slipped into the trailer and dashed across the room. The cat leapt upon the coffee table that held both the wretched infant and her bloody afterbirth. Michelle, still applying pressure to Sandy, watched in helpless horror as the cat took two quick bites of the placenta.

Something snapped inside her. "Get the fuck out!" she screamed. She felt hysterical, mad with rage and horror. "Fuckin' thing!"

She stood up, dropping the bloody towel. The cat stood her ground, defending its prize meal, arching her back and hissing at Michelle. Gore dripped from her whiskers. Michelle grabbed for the cat and Midnight swiped out with claws extended. She scratched Michelle across the knuckles, through the already bloody glove. In Michelle's fury, she barely felt the scratch. She grabbed the fucking cat by its scruff, lifted it yowling and twisting, and carried it to the door. She tossed the cat into the night and slammed the interior door closed.

Michelle pulled off the ruined glove, covered with sticky blood and black cat hair, and threw it in disgust to the floor. She turned again to her patient on the couch. Sandy gave a final shuddering convulsion, and then she was still.

CHAPTER 11

9:15 PM

*G*OD THESE PEOPLE *are morons,* Gillian Hudson thought.
The community meeting was well into its second hour and she'd endured tirades by more than a dozen citizens, aired with varying degrees of quivering outrage. Old Annie Lutz claimed some of the water had got into a cut while she was shaving, and that she now had a strange growth on her armpit. She began to unbutton her shirt to unveil this alleged tumor, and had it more than halfway open before cries of protest from the crowd compelled her to keep her top on. Henry Bourne, who managed the Casey's General Store, complained that the water had left such a sludgy residue in his frozen fountain drink machines that he'd already replaced two units. Bobby Trott drunkenly insisted the city pay for damages the water had done to his rose garden, which had lost the top prize at the Great Lakes District Festival of Roses for the first time in five years. This, he claimed, had caused, "inestimable injury to the Trott family's national standing and reputation." Though Gillian's cheeks were on the verge of cramping from the strain of keeping it pasted on her face, she maintained her well-practiced PR smile through all their petty bitching. This was her job, and she was damn good at it.

Drinking the vile water at Bill Potter's challenge had been a master stroke, though the stuff had left a foul-tasting black paste on Gillian's tongue. No polite way to put it, the water really did taste like ass. More than one person had made the lame joke that it was as if King Chip, the ridiculous cow turd mascot painted on the side of the tower, had somehow tainted the reservoir within.

King Chip wasn't responsible, of course. Gillian's employer was. Malovo Agricultural Development had, at great expense, pumped thousands of gallons of a chemical into the town's water supply, to counteract the effects of Lot 472. That was the experimental substance inadvertently released into the population back in May, which had caused a short-lived outbreak of mass sleepwalking. If not for the company's decisive actions, much of the town would still be wandering around, acting out their tawdry small-town dreams. Even if they knew this, the citizenry probably wouldn't be grateful. They'd probably still be griping about their lumpy armpits and goddamn slushy machines.

Bobby Trott's comments had devolved into an angry, half-coherent diatribe against the rose judge's insistence on weighing a flower's form over its color and substance, which did not seem germane to the water issue in any way. Mayor Sager, as self-proclaimed arbiter of the proceedings, banged three sharp raps with his gavel.

"That'll do, son," Sager said. "Why don't you have a seat, all right? I know you're upset, like most of the folks here tonight. And you have a right to be. But I will swear on a whole stack of Bibles we in the village government are not responsible for what's going on here. Trust me, it goes a little higher up than that. If y'all don't mind, I'm going to take the floor for a few minutes and say some things that need to be said."

Across the long table, Gillian saw Diana Clayton, the Village Board Chairperson, roll her eyes. Gillian was a fair lip-reader and was reasonably certain the other woman had mouthed the words: "Oh boy, here we go." Gillian shrugged. It was the town's own fault for electing this guy. Sager had just started his fourth term. In a village full of idiots, the biggest idiot among them served as king.

"I was sitting on my back porch this morning," the mayor began. "Now, I know it ain't politically correct to say this. Hell, I'll probably get drummed out of office for admitting it, but I was having a smoke. I'm down to one cigarette every day before breakfast and let me tell you, some days it's all downhill from there. Anyway, I'm looking up at the sky and I notice all these trails left behind by jet airplanes, criss-crossing up in the air and kinda spreading out into the clouds. I'm out there every morning, so I see this a lot. Some days there's hardly anything up there and on other

49

days it's like the whole damn sky's covered with the stuff. Got me thinking, what in the hell are they spraying up there?"

Gillian, resisting a powerful urge to bang her forehead on the table, managed to keep an expression of polite interest on her face.

"Now ask anybody who really knows and they'll tell you this is a pretty recent phenomenon. Nobody was spraying chemicals up in the sky twenty years ago, and the whole thing really kicked into high gear in the past ten or fifteen years, back when so-called scientists first started squawking about 'global warming.' Hell, that's just a smokescreen. They're able to get away with perpetrating this hoax because most people are ignorant when it comes to simple science. They'll believe just about anything if a fella in a white lab coat sells it to them using big enough words. So let me give you one simple word that explains the whole thing." He paused here, for dramatic effect. "Control."

"Weather control." The mayor banged his gavel to emphasize the point. "Mind control. *Population* control." Bang bang. "The no-longer legitimate US federal government, under control of the United Nation's New World Order for at least twenty years now, has airplanes that release chemical trails into the atmosphere. These trails form clouds, which make rain, which falls to earth and fills up our lakes and streams, pouring these chemicals into our water supply. Messing with the water is nothing new, really. They've been slipping fluoride into the reservoirs since the fifties, but all that does is make people docile and stupid. That's how the Nazis came to power. No, really. Know your history. Look it up. But these new chemicals they got now are way more sophisticated. They actually make people open to suggestion, so you can program 'em, like robots. And how do they deliver these suggestions?"

He's going to say HAARP, Gillian thought.

"Let me tell you about a little-known government program called HAARP." The mayor laid out the acronym, punctuating it with his gavel. "High-altitude. Aerial. Radio. Pulsation. Your tax dollars at work, folks. Bombarding us with radio waves, sending out messages that our brains, rewired by the chemical-tainted water, receives and decodes, taking them for our own thoughts. They can change the very way we think. Let me give you a just-for-example."

Don't say gay marriage, Gillian silently begged.

"Gay marriage," said the mayor. "This was a little experiment they did, just to see if they could pull it off. Back in the early nineties, when they first set up this program, hardly anybody supported homosexuals getting married. The very idea was repugnant for all right-thinking individuals. Now, though, after two decades of bombarding people's waterlogged brains, three out four people out there will tell you it's perfectly fine. And they expect us to believe that's a coincidence? That's how insidious this thing is. It can convince a majority of the US population to swallow an idea that flies in the face of all common sense and decency. And what's next? You think it's another coincidence that every time they take a poll to see how many people call themselves a Christian, that number goes down? I don't want to sound like a paranoid crank…"

A little late for that, Gillian thought.

"…but I suspect a satanic influence."

Oh, Jesus.

She tuned out a little at that point. The mayor's spiel continued, hitting all the predictable touchstones. Obamacare, gun control, compulsory vaccination, the looming threat of global sharia law. The promise of the coming Rapture. It was almost fascinating how the mayor managed to weave all these disparate threads into his epic tapestry of bullshit. Gillian was tired, though, and she'd heard all this before. It always amazed her how the tin foil hat crowd could correctly sense there were powerful, nameless forces shaping their lives, but be so fundamentally wrong about all the specifics.

True, Malovo had experimented with using aircraft to disperse various chemical agents into the upper atmosphere, with the goal of wide-scale pest and disease eradication. But they'd abandoned those trials back in the eighties, for the simple reason that even highly concentrated agents diffused to completely ineffectual levels when delivered at that altitude. It was also true Malovo was investigating the possibility of using high-altitude aircraft for both solar radiation management and carbon dioxide removal, global geoengineering programs for mitigating and controlling climate change. But the SRM and CDR programs were at least two years from practical implementation.

The other perennial conspiracy bogeyman the mayor had invoked, HAARP, actually stood for High-frequency Active Auroral Research

Program. This was a completely innocuous research facility in Alaska, designed to study the ionosphere using high-power radio transmitters. Paranoid claims the facility was used for mind control experiments were completely baseless, of course, but if the cranks who subscribed to the HAARP theories ever caught wind of Malovo's Project Toxo, their heads would explode.

Project Toxo scientists had successfully used radio waves to affect, not only mental imagery transmission and reception, but literal mind control in laboratory animals injected with the versatile 472 substance. Pigs with telepathic interfaces. Remote control monkeys. There was no need to build a massive antenna array, either. These psychic exchanges had been accomplished with ordinary cell phone and wi-fi transmitters. Human trials could begin as early as next year.

Gillian supposed these experiments *could* be part of a satanic conspiracy to destroy Christianity and turn the whole world gay. If that was the case, though, those details were classified above her pay grade.

The mayor was wrapping up his rant. Gillian snapped back into the moment when she saw he was pointing directly at her, and he was on the verge of foaming at the mouth.

"...this company we allowed into our town, poisoning our air and our water," he was saying. "They've got our economy all tied up, with half the folks in town working at their ethanol plant and all the farmers within fifty miles under contract to buy their damn GMO seeds. They've got airplanes and drones, too. I've seen 'em. And they give full spousal benefits to same-sex domestic partners. They've been doing it for years." He concluded his statement with a final, resounding bash of his gavel.

"Mr. Mayor!" Diana Clayton wrenched the gavel from his hand. "That's quite enough. I'm so sorry, Ms. Hudson. Do you even want to dignify that with a response?"

Gillian looked out into the crowd. Judging by facial expressions, the split between citizens embarrassed by their mayor's tirade and those who agreed with at least parts of it was more or less even.

"It's all right," she said. She turned to face the mayor directly. "Mr. Mayor, you've raised some troubling and provocative questions. I can't speak to these trails you've seen in the sky, other than what I've been told, which is that they are the perfectly harmless condensation trails left by the water in jet engine exhaust. But I can tell you, categorically, Malovo does not conduct *any* chemical spraying. In fact, with our patented pest-resistant seed stocks, we've even eliminated the need for ordinary crop dusting. As to the water issue, we're part of this community, too. Both the ethanol plant and the Lawndale Manor subdivision, where I and most of the Malovo executive team live, draw from the same municipal supply as everyone else." This was a white lie, Lawndale imported their water, but Gillian delivered it so smoothly that had she been strapped to a polygraph at that moment, the needle would not have even twitched. "We're all in this together. Bickering and finger-pointing are counter-productive. We all agree there is a problem here, and we should all work together in order to find a solution. Mr. Mayor, I can pledge on behalf of the Malovo corporation that we'll put our full and considerable resources behind whatever measures you and the Village Board decide to take."

There was actually some applause at that. The mayor sputtered a bit, but offered no rebuttal. Gillian favored him with a warm, gentle smile and mentally composed her Oscar acceptance speech.

CHAPTER 12

9:25 PM

BY THE TIME Alice pulled into James Delany's driveway, her nausea was in full force again. She had some medicine in her glovebox, an Eden Apple flavor Chronic Lolly. She'd been into the lollipops recently. The dose took effect more quickly and evenly when it came in the form of something she could suck on, which of course also fed into her oral fixation. She wondered if the combination of lollipop and eyepatch could be sexy enough to overcome James's stubborn refusal to even consider heterosexuality as an option.

Walking up to the house, she heard music was blasting at a window-rattling volume. Alice happened to recognize the tune as the live version of "Transgender Dysphoria Blues" by Against Me! The neighbors had to love that.

James was the most interesting person of her own age Alice knew in town. Granted, Bakersfield High School didn't offer much in the way of competition for that particular title, but still, James was special. The music was a good example. James was into punk and hardcore. Metalcore, deathcore, queercore. Any kind of core, basically. The musical tastes of most other guys at her school began and ended with whatever happened to be on Johnny Six-Pack's current rotation on WBIL. Country music nauseated Alice almost as much as her chemotherapy did.

Outwardly, though, James didn't look like a punk. He dressed and groomed himself like a Mormon missionary on casual Friday, which meant he wore his collar unbuttoned and usually didn't have on a tie.

James was also openly and unashamedly gay, which in a town like this, was an act of daily courage. Alice admired him for this, but she couldn't help but find James's sexual preference to be, on a purely personal level, deeply disappointing.

Alice stepped up to the door. She knew James wouldn't hear if she knocked or rang the bell, and she further knew the door would be unlocked, so she let herself in. She followed the pounding music back to his bedroom, with the slim hope she might walk in on him committing some solitary act of adolescent release.

No luck there. He was bent over his keyboard, typing away. Probably working on his blog. He wrote about vampire and horror fiction, which qualified as another act of provocation in Bakersfield. Reading books for entertainment was suspect enough, but reading about such dark, occult subject matter probably put him on the town's official Satanic Cult Watchlist, if such a thing existed. (Alice would not be even slightly surprised if it did.)

"Hey, James," she said.

He jumped about a foot. "Whoa, hey," he said, clutching his heart. "You scared the heck out of me." Alice had never once heard him swear.

"Sorry," she said. "Door was open."

He tapped the keyboard to nudge the volume on the music down.

"Cool eyepatch," he said. "Where'd you get that?"

"That new Christian gift shop downtown, believe it or not. You like?"

"Yeah. It's really cool."

"Does it kind of make me look like Nick Fury? In a scrawny white girl way, I mean."

"Ah. Not really, no."

"I am bald," she said, tipping her wig. James looked away and Alice regretted making the joke. Any reference to her cancer made him uncomfortable.

"The house is so quiet," she said, deflecting. "Where's your uncle?"

James chuckled a little. "You won't believe this, but he's actually on a date."

"No shit?" Alice laughed. "Who went on a date with him?"

"Some girl he works with," James said. "I haven't met her."

"Wow. I thought he was still hung up on your Aunt Michelle."

"Oh, he totally is. I don't know. Maybe this will help him finally move on."

"Yeah, Jesus," Alice said. "If ever a man needed to get laid, it's your Uncle Mark."

James nodded and looked away. He also had a strange modesty whenever the subject of sex came up.

"Mmm," she said. The lolly was kicking in. That familiar reeling sensation of fuzzy detachment, delivered via the sour apple sweetness on her tongue. The pain and nausea and hopelessness were still there, but were fading into manageable background noise. God, she loved weed. It was almost worth dying, to feel this sensual and alive. "Taste this. It's really good."

"Ah, no." James regarded the proffered sucker with mild horror. "For one thing, that's been in your mouth, so ew. For another, I do not want to get stoned."

That was another thing. James was totally straight-edge. Alice had never even seen him take a drink. He wasn't judgmental about it, though. He usually seemed amused by her stoniness. Still, she would love to see him let loose and get high sometime.

"You sure?" she said. "It might help you work up the nerve to talk to Jose at the party."

"Yeah, about that..."

"No. You are *not* backing out. You promised you'd go with me."

"I didn't promise," James said. "I said I'd think about it."

"Same thing."

"I don't know any of the people who'll be there."

"You know all the people," Alice said. "They're the same people you go to school with every day."

"Yeah. My point exactly. Why would I want to hang out with those jerks? I don't think they'll be any more charming or tolerant when they're drunk. Just the opposite, probably."

"They're not *all* jerks. Besides, didn't you hear me? *Jose* will be there."

"Yeah, well, that's not..." James was blushing.

"Oh, come on. You told me you're into him."

"Maybe," he said. "Maybe. But I don't think he's into me. I don't even think he's gay."

"You told me he was."

"I said it was a possibility." James sighed. "He, uh, talked to me again yesterday."

"You mean flirted?" Alice pressed.

"No, *talked*. Normal stuff about Mr. Perkin's calculus homework. But...it was in the locker room after gym class."

"Oh my God. Were you guys *naked*?"

"No!" James said, blushing furiously now. Alice was feeling the flush herself. "We were, you know, getting dressed."

"Jesus." Alice closed her eye to savor the mental image. Jose Collier was on the basketball team, six-foot-plus and nicely muscled. His Mom was Costa Rican or Puerto Rican, some kind of Rican anyway, which made him intriguingly ethnic by lily-white Bakersfield standards. Maybe not the brightest guy at BHS, but he seemed amiable enough. And definitely hot. The thought of him and James having a casual underwear-clad conversation filled Alice with a whole stew of feelings. Jealousy was only one component.

"And then he texted me after school."

"What? And you didn't you call me right away?"

"It's not a big deal. I don't even know for sure if he knew he was texting *me*."

"Let me see it. Now."

James surrendered his phone. Alice pulled up the text:

-whas up?

-I'm just doing homework. What's up with you?

"He never replied," James said. "So I don't know what that means."

"'Whas up?'" Alice read. "Oh my God, he's *begging* for it."

"I don't know."

"James, straight guys don't go up and talk to out-and-open gay guys half-naked in the locker room. And then text them 'whas up' after school. Trust me. He's into you. You *have* to make the next move."

"I still don't know." Poor James looked like he might hyperventilate.

"I am going to make this happen. If I accomplish only one more thing before I leave this earth, it's going to be hooking you up with Jose Collier."

James's expression changed at that, grew harder.

"Don't say things like that, Alice."

"Sorry. I'm just really determined about this. Come on, let's go. Right now."

James took a deep breath and nodded twice. He saved his work on the computer and then looked down at himself. "You don't think I should get changed?"

"You look great." He did, too. Flustered desire suited him. "You should drive, though. I'm going to suck another lolly on the way over. I want to be really ripped for this."

"Okay," James said, steeling himself. "Okay."

"So," Alice said as they walked out of the house, James turning off all the lights in what was probably a stalling maneuver. "You've seen him naked in the locker room, right?"

James's face was the approximate color of a ripe plum. "I guess so, yeah."

"So is he...you know?"

"Is he what?"

"You know." Alice rolled her eye. "*Big*?"

"I don't look at that," James insisted.

"You don't look," Alice scoffed. "Everybody looks. I check out other girls and I'm less into females than you are."

"He's..." James was literally quivering. "I don't want to talk about it, okay? Let me write a note for my uncle, in case he comes home."

"Wow," Alice said. "What are the odds? You both might get lucky tonight."

CHAPTER 13

9:30 PM

MARK HAD NO idea where in the hell they were, but he was pretty sure they were nowhere near Mason City. Ellie wove an eccentric, winding path through the dark Illinois countryside. She changed directions seemingly at random, blasting up the straightaways at terrifying speeds only to brake suddenly to take some side path or remote gravel road. It was difficult to tell for sure, one harvested cornfield looked pretty much like any other in the moonlight, but it seemed they were heading more east than north. He wondered if Ellie was hopelessly lost, or if she was for some reason deliberately trying to disorient him. He wasn't sure which of these possibilities was more troubling.

Terror and arousal competed for dominance in his mind. Mark would have felt insecure perched on the back of the motorcycle even if Ellie wasn't a complete maniac. But she was certainly that. She alternated between unsteady wobbling and bursts of white-knuckle speed, treating the lines of the road as carelessly as kindergartner with a crayon in her fist. But every time he began to give serious consideration to hopping off the bike and taking his chances on foot, she would take one of his hands, desperately clutching her waist, and move it a few breathtaking inches either up or down. Pressing Mark's half-frozen fingers against one of the soft, warm secret places on her body. It had been a long time since he'd known the tactile wonders of feminine flesh. There was also the unavoidable circumstance of her hindquarters being pressed so intimately close to his frontquarters, the contact further aggravated by the warm vibrations of the bike. Their clothes were a wholly inadequate barrier between them. Mark entertained a justifiable fear he might climax before they even reached their destination. Wherever in the hell that might be.

One thing about it. Being simultaneously so lost, afraid, sexed up, and cold (late October in Illinois being less than ideal motorcycle weather), there was no room left in Mark's mind for drunkenness. He felt as sober as he'd ever been in his life.

Then Ellie pulled to a sudden halt, nearly toppling the bike. Even with the rumbling motor, he could feel her shuddering beneath his touch.

"What is it?" he said, awkwardly propping the weight of the bike on one leg. "Is something wrong?"

The headlamp illuminated the road ahead. There was a short bridge with metal guardrails, crossing over a small stream. Still grasping for the geography, he wondered if this was perhaps the southern branch of Sweetwater Creek.

"You're going to have to drive the bike," she said.

"What? I don't know how to..."

She slid off the bike and turned to face him. He could see how afraid she was. "Please, Mark. I don't do bridges. When I was fourteen..." She was actually crying now.

"What?" he said. "What happened?"

"Okay." She took a deep breath. "When I was fourteen, my mom left my dad and took me with her." Ellie leaned in close. "They had a huge fight one night, like a tooth and nail kind of fight. She woke me up and made me pack a bag. We left for the bus station in the middle of the night. My Aunt Lacey lived in New York and we were going to go stay with her. I didn't want to go..."

Ellie was trembling, and pressed herself even closer to Mark as she sobbed out her story. Mark held her, awkwardly, trying to prop up the bike at the same time.

"We were crossing the Ft. Henry Bridge over the Ohio River in Wheeling, West Virginia. I was reading a book. It was the first *Hunger Games* book, actually. Mom bought it for me at a truck stop. So I didn't see it happen."

"See what happen?"

"A drunk driver in a car was going the wrong way on the bridge. The car hit the bus and we went over the edge. Into the water."

"Oh my God."

"I broke my collar bone and three ribs. My neck was so bad they thought for a while I was going to be paralyzed. But my mom, she drowned."

"Jesus, I'm sorry."

It was strange. Mark was almost positive the story she was telling was made up. There was something canned and rehearsed about the details she rattled off. Plus the thin trickling stream before them bore about as much resemblance to the Ohio River as an earthworm did to an anaconda, so he didn't see how this situation could remind her of that one, even if it had been true. But at the same time, her terror seemed completely genuine. Either that or Ellie was an actress on a par with Meryl Streep.

"Since then, whenever I drive over a bridge, I have this *urge*. Like a *compulsion*," she said. "I want to go over the edge. Like my mom is still down in the water, calling to me. She wants me to go to her, so I can be with her. It's really strong sometimes. Like right now. I can almost hear her. I'm so afraid, Mark. Please, just drive over the bridge."

"I've never even driven a motorcycle," he said.

"It's easy." Ellie sniffed. "Can you drive a stick-shift car?"

"Yeah."

"Same thing. Except backwards. You work the clutch with your hand and shift the gears with your foot."

"That doesn't make any sense. Can't we walk the bike over?"

"No." Ellie moaned, a strange frustrated note. "We'll be over the water too long. Please do this for me, Mark. My friend's house, where I'm staying? It's just on the other side. We're almost there."

"Where?" Mark could see only dark timber across the bridge, on both sides of the road.

"When we get there, I will *fuck your brains out*," she panted. The erotic promise of Ellie's words was at serious odds with her tone, which came out with an almost hysterical hostility. "I wanna lose my fucking mind with you. Is that okay? Would that be all right with you?"

Her eyes were wide open, black and crazed-looking in the moonlight. A million alarm bells were going off in his mind and yet...

Twenty-eight months was a very long time.

"Alright," he said. "Fine."

"Thank you." Her laughter came out as jagged as her sobs. She kissed him, deeply, her lips salty with tears. "Oh, God. Thank you, Mark."

They traded places on the bike. Mark in front, Ellie wrapping herself around him from behind. She clutched him tight, running her hands over his chest.

"Your right hand does the throttle and the brake," she said, her hands guiding his. "Left hand is the clutch. Pull it in. Good. Now put it in gear and let out the clutch."

The bike lurched forward and stalled out.

"It's okay," Ellie said. "It's okay. Just...smooth. Like a car. Push the button to start it up again."

Mark put the bike into neutral and pushed the button to start the engine. Again, he managed to put in into gear, but this time when he let out the clutch, the bike didn't stall. They rolled forward, wobbly but upright.

"Good," Ellie shouted behind him. "Give it a little gas."

Mark twisted the throttle back a few timid millimeters. The bike propelled forward, straightening out. The engine whined.

"Now shift," Ellie called.

The gears ground a bit, but Mark managed to find second. They slid over the bridge at an unsteady fifteen miles an hour. Mark laughed. It was exhilarating. "Born to be Wild" began to play in his head.

"Good!" the woman behind him yelled, nuzzling into his back. "Keep going!"

Ellie's hand slipped around his waist and then reached down to grab his crotch. She clutched him, hard and stupefied in her hand.

This distraction proved to be fatal. Mark's right hand slipped the brake and instead gave the throttle a squeeze, an involuntary mirror action to what Ellie was doing to his lap. The bike leapt forward with a burst of speed. Mark managed to hold a steady course for about thirty feet before the needle skipped on the Steppenwolf record. The bike launched off the side of the road, into the dark woods beyond.

By some terrible miracle, the motorcycle remained upright as the ground sloped sharply off the road into the timber. Ellie screamed in his ear, or maybe Mark was screaming. He couldn't really tell for sure. The bike rolled down the hill, picking up speed. He was afraid to try the brake for fear of hitting the throttle again, and instead held on for dear life as the headlamp illuminated tree trunks streaming past on both sides. The bike bounced on the hard rutted slope, dust flying all around. Mark saw a pair of glowing green eyes floating in the night before him that turned out to be a terrified raccoon. The creature made a high, wailing scream (or, again, this frantic sound may have come from Mark's throat) and barely waddled out of his path in time.

The bike hit a half-buried tree root and was airborne for about half a second. Mark's eyes took in a baffling sight. A wooden cross-hatch pattern flying towards him. He had a scant half-second to wonder what in the hell it was before they flew through it, the wood splintering into a million pieces, shattering like glass.

The bike had punched through a wooden trellis on the side of an enclosed porch. Landing on the porch, Mark finally lost balance. The bike spilled over and tossed its two riders aside, into what appeared to be a large tarp of some kind rolled up against the side of the house. It smelled like fresh paint.

The tarp did cushion their crash landing somewhat, but it was still a hard fall. Mark landed awkwardly and painfully on his left wrist, twisting it beneath him. His left leg was pinned beneath the bike. He and Ellie lay there for a few dazed seconds in a tangled pile of limbs, torsos and idling motorcycle, with dust and exhaust smoke swirling all around them.

Mark might have blacked out for half a second, because he came to with the sound of Ellie's laughter in his ear. She was actually laughing.

"Oh my God," she crowed. "You are a *shitty* driver."

Mark managed to extricate himself from the bike. He had the presence of mind to turn off the motor. "Are you all right?" he said.

"No," Ellie sat up and grunted, then laughed some more. "I fucked up my shoulder."

"Where are we?" Mark said. The house's existence here in the middle of the woods seemed utterly incongruous.

"We're here," Ellie said. "This is where I live."

"What?"

At that moment, the front door burst open and a woman stepped out onto the porch. She was upper middle-aged, tall and stocky, with long gray hair. Also worth noting, she was completely naked.

"What in the holy hell?" the nude woman exclaimed.

"Oh hey, Berta," Ellie said. "Mark, this is my roommate, Roberta. Berta, this is Mark Davies." She let out another volley of laughter as the irresistible pun rose to her lips: "I hope you don't mind if he crashes here tonight."

CHAPTER 14

9:44 PM

MICHELLE RAN THE damp cloth down Sandy Aswell's body, gently washing her as well as she was able to with the strange-smelling, cloudy water. Michelle dabbed away the dried vomit from the side of Sandy's mouth and the sweaty dirt from her neck. She tenderly swabbed under the dead girl's arms and washed her breasts and her belly, dipping the cloth in the cereal bowl that was one of the only clean dishes she could find in the trailer.

She had only meant to wash Sandy's feet at the start. The sight of the black, caked-on dirt on her soles had seemed sad and undignified to Michelle. Rinsing them off seemed the least she could do, considering how she had failed to help Sandy in any other way. But once she cleansed the girl's feet, she remembered reading about the Jewish ritual of washing the dead. She found comfort and solace in the task, and hoped she had in a small way restored Sandy's dignity.

Michelle pulled a relatively clean sheet over Sandy's body, covering her slack face. Then she broke down for a moment, and quietly sobbed for a while. She knew she should leave. She should go get help, maybe find a neighbor with a landline telephone. Report the death. Start whatever grim processes needed to be set in motion. But it seemed wrong to leave Sandy alone in this terrible place.

Michelle pulled the bloody, filthy towels out from beneath Sandy, wadding them up and placing them on the floor. She laid the comforter from Sandy's bed over the body, tucking the dead girl in on the couch with only her white-shrouded head sticking out. As if she'd merely fallen asleep watching television, like Ben often did.

She was bent over the blanket-swathed body, whispering an incoherent prayer, when the trailer door burst open behind her.

"What are you doing there?" a harsh male voice called out. "Step away from that!"

Michelle stood up and spun around. A tall black policeman in a state trooper uniform had entered Sandy's tiny trailer, his bulky frame seeming to take up half the space in the room. She hadn't noticed until that moment that the flashing red and blue lights of his cruiser had filled the night outside the trailer, spilling strobing light in through the windows. Michelle's first reaction was relief. Someone had finally arrived. She was no longer alone.

"Are you Michelle Blair-Delany?" he demanded.

Michelle was thrown, both by the fact the trooper knew her name and by the expression on his face as he spoke it. A look of pure disgust. This was so strange to her that for a moment she could not answer.

In that speechless moment, Sheriff Nathanial Bates stepped into the trailer behind the trooper. Now fear and hatred penetrated Michelle's confused daze. Here was the man who had murdered her sister, shot her down in the street right before Michelle's eyes. She gritted her teeth at the sight of him.

"Is this her?" the trooper asked Bates.

"Yes," Bates said. He nodded at her. "Ms. Blair-Delany, this is Master Sergeant McMurtry with the State Police. He asked me to come along because he received a call—"

"Is that Sandy Aswell?" McMurtry barked, crossing the room and tearing the sheet from Sandy's face. "Jesus! She's dead!"

Michelle raised her hands slowly, and stepped back away from the body. Bates removed his hat, an oddly chivalric gesture under the circumstances.

"What did you do to her?" McMurtry said. His eyes locked red and furious upon Michelle for a second, and then lit on the bloody towel-covered lumps on the coffee table. "Is that..." He pulled one of the towels away and staggered back with a cry of genuine alarm. "What the fuck is that?"

"It's a baby," Michelle said. "A stillborn child."

"Stillborn?" McMurtry hissed. "Have a look at this, Nate. Are those *horns*?"

The sheriff stepped over and took a look at the dead infant. He frowned curiously.

"By God," he said. "Those do look like horns. Charlie, I'm going to get a picture of this, for evidence." Bates pulled a camera phone from his pocket and snapped a few shots of the malformed infant.

McMurtry lifted the other towel. "What the fuck is *this*?"

"Afterbirth," Michelle said. "That's normal."

"Normal?" McMurtry barked. "There is not one goddamn normal thing about this." He stepped close to Michelle. "Ms. Blair-Delany, you are going to come with me to answer some questions at the state police barracks in Springfield. You have the right to remain silent..."

"Wait a minute," Michelle said. "You're *arresting* me?"

"...and you have the right to legal counsel. If you cannot afford counsel, such will be provided for you."

"Why in the hell are you arresting me?" Michelle's voice shook with rage, spilling out from deep inside her. All the terror and helplessness she'd absorbed for the past two hours now spilled out, manifesting as naked fury.

"Ma'am," Bates said, and this enraged Michelle even further. This man had murdered Jennifer, and not only did he walk free, not only did he now come here to dare to accuse her of some crime, but he actually dared to call her *ma'am*? "The State Police received an anonymous tip that you were coming here to perform an illegal post-viability abortion."

"Abortion?" Michelle choked out. "You think this was an abortion? Are you fucking insane? What do you think I performed an abortion with? My bare fucking hands?"

"Cool it, miss," McMurtry said. "Just calm the hell down. I'm confident a search of this trailer will reveal your instruments."

"Instruments? Jesus. If I was here performing an abortion, why would I make twenty fucking calls to nine-one-fucking-one?"

"We didn't receive any 911 dispatch calls," Bates said.

"I can prove it," Michelle reached in her pocket, a sudden move that provoked Master Sergeant McMurtry's hand to drop to the butt of his pistol.

Michelle looked down at the weapon on his belt. She recognized that perhaps she should be afraid, but all she felt was rage at these men and their fucking guns.

"I'm getting my phone." She pulled out the phone and tapped the black screen. It stubbornly refused to light. The battery was dead.

"Shit," Michelle said. "Look, if we can charge my phone somehow, you'll see I made several calls to 911. I don't know if they were going out, because the coverage down here is for shit, all right? But I did make them."

"She's right about the signal," Bates said, frowning down at his own phone. "I tried to e-mail these photos to headquarters, but I got that darned little hourglass. I don't know, this is a new phone and I'm still not a hundred percent on how to use it."

Both Michelle and McMurtry flashed a curious look at the sheriff, whose tone seemed oddly disconnected to the tension in the room. When the state trooper returned his gaze to Michelle, though, his fury was undiminished.

"Let me tell you what I think happened," he growled. "I think Ms. Aswell there found out she was carrying a baby with birth defects. She couldn't kill it legally, because in this state there's laws against late-term baby murder, at least. So she gave you a call. How many of these have you done?"

McMurtry was was right up in Michelle's face, close enough so she could see the tooled leather band on his Stetson hat. It looked like the one Timothy Olyphant wore on *Justified*. This detail struck her as ridiculous. Wannabe cowboy cop.

"You know I got a daughter with Down syndrome?" he snarled. "The doctors detected that in the pre-natal screening and they offered me and my wife the chance to abort her. Doctors, *recommending* murder. Leslie's eleven years old now and she is the sweetest, purest soul I've ever known. She's the light of our lives. So I take this shit real personal."

"That's..." Michelle was struck nearly speechless by the absurdity of this. "I'm happy for you and your family, but that has nothing to do with..."

"What is this, really? Some kind of lesbian voodoo thing?"

"*Lesbian voodoo?*" Michelle hardly believed what she was hearing. "Are you kidding me? Yeah. You got me. You finally uncovered the global lesbian voodoo abortion conspiracy. We harvest fetuses for the blood, so we can pour it over our bodies while we dance naked in the moonlight. We whittle their little shin-bones to make our dildos. You didn't know that?"

"Just stop right there. That's enough."

"You ignorant motherfucking cowboy," Michelle snarled. Something inside her had broken. She was aware of the danger of what was flowing from her, but was powerless to stop it. "This woman here died because she didn't have access to kind of pre-natal care your wife was fortunate enough to receive. Why? Because she's poor and pro-life shitheads like you shut down women's health whenever you get the chance. She *should have* had an abortion. If she had an abortion, she'd be alive right now. Because that baby fucking killed her. Jesus fucking Christ!"

"Watch your mouth," McMurtry growled. "I will not tolerate blasphemy from a murdering dyke bitch like you."

Michelle slapped the State Trooper across the face, with every ounce of her fury behind her open palm. She struck McMurtry hard enough to knock his stupid Raylan Givens hat askew.

Shocked silence filled the room for a long second, the three of them gaping at each other in disbelief. Michelle, her hand stinging, actually opened her mouth to apologize. Before she could make a sound, though, McMurtry's hands were on her, spinning her around and slamming her against the thin wood paneling of the trailer wall.

The takedown was swift. McMurtry tossed Michelle face-down onto the filthy floor, hard enough to knock the wind out of her. Dusty cat hair tickled her nose and unidentifiable grit pricked at her cheek. The policeman's knee drove brutal weight into the base of her spine. He wrenched her arms behind her, clamping cold steel hard to the bones of her wrists.

From Michelle's pinned vantage on the ground, she looked over and saw Midnight the cat, sitting in the open doorway.

You know, the cat seemed to say, casually licking a paw. *I really hate to say I told you so.*

CHAPTER 15

9:55 PM

BEN AND EMILY sat in a deer stand, up in a big maple tree. Emily said her dad came out here to hunt sometimes and that's how she knew it was there. They were a little bit away from the party in the woods, but not too far for the strange pounding teenage music and bonfire smoke to waft up to their perch.

A deer stand, Ben had just learned, was pretty much a tree house for grown-ups, with little windows to stick their guns out. It seemed a little unfair to him. He'd thought hunting was about stalking your prey through the woods like a real predator beast, not sitting up in a tree waiting for some unsuspecting animal to come along so you could blast it from above. But what did he know? His father didn't hunt. He hadn't grown up with rifles and venison as Emily had.

Emily took a drink of hot chocolate from the Thermos she'd brought along, and then passed it to Ben. He took a swig of the warm sweetness and wondered if maybe he was in love.

Ben's feelings for Emily weren't anything like the love stories he came across sometimes in books and movies and TV shows. He didn't quite grasp all that moony, huggy-kissy stuff anyway. It was more like he was so comfortable being around Emily that it was almost like being by himself. And when she wasn't around, he often found himself wondering what she was doing at that same moment. Watching television, he'd wonder if she was watching the same show. Eating dinner, he'd think of hilarious comments he could share with her later about what a terrible cook his father was. It wasn't "desperate longing," like people in love in books seemed to feel. (Many of the things he'd read made love seem like a debilitating mental illness.) Ben's feelings for Emily were closer to other stories he'd read, about twin siblings who felt a mysterious connection to one another even when they were miles apart.

Is that what his father had felt for his mother, back when they'd been grade school friends? Had Dad thought of Mom as Ben now thought of Emily, only to have this feeling change and grow as they changed and grew, until it turned into that other kind of love? The moony, huggy-kissy kind that had ultimately led to Ben's conception and birth? Maybe that's where things had gone wrong for them. Ben hoped he could keep his feelings for Emily pure, and free of all that crazy stuff. Maybe that way it would last forever.

"They're doing it wrong," Emily said, peering through her binoculars.

"What?"

"Look." She passed the glasses to him. "That girl in the tiger mask has a *teddy bear,* for gosh sakes. I think that's what they're going to bury. It's supposed to be a sock monkey."

Ben looked through the binoculars down at the bigger kids around the fire. It was hard to tell what was going on. Mostly the party-goers were silhouettes in front of the fire, or dark shadows off to the side. Every so often, one of them would step into the warm flickering light long enough to make out the outlines of the strange animal masks they were all wearing. Ben didn't see a tiger girl holding a stuffed bear, but he did see a tall boy in a black hoody and what looked like a wolf mask. Wolf-boy tried to drink from a bottle of beer without taking his mask off, and ended up spilling the stuff all over himself. Even from this distance, Ben heard him and his friends laughing about it.

"And it's not even Halloween yet," Emily said. "I think it actually has to be on Halloween night, or it won't work."

"What's the monkey supposed to do, anyway?" Ben asked.

"Protection spell," Emily said impatiently, as if repeating a lecture he'd somehow missed. "It's what holds the bad spirits back. And if they're doing it wrong, that means we won't be protected for a whole year."

"How do you know all this?"

"My Uncle Emmett used to be friends with your dad," Emily said. "He told me about all kinds of crazy stuff they used to do together. Hey, there's another car coming. See if you can tell who it is."

71

Ben swung the lenses around to the little gravel pull-off where everybody was parking.

"That's my cousin," he said, a bit surprised. This didn't seem like James's kind of scene at all. Then he saw Alice Kiernan getting out of the passenger side. That made more sense. Ben understood James and Alice's friendship was similar to the one he had with Emily. Alice could, and often did, talk James into doing things he would never do on his own.

"Is that the girl who has cancer?" Emily said.

"Yeah. Alice."

Ben watched as James and Alice went over to the fire. They were greeted by the girl Emily had seen before, the one wearing the tiger mask. Tiger-girl handed James a mask that looked like it was maybe supposed to be a lamb or a goat or something. Ben could tell even from up here that there was a little bit of discussion, convincing James to put on the mask, but he finally did it. Alice was wearing an eye-patch. That was apparently enough of a disguise on its own, because the Tiger-girl didn't make Alice put on an animal mask. Then Wolf-boy came over carrying a couple bottles of beer. Alice took hers without hesitation, but James tried to refuse. Again, there was some kind of discussion and James finally accepted the beer. He took a timid sip as Ben watched, a little surprised. He didn't think James did that kind of thing.

"What's going on?" Emily said. "Let me see."

Ben passed the glasses back. Emily watched for a while without saying anything, and Ben helped himself to more cocoa.

"Well, that's interesting," she said finally.

"What?"

"Your cousin is going off into a car with that wolf kid."

"Really?" Ben didn't have much of an idea how that kind of thing worked, but he wondered if that meant James was finally getting a boyfriend.

"Hey," Emily said. "Look down there with your ghost camera and tell me if you see anything strange."

Ben pulled the digital camera from his kit. The little monitor screen on the back rendered the scene below in an eerie gray-green monochrome. The camera didn't have a zoom lens, though. From this distance, he couldn't make out any more than he could with his naked eye. But something about the view on the screen bothered him. It reminded him of the dream

72

he'd been having before Emily had crawled into his bedroom window. It seemed he'd been looking through the camera in the dream, too. Maybe even down at a fire in the night. This sense of déjà vu was so strong that he was not surprised when something black and fluttering passed in front of the camera. A bat or perhaps an owl, some night flyer on the wing.

I remember that, he thought.

He wondered, as he sometimes did, if perhaps he was not asleep and dreaming right now. This thought came to him more and more often since the weekend when all the people in town were sleepwalking. Ben himself had not succumbed to the Sickness, but he imagined the people who did fall asleep had slipped so smoothly into their dreams they hadn't noticed the change. The situation at hand- perched in a tree with Emily Grady, watching masked revelers around a fire in the night—was certainly strange enough to be a dream, but he knew somehow it was real. He'd often had dreams he had confused for reality, but never had his waking life been mistaken for a dream.

"What?" Emily said. "What do you see?"

Ben looked back up at her. "Nothing."

"Nothing?" she said. "You have this look on your face like you saw a whole pack of ghosts down there."

"No, it's just..." At that moment, he remembered something else from the dream. His mom washing another lady's feet.

"Just what?"

And it was strange and scary because the lady with the dirty feet was dead.

"Ben?" Emily said. "What's wrong? You're freaking me out."

And then the police came. They blamed his mother for killing the lady with the dirty feet. They hurt her and then they took her away.

"Ben?" Emily called, but her voice was far away because the bad thing happening to his Mom was real and it was happening right now and he had to get out of this tree to see if he could help her. If it wasn't too late.

They'd climbed up to the blind with ladder rungs nailed to the side of the tree but Ben, in his hasty panic, leapt from the stand. He dropped a good twelve feet and landed hard on the forest floor.

"Ben!" Emily screamed after him.

Half-blind in the dark woods, Ben ran towards the bonfire like a moth's doomed bid for the light.

CHAPTER 16

10:08 PM

DIANA CLAYTON RUBBED her dry red eyes and massaged her pounding temples. She cast her thoughts towards the bottle of red wine in her refrigerator at home with an almost erotic longing. Diana looked back and forth across the table, at her fellow board members and the two guests. They were obviously as sapped as she was. Daniel Holder, the village clerk, was openly playing Candy Crush on his i-Pad. Both Mayor Sager and Wayne Wilson, the water inspector, were dozing in their chairs. Even Gillian Hudson was looking ragged, her permanent PR smile noticeably sagging.

Most of the townspeople had already left, discreetly shuffling out of the meeting hall in groups of two or three for the past hour. The weary board was faced with only the real die-hards now, and even they were winding down. Ten o'clock in Bakersfield was like two AM in a city.

Tim Black, who owned the motel north of town, let out a huge yawn in the middle of the rambling litany of complaints he was reading straight from guest comment cards. Looking as embarrassed as if he'd belched, he chose to end it on that note.

"I guess you all get the point by now, anyway," he said, and then re-took his seat.

"Thank you, Mr. Black," Diana said. "I think we're all pretty tired. On behalf of the entire Board, I'll say yet again that we hear your concerns loud and clear, and we are actively working to find a solution. So if there isn't anything new to add, I'm going to move to adjourn. All in favor..."

"Excuse me, I haven't had a chance to speak yet." Joyce Frank stood in the aisle, swaying back and forth with her usual hypnotically slow agitation.

"Oh, crap." Diana was so tired she let herself speak that aloud.

Joyce had once been an active and vibrant member of the community, and had actually sat on the board herself for two terms. But that was before her daughter Tammy was murdered by the Holiday Killer, on Independence Day twenty years ago. After that, she went into a tragic public tailspin. Her husband left her, taking full custody of their surviving son, and she lost her real estate business due to the complete collapse of her mental health. On a sliding scale of crazy, she was a perfect ten. Scored against her, even the Mayor himself didn't rate more than a five or a six.

"The board recognizes Joyce Frank, but after that we're going to call it a night," Diana said. In a way, Joyce would provide a perfect capper. Might as well end with her. "You have five minutes, Joyce."

For a moment, Joyce looked around the room, her thick glasses magnifying the madness in her eyes, casting a glaring projector beam of lunacy onto the faces of her fellow citizens. The cigarette always present in her mouth was unlit now, in deference to the indoor smoking regulations she complied with only grudgingly. With quick little purses of her lips, she caused the thing to make little wagging, stabbing motions, like a carcinogenic accusatory finger. Then she tucked it behind her ear.

"You know me," she said by way of preface. "You know I know the difference between darkness and light. Can you tell me then how it is that I have found nine bats dying on my doorstep in nine days? Those black things do not wing beneath the sun!"

Diana felt a dreadful sinking sensation. She made a mental note to move to repeal the short-sighted city ordinance guaranteeing every citizen the right to public comment, no matter how nuts they were. She'd bring it up at the next closed meeting.

"I have heard too the cries of owls in the daylight. Possums and coons rooting through my trash at high noon. Why do the night things come to me in the day? Well, I will tell you, though you will not like the answer."

She paused then, either for dramatic effect or because her troubled mind had frozen like a slow-loading website. The silence dragged out for an entire minute, long enough for Diana to build up slender hope Joyce had simply stopped and they could all go home now.

No such luck there.

"Witches!" Joyce cried, causing at least a few people to jump out of their seats. "Yes! I spoke it aloud! All these things have happened before, you know. The bad water, the night beasts daring the day, the masked girls dancing in the woods who stick pins in my mattress. Pins! Oh, and the babies. The poor little babies, dying on the vine, all wombs barren except those that have sealed their pact with the devil by kissing his backside! Yes, they do that! I've seen it! History repeats itself over and over because you people never learn. You never learn that the witches have always been here, in this town, waiting for their time to *rise*! Those who have eyes to see the signs know that their time is *now*!"

The lights went out.

The power died at the precise moment Joyce Frank incanted the fatal word, "now." The overhead fluorescents snuffed out without so much as a flicker, thrusting the assembled citizens and the village board members into absolute darkness.

The first reaction was laughter. Those who laughed no doubt found the timing comical in its perfection. In that moment, many perhaps believed this was a flawlessly executed Halloween prank. Maybe Joyce Frank had feigned mental illness for two entire decades, just to deliver this crushing punchline.

"You see?" she cried ironically into the blind darkness. "Now finally do you see?"

The dark room echoed with a cacophony of whistling tones and chiming bells, chirping birds and wailing sirens, animal sounds and snatches of popular song. A dozen or more cellphones simultaneously played their incoming text notifications. The darkness was filled with the ghostly blue light of dozens of illuminated screens, reflecting off the anxious downturned faces of the people checking to see what they had been sent.

Diana's own phone went off with its familiar bluegrass banjo riff. She picked it up, but cries of alarm came from around the darkened room before she could even unlock the phone to check the text. She saw with a prick of foreboding the message was from the Logan County Sheriff Department's

Emergency Notification Service, designed for rapid dissemination of news about tornado warnings, school shootings and AMBER alerts. Stranger still was the notice "MSG CONTAINS MEDIA CONTENT."

She tapped the message to open it. At first her mind could not process what her eyes were seeing. If only the people in the room would stop shouting, perhaps she could make sense of it.

Whatever it was, it was bluish-white, covered with patches of bright, glaring red. Glistening and wet. It looked at first glance like a surgical photo of a diseased organ, but the small shape bore a twisted face and shriveled limbs. Diana blinked twice and only then did she grasp she was looking at a fetus. A horribly deformed human fetus, with eyes and arms and—God help her, were those horns? Yes. The misbegotten thing on her cell phone screen wore demonic horns on its head.

The emergency lights finally kicked on, and the dull shadows they cast seemed worse than the total darkness had been. No one was laughing now. They were screaming instead.

"They're here!" the madwoman Joyce Frank called, her own terror edged with what sounded like manic glee. "The witches are here among us! May God save us all!"

CHAPTER 17

10:18 PM

THERE WAS A brief skirmish over by the portable speakers. Icona Pop was unplugged and replaced mid-song when somebody patched Blake Shelton in.

"God damn it." Gemma Gordon half-stood. She exhaled an irritated dart of smoke. "I told Luke he couldn't play that shit-kicker music at my party."

Alice thought maybe Gemma was going to go over and kick her boyfriend's ass for messing with her music, but she sat back down on the log beside Alice. Gemma had pulled Alice over away from the fire so they could smoke a joint without having to share it with a dozen other people. Gemma passed it back to Alice and shook her head.

"I knew I shouldn't have invited that asshole."

Gemma was an interesting case. Her mother was a Malovo lawyer, and Gemma definitely projected the rich-bitch mean-girl vibe shared by most of the Lawndale clique. In fact, she probably would have been the Queen Bee among them, if she didn't demonstrate the same contempt for her country club peers that she did for the redneck farmer kids. She liked Alice for some reason, though. Maybe she saw her as one of the only people going to BHS who wasn't her obvious intellectual inferior. That, plus they shared a connoisseur's taste for quality herb.

Gemma had also, as it turned out, used to date Jose Collier. This made the fact that he and James had gone off in a car together a subject of vital curiosity for the both of them.

"Do you really think they're…" Alice said, holding in her smoke. After two lollies on the way over, the joint was putting her into a low stratospheric orbit.

"I'd put the odds at about fifty-fifty," Gemma said.

"So Jose *is* gay?"

"I'm pretty sure, yeah." Gemma took the joint back. "If *I* couldn't past second base with a guy, he's gotta be into dick. I mean, he's Mormon and all, so he does have that, 'I don't want to go to hell' thing going on. But believe me, I've cracked tougher nuts than that."

"Why did you go out with him for so long then?"

"Lemme tell ya, honey." By the way Gemma was slurring her words, Alice was pretty sure she was drunk as well as high. "In a town like this, being a beard for a gay boyfriend is one of the best deals a girl can get. All the social benefits, and you don't have to worry about getting knocked up with some white trash baby."

"Yeah, but don't you get...horny?"

"That is why the Goddess, in her infinite beneficence, has blessed us with the gift of the sacred vibrator."

"Oh."

"You *do* have a vibrator, don't you?"

"Well, no."

"Girl." Gemma grabbed Alice's knee. Hard. "You *need* vibration. James is sweet and cute and all, but that boy's obviously not going to help you out there. When's your birthday?"

"Um." Alice cleared her throat. "June." A month she was pretty sure she wasn't going to see come around again.

"Oh, that's past your due-by date, isn't it?" That was another thing about Gemma. She was one of the only people Alice knew who wasn't totally freaked out by her imminent death. Alice found this refreshing in a way, though it was a little strange just *how* comfortable Gemma was with the subject. "That sucks. Tell you what. Even though it's not your birthday, tomorrow I'm going to go on Amazon and order you a pink Buzzy-Bee like the one I have. It's amazing. I mean, like roll-your-eyes-back-in-your-head *amazing*."

"You don't need to..."

"No, I do," Gemma said. "Oh, I've got something else for you, too."

Gemma, the joint crooked in her mouth, leaned back and reached into her jeans pocket. She pulled out a little chain necklace and handed it to Alice.

Alice held the necklace up to have a look at the little silver charm in the firelight. It was a really strange design. A nude woman with her legs wrapped around a crescent moon.

"I've got one just like it," Gemma said. "Actually, I'm going to get a tattoo of that design done next week. Do you like it?"

"Yeah," Alice said. Gemma was looking at her with an uncomfortable intensity. *Is she hitting on me? Is that what's happening here? What do I do with that?* "It's really..."

"I know, you're probably getting a weird lesbian vibe off me right now, what with me buying you a sex toy and giving you a necklace with the moon going down on some chick. But trust me, it's not that. I'm hopelessly straight. Unfortunately. See, I'm in this...I guess you'd call it a group or a club or whatever. The lady who runs it is always asking me if there are any girls at school who'd be a good fit. But, you know. Most girls at our school are either stupid redneck country bitches brainwashed by that Church of the Shepherd crap, or else they're shallow Lawndale rich girls without a goddamn brain in their pretty little heads. But then there's you. I've talked to her about you. She's definitely interested."

"Wait," Alice said. "Who is this person you're talking to about me?"

"Her name's Roberta. She's really cool. I told her about how good you are with computers, and she said that could be useful. And I told her about your cancer." Gemma took a big drag and held it in for several seconds. "She said maybe we can help you with that."

"How could you help me with my cancer?"

Gemma passed the joint back to Alice and paused before answering. Alice got the sense she was choosing her words carefully.

"There are...forces," she said. "In and around this town. I know Bakersfield seems boring as hell, but it's a really unique place. Did you know it's at the exact geographic center of the state of Illinois?"

"Yeah, of course," Alice said. There was even a plaque marking the exact spot, out in front of the elementary school. "But I don't see what that has to do with me."

"It's the exact center of...other things, too," Gemma grasped. "Roberta explained it to me this way once. So you know how people say good and evil are two sides of the same coin?"

"Sure."

"Well, imagine the coin, the good and evil coin, is spinning. Okay? Spinning, so perfectly balanced it doesn't even wobble. And it's spinning right on the pivot of a perfectly balanced teeter-totter. That's Bakersfield."

"Okay..."

"See, there's balance, but it's precarious," Gemma continued, frustrated Alice wasn't getting it. "Even small shifts can knock off the equilibrium. And that creates energy. Energy we can use to accomplish amazing things. That's what we're doing here, tonight."

"I thought we were just partying in the woods."

"It's a ceremony," Gemma insisted. "A ritual. Burying the doll, wearing the masks, the whole Dionysian hedonism thing. What we're really doing is knocking off the balance a little bit, to create energy for the real work that's going to happen in the next couple days. It's going to be an interesting Halloween."

Alice stubbed the joint out on the log. "Either I'm too stoned to follow what you're saying, or I'm not stoned enough for it to make any sense."

Gemma laughed. "That's all right. You'll see. Tomorrow I want you to come..."

She stopped when she James stalking over towards them, holding his hand up against the side of his forehead.

"I want to go home, Alice," he said, his voice shaking.

"James?" Alice stood up and got a glimpse of his tear-streaked face in the dim light. "Are you *bleeding?*"

He pulled his hand away from his temple and looked down at the blood on his fingertips. "His ring must have cut me."

Gemma stood up beside Alice. She grabbed James's hand. "Jose hit you?"

"I don't want to talk about it," James said, pulling away. "I want to go home." He looked desperately to Alice. "Can we just go home?"

"Where'd he go? Jose!" Gemma barked.

"I'm okay, I swear," James said. "I'm just embarrassed. Can we get out of here, please?"

"No," Gemma said. "You can't let this go. *I* won't let it go. *Jose!*"

She saw him standing over beside the fire, starting in on a fresh bottle of beer, talking to a couple of other guys.

"Get your ass over here!"

Jose exchanged an obnoxious "better see what this crazy bitch wants" look with his buddies, who gave him some commiserating laughter. Reluctantly putting his beer down, he walked over towards them.

"What?" he said.

"Did you hit James?" Gemma demanded.

"Yeah. Because he grabbed my dick."

"I did not," James protested.

"Yeah you did, you little faggot."

"Hey!" Alice felt fury rising up inside her, penetrating many levels of stony mellow. "You can't call him that!"

"No, I didn't," James said to Alice. "I...I touched his knee."

"And then he tried to kiss me!"

James nodded. "I did. But he..." He looked Jose in the eye. "I thought you wanted me to. The way you were talking to me. The things you were saying."

"No." Jose looked away from James, appealing to Gemma. "I'm not a queer like him."

"Yes, you are," Gemma's face twisted in disgust. She punched Jose in the arm. "Shithead. Just because you don't have the balls to admit it doesn't give you the right to *punch* somebody because he got confused by your mixed fucking signals. God."

"I'm not gay!" Jose looked like he might start crying now. "Why does everybody keep saying that?"

"Jesus, I wonder," Gemma said.

"It's not a big deal," James said. "Let's just go, okay?"

"James!" Somebody else was calling to him, from over by the fire. It sounded like a little kid. Alice looked up and saw James's ten-year-old cousin Ben running towards them. How he happened to be there, she had no idea.

"Ben?" James said, sounding as baffled by his cousin's appearance as Alice was. "What are you doing here?"

"There's something wrong with my mom," Ben said. "Can you take me home?"

A young girl appeared behind Ben. She looked as confused as Alice felt. Something strange was happening here.

"We came out here to spy on the party," Ben said. "But now I think my mom's in bad trouble. Please, James, take me home, all right?"

James's cell phone rang right at that moment. He pulled it out of his pocket and looked down at the screen. "It's Lana."

"See?" Ben said. "She's going to say something bad happened with my mom."

James flashed Alice a worried look. The phone rang two more times before he gained the courage to answer.

"Hi," he finally said. He frowned. "It's okay, Lana. He's here with me. No. What happened?" He pressed the phone close against his ear and plugged a finger into his other ear. "Arrested? What for?" He flashed Alice a worried look as he listened. "No. Go ahead and go. I'll take care of Ben, okay? Don't worry about him. Call me when you find out what's going on."

James hung up. All five of the others, even Jose, were looking at him for explanation.

"I don't know how you could have known that, Ben," James said. "But your mom just got arrested. They're accusing her of performing an illegal abortion."

"What?" Alice said.

"I don't know," James said. "That's all Lana told me. The sheriff's transporting her to the jail over in Lincoln."

"The sheriff?" Ben said, his voice breaking. "Sheriff *Bates*?"

"Don't worry, Ben," James said. "She'll be okay. Let's get you home, okay? Your little friend, too."

"Our bikes are parked over by the tree," the girl said. "We can't leave them there."

"Let's go get them," James said. "We can put them in my trunk."

"I'll help," Jose said. Everybody looked at him curiously for a second. His face revealed some kind of inner turmoil.

"I'm sorry," he said. "Sorry I hit you. I was..." He shook his head. "I'm sorry about your aunt, too. Can I help you with the kid's bikes, please?"

"Sure." James gave Jose a look Alice couldn't quite decipher. "Come on."

James and Jose left with the two kids to get their bikes. Alice was left alone with Gemma, who was looking at her with an odd elation.

"See?" Gemma said. "I told you it was going to get interesting."

CHAPTER 18

10:24 PM

BLOOD DRIPPED FROM a fresh cut on Michelle's right cheek. She wasn't sure when she'd received the injury. It might have been when Sgt. McMurtry had slammed her against the wall of Sandy's trailer, or when he had thrown her to the floor, or when he had shoved her into the back of Bate's sheriff's department cruiser, banging her face into the door frame. With her hands cuffed behind her, she had to wipe her cheek on her shoulder. Her top was already ruined, splattered with Sandy's blood. Adding a bit of her own wouldn't make much difference.

They were on the dark country highway, heading north towards the Logan County jail in Lincoln. A good twenty minute drive normally, but Bates was taking the nearly deserted road at enough of a clip to make it in fifteen. Bates had talked McMurtry into allowing him take Michelle to the county lock-up instead of a state police holding cell in Springfield. Michelle honestly didn't know which was worse. Sgt. McMurtry was gripped with rage and contempt for Michelle, seeming to take her very existence as an affront. Bates, shockingly, was calm and reasonable in comparison. That had been the gist of his argument as well.

"You're too dang mad, Charlie," Bates had said back at the trailer. "You take this lady into custody, you're going to do something you regret. You're too dang mad. So why don't you take charge of the crime scene here. I'll book her in Lincoln. She's not going anywhere."

Michelle wondered if they were playing some good cop/bad cop gambit on her. If they were, she was reasonably certain Bates had never fallen on the "good" side of that divide before. He was definitely a bad cop.

Still, he had so far treated her with nothing less than courtesy. He'd even allowed her to call Lana from his cellphone, dialing the number for her and holding the phone up to her uninjured cheek. He didn't have to do that. Thankfully, the call had gone through and, thankfully, Lana had actually answered. She was going to make some calls to try to get her a lawyer, though Michelle doubted she'd have much luck with that at ten o'clock on a Saturday. She was resigned to spending at least one night in jail.

After the call, Michelle did something she never thought she'd do. She said, "thank you" to her sister's murderer.

"Heck, Ms. Blair-Delany," Bates had replied. "It's the neighborly thing to do."

She leaned back in her seat now, trying to find a halfway comfortable position sitting on her tightly clamped wrists. There wasn't one to be had.

"You doing all right back there?" Bates asked.

Michelle didn't know how to respond. She didn't trust this man, and didn't understand why he was feigning kindness now.

"I've had better days," she finally said.

"You're bleeding there, on your cheek. There's blood there."

"Thanks to your friend."

"Yeah, well," Bates said. "You have to know Sgt. McMurtry's a good guy. A good cop, one of the best I've known. But you did provoke him. You struck a police officer. That never ends well."

"He called me a dyke bitch."

"I'm sure he'd take that back if he could, but you really touched a nerve with him. He's a good cop, one of the best I've known, but he's got a particular soft spot for unborn babies. Sayin' the word abortion to him's like wavin' a red flag to a bull."

"It wasn't an abortion," Michelle insisted again. Having to repeat the denial, to this particular man, both wearied and aggravated her. "I'm a pregnancy coach. Sandy called me over because she was having pains. It turned out they were contractions. She was in premature labor. I did all I could for her, but the baby...those horns. They tore her up."

Telling it, Michelle relived the horror a little. She forced herself to swallow the fresh grief, though. She would not allow herself to cry in front of this man.

"That all may be true, Ms. Blair-Delany," Bates said. "And I'm sure our investigation will get to the bottom of what really happened there. But from our point of view, it looks pretty darn bad. We got an anonymous call, saying you were performing an abortion."

"Yeah, where did that call come from? Nobody even knew I was down there."

"Well, see. That's the funny thing about anonymous calls. Half the time, you don't know who's makin' 'em."

Is he fucking with me?

"So we walk in on that scene and there's blood everywhere. Dead woman, dead baby. Blood everywhere. Well, you have to admit it all looks pretty darn bad from our point of view."

There was something odd about the way Bates was speaking. His polite country Sheriff drawl—an affectation that didn't suit him—came and went. It was overly strong at times and at other times was barely there. He was like a comedian doing an Andy Griffith impression that still needed some practice in the mirror at home before he attempted it on stage. He was repeating himself quite a bit, too.

The whole thing was deeply strange, now that she had time to think about it. In hindsight, it almost seemed like an elaborate set-up. She'd been lured down to the trailer, where the phones were somehow disabled. An anonymous call had been made to the police while she struggled to save a woman and a child who were beyond saving. Michelle sensed she'd been manipulated into this position. But why and how and by whom were unfathomable questions.

Could Bates have set this whole thing up somehow, to trap her? Was she headed now for a jail cell "suicide"? That didn't make sense, though. Even if Bates did want to eliminate her for some reason, there were surely simpler ways to accomplish it. Why the elaborate production?

Her mind chased itself in paranoid loops for a few dark highway miles until Michelle gave up trying to understand. She was weary to the point of collapse, the adrenaline overdose of the past two hours finally depleted.

"Say, Ms. Blair-Delany," Bates said from the front seat. "I got something I been meaning to say to you for a while now."

Michelle looked up into the rear-view mirror. The sheriff's eyes were just visible there, in the reflected glow of the dashboard lights. He seemed to be leering at her, his gaze a hard contrast to the odd softness of his voice.

"I'm real sorry, about what happened with your sister."

"What *happened?*" she said, not quite believing what she was hearing. "You mean when you shot her?"

"Yes," he said. "I shot her. But she attacked me. Bit me on the neck. I still got a scar. Assaultin' a police officer never ends well. So I shot her. I still got a scar, on my neck, where she bit me. But I am real sorry, about what happened with your sister."

Michelle opened her mouth, but couldn't form a response. She didn't know if she was more thrown by the fact that he was apologizing, something she had never would have expected in a million years, or by the disjointed, record-skipping stutter of his words.

"That was a confusing time, for all of us. I suffered loss, as well. Not as much as you, but I suffered loss as well. My wife left me. My father, well he was in a nursing home with Alzheimer's and he passed away shortly after that. So I suffered loss as well. That was a confusing time. For all of us."

"I'm sorry," Michelle almost said. She managed to catch herself at the last second, retracting the words so they came out as barely a whisper, little more than mouthing them. She had no sympathy for this man.

"I like to think I've changed since then," Bates said. "I'm a changed man. I like to think so, anyway. I'm not so...angry anymore. I've been goin' to church again, tryin' to get right with the Lord, you know? He was in a nursing home with Alzheimer's and he passed away. That was a confusing time."

"For all of us," Michelle seconded, to see how he'd respond.

"That's right." Bates nodded in agreement. "For all of us. We've all suffered loss."

A car was approaching in the opposite lane, the bright headlights filling the car with white light. "I'll take care of you, miss," he said. In the rear view, Bate's briefly illuminated eyes glared at Michelle with gleaming fury, a direct rebuke to the mildness of his words. "I'm a changed man." The other car passed, and its retreating tail lights flooded the rearview with bloody light. Bate's furious gaze was stained with hellfire red.

"I'm not so angry anymore."

CHAPTER 19

10:33 PM

THE FIRE WAS burning down and the moon had disappeared from the skylight overhead. The wine bottle was empty. The memory of the last glass was a radiant, buzzing glow in Mark's belly and in his brain. He was warm and drowsy, sinking into the softness of the couch and of the woman in his arms. Ellie turned to him and finally whispered with winey breath the words he'd been longing to hear for almost an hour: "Let's go to bed."

Even from across the room, Lizzy heard that.

"You're going up to Ellie's room?" The naked girl relaxed her pose, tilting her head at Mark with a childlike curiosity. Her eyes grew wide with genuine concern.

"Lizzy!" Roberta snapped. She looked up from the charcoal sketch she was scratching onto the canvas draped across most of the room's north wall. Mark's knowledge of the artistic process was limited, but he thought it was unusual for the artist to be nude as well as her model. "Please hold still."

Roberta was painting a huge mural, a surreal night-sky scene. Shadowy flocks of night-birds swarmed a purple sky dotted with fiery stars and a single streaking comet. The centerpiece of the mural was a life-size version of the image Mark recognized from the tattoo he'd glimpsed on Ellie's neck. A woman rode astride the crescent lunar face, her legs open to receive the moon-man's oral adulation. The mural appeared complete save for the central figure of the woman, which was still a skeletal sketch.

Lizzy, serving as the model for the moon-ravaged woman, snapped back into her awkward position. She sat backwards astride the hanging hammock chair that stood in for the shape of the crescent moon.

"Head back," Roberta called. "Relax your arm." She walked over and made fussing manual adjustments to Lizzy's pose. Only when she was satisfied did she resume her sketching.

"You shouldn't go up into her room," Lizzy warned, this time without breaking her pose. "There's a ghost in there."

"Oh my God. There's no ghost," Ellie said, with the irritated air of a teenage girl embarrassed in front of a boyfriend by her little sister. She stood up and, taking Mark's hand, pulled him to his feet as well. "Come on."

"There is too a ghost," Lizzie said, her airy little girl voice utterly without guile. "I've seen it. It pushes books off the shelf."

"You push the books off my shelf," Ellie challenged.

"Nuh-uh."

"You shouldn't even go in my room, anyway."

"It was my room before it was your room," Lizzy pouted.

"Well, it's my room now." Ellie pulled Mark a few paces across the room, but she seemed hesitant, possibly a little anxious. Maybe there *was* a ghost.

"Are you going to do sexy stuff in there?" Lizzy asked.

"Jesus, Lizzy!" Ellie said.

"That's none of your business, Elizabeth," Roberta said, not looking up from her work. "Ellie and Mark are adults. They can do whatever they like."

"I'm an adult," Liz countered petulantly. "You never let me do what I want."

That comment hung in the air. Ellie pulled Mark over towards the staircase. He was limping slightly, his left ankle twinging a little where the motorcycle had landed on it.

"Goodnight," he said sheepishly, uncomfortable with the scrutiny cast his way by both the nude mother artist and her equally nude model daughter. Grasping the bannister for support, he followed Ellie up the stairs. Anticipatory lust rose in steady increments with every painful step, gradually overtaking the awkwardness they were leaving behind them on the ground floor.

They'd spent the past hour or so down there, out of what Mark assumed to be an unspoken house rule. He got the feeling Roberta would have considered it rude of him and Ellie to simply go upstairs and hop into bed. First, they had to undergo the strange social ritual of sharing a bottle of wine and watching Roberta work, pretending all the rampant nudity didn't make anyone uncomfortable.

"It gets hot in this house and I don't like getting paint on my clothes," Roberta had explained to Mark when he first came inside. "I'll put on a robe if it disturbs you."

"No, it's cool," he'd said. Truthfully, Roberta's wizened nakedness didn't bother him. She was completely unabashed, obviously comfortable in her skin, and Mark was worldly enough not to be shocked. Roberta's body was a decade or two past the point where he would have gazed upon it as a sexual object, though he could still see the foundation of the curvaceous beauty she had probably once been. Now her nudity had the quality of the white shirt and leather smock he wore in the New Salem blacksmithing shop. It was simply the uniform she wore while she plied her trade. "It's your home."

Lizzy, though, was a different story. Her nakedness did unsettle him, just a bit.

He first saw her when they stepped inside, straddling the hammock swing in front of the breathtaking mural. Lizzy was young, perhaps younger than Ellie, and almost ridiculously voluptuous. Her flawless skin and long brown hair glowed with golden light, as if illuminated from within.

"This is my daughter, Lizzy," Roberta said. She gave Mark a hard look, perhaps scrutinizing him for any signs of untoward lust. Ellie mirrored the expression, but her intent was clearer. She was blatantly daring him to find the other girl attractive.

"I'm not really her daughter," Lizzy informed him. "I'm adopted."

While her body looked like a painting Vargas would have rejected as being too implausibly sexy, Lizzy's face was vacuous and juvenile, with dull brown eyes and a slightly slack jaw. Mark wondered if she was, if not mentally handicapped, perhaps not quite all there.

"Lizzy, this is Mark Davies," Roberta said.

"Mark Davies, who wrote *Blood World?*" Lizzy said in her childish voice.

"That's me," he replied, surprised.

"Roberta reads me those books at bedtime," Lizzy explained.

"She likes anything with vampires." Roberta walked off into the kitchen adjoining the front room studio and continued talking from the other room: "I tend to skip over the more violent parts. And the sex scenes, which are a bit phallocentric for my taste."

"*Blood World*'s pretty good," Lizzy said. "But I like *Twilight* better."

Jesus, Mark thought. *Everyone's a goddamn critic.* Still, it was strange. It had been months since he'd met anyone who would admit to being a reader of his, and now he'd encountered three in one night.

Roberta returned from the kitchen, bearing a bottle of red wine and three glasses. She set them down on her work bench, where a corkscrew was conveniently at hand.

"Sit," she invited, with the force of a command. "Have some wine. Talk for a while."

So Mark curled up beside Ellie on the couch and accepted the glass that was pressed into his hand. Ellie pointed up at the skylight directly above them. The moon was perfectly framed in the center of the clear glass pane. Unlike the waning crescent presented in the mural, the overhead moon was a brilliant, pregnant gibbous.

"It's almost full," Ellie whispered to Mark. There was something suggestive about the way she phrased this. The words were filled with erotic promise, like a double entendre which he caught the intent of, but not the meeting. She unclasped her choker necklace and slid it from her throat, finally revealing her tattoo, which was a miniature of the grand-scale mural before them. To Mark, the baring of her neck was as provocative as if she'd taken off her top. On impulse, he kissed her ink-stained flesh, with the taste of the blood-red wine still heavy on his tongue. Ellie gasped as if bitten.

Now, following her up the stairs to the promised land of her bedroom, Mark recalled that daring kiss with mounting anticipation of all the other places on her he'd like to taste.

He glimpsed her cluttered room for a second before she turned out the lights and shut the door behind them. A small nightlight plugged into the wall now provided the only illumination. Ellie shed her clothes in the long shadows it cast, dropping them carelessly to the floor. She kissed Mark with a cannibal's fervor. Mark held her close, exploring the wondrous contours of her body, frantic with the warm electric feel of unfamiliar flesh beneath his hands.

They stumbled closely entwined over to the bed. Half-blind and clumsy-drunk, tripping over crap on the floor, they fell laughing onto the mattress. The bed was unmade, the twisted sheets mounded with bunched-up blankets and seemingly dozens of pillows. All of it smelled of Ellie's strange, spicy aroma. *Oregano?*

In the short trip from the door to the bed, Ellie had managed to unfasten and unzip Mark, with a pickpocket's dexterity. His clothes thus loosened, her hands and his conspired to pull them off and toss them away. A minute later, Mark and Ellie were writhing naked in the soft dunes of bedding. They inhaled the fog of their mingled arousal, grappling together for the sake of the tingling friction of flesh on flesh. Ellie and Mark covered one another with hungry nibbling kisses, crazed with the narcotic taste of each other's salt and sweat and skin. Mark latched onto a nipple, a pebbly surprise to his tongue.

"Mark," Ellie gasped. "Do to me what the moon's doing to the girl in the insignia."

Insignia. Even in the throes of his delirium, he found that to be a curious word to use. "Mmm," he made a moaning assent, abandoning with some regret the sweet cap he suckled. His lips and tongue traced a sluggish trail down her smooth flat belly.

"You'll do that for me?" Ellie said. "Some guys won't the first time."

"Mmm," Mark re-iterated. He was already almost there, but it seemed a waste to hurry. Every inch of her was delicious. His fluttering tongue dipped for a second into the hard little pit of her navel, and then continued downwards towards the humid pulsing heat source that was drawing him like a magnet.

"God, yeah," Ellie begged. "Please."

Her legs opened before him. Mark burrowed into the center of her being. Ellie writhed and gasped and surged against his puckering.

"Oh, Mark." Ellie's moan contained a strange note of regret, as if she'd goaded him into committing a fatal error. He was too far gone to be dissuaded by her contradictions anymore.

Mark had long promised himself that when he finally found himself with another woman, he would not compare her to Missy. But memories of his ex-wife came helplessly to mind. He had loved doing this very thing to her, too. Mark was startled by how different Ellie tasted. Wilder than

Missy, not as sweet. Ellie's juices were red wine to Missy's white; dark chocolate to Missy's milk. Mark lapped Ellie's bittersweet resin. She cried out when he penetrated her with his tongue and Mark groaned in empathy. He was exultant, delirious, lost in a dream.

"Go up a little," Ellie panted. "Up, up." Another difference. Missy had always received this gift in silence, Mark relying upon his well-learned knowledge of her body's responses to gauge his efforts. Ellie, though, was a talker. "There. Yeah, right there."

She grabbed him by the hair and held him firm, keeping him on point.

"That feels so nice, Mark," she said. "It's almost worth it."

"Uh?" Mark made a muffled, questioning vowel sound. That seemed a strange comment, even coming from her.

"Don't stop," she said. "It's really relaxing. Even if I fall asleep, keep going."

"Urm," he hummed against her, making her giggle and squirm.

"This was my room when I was a teenager, too," she said, leaning her head back and looking up at the ceiling. "Roberta was friends with my dad. After Mom died, we stayed with her for a while. In fact, we slept together in this very bed."

Mark lifted his head to look at her curiously, but with a tug on his hair she bid him to continue his work.

"It was nothing like that," she chided. "I couldn't stand to be alone then. Actually, he was murdered in this room. I saw it happen."

At that, Mark did stop. Weird, he could handle. Weird, he even kind of liked. But this was getting to be a little *too* weird.

"Some men came for him." Ellie didn't seem to notice Mark had stopped, but she still clamped his head tightly between her thighs and retained her grasp on his hair. Breathing, he fretted, might become an issue if he couldn't lift his head soon. "Dad heard them coming. He liked to gamble, and he owed a lot of money to some people, so he was always on edge. He made me hide in the closet. That closet over there. The door was open, though, just a crack."

Mark squirmed, but she would not release him.

"There were two of them, wearing masks. I think they were just Wile E. Coyote masks from Wal-Mart, but they were painted black and day-glow red, with crazy spirals around the eyes and blood dripping from the mouths. They looked like freaky-looking African tribal masks or something. The guys in the masks shot my dad seven times. I counted." Ellie arched her back and let out a breathless shudder. "Berta filled in the bullet holes with spackle, but you can still kind of see them. There's one on the wall there, right above the headboard. I look up at it sometimes and wonder if that was a bullet that had actually passed through my dad's body, or if it was a shot that went wild. If it went through his body, maybe some of his blood is left inside the plaster."

"Okay." Mark pulled away, wrenching his head free. He stood up. "I'm done."

"What?" Ellie looked genuinely surprised. "What's wrong?"

"What's wrong?" He scanned the dark floor, squinting for his clothes. "Your pillow talk is a little on the intense side, Ellie."

"I was opening up to you," she said, sitting up and pulling a blanket over herself. "I've never told a guy about that before. I felt like I could trust you."

"I appreciate that," Mark said. He spied something white on the ground. He picked it up thinking it might be his underwear, only to find it was a discarded pillowcase. "I'm glad you feel that comfortable with me. But that was not the appropriate moment to share the 'my father was killed in this very room' story."

"Appropriate?" she gasped, outraged. "You didn't think it was *appropriate*?"

"Listen, Ellie. If you want to open up and share traumatic childhood stories, I'll do that with you. I've got some crazy shit I'd love to get off my chest, too. But, just so you know, as foreplay, it's kind of a mood killer."

"Sorry if me telling you about my father's murder wrecked your boner."

"You don't need to be sorry, but actually, yeah it did." By happy accident, Mark found his pants. "So, do you want to get dressed and talk?"

"Just go."

"That's fine, too. If that's what you want. Can you turn on the lights, though, so I can find my clothes?"

Ellie switched on a bedside lamp and turned away from him. If she was crying, she was doing so silently. Mark found his shirt, his shoes and one sock. He wrote the other sock and his underwear off as acceptable losses.

"Ellie," he said as he was pulling his clothes on. "I'm sorry it ended like this. I did have fun with you tonight. Maybe we just drank too much and so things moved too fast. If you want to try it again, I'd like that. If not, I hope we can at least be cool with each other at work."

No response. She didn't even move. Mark went over and put a hand on her bare shoulder.

"Don't fucking touch me," she growled.

"Sorry," he said again. "I am sorry, Ellie. Are you all right?"

"Get the fuck out of my bedroom."

"Okay."

He stepped out of the room and walked down the stairs. Most of the lights were out downstairs, except the track lighting along one wall that illuminated the unfinished mural. Roberta was sitting in the dark on a couch, studying her work. She was wearing a bathrobe now, signifying that she was done for the night. Mark didn't see Lizzy anywhere and assumed she'd gone to bed. Roberta looked up when she saw Mark descend the stairs.

"Didn't work out?" she said.

"You know, I..." Mark was at a loss.

"You don't need to say anything. I've known Ellie all her life. She can be difficult."

"That's a good word to describe her, yeah."

"She's a remarkable young woman, though," Roberta said. "If you can get past her defenses, it's well worth the effort."

"I don't know that she wants me to anymore."

Roberta shrugged, continuing to stare at her mural. "What are you going to do now?"

"Well, if you tell me what direction Bakersfield is, I'll just hobble my way home. Maybe I can make it there by morning."

"Nonsense," Roberta said. "I can give you a ride."

"That would be so great. I would appreciate that like you would not believe."

"Not a problem, Mark. Just give me a few more moments with my painting. I always stare at it for a while after a session, to plan my next move. It's part of the process."

Mark sat beside her. "It's an amazing piece," he said. "Breathtaking, even."

"Thank you."

"Did you do Ellie's tattoo, as well?"

"Yes. I think sometimes needle on skin is more my true medium than brush on canvas. I do appreciate the bigger scale, though."

"They're both remarkable. What does it mean?"

Roberta stared at the painted wall for a few moments, and Mark wasn't sure if she was going to answer him.

"It's a power symbol, primarily," she said. "A reclamation of power women once had and can attain once again. Most cultures throughout human history have identified Luna as a goddess, which seems obvious considering her cycles. But of course modern western culture, with its engrained gynophobia, has denoted the moon as masculine. 'The Man in the Moon,' they say. This image seeks to balance that. It's a sexual image, but without the connotations of male dominance that pornography carries. The man in the moon is placed in a subservient position, servicing the woman, pleasing her. Cunnilingus removes the phallus from the equation and, in a way, feminizes the masculine moon."

Mark wiped his face, a bit guiltily. Roberta looked over at him.

"I bet now you're sorry you asked," she said. She set her hand above Mark's knee, a bit higher up the leg than he was prepared for, and then stood up. "Let me put some warmer clothes on and then I'll get you home."

"Thank you."

While she was out of the room, Mark pulled his cell phone from his pocket. He'd turned the phone off before his date. When he re-activated the device, it came to life with an alarming cascade of chimes. Mark looked down at the screen. Twenty-eight new texts and twenty-one voice mails, more communication than he typically received in a month.

"What the fuck," he said out loud.

THE DAY BEFORE

HALLOWEEN

CHAPTER 20

12:36 PM

T HEY WERE ON 121, south of Lincoln, when the rain began. Cold desultory spatters on the windshield at first, gradually building into a steady misty dowsing. There is nothing in the world as gray or depressing as a late October rain in Illinois. Mark looked out on empty dirt fields devoid of color, intersecting at the horizon with the drab gray sky. When he lived out west, Mark had loved to drive through the desert and look out on vistas of stunning oblivion. In terms of utter desolation, though, nothing held a candle to Illinois farmland on a rainy day after the harvest. Even the occasional farmhouse they drove past did nothing to lessen the bleakness. The houses appeared dark and lifeless and empty, like structures left standing after an apocalypse. It was difficult to imagine people living inside them.

James was driving, as Mark's car was still parked down in Springfield. Lana and Ben were in the backseat. There was little conversation on the drive. All four of them were suffering hangovers (in Mark's case, a literal one) from the previous night's traumas. James had a bruised cut on one temple he didn't want to talk about. Likewise, Ben hadn't fully explained how he'd come to be out in the woods when he should have been home in bed. He gazed anxiously out into the scrolling distance, his worry for his mother as plain as the creased furrows on his forehead. Lana had done her best to soothe him, but these efforts seemed to have exhausted her. She was dozing now, with her head resting against the window.

Mark had plenty of time to think on the quiet drive over. Half his mind was devoted to replaying his ill-fated date with Ellie. He went over and over it, shamefully lingering on the evening's physical aspects. The feel and the taste of her skin. How she'd looked, how she'd smelled. He constructed hypothetical fantasy scenarios in ways the night might have ended differently if he'd played it better. But then Mark would catch himself in the midst of one of these adolescent fancies, and the other half of his mind would chide the first for such selfish thoughts. He should be entirely focused on helping Missy.

What had happened to her was unbelievable, her arrest a grave injustice. Mark knew she wasn't even capable of what she'd been charged with. Missy was the most empathetic person he'd ever known. Being present for the death of a mother and a still-born child must have been horrible for her. His travails of the previous night were inconsequential in the face of her ordeal.

Mark hadn't talked to her himself, but Lana had told Mark that Michelle had said the baby was severely deformed. Mark couldn't help but wonder if the fatal birth defect had anything to do with whatever crap Malovo had dumped into the water to counteract the sleepwalking sickness. Lots of women in town had been impregnated on that wild weekend, and there were rumors several of them had miscarried. He'd also heard that other women who were already pregnant when the outbreak occurred had delivered babies with birth defects.

If Mark were to confront his mother about this, he knew she'd have some slick explanation about how her beloved employer could not possibly be responsible. It made him angry, that this company could so casually manipulate the lives of everyone in town, with no fear of culpability.

Still, even with Malovo being such a handy scapegoat, Mark couldn't shake the guilty sense that none of this would have happened if he had simply not gone out with Ellie. Thinking with his dick was a trait he'd almost certainly inherited from his father. If he'd stayed home, maybe he could have somehow prevented Missy's arrest, and whatever had happened with James, and whatever had happened with Ben, too. The whole world had fallen apart while he was out trying to get laid.

There you go again. As usual, the scolding voice in his head was his ex-wife's. *Thinking everything's about you.*

When they finally pulled into the parking lot at the jail, Ben tried to shake Lana awake. Her eyes fluttered open for a second, but then she curled up against the side door and went back to sleep.

Mark turned around in his seat. "Lana," he said, touching her leg. "We're here."

"What?" she mumbled.

"We're at the jail."

"Jail?" She blinked at him, confused. Comprehension slowly dawned. "Oh, Chelle." She shook her head, to clear the cobwebs. "Sorry. I don't know what's wrong with me. I'm so tired."

"It's all right. Are you up for this?"

She nodded. "Ready as I'll ever be."

The rain was pouring down now. They dashed across the lot, but still got soaked as they made their way inside. The sheriff's department headquarters was nearly deserted on this Sunday afternoon, and so dimly lit inside it seemed they could hardly be bothered to leave the lights on. The front desk was manned by a lone deputy, whose name badge read "Anderson." Deputy Anderson was an older, balding man with a soft weathered face and sharp eyes. He leaned back in his seat and watched the four of them approach, dripping all over the floor. He had a bored expression, though his eyes were keen and suspicious.

"Really coming down out there," he observed.

"Cats and dogs," Mark affirmed. "We're here to visit a prisoner. Michelle Blair-Delany."

Anderson scanned the four soaking wet individuals standing before his desk with distrust, though his face retained the weary half-smile.

"Prisoners are allowed only two visitors at a time," he said.

"Okay, that's cool," Mark said, stepping aside. He looked over at Lana. "You and Ben should go first. James and I can wait out here."

The deputy sighed and picked up a sign-in clipboard. "I need to see some ID," he said, slipping on a pair of glasses.

Lana fetched her license from her purse and slid it across the desk. Deputy Anderson barely glanced at it. "For both visitors, please."

Lana put her hand on Ben's shoulder. "He doesn't have an ID. He's eleven."

Anderson squinted in turn at Lana and Ben, their racial disparity apparently causing him a twinge of pain. "Are you the boy's mother?" he asked, with pointed irony.

"No," Lana spoke very slowly, which Mark recognized as a sign of her incipient anger. "His mother is who we've come here to visit."

"And who are you?"

"I'm her wife."

"You're kidding." The deputy's chuckle sounded genuinely incredulous, as if he'd never heard of such an absurd thing.

"Do I look like I'm kidding?" Lana's former sleepiness was gone. She looked across the desk, her gaze hard and sharp.

"Minors are only allowed visitation if accompanied by a parent." Deputy Anderson's voice had grown sharper, too, rising to meet Lana's antagonism.

"Look," Mark put in, trying to defuse the scene. "I'm his father. Lana has my permission to take Ben back there to visit his Mom."

"I don't need your permission," Lana said.

"If you're his father, you're free to take him back," Anderson said. "She's not."

"You don't understand the situation," Mark said.

"You're right about that," the deputy said. "I've never seen a deal like this. What is it, some kind of polygamy thing?"

"Oh, for God's sake," Lana spat.

"No," Mark said. "It's actually pretty simple. I'm Michelle's ex-husband. Lana here is her current wife."

"Ex-husband?" Anderson frowned. "So is she a gay or not?"

Lana closed her eyes for a moment, swallowing her rage before it could surface. "I am legally married to Ben's mother. That makes me his legal guardian, and entitles me to escort him to visit his mother in your jail. Are you going to do your job and let me pass?"

"Don't take that tone with me, lady," Anderson said. "Visitation is entirely at my discretion and this whole situation seems damn fishy to me. Do you have any documentation of your, uh, alleged relationship?"

"You mean my *marriage license*? No. I don't carry my goddamn marriage license around with me."

"Well, then there's not a hell of a lot I can do for you."

Lana let out a little cry of frustration and stepped back from the desk.

"I won't tolerate tantrums, miss. If you can't control your temper, I'm going to have to ask you to leave."

Lana's eyes flared. For a second Mark, thought she might actually leap across the desk and throttle the asshole.

"We're not going to get to see Mom?" Ben cast wide, anxious eyes up at Mark.

"You're not going to leave here without seeing her," Mark assured his son. The best solution might be for him to take Ben back there himself. Lana could take her turn afterwards and see Missy one-on-one. This was a delicate situation, though. Not only was he unsure how Lana would take this suggestion, he was afraid to leave her alone with this homophobic cracker. He didn't want Ben to end up with both his moms in jail.

"There a problem?" came a voice from behind Deputy Anderson.

Mark looked up and saw the bulky frame of Sheriff Nathanial Bates emerge from a back office. Though he should have anticipated the possibility of encountering the sheriff at the sheriff's department headquarters, seeing Bates provoked an automatic fight-or-flight flush of adrenaline in Mark's blood. Fighting not being a viable option against an armed opponent twice his size, his first instinct was to grab Ben and fly right the hell out the door. The last time he'd seen the sheriff, Bates had tried to bury him alive after beating him senseless on a golf course.

Deputy Anderson glanced back at his boss. "These folks want to go back and visit the prisoner, but this lady here is not the boy's mother."

"Heck, Bob," Bates said mildly. "This family might be a little unconventional, but it's still a family. And Ms. Blair-Delany's the only prisoner we got back there right now, so it's not like the visiting room's going to be too crowded. Why don't you all go on back there?"

Mark looked over at Lana. His distrust and confusion was plainly mirrored on her face.

"You too, Mr. Davies." Bates smiled at Mark. He actually *smiled*. "I know you're on pretty good terms with your ex, and I admire that. Heck, I wish Mara and I could have stayed that friendly."

"Ah..." Mark was at a loss. "Thank you?"

"You're welcome," Bates said. "Your family might be a little unconventional, but it's still a family. It's love that defines a family, in my humble opinion. More so than traditional notions, anyway. So why don't you all go on back there? We only got the one prisoner right now, so it's not like the visiting room's going to be too crowded."

Bates came out and actually held the door open for them. Uncertainly, exchanging baffled glances, the four of them walked back to the little visiting room.

"Make yourselves nice and comfortable in here and I'll go fetch Michelle," Bates said. "You want me to have Bob put on a pot of coffee for you?"

"No thanks." In Lana's astonishment, she was barely able to speak above a whisper.

"All right, then," Bates said. "Have yourselves a nice long visit. I know Ms. Blair-Delany's got a lawyer coming by later on for our interview, and I'm looking forward to getting to the bottom of what happened. Frankly, I was real surprised to see her mixed up in this sort of business. I'm sure there's an explanation for it all." He looked right at Ben. "Hopefully, we'll be able to send your mama home today. How's that sound, champ?"

Ben cast a doubtful look over at Lana before answering. She nodded at him.

"That sounds real good, sir," Ben said.

"Yep." Bates chuckled. "Boy loves his mama. I think love defines a family, more than traditional notions. In my humble opinion, anyway. So you all get comfortable while I fetch Ms. Blair-Delany. I can have Bob put on a pot of coffee, if you like."

"Uh, no thanks," Mark said.

Bates exited the room, the smile plastered on his lips.

Mark turned to Lana when he was gone. "Who the hell is *that*?" he said.

CHAPTER 21

12:58 PM

AFTER THE ELEVEN o'clock services ended, Pastor Tom Peters of the Church of the Shepherd excused himself from the monthly Last Sunday Senior Lunch and drove up to Lincoln to meet with Sheriff Bates. Nathanial had summoned him with a rather mysterious text:

I need to see you matter of great spiritual import Lord's business

Of course, he didn't respond when Tom texted him back asking him to clarify that a bit, and he didn't pick up when Tom called, either. That was typical. Nathanial preferred face-to-face conversations, especially when it came to serious matters. In the months since Bates had experienced his stunning conversion following the Sickness, Tom had become something of a personal spiritual advisor for the man. This was a responsibility Tom did not take lightly. In saving Nathanial's soul, Tom knew he was also redeeming his own. They were like two drowning men who were able to stay afloat only by clinging to one another.

Before the Sickness, Tom had been under the thrall of Barry Tuttle, a man who was the embodiment of spiritual struggle. Love and hate, light and dark, good and evil—all these conflicts had been perfectly incarnated in Tom's relationship to the Church's former pastor.

Barry had led Tom to Christ, that couldn't be denied. Tom had been in a free-fall after his brother Toby was murdered by the Holiday Killer. Well on his way to sinking into despair and drugs. Maybe even suicide. Then his family had started attending the Church of the Shepherd. Pastor Barry facilitated Tom's call to service, getting him involved in the church from the start. Tom began serving as youth outreach director when he was a still teenager and he later became one of the administrators of the Loaves and Fishes International charity. Through the church, he'd also discovered his love for music and had started his band, Young Lions. The group was going stronger than ever. They'd just signed a deal with a Christian music label that would let them spread the Word through the power of song on a whole new level.

That was the good. That was the light. But there was darkness as well.

Barry had corrupted Tom's body. There was no other way to describe it. In shameful, dimly recalled encounters in Barry's office at the church (which was Tom's office now) or at the pastor's house. Barry had convinced Tom that these sessions, fraught with both pleasure and pain, had been conducted with the purpose of rooting out the sin he'd seen within Tom's heart. "To cast out sin, you have to bring it out into the light," Pastor Barry had told him. "You have to confront it head-on, if you want to get pure again." Tom was ashamed now at how easily he had swallowed that treacherous lie. For the longest time, he'd actually believed the fault had lain within him, and that Pastor Barry had set him free.

Even worse than what the pastor had done to Tom's body was the damage he'd done to his soul. Pastor Barry, along with Sheriff Bates, had been involved with running drugs into Central Illinois. In fact, the operation Bates had built made them essentially the sole source of cocaine, heroin and methamphetamine for the entire middle third of the state. Tom had been a loyal soldier in this evil enterprise, believing Pastor Barry when he'd said God's plan was mysterious and that evil acts can serve a greater good. Tom had done terrible things with this rationale. Some were so terrible he had not yet been able to confront them. Like what had happened to Jacob Norrell.

Jacob was another young man with whom Pastor Barry had become "involved." But then Jacob had threatened to reveal their relationship, and had blackmailed the pastor for drugs. Tom remembered being left in a church basement room, alone with Jacob Norrell. He also remembered there had been a gun in the room, resting on the table before him. After that, his memories broke down into the disjointed nonsense of the sleepwalking Sickness. Jacob Norrell was gone, though. That was undeniable. Nobody had seen him since. And there were bloodstains on the wall in that room. Tom had painted over them himself.

When Tom awoke from the Sickness, he learned Pastor Barry was dead. Suffering his own sleeping visions, Barry had murdered his wife Eve, then taken his own life. Tom, for the first time in decades, was free from the man. He was able to mourn the good that had been lost, and to bury the bad deep inside.

Sheriff Bates was missing for almost a week after the Sickness, and Tom had feared the worst for him as well. But when he reappeared, he had changed, as dramatically as Saul becoming Paul on the road to Damascus. Before, Bates had barely bothered to mask his contempt for people of faith. Afterwards, he came to Tom, literally on bended knees, sobbing, begging for help in finding his way back to the light. He repented, and immediately closed the drug operation. A multi-million dollar enterprise disappeared overnight. Addicts all over the middle part of the state were thrust into cold turkey withdrawal, Central Illinois having become perhaps the one place in the entire nation where there were simply no drugs to be found. The Barber clan, the sheriff's trusted criminal deputies, suddenly found themselves unemployed.

Like them, Tom had come to rely on the income the drugs brought him. It hurt at first, but he did have some savings, and there was a slight salary increase when he was named as Pastor Barry's successor. He and his wife Liz made it work. Things were better now than ever before. Not as much money coming in, of course, but now there was no guilt about the source of their income, no fear of being discovered.

Tom's heart was pure and clean, as long as he could keep the memories down in the hole.

It was almost one o'clock when he made it up to the Sheriff's Department headquarters. Deputy Bob Anderson was working the desk, as he had done since the previous sheriff's administration. Probably the one before that, too.

"Hello, Tom," Anderson said.

"Hey, Bob. The sheriff in his office? He wanted to see me."

"He's back in the men's room."

"All right," Tom said. "I'll wait."

"No, he told me to tell you to go on back there."

"Into the men's room?"

Anderson gave a "don't ask me, I just work here" shrug.

Tom thought that was a bit strange, but not completely out of line. Nathanial had gained a few eccentricities since his conversion. Tom didn't understand completely, but he accepted the odd speech patterns and strange little behavioral quirks as part of the sheriff's new personality. On balance, it was a definite improvement. Perhaps Nathanial simply thought the men's room would be a more private place to talk.

He found the sheriff standing before the bank of sinks along one wall, staring into the long mirror.

"Come over here, Tom," he said without looking up. "I want to show you something."

Tom went over and stood beside Nathanial, who pointed at something in the mirror. A bit of graffiti, written in black magic marker, high on the opposite wall above the urinals. "Save a chikin eat mor pussy," it said.

"Notice anything strange about that?" Nathanial asked.

"It's obscene," Tom noted. "Whoever wrote it can't even spell."

"Not that," Nathanial said. "Turn around and look."

Tom turned around. He saw now that the idiotic slogan had been written on the wall perfectly backwards.

"Whoever put that there meant for it to be read in the mirror," Nathanial said. "Now, why would somebody do that?"

"I don't know why anybody would write that in the first place," Tom said.

"Me neither," Nathanial said. He was still staring into the mirror. Tom met his eye in the reflection and saw something of the sheriff's old steely gravity there. "There's strange doings afoot, Tom. I don't mind telling you, I'm a little worried."

"What do you mean, Nathanial?"

"Do you know who I arrested last night? She's in the visiting room right now."

"Michelle Delany?" Tom said. The news of the arrest had spread quickly through town, spurred on by a crime scene photo of the deformed baby that had somehow been sent out via the sheriff department's emergency notification service.

"Yep." In the mirror, Nate grinned. "Do you know why I arrested her?"

"I heard she performed..." The word itself was difficult for Tom to say. "...an abortion. And the woman died. And the baby was abnormal."

"It wasn't an abortion," Nathanial said. "It was something even worse."

"What could be worse than…"

"Did you see the picture?"

"Yeah," Tom said, closing his eyes. The image was still burned there behind his lids. He wished he could un-see it. "It was horrible. I didn't want to look."

"The funny thing about it is, I never sent out that notification." Nate still hadn't turned away from the mirror. He met Tom's eyes in the reflection. "I e-mailed it to Janice in dispatch, purely for evidentiary purposes. She swears she has no idea how it got sent out."

Tom got a chill when Nathanial said that.

"What's the first thing you noticed about that dead baby?" Nathanial asked.

"Horns," Tom whispered. He was beginning to feel afraid. "It had horns."

Nathanial nodded grimly. "Do you know who Thomas Gorman is?"

"Yeah, of course." Gorman was something of a celebrity, an expert on occult crimes who'd written several books on the subject. He frequently appeared on talk shows and news programs, and spoke often at churches and law enforcement seminars. Tom had looked into having him lecture at the church, but Gorman's speaking fee was well outside their budget.

"I talked to him this morning," Nathanial said.

"Really?"

"Yeah. I e-mailed him that picture, to see if maybe he'd want to serve as a consultant on this case."

"Why?" Tom asked.

"When I saw that dead baby with the horns on its head, I got this terrible feeling, like I was looking at the devil himself. I knew there was something sinister going on. You want to know what Gorman told me?"

Tom shivered. He almost didn't want to know. "What?"

"He said there's this trend now, among cult groups, to try to summon demons to possess the souls of unborn children."

"No," Tom moaned.

"I'm afraid so, Tom. The good news is, he said that because the child was stillborn, this was an unsuccessful attempt. The baby's poor little body couldn't handle the demonic presence in its soul. It died. All things considered, we have to take that as God's mercy."

"Yes." Tom's eyes were actually watering.

"The bad news is, we may have a satanic coven, right here in Bakersfield. I don't know if that woman in there is the ringleader, or just a follower, but the one thing that's clear is that she is a real, practicing..."

"...witch." Tom spoke the word that chilled him to the core. "I know she is. She's been into that stuff since she was a little girl. I remember."

When Tom was a teenager, before he was saved, he was involved in some scary things. For a couple of years in a row, on Halloween night, he'd attended what he thought at the time was just a party. His teammate on the football team, a black kid named Boone Tate, had set it up. They went out to a corn field to drink liquor and smoke marijuana around a big bonfire. And then, in a strange ritual, they'd buried a sock monkey in the field with handfuls of candy. After this weird ceremony, Tom had even engaged in pre-marital sex with Sherilyn Torrance, his girlfriend at the time. Back then, he'd thought that was the whole point of the thing. Getting the girls so worked up with fake mumbo jumbo magic that they'd let the boys do their dirty stuff.

After the second time they buried the monkey, though, the true meaning of the ritual became clear. The magic was real. They called up the devil that night, and he came. The newspapers called him the Snowman, or the Holiday Killer, but Tom knew the truth. Satan himself killed five children in Bakersfield over the course of that terrible year, including Tom's little brother Toby. The sweetest kid you'd ever want to know.

Even after the truth came out, there were kids who wanted to do it again. Missy Delany was one of them. Mark Davies was another. But they were just followers. Boone Tate's little brother Jess had been the ringleader. At his command, the other children buried another monkey on the next Halloween. Something went wrong with their spell, though, and the devil killed Jess Tate. That was the end of it, thank Jesus.

Missy ended up marrying Mark Davies right out of high school and they moved away, good riddance to the both of them. But then, last year, Missy had moved back. Married to a black lesbian. Flaunting their wickedness, without shame. So Tom was not surprised to learn they were witches. Not surprised at all.

"This thing goes deeper than one poor little baby," Nathanial said. "You know how bad the water is."

"Are the witches poisoning the water?" Tom gasped.

"I honestly can't say, Tom. But I'll tell you something not a lot of people outside my department know about. A couple months ago, we found out somebody broke into the fence around the water tower. Now that ain't unusual. Punk-ass kids get in there a couple times a year, to try to graffiti the tower. There was no graffiti this time, but the water maintenance people told me somebody pried open the vent on top of the reservoir. They did a visual inspection and found a dead cat floating in the water."

"A cat?" Tom said, aghast.

"A *black* cat. They told me one dead cat more or less wouldn't be enough to taint almost a million gallons of water, but that's damn peculiar, don't you think? Who'd climb all the way up there just to toss a cat inside?"

"Do you think that's some kind of spell?"

"I don't know, Tom. I honestly don't know. But I can tell you since then, there's been at least six women who've suffered miscarriages right here in town. Those are just the ones I know about. And then there's, you know..."

Tom gulped and nodded. His eyes watered. "The babies who die."

Tom's twin daughters had been born in August. Little Katie was strong and healthy, thanks to God. But her sister Faye, born eight minutes later, only lived for twelve days. There was no explanation for her passing. Sudden Infant Death Syndrome, the doctors called it. They even did an autopsy on her poor little body, but had found nothing. Liz had been heartbroken, devastated. Tom was tasked with explaining to his two oldest how Jesus could have let such a thing happen.

"Heaven must have needed another angel," he'd told them, simple terms even young kids could understand. "I know it's sad, but she'll be waiting for us when we get there."

Veronica and little Toby had accepted that, without question. Tom wished his faith was as strong as that which he had instilled in the hearts of his children.

"I can't say for sure all these things are related," Nate said into the mirror. "But that's why I called you up here. I'm going to do all I can to combat this thing, but you know my hands are tied somewhat by the constraints of the law. You need to warn your people. Have them be on their guard. There's nothing more powerful than a fellowship committed to zealous prayer. And *vigilant* resistance to evil."

Tom nodded. "I understand, Nathanial."

"These next couple days are going to be crucial. You know what tomorrow is, right?"

"Halloween." Another word Tom didn't like to speak aloud.

"That's the unholiest day of the year to these people. It's going to be a full moon, too. Based on these signs I've seen, I think they've got something big planned. I don't know exactly what, but we gotta be..."

The bathroom door opened then and none other than Mark Davies himself walked into the room. He gave a start when he saw Nathanial and Tom standing there. He almost stepped right back out.

Nate turned from the mirror for the first time and his whole demeanor changed. He favored Mark with an easy smile.

"Mr. Davies," he hailed. "Don't mind us. Me and Tom got to gabbin'. Shootin' the you-know-what. There something I can help you with?"

"No," Mark said, eyes darting around. "I just need to use the..."

"Right, of course. Say, you getting along all right in there? Everybody comfortable?"

"Sure. It's a real cozy jail you got here."

Nathanial laughed at that, long and hard, until both Mark and Tom were staring at him.

"Say, if you want some coffee, I can have Bob put on a pot for you."

"I think we're about to leave anyway, so no thank you," Mark said.

"Suit yourself, he brews a mean pot. Hey, I don't want to get too personal, but even if you're planning on going number one, I'd steer you towards using the stall. Somebody wrote some filthy stuff above the urinals there. Nobody needs to look at that kind of garbage."

Mark glanced over at the graffiti on the wall.

"See that?" Nathanial said. "Disgusting, really. I don't know what kind of sick mind comes up that stuff."

"I've seen worse."

"I'm sure you have, son." Nathanial shook his head sadly. "I'm sure you have. Still, I'd steer you towards the stall, even if you are going number one."

"Okay," Mark said, easing towards the stall. "Thanks."

"You're welcome, son. I've gotta be moseying. I'll have Bob put on that pot for you."

"Sure."

Mark stepped into the stall and closed the door. It locked with a little click. Nate turned back towards the mirror. Tom caught his eye there again and Nate's reflection winked at him.

"Don't forget what I said, Tom," he whispered. "Be ready."

Tom followed him out. Before he drove back to Bakersfield, he sat in his car and made a few calls. Putting together an emergency meeting with key members of his congregation. He wanted to confront this thing head-on.

CHAPTER 22

1:49 PM

ALICE HAD PUSHED it too hard the night before, and now she was paying the price. She should have known better. Partying in the woods and driving around for half the night were things most people her age did with hardly a second thought. But not her. Not anymore. Probably not ever again.

She woke from edgy dreams of the grave into half-conscious queasiness and pain. In and out she faded, until she could no longer find a way to position herself on the bed that didn't make every bone in her body ache. Still, she couldn't bring herself to get up until the need to urinate rose to undeniable levels. That was a real concern with her. During her lowest ebb so far, back in February, she'd actually pissed the bed a few times, and was so weak she couldn't even change her clothes or the sheets herself. Her dad had to do it. That was humiliating. She'd sworn she'd never let herself get in that position again.

Until she was officially up, though, the day's status as a "bad one" was still hypothetical. She relished this uncertainty until her bladder felt like it was about to rupture. Then she rolled out of bed. The joints connecting her legs to her pelvis felt like they were filled with ground glass when she put her scant weight on them. She knew then it was going to be a very bad day indeed. She hoped that didn't mean this was going to be bad week. Or a bad month. Or that all her good days were finally behind her.

Forcing herself not cry or even groan, she shuffled like a *Walking Dead* extra into her bathroom. Once her business was done, she pulled herself over to the medicine cabinet and doubled down on the oxycodone. She washed the pills down with water straight from the faucet. Though she tried to look away in time, she caught a glimpse of herself in the mirror.

Pale white, with huge black bags under her eyes. She looked like a ghost already.

She staggered back over to the bed and lowered herself onto the mattress like a fragile piece of crystal. Then she did cry, for a little while. Quietly, though, so Dad wouldn't hear.

Maybe twenty minutes or so passed before the pain pills began to kick in. They didn't kill the pain, only dulled its sharpness a bit. She felt weak, too. Exhausted, no energy at all. She didn't even have the will to go out into the kitchen, where she kept her weed meds. She felt beyond their help, anyway. That's how bad it was.

Lying down made her neck and her jaw hurt, so she propped herself up the best she could with her body pillows. This made her chest hurt, but not quite as badly. She opened up her laptop, to see what was going on and maybe take her mind off her pain for a minute.

She clicked around a few social media sites. James's Aunt Michelle was the only thing anybody was talking about. Alice saw that disgusting picture of the horned baby posted in about twenty different places. Some of the posts condemned Michelle with harsh, misspelled caps-lock fury. "THIS ABORTIONIT MURDERER BITCH DESERVES DEATH PENELTY!!!!" somebody with the handle sithlourde99 proclaimed. Others took the "sick joke" tack. "Looks like Satan fucked a garden gnome," quipped Josh2.0. (That was really Josh Milton, the self-proclaimed "class comedian," who Alice found about as hilarious as her chemo treatments.)

On Facebook, she saw a post by Travis Chasen. He was the leader of the Church of the Shepherd's Youth in Action club, and this position apparently compelled him to issue the group's official statement on this case. He didn't post the picture, Facebook probably would have blocked that anyway. Instead, he'd put up a link to the Springfield newspaper website's article about Michelle's arrest, with the headline: "CRIME SCENE PHOTO MISTAKENLY TEXTED AFTER ALLEGED ABORTION ARREST."

"We in the COTS-YIA club were saddened but not really surprised to finally have confirmation of what we've suspected for a long time," Travis's post read. "There is organized occult activity right here in Bakersfield.

Hopefully, our repeated warnings will no longer fall on deaf ears. The 'Sickness' wasn't enough of a wake-up call for our town, but hopefully this will be. Finally, we have proof the occultists' sinister plans involve crimes against the most innocent and vulnerable of our town's citizens—unborn babies. If you want to help us take action and show our unified resistance to this satanic threat, please join us for a presentation and prayer meeting 8 PM TONIGHT at the Underground Club downtown Bakersfield."

The post had received thirty-one likes and eighteen comments in the hour or so since it had been posted. Scrolling through them, Alice found most of the replies were supportive. But then, posted a few minutes ago, there was a long comment from Gemma Gordon:

"Now I know why they call it the Church of the Shepherd," she wrote. "Because you're all a bunch of ignorant freakin' SHEEP. You don't know the woman who died or the woman who was arrested. You have no idea what really happened there. All you have is this 'conveniently' leaked pic that shows a baby with a bad birth defect that's probably what killed it, not an abortion. But toss something like that to a bunch of superstitious bumpkins like you sheep shackers, and all of the sudden it's a satanic conspiracy. You think starting a hysterical panic like this will finally get people to come to one of your stupid 'underground' meetings? Sad thing is, in this stupid hick town, it'll probably work. Devil baby should be your poster child. She's the best thing that ever happened to you."

Alice timidly moved her cursor over the little thumbs-up 'like' button and hesitated for a moment before finally clicking. This seemed like a daring, controversial stance to take. So far, no one else had shown support for Gemma's statement.

It got Alice thinking, though, about Gemma and all the strange things she'd said last night about secret clubs and spinning coins balanced on teeter-totters. And how all that could somehow help Alice with her cancer. Because she was curious, and had nothing better to do on a bed-ridden Sunday, and because it would distract her from her misery, Alice went in and hacked Gemma's e-mail.

This wasn't really a great feat of cracking. Alice was something of an unofficial IT person for her classmates, and even some of her teachers. A couple weeks ago, Gemma's laptop had been running really slow and wouldn't synch with her phone. In exchange for fixing it, she gave Alice a gram of purple kush and her mom's Malovo wi-fi password. The weed was a nice thought, though with her prescription, Alice could get comparable product on her own. The password was the real prize. The Lawndale Manor subdivision had a free wi-fi network for all its residents that was about four times faster and way more reliable than the box Alice's dad rented from the cable company. More to the point, Gemma had also given Alice her personal e-mail password. "GGGbitchez!98." So far, she hadn't changed it and, like most people, she used the same password or slight variants of it for *everything*.

Feeling a bit of perverted stalker's shame, Alice slipped like a panty-sniffing ghost into her friend's digital dresser drawers. She snooped around, careful to cover her tracks behind her. There were some interesting things to be found, so much so that Alice lost track of time and nearly forgot how goddamn sick she was.

Her dad knocked on her door sometime later, it may have been an hour or more. He timidly stuck his head into her room.

"How you feeling, honey?" he asked. Dad looked almost as tired as she felt. She knew he wasn't sleeping well since he'd quit drinking.

"Moderately shitty, Dad. Why?" she said, a little more sharply than she'd meant to. Looking up from her screen even for a second made her snap back to the pain of the real world.

"Well, uh, James is here. Do you want me tell him you're not up for a visit?"

"No. Send him back. James I'll talk to."

"You sure? You don't look well."

"Yeah." Alice winced a little. "It's cool. Have him bring back my medicine, though."

"What kind do you want?"

"Are there any of those brownies left?" She was feeling a little hungry. Maybe she could keep one of those down.

"I'll check."

Her dad went away. James showed up a few minutes later. She could tell by his expression when he saw her how bad she must have looked. He made himself smile, though. James had two plastic-wrapped brownies in his hand. "Your dad didn't know if you wanted chocolate mint or peanut butter."

"Mint," Alice said, sitting up with a groan. "The peanut butter ones have this kind of dog shit aftertaste."

"That sounds lovely."

She unwrapped the brownie he handed her and took a small bite. Chewing and swallowing seemed like a lot of effort for such a meager reward.

"How are you doing?" James asked, with a level of sympathy that was a little irritating.

She turned it back around on him. "Better than you, from the looks of it." She touched the side of her forehead. James's bruise from the night before was swollen and purple.

"Oh," he said. "That."

"Jose seemed like he was starting to warm back up before we left."

"I'm done with that guy. Trying to date someone *that* repressed is way more frustration than I need. Plus, I don't appreciate getting punched in the head and called a faggot."

"Good for you." Alice nodded, though it felt like her neck was on a badly rusted hinge. "Did you get in to see your aunt?"

"Yeah. She's a little banged up, a little freaked out, but she's okay. Lana hired a lawyer who's driving up there for the interview with the sheriff later today. Everybody's pretty sure she's going to get released without even being charged once all the facts come out."

"Well, in the court of Bakersfield teen social media, she's already been tried, convicted and sentenced to death."

"That's why I'm staying off-line. I'll get pissed off if I start reading that stuff."

"She does have some defenders," Alice said. "Gemma's on her side."

"Huh. Maybe there's hope after all."

"I'm finding out some interesting things about our friend Gemma Gordon. Here, look." Alice scooted over so James could sit down next to her, adjusting the pillow desk so it rested on both their laps. She was not too far gone to be gratified by his warm presence beside her in bed.

"This is her e-mail?" James said. "Did you *hack* her?"

"Just a little."

"Wow. Remind me to never get on your bad side."

"She was expelled from her old school in Portland for bringing a gun to school," Alice said. "Arrested for *cocaine* possession when she was fifteen."

"Wow. Wild child."

"Yeah. Her parents sent her to a shrink after that, but get this. She ended up sleeping with the guy. Got *him* arrested. She's like a real-life Laura Palmer."

"Wait, what's..."

Alice clicked onto another screen. "And look at this, she blogs under the name Rosie Thorne. It's all really strange stuff about getting your period to synch with the moon and how to have out-of-body experiences. Here's one about how to summon an incubus so you can have sex with it."

"What was that screen you were on before?" James sounded frantic. "Go back, go back."

Alice clicked back into Gemma's sent e-mail folder. "What's wrong?"

James tapped his finger on the screen. "There, look. She sent an e-mail to Sandy Aswell!"

"Who's that?"

"That's her! The girl who died. The baby's mother."

"No shit?"

Alice looked down at the screen. The e-mail had been sent on 10/21. Nine days ago.

"You made your bed now you have to lie in it," the subject line read. "Bitch you're on your own."

Alice clicked open the e-mail. It was long and rambling and cryptic, the meaning difficult to discern. What came through clearly was the ire. There were numerous references to an unnamed "betrayal" and Sandy's "refusal to honor the agreements you made." "You were never really one of us," Gemma said. "We all did our parts. We all made sacrifices. We're not a bunch of selfish, precious little bitches like you." "Don't go crying to Roberta," Gemma warned towards the end of the rant. "She may forgive you, but the rest of us won't. It's way too late for you to come crawling back to us now. We're going to plan B and we don't need your sorry white trash ass for that. I know you got problems now but you know you brought them on yourself." She closed with a re-iteration of the subject line: "Bitch, you're on your own."

"What the hell is that about?" James wondered aloud.

They were reading it over again, trying to puzzle it out, when Alice received a text message on her phone.

"Oh, shit," Alice said. "It's Gemma."

-Do me a favor?

-What do you need? Alice texted back.

Gemma replied: *-I'm in 7 diff flame wars with sheep shacker asshats. They're getting really fucking obnoxious. I think 1 even hacked me. I keep seeing things shift around on my email. Surprised any of them are smart enough to pull that shit off.*

"Oh, crap," James said, reading over Alice's shoulder.

Alice, feeling flushed, typed: *-That sux. What do you want me to do?*

-They're meeting tonight @ stupid underground club. I think they're planning something big. Can u go & tell me what they're up 2?

"You can't, Alice," James said. "You can barely sit up in bed."

-You want me to be your spy? Alice typed.

A brief lag, and then Gemma replied: *-LOL. Yeah, totally. Wear yr i-patch. You'll look totally badass.*

Alice smiled at that.

-OK I'll go. James'll help me.

-Awesome. Yr my fuckin hero.

"What are you doing?" James said. "You're too sick."

Alice let out a long exhalation that made her ribcage rattle with pain. She nodded, though.

"I can do this," she said. "But I'm going to need a lot of drugs."

CHAPTER 23

2:01 PM

A FTER THE VISIT with Michelle at the county jail, James dropped Mark off in Springfield, so he could pick up his car from the lot where he'd left it the night before. Lana and Ben went back with James, to await word on what was going to happen with Missy, and so Mark drove home alone. Finally returning from what felt like hours on the road, Mark found Abraham Lincoln waiting for him on his front porch.

Abe worked with him at New Salem, although Mr. Lincoln's devotion to the job placed him on an entirely different plane from his fellow interpreters. Mark didn't know what the man's birth name might have been, but at some point he'd legally changed it to "Abraham Lincoln." Mark had even seen his driver's license. That Abe actually had a license was one of the few anachronisms about him. He took his method acting to ridiculous extremes. Next to him, Daniel Day-Lewis looked like an amateur.

At six-four, he was the same height and, with his thinning hair and slightly asymmetrical features, bore a distinct resemblance to the great man—though most maintained that the imposter was somewhat better looking than the original. Abe dressed exclusively in clothes the earlier Abe Lincoln might have worn during the period of his life when he lived in New Salem, and in his early thirties was close to the same age. (The real Lincoln left New Salem to seek his fortune in Springfield when he was twenty-eight.) He walked and talked as Lincoln might have, and was a walking encyclopedia of Lincoln lore. Tourists loved him. Few people left the park without getting a selfie with Abe Lincoln.

Abe did not live within the park itself, but had built a strenuously authentic log cabin for himself just outside nearby Athens. He lived there without electricity or plumbing, shitting in an outhouse and reading by firelight every night as his hero had done almost two centuries prior. He did drive to work, though, the commute being too distant for horseback to be practical. Naturally, he drove a Lincoln. The car was now parked in Mark's driveway.

Mark pulled in beside it. Abe was sitting on the porch swing, his long legs stretched out before him, crossed at the ankles. Mark had never seen him outside of work before. He seemed completely out of place in the context of a modern front porch. He wore a striped cotton shirt and handmade denim blue jeans with suspenders, which Mark had no doubt were historically accurate down to the thread count. The garments were ill-fitting by design, conforming to eye-witness accounts of Lincoln's manner of dress as a scruffy young bachelor.

"Afternoon, Mark," Abe hailed as Mark stepped up onto the porch. He stood up and extended his authentically work-calloused hand.

"Hi, Abe," Mark said, shaking his hand. "What brings you by?"

"Bad news, I'm afraid." Abe wore the simultaneous warm politician's smile and melancholic wrinkling of the eyes that he had cribbed from portraits of Lincoln. Though these were obvious affectations, they nonetheless came across with a heartfelt authenticity. Abe's performance had been internalized to such a degree that it had long ceased to be an act.

"What's wrong?"

"I'm sure you're aware of the budget stalemate between our governor and the state legislature." Abe shook his head sadly. "Proving once again, not that further proof was needed, that a house divided against itself cannot stand. Both sides have proven unable or unwilling to compromise or concede any point to the other, putting their opposing political agendas above the needs of the people of this state. And now, a day of reckoning has come, for the humble venture in which we both proudly participate."

It took a moment for the dense cloud of words to absorb, but Mark finally grasped what Abe was saying.

"They cut our budget." This wasn't too great a shock. There had been talk of this happening for a while. State agencies and programs were getting slashed left and right as the impasse wore on, including social services certainly more essential than state-run historic sites like New Salem.

"Succinctly, yes," Abe nodded. "Effective immediately, New Salem is to be closed to the public. Certain essential maintenance and administrative personnel will be retained, with an eye towards a future re-opening. Historical interpreters, such as you and I, are deemed inessential, as there will be no one to interpret history to."

"Shit." Mark sat down on the porch swing, the weight of his unemployment coming over him all at once. On top of everything else, this was a crushing blow.

"I want you to know that this in no way reflects your job performance, Mark," Abe said, sitting down beside him. "It's purely a budgetary decision. You are as fine a smith as I've ever worked with. I'm sure you'll have no problems finding employment."

"Thanks," Mark said. He closed his eyes and felt really sorry for himself for a few moments, before looking up at Abe. Mark had at least some job skills and experience applicable to this century. Abe was a man completely out of time. "What are *you* going to do?"

"Don't worry about me," Abe smiled. "I am a frugal man who lives very simply. I have faith that I can weather this storm. The park will re-open, eventually. People need their history. The past is the cause of the present, and the present will be the cause of the future. All these are links in the endless chain stretching from the finite to the infinite."

"That's nice. I like that," Mark said. "Hey, do you want to come inside? I think I have a couple beers left in the fridge. I don't know about you, but I could use one right now. It's been a hellacious twenty-four hours or so. Really, getting laid off is just the shit cherry on top of the turd sundae."

"Beer's a fine thing," Abe said. "I'm a firm believer that the people can be depended upon to meet any crisis, provided with real facts and beer. But I'll decline. I still have several stops to make on this grim errand. I must say, you've taken the news better than most."

"You're driving around, personally telling everyone the park's closed?"

"I thought it would be easier to take coming from me. Laura sent out an e-mail, but that lacks the human touch."

"Laura lacks the human touch." Mark bit his lip thoughtfully. "So, uh, have you been to see Ellie Tarwater yet?"

Abe chuckled. "I heard a rumor you two went out last night. How did that go? Or is that part of your 'turd sundae?'"

"That's the fecal fudge ice cream part, yeah."

"Well, as Abraham once said, I believe in a letter he wrote to Horace Greeley, 'One must never stick his dick in crazy.'"

It took a second for Mark to get that, but then he burst out laughing.

"Abraham Lincoln said that?"

"I saw the quote next to his picture on the Internet, so it must be authentic."

"He was a very wise man," Mark said. "Unfortunately, or maybe fortunately, it didn't get that far."

"I myself have had some experience in this area," Abe said. "Being intimately involved with a madwoman, that is."

"Mary Todd?"

Abe shook his head. "Carrie Franklin."

"Was she before or after Ann Rutledge?"

Abraham's expression loosened a bit. The mask slipped from his face and then Mark was looking at a completely different person. Even his voice changed, from the high, piercing nasal of his Lincoln voice to a lower, more relaxed cadence. "This is from my pre-Abrahamic days, Mark. When I was a struggling college student."

"Oh." Mark could not remember ever seeing Abraham break character before.

"I was working for a service that hired out male strippers to dance at bachelorette parties and the like."

"Wait." Mark must have heard that wrong. "You what now?"

"Don't be so shocked. I'm not the only president with a sordid past. Ronald Reagan was infamous for his Hollywood orgies."

"You're fucking with me."

"About Reagan, yes. The man was a dolt, even then. But I did do some stripping. The money was good and I have to admit, it was gratifying to be the object of so much female attention. In any case, the same agency I worked for managed female strippers as well. That's how I met Carrie."

He shook his head, lost for a second in his past.

"She was literally, without exaggeration, the most beautiful woman I've ever seen. Fair hair and skin, a face so pretty you just wanted to hold it between your hands and gaze upon it. And her body was...astounding. Flawless. All the girls that worked there were attractive, they had to be. But Carrie shone so brightly that the others just faded to obscurity beside her. And she chose me."

"Sexual relations with her were...unworldly. There was a ferocity to her lovemaking. A desperation. It was intoxicating. But she was so...goddamn... *crazy*. Her ex-boyfriend contacted me shortly after we started dating, and tried to warn me about her. He told me that she'd burned down his house. Of course, I was so drunk with love at that point I wouldn't hear anything that could turn me away. But the moods she went through. Manic elation, jealous fury, the blackest of depressions. She could turn on a dime from one to another without warning."

"The first time I broke up with her was because she verbally attacked my mother. Carrie called her a 'controlling whore,' because she was jealous that Mom took me out to lunch on my birthday. We got back together when she told me she was pregnant, and then broke up again two months later when I found out she'd been faking it. Then she beat herself up like Edward Norton in *Fight Club* and called the police, saying that I did it. I spent almost a week in jail before she recanted her story. Even after that, she still wanted to get back together. And I would be lying if I said there were no incidents of...backsliding. My own behavior, I see in hindsight, was similar to that of a drug addict. Seeking out that which was destroying me because of the fleeting ecstasy it made me feel."

"Jesus," Mark said. This was not a story he would have expected from the mouth of Abraham Lincoln. "So what finally happened?"

"I moved to another town, transferred to another school, just to get away from her. She became involved with someone else after I left, which filled me with both jealousy and relief. I considered contacting this new boyfriend, as her ex had done with me, to warn him. But I lacked the will and the courage. I don't know if it would have made any difference, anyway. If he was as under Carrie's spell as I had been at the beginning of our relationship, I'm sure he wouldn't have listened to me. In any case, I later read in the newspaper that she shot him in his sleep and then shot herself. Murder-suicide."

"Oh my God."

"When I look back on that part of my life now, I don't feel the relief one might expect. I don't say to myself, 'that could have been me, but for the grace of God.' Rather, I feel a profound regret. Though the evidence suggests that she was beyond saving, I still wonder if I might have been able to save her, if I had treated her with more kindness. In my darker moments, I even envy the man she died with. Through the distorted lens of her madness, which I had come to share to a degree, the fact that she killed this man and then herself proved that she loved him more than she ever did me."

"Woah, Abe. That's crazy."

"I'm sorry, I get lost in my storytelling sometimes. I tend to go off on irrelevant tangents. I'm not saying that Ellie is in any way like Carrie. I'm neither warning you away from her, nor am I saying that you should give her another chance. I suppose I'm just saying that I understand the allure of the wounded angel."

Abe stood, reclaiming the Lincoln persona as he stretched to his full height. "As it happens, I'm seeing Ellie next. Is there any message you wish me to convey to her?"

"I guess...just tell her I'm sorry."

"I'll do that. But now I want to leave you with something else Abraham said." He cleared his throat and was fully in character as he said: "An eastern monarch once charged his wise men to invent him a sentence to be ever in view, and which should be true and appropriate in all times and situations. They presented him the words: 'And this, too, shall pass away.' How much it expresses! How chastening in the hour of pride! How consoling in the depths of affliction!"

Abe smiled and put on his hat. Not the trademark stovepipe of the presidential years, but a more modest and period-accurate straw hat.

"This too shall pass away, Mark," he said.

Abraham got into his Lincoln and drove away. When he was gone, Mark walked back inside the house and straight to the kitchen. He opened the fridge, and was dismayed to find that he'd been wrong about there being beer left. He sure as hell could use one right now.

CHAPTER 24

2:47 PM

MICHELLE SAT ALONE in the interview room, waiting. She'd been there for a long time. She couldn't say how long, there was no clock in the room, but it felt like it might have been an hour or more. The room was smaller than Michelle would have supposed, though her only frame of reference for police interrogation rooms came from watching movies and television. Instead of the long table with handles installed to shackle the suspect, like she'd seen in every cop show she'd ever watched, there was a regular office desk and three chairs. Sitting in one of the chairs facing the desk, Michelle felt like she'd been summoned to the principal's office for smoking on school grounds, rather than about to be interrogated by the sheriff for felony crimes.

The one aspect of the room that did conform to the cliché was the big mirror covering most of the wall facing her. Two-way glass, of course. By re-focusing her eyes, she could just make out the silhouette of a video camera on a tripod through the mirror. Its steady red light indicated that it was impassively watching her.

Michelle understood that making her wait in this room facing her own reflection was part of the overall psychological strategy of interrogation. They were letting her stew, stoking her paranoia, making it more likely she would slip up and confess. Honestly, Michelle was too tired to care. All she wanted was sleep in her own bed and a long, hot, cleansing shower. Lana had least brought a clean shirt from home for her to change into, but she kept finding spots of Sandy Aswell's blood on her skin, under her nails. It was in her hair, too. She smelled like it.

In her boredom and exhaustion, Michelle slumped in the hard chair and dozed off for a few moments. She snapped awake when the door opened. A woman stepped into the room, cool and professional-looking, in a suit-dress with her dark hair pulled back.

"Michelle?" the woman said. "Hi, I'm Leslie Grady. I'm your attorney."

Michelle stood up and shook her hand. She'd never formally met Leslie, but she knew who she was. Leslie was married to Gerald Grady, who ran the feed store downtown. Their daughter Emily was Ben's best friend at school.

Like Michelle, Gerald Grady had escaped from Bakersfield, only to be pulled back in by the hometown gravity that sucked as relentlessly as a black hole. In Gerald's case, he'd moved back following his father's stroke, to run the family business that could not be entrusted to his idiot brother Emmett. When Gerald came back home, his big-city wife had come home with him. Leslie had been a criminal lawyer in Chicago, apparently a successful one, but she'd moved her practice to Springfield. She had a good reputation, and Michelle felt comforted by her obvious competence. There was one thing she didn't get, though.

"I'm sorry, but I already have a lawyer," Michelle said. One of Lana's fellow teachers had a sister-in-law who'd recently started practicing in Decatur. Lana had already talked to her, and she was willing to give them a discounted rate.

"Alma Goodman of Ketchum and Hall?" Leslie said. "She's not an experienced attorney. I don't think your case is going to be very complicated, but you're better off with someone who's actually handled this sort of thing before."

"I'd like that, I've heard nothing but great things about you, but the thing is...we looked into your rates. We can't afford you."

Leslie smiled. "Your former mother-in-law hired me. She'll be taking care of all your legal expenses. You don't need to worry about that."

"Gillian?" Michelle said. "Really? Why?"

"Maybe she still thinks of you as family."

"I don't think she thought of me as family when I was married to her son."

"Whatever the reason, she's taking care of everything," Leslie said. "Can we sit down? I want to ask you a few questions before the sheriff comes in."

Michelle re-took her seat. Leslie took the seat behind the desk, and flipped open her iPad case. Michelle now felt a bit like she was about to undergo a job interview.

"First of all," said Leslie. "I need to apologize to you. My daughter took it into her head last night to abduct your son."

"Yeah, I heard a little bit about that. Ben didn't really want to talk about it, and with my situation, his sneaking out kind of took a back seat."

"Perfectly understandable." Leslie nodded. "I wanted you to know that it wasn't Ben's idea to traipse out into the woods in the middle of the night. That was pure Emily. My daughter has a wild imagination and an iron will. That sometimes makes for a dangerous combination."

"She reminds me of myself at that age," Michelle said. "Which is probably why Ben's so crazy about her."

"I know. Young love." Leslie leaned forward and snapped almost instantly from informal to business mode. "So. Gillian told me that you have some personal history with Sheriff Bates."

"That's one way to put it. Another would be to say he murdered my sister."

"In the line of duty, as I understand it. Was there an investigation?"

"It happened during the Sickness," Michelle said. "Nobody looked very closely at anything that happened over that weekend."

"Sheriff Bates has always had a reputation for brutality. Nobody's ever been able to pin anything on him and have it stick, though." She squinted across the desk at Michelle. "Did you get that cut on your cheek when you were arrested?"

"Yeah, but Bates didn't do it. That was Sgt. McMurtry, the state trooper."

"The state police at least have a review board for allegations of excessive force. I'm not sure much will come of it, but I'll request a formal review of your arrest." Leslie tapped her tablet screen with a stylus, making notes of some kind. "Do you know why you were taken here for processing rather than the state police barracks?"

"McMurtry is a serious pro-lifer," Michelle said. "He really thought I was performing an abortion, so he flipped out on me. Completely. I kind of flipped out right back at him, and things just escalated. Bates was...calmer."

"He took you here for your own protection?"

"Yes, but..." Michelle frowned, remembering how *off* Bates had been on the ride to the jail. "There's something wrong with him," she whispered. "He's changed."

"Changed how?"

"He's...*nice*."

"Nice?" Leslie looked up at Michelle, an eyebrow raised. "This is a problem?"

"I don't know how to explain it. Having dealt with him before, it's like...somebody broke him and didn't put him back together quite right."

Leslie shook her head and returned to her notes, obviously dismissing Michelle's comments as irrelevant.

"One more thing," she said. "Do you have any idea who made the anonymous call?"

"Not a clue," Michelle said.

Leslie looked like she might have been about to follow that up with another question, but then the door opened again and Bates stepped into the room.

"You ladies ready for this interview?" he asked.

"We're ready," Leslie said. She stood up. "I think sitting I'm in your chair, though."

"Nah, don't bother," he said. "Sit back down. We'll keep this casual. I don't think it'll take long."

He sat in the chair beside Michelle. Both of them now faced Leslie, who was seated behind the desk, and the mirror on the wall behind her. This seating arrangement seemed improper to Michelle. In terms of physical space, she was aligned with Bates, and in opposition to her own counsel. She wondered if this was a subtle manipulation, something else meant to throw her off guard. Leslie seemed troubled by it, too. She tilted her head curiously at Bates.

"Good to see you, Mrs. Grady," he said, with no apparent guile. "How's Gerald doing?"

"Very well, thank you," Leslie said coolly.

"I saw him last week. He called me because somebody busted in through a side window over at the feed store. They didn't find anything worth stealing inside, but they did pry open a cash register. I swear, this new class of criminals we got now is so dumb they don't know that stores don't leave money in their drawers overnight. It's a safe bet drugs were involved. I tell ya, this crystal meth stuff is a plague straight outta Egypt. Did your insurance give you any hassle about paying to replace the glass?"

"Gerald didn't mention anything about it to me," Leslie said. "Sheriff, I'd like to begin this interview now, please."

"Oh, sure. Sorry." He turned to Michelle. "Ms. Blair-Delany, do you mind looking straight ahead, into that mirror there? See, that's what they call a 'two-way glass.' You can't see it, but there's a camera on the other side. We record these sessions, you know, in case we have to go to court. To tell you the truth, I don't know why we bother with the mirror. Do you think there's anybody's who's actually fooled by that?"

Michelle looked up at the mirror. Bates, sitting beside her, leered at her in the reflection, grinning with an almost sadistic glee. But when she turned away from the mirror and faced him directly again, he was still wearing the same genial smile. It was almost like the man and his reflection were two different people.

"No, no. Keep facing forward. We want to see your pretty face." Bate's sneering reflection winked at her, but his voice maintained the lazy country drawl. "All right. Last night, which for the record was Saturday, October twenty-ninth, did you visit Sandy Aswell at her Southern Villas home?"

"Yes," Michelle replied warily.

"How were you acquainted with Ms. Aswell?"

"She hired me to be her pregnancy coach."

"Pregnancy coach." Bates, in the mirror, actually bared his teeth at Michelle. It was an unmistakably aggressive gesture. Leslie, though she was facing Bates directly, didn't seem to notice anything amiss. Michelle wondered if Leslie had seen anything at all. "Could you, just for our benefit, explain what a pregnancy coach does?"

"Sure. I offer advice and guidance on every aspect of my client's pregnancy. Exercise, nutrition, things like that. Also, emotional support. I make myself available for any questions or concerns my client might have.

If she wants me to, I can also accompany a client on doctor and hospital visits, up to and including the birth itself."

"Did you go to school for that, school for that?"

At that weird little stutter, Leslie did glance curiously up at Bates. Michelle was sure, though, that Leslie did not see the face he pulled in the mirror. He tilted his head and stuck his tongue out of the side of his mouth, like a man in a noose.

"I trained as a midwife, in Colorado," Michelle said, doing her best to keep her voice level. "I couldn't practice here in Illinois, but most of the training is still relevant to coaching."

Bates nodded. "Have you ever performed an abortion?"

"No."

"But you consider yourself pro-choice, right?"

"Don't answer that, Michelle," Leslie warned. She cast a hard glance at Bates. "My client's political opinions are irrelevant."

In the mirror, Bates rolled his eyes crazily, but his voice was unperturbed as he moved to the next question: "If one of your clients decided she wanted to, you know, terminate her pregnancy, what would you?"

"I'd drive her to a clinic."

"Unless she's too far along, like Sandy was. The clinic would turn her away. If that was the case, would you whip her up some kind of home-brewed herbal potion?"

"No."

"But I bet you know how to," Bates pressed. "Isn't that something they teach in midwifin' school? How to mix to mix up pennyroyal and whatnot?"

"Not for at least a century," Michelle said. "I did take a course in the history of midwifery, where we discussed the traditional use of herbal abortifacients."

"Ooh," Bates chuckled. "Ain't that a fancy word?"

"Where are you going with this line of questioning, sheriff?" Leslie asked.

"Well, I'll tell you. In the search of Ms. Aswell's trailer, they found a jar containing a strong-smelling liquid residue. We won't get the lab results back for maybe a week or more. Same with the toxicology report on the deceased. So we were hoping maybe Michelle could shed some light on what the stuff might be. Did you slip her some witchy little potion to ease that baby on out of there?"

"Absolutely not."

"Okay," Bates said. "I guess you're free to go, then."

"What?" Michelle said.

"Sorry we had to keep you overnight, but you were the one who insisted on having a lawyer present. We could have cleared this up a lot sooner."

"Am I correct in understanding that you're not charging my client?" Leslie looked as dumbfounded as Michelle felt.

"What the heck would we charge her with?" Bates said. "She just said she didn't do it."

"So that's it? I can just go?" Michelle looked from her lawyer to her captor. It seemed she'd missed something important.

"Unless you really want to stay. Tonight *is* meatloaf night."

"No," Michelle said, standing. "That's quite all right. Can I get my phone back, so I can call my wife?"

"Sure, you'll get all your personal effects back," Bates stood up and went to the door, holding it open. "You know they're going to tear you to little pieces, don't you?"

"What did you say?"

"I said you'll get your effects back. They're in a locker just down the hall. I'll go grab 'em while Bob's working up your papers."

"No, you said 'they're going to tear you to pieces.'"

Nate frowned. "Uh, I don't think so."

"You did." Michelle looked to Leslie. "Didn't he?"

"You did say that, sheriff," said Leslie. "What did you mean by that? Who's going to tear her to pieces?"

Bates looked back and forth between the two women like they were pulling a prank on him. "I have no idea what you're talking about. Look, why don't you both get on home? It's Sunday. That's family day. I wish I had a family to spend my Sunday with. Leslie, you'll say hi to Gerald for me?"

"Yes, sheriff. I'll do that."

"And Michelle, sorry again for the inconvenience. They're going to burn you alive. You go on home to your boy. I'm sure he misses his mama."

Bates walked away down the hall whistling, leaving Michelle and Leslie standing there stunned. Michelle wasn't any less flummoxed when she recognized the tune he was whistling.

It was the theme from *The Andy Griffith Show.*

CHAPTER 25

4:12 PM

AFTER A COUPLE of hours of bored sober solitude at home, Mark drove into town through the dribbling rain, in search of alcohol. The thought of drinking at home alone seemed far too depressing, so he decided to go to Wolfy's. Drowning his sorrows at the local watering hole was an irresistible cliché, a perfect expression of his gloom.

He'd never actually been inside the place before. The tavern had been a Bakersfield fixture since long before he was born, with a reputation as a hardcore redneck bar. A real fights-in-the-parking-lot, both-kinds-of-music-on-the-jukebox, Confederate-flag-on-the-wall kind of joint. He stepped into the dimly lit room, shaking off the rain, and glanced around nervously in case there might be some kind of detector built into the doorframe that would identify him as an Obama voter and set off an alarm. The smells of sour beer, antique nicotine, and lemon-scented urinal cake were saturated into the woodwork. Mark saw right away that he'd been right about the Confederate flag, as absurd as that seemed in the heart of Lincoln country. The flag, in fact, hung directly over the jukebox that was at that moment pumping out a Toby Keith song. Mark made a silent vow to avoid the parking lot at all costs.

The place was almost deserted on this rainy Sunday afternoon. Other than Mark and the bartender, the only other two people in there were an old drunk, propped in one corner with the dusty permanence of a piece of furniture, and a waitress, sullenly wiping down a table. The waitress was thin and boyish, with short, spiky hair. In her faded sleeveless Sonic Youth t-shirt, she looked as out of place as Mark felt. She gave him a curious look as he stepped up to the bar.

The bartender, Wolfy himself, was a grizzled piece of leather in a denim shirt, sleeves rolled up to display unidentifiable blue splotchy tattoos on his hairy beef jerky arms. He had a frayed white beard like a hobo Santa, but his eyes were lively and sharp—a light, piercing blue. These eyes gave Mark an appraising scan.

"Help you with somethin', pal?" Wolfy asked. By his tone, he seemed to have concluded that Mark had wandered into the bar by mistake, or perhaps to ask for directions to a more suitable place.

"Yeah," Mark said. Out of sheer perversity, he considered asking what microbrews Wolfy carried here, or if he had a list of his bottled imports. Luckily though, Mark's self-preservation instincts kicked in at the last possible second. This was not that kind of bar. "I'll have a Coors... ah, Miller."

"Corsamiller?" Wolfy said.

"Miller," Mark said. "High Life. Please."

"Right." Wolfy drew the beer and slid it across the counter to Mark.

"Thanks." Mark paid for his drink and took the foamy mug over to a table by the jukebox, which had just segued into a Hank Williams Jr. tune. Mark wondered if a track by the man's father would be too much to ask for.

The waitress stepped over from the shadows. "Never thought I'd see you in here, Mark."

She was vaguely familiar looking. About Mark's age, so he'd probably gone to school with her. He couldn't place her, though. Mark had experienced this a lot since moving back. Everybody seemed to remember him, but his former schoolmates tended to blur together in his mind. Maybe it was because after he moved away, he'd tried so hard to forget this place. Or maybe it was just because he'd smoked so much pot in high school.

"I'm a local now," he said. "Might as well act like one."

"You were never a local," she challenged. "You don't remember me, do you?"

"We went to school together, right?"

"Wow. Good guess. It's all right. Nobody remembers me." She shook her head with disappointment, though. "I'm Sally Wolf."

"Wolf, so you're..." Mark cocked his thumb over at the bar.

"Wolfy's daughter, yeah. Why the hell else would I work in this goddamn place?"

Mark should have guessed that. She had the same eyes as her father, so light blue they appeared to be lit from within. Other than that, there was zero resemblance.

"I just thought maybe you'd remember because I was on the swim team, with Missy. You went to all our meets."

"Oh yeah." That clicked. Sally had been even smaller then, like a junior high schooler who'd been promoted a few grades. "Didn't you shave your head for a while?"

"Oh, yeah. My Sinead O'Connor phase," Sally said. "I probably just did that to try to impress Missy, actually."

"Really?"

"I had such a crush on her." Sally sat down across from Mark, and leaned in confidentially. "Remember those yellow suits we wore? They made everybody else look like shriveled-up lemons, but not her. God, the way she looked when she got out of the pool, dripping wet, especially if the water was *cold,* if you know what I mean."

"I do." That triggered a sense memory so vivid he could smell the chlorine.

"I just wanted to lap the bleachy water right off her," Sally said.

"Oh my God," Mark laughed, sipping his beer. "Stop."

Sally laughed along with him. "She was an amazing swimmer. Cut through the water like an arrow. She could have gone really far if the rest of us didn't suck so bad and drag her down. I always thought she could have even gone to the Olympics if she tried hard enough."

"She was really good," Mark said. "She didn't keep up with it after graduation, though. I always thought she should have."

"How's she doing? I was really shocked to hear about her getting arrested."

"I saw her this morning. She's doing well. I think they're going to let her go. There's nothing to these charges."

"Of course not," Sally said. "Duh." She shook her head and gave a dreamy smile. "She was really my first love, you know. She was actually nice to me. Most of the other girls on the team were catty little bitches, but Missy...for a while I even thought maybe I had a chance with her. But then she started going out with *you.*"

"Sorry about that."

"I've had some time to get over it," Sally said. "But I was super jealous for a while. I actually put a curse on you."

"That was you?" Mark laughed. "Wow. That explains a lot."

"Then she moves back to town, married to this gorgeous woman. I have to admit, even after all those years, that stung a little bit."

"Tell me about it."

"Sally!" Wolfy barked from behind the bar. "You clean the men's room yet?"

Sally rolled her eyes at Mark, and then called back: "I was just getting to that, master."

"I have to go," she said. "These country boys' mamas never taught them not to piss all over the floor. But that's why I love my job. Enjoy your Miller High Life."

"Good talking to you, Sally."

Mark slowly finished his beer. Towards the bottom, he didn't even mind the taste anymore. The cheap beer, mainstream country music and the memories Sally had given him to brood over worked well together, bringing Mark to a satisfying level of melancholy. He decided that he'd like to keep this going, so he went back up to the bar to have another. Wolfy, a true professional, already had one poured for him.

"Thanks," Mark said.

"Hey, I saw you talking to my daughter there."

"Yeah, we went to school together."

"Right. She seems to like you. That's rare, you know. For her to hit it off with a man like that, if you know what I mean."

"Yeah, I guess," Mark said, taking an evasive sip of the beer.

"Say, I wonder if you'd do me a favor." Wolfy opened up the cash register and pulled out a bill. He laid a hundred down on the counter in front of Mark. "Take her out. Show her a good time. On me."

"You want to pay me to take Sally on a date?"

"Yeah. Maybe it'll straighten her out a little bit."

"You know it doesn't work like that, right?"

Wolfy dismissed that comment with a wave of his hand.

"I'm not some kinda bigot, you know?"

"That's good."

"I know how it is," Wolfy said. "Kids have to get this stuff out of their system when they're young. I understand that. But Sally's almost thirty. She doesn't have a lot of time left, you know? She's old enough to put this kid stuff behind her and grow up. Or else I'm going to die without any grandkids."

"Wow." That was about all Mark could bring himself to say.

"I know who you are," Wolfy said. "You were married to a lady like that, right? A gay lady. And you had a kid with her."

"I did."

"I know Sally ain't the prettiest girl in the world. But she's a real sweetheart. You ought to give her a chance."

"Thanks," Mark said. "But I think I'm going to pass."

He dug in his pocket to pay for the beer, but Wolfy waved this off. "Beer's on the house. Just go sit down and think it over."

Mark went back over to the table, shaking his head. As soon as he sat down, he received a text message. He looked down and saw it was from Lana.

-*Chelle just got released. No charges filed. I'm heading to pick her up now. Come over tomorrow night for dinner to celebrate.*

This was great news, a tremendous relief. But it contained within it a slight note of rebuke. Telling Mark to come over to celebrate tomorrow meant that he didn't rank the private family celebration that would no doubt occur tonight. Why? Because he wasn't part of the family. Not really. As close as he was to his ex-wife and her current spouse—closer, he knew, than he had any right to be—this was still a circle that he was shunted from. A circle that contained his son, but not him. Mark tried to not let this bother him. He texted back with his sincere congratulations and then drained the rest of his beer in a single pull. He was debating the wisdom of beer number three when Sally returned from the restroom.

"Hey," he told her. "Just got some good news. Missy's being released from jail. They're not going to press charges."

"That's great," Sally said. "I was kind of worried. I knew it was bullshit, but in this town, you never know what people are going to believe."

"That's too true," said Mark. "Oh, I should probably also tell you I had a really strange conversation with your dad."

"Did he tell you his theory that I'm only gay because I haven't met the right man yet?"

"In so many words, yeah."

"And he tried to pay you to take a swing at being my Mr. Right?"

"You got it."

"So, are you ready to go or what?" Sally held up the hundred dollar bill.

"What, really?"

"Look," Sally said. "I'm not into guys, but I am into getting nights off from this dump. And, this might make me a bad person, but I'm not above exploiting my Neanderthal father's ignorance to get a free dinner. Please don't tell me you have moral qualms about that."

"Not really, no."

"Do you have a problem with hanging out with a woman you don't have a chance of going to bed with?"

"Trust me, I'm used to that."

"Okay then, what do you say?"

"Sure," Mark said, standing up. He had nowhere better to go, and Sally seemed like good company. It would sure as hell beat sitting home alone. "Let's go."

"Thanks Dad," Sally called, grabbing her coat on the way out the door. "Don't wait up."

"You kids have a good time," Wolfy beamed after them.

"Idiot," Sally muttered as they stepped out into the rain. She flashed Mark a look. "You know, if you got me pregnant, he'd probably buy you a car."

CHAPTER 26

4:46 PM

AFTER THE INTERVIEW with Michelle Blair-Delany, Nathanial wasn't feeling well, so he decided to take the rest of the evening off and drive back home to Bakersfield. His head felt like there was a crew of roofers up there, installing shingles on his skull with a bunch of high-power nail-guns. Pop! Pop! Pop! He knew he'd feel better if he could get away from all the mirrors up at headquarters. There were mirrors in the john, mirrors in the interview room. Why the heck did they need so many stinkin' mirrors, anyway? Nathanial had considered taking them all down like he'd done at home, but he knew people would think that was pretty gosh-darn strange.

Nathanial didn't even like to use the mirrors in his cruiser while he was driving, if he could help it all. He'd picked up the habit of changing lanes without looking, trusting in the Lord that no one was behind him. He'd had a couple close calls, some horns honked at him, but better that than catching a glance of the leering, taunting devil that lived in his reflection.

The rain finally let up on the drive over, and by the time he got home the clouds were clearing away. Nate pulled into his driveway. He didn't park in the garage anymore because that's where he was keeping all the mirrors he'd taken down from inside the house. It gave him the horrors to think of them all stacked out there like that, propped up facing backwards, but he was afraid to break them, too. No telling what might happen if he did that.

The worst part was, it wasn't even just mirrors he had to watch out for. Any reflective surface would do the nasty trick. Panes of glass. The screen on his phone. Even the old chrome toaster he used for his English muffins.

No matter how hard Nathanial tried to sneak up on his reflection, Nate was always waiting inside, looking him right in the eye.

Nathanial let himself into his dark, empty house. It was so quiet all the time since Mara had left. The quiet aggrieved him almost as much as mirrors did. When it was real quiet like this, Nathanial could sometimes hear Nate inside his head and that was even worse than seeing him in the mirror. He liked to leave the TV on most of the time, even when he slept. For the sound, and for the company of living human voices. The Weather Channel was the best for this. The news sometimes got Nate riled up, and those reality shows that were on all the time were so asinine that Nathanial felt dumber just watching them. But it soothed him to hear about the low—and high—pressure fronts moving around the country, visualized on colorful maps. When there was stormy weather down in Texas or Oklahoma, it was as exciting as any Hollywood movie, but without the guns and the violence and all the shouting and cussing. The weather-ladies were pretty without being overly sexed-up, which was good because sometimes that kind of thing got Nate riled, too.

Nathanial warmed up his supper, Healthy Choice Chicken Fettuccini Alfredo, careful to glance away from the reflective glass front of the microwave door. In terms of flavor and nutrition, the meal was only marginally better than the cardboard carton it came in, but cooking for himself seemed a pointless task. Mara had never been great shakes in the kitchen—she seemed to think the whole point of cooking was the glass of wine you got to drink while you were doing it—but Nathanial would have given his back teeth for one of her undercooked chicken casseroles or dried-up pork chops right now. The pleasure a man took in having a woman cook for him had little to do with how the food actually tasted.

Nathanial carried the steaming carton with him into the living room and plopped down on the couch. He reached over to grab the remote, but then he made the fatal mistake of looking up at the dead black television screen. The late afternoon sunlight pouring in through the west window cast his reflection perfectly on the screen. Nate sneered out at Nathanial, clear as day.

"Put that goddamned remote down," Nate said. "You and I gotta talk."

"I got nothing to say to you." Nathanial pointed the remote at the television, but Nate put it down before Nathanial could switch the set on and obliterate his hated reflection.

"I *am* you, you goddamn dumbass. The *real* you. You're just a robot those Malovo fucks wired up inside my brain."

"That's not true," Nathanial said. "You're not the real me. You're a *cancer*. A tumor they cut out of my head."

"Yeah, they did a real fucking good job of that."

"I need to go back in, for a follow-up. They said I might have to."

"That's the last goddamn thing you want to do, son," Nate said, and Nathanial thought he might have detected a note of fear in his voice. "Let those brain butchers back in there, hacking shit up again? We'll end up a goddamn vegetable, pissing into a bag."

"Why can't you let me be? Just let me live my life? Things are starting to go well."

"Oh, things are going well, are they? So says the man-eating microwaved crap in a house by himself, afraid of his own goddamned shadow. You fucked everything up. Fucked up my business. Fucked up my marriage."

"Mara left because of *you*," Nathanial countered.

"Yeah, well *I* would have got her dumb ass back by now. You know all that woman needs is one decent fuck to set her straight, and she sure as shit isn't getting that from Bill goddamn Potter. It's fucking disgrace, letting a dipshit like that steal *my* wife. Jesus. You're not even half a goddamn man. I know for a fact you can't get a hard-on without me."

Nathanial had never noticed before, but it hit him now. Nate spoke with the same hard, reproaching tone of his father, who had rarely let a day go by without reminding his son of his worthlessness. Ted Bates had known by some sadistic sixth sense the precise words to penetrate whatever defenses Nathanial had managed to acquire. He found all the soft spots and prodded them with hateful jabs and, if Nathanial dared to talk back or stand up for himself, he took it up a notch and started using his fists.

In a way, this realization was comforting. It seemed like something the shrinks would pounce on, Nathanial projecting all his daddy issues onto this raging hallucination. That made more sense than the preposterous notion that he'd been programmed like a machine to suppress his true nature and that this beast in the mirror was in fact his essential self.

"Oh boo hoo, Daddy was so mean," Nate snarled from the television. "God damn, you sound like one of these whiny liberal faggots blaming all their problems on their crappy childhoods. That is such a crock. I made a man out of myself *because* that fuckin' asshole toughened me up. You never heard me crying about it. Jesus, you turn my fuckin' stomach."

"You're not real," Nathanial said. "Please just go away."

"What, and let you fuck things up even more? You're gonna get us killed. You think Suzy and her boys are just going to roll over and accept that you've destroyed their livelihood?"

"I can handle the Barbers."

"Shit," Nate hissed. "You can't even handle your own dick. You know they've got a new supplier hooked up, right?"

"Yeah, I figured they would."

"So what are you going to do about that? You're stuck between the rock of your law enforcement duties and the hard place of your past affiliation with a criminal enterprise. What do you think the first thing those boys will do if one of them gets arrested?"

"Probably float my name," Nathanial sighed.

"*Our* name," Nate said. "You can't let that happen. There's lots of mirrors in prison, shithead. Those polished metal kinds you can't break. I will make your life hell."

"It already is," Nathanial moaned.

"Oh, quit your blubbering. Jesus. Anyway, the Barbers are kind of a back burner problem right now, considering."

"What do you mean by that?"

Nate gave a crooked grin. "Why don't you scoot over and let me drive for a little bit? The next couple days are going to require some delicate maneuvering."

"What the heck are you talking about?"

"That dyke broad, Michelle Delany," Nate said. "Did you happen to notice that she *saw* me? Most people are too goddamn dense to realize anything's off, but she's a sharp one. I've already got a plan in motion to deal with her, though."

"What plan?" Nathanial said, starting to panic.

"If everything goes right, this'll finally let us take care of that Mark Davies motherfucker, too. That's why you need to let me take the reins, at least through tomorrow. I'll give 'em back." Nate chuckled. "I promise."

"Just tell me what you're talking about!" Nathanial Bates shouted at his television.

"What time is it?" Nate glanced at his watch, and Nathanial felt the awful, creeping sensation of someone else lifting his wrist and turning his head down to look. "Ooh, it's going on five right now. Quick, turn on the news. Channel two. You're going to wanna see this shit."

Nathanial, or Nate, he wasn't sure who was in control at this point, picked up the remote again and turned the set on to the Springfield station. Nate's leering reflection was replaced by the local news's bombastic opening credits.

"In our top story," said Bridgette Coy, the pretty dark-haired anchor lady, "the tiny Logan County community of Bakersfield is once again in the news."

Because the graphics department of the local news station was hopelessly literal-minded, a picture of the "Welcome to Bakersfield! Pop: 6500" sign appeared over her shoulder.

"Last night, local resident Michelle Blair-Delany was arrested under suspicion of performing an illegal abortion." The screen cut to a shot of Michelle's mug shot, her brown eyes staring into the camera with weary defiance. "The Logan County Sheriff's Department released Blair-Delany earlier this afternoon with no charges filed, but the entire community is on edge following the accidental release of a gruesome crime scene photo. Two News has determined that the image, showing the body of a deformed fetus, is too graphic to broadcast, but hundreds of residents received the photo in a text notification last night. A representative from the sheriff's department issued a statement apologizing for the photo's release, which they claim was 'completely inadvertent.' The statement also claims that an internal investigation is pending to determine how the photo was released."

"You did it, didn't you?" Nathanial said aloud. "You sent it out."

"Shhh," Nate shushed inside his head. "They're getting to the good part."

"In an even more troubling twist, Two News has learned that Logan County Sheriff Nathanial Bates has sought consultation from Thomas Gorman, a noted expert on occult crimes. The department declined to comment on the possibility that this case has a connection to the occult, but we contacted Dr. Gorman via Skype at his home in Austin, Texas."

The screen was filled with a jagged, jittery-digital image of an overweight man in a pastel tie and glasses.

"Obviously, I can't comment directly on an open investigation, but I can say that there are numerous black magic rituals that call for the blood of an unborn child," he said with authority. "And deformations of the type seen in this photo are common in cases where occult practitioners deliberately induce birth defects. This is done in an attempt to summon a demon to possess the baby's soul. Also quite alarming is the fact that this birth occurred so close to Halloween, which is the most profane holiday on the satanic calendar."

"He said he would be discrete!" Nathanial hollered, standing up from the couch.

"*Discrete*," Nate sneered. "That shithead can't stay off TV more than five minutes at a stretch. That's why I called him in."

"But he's spouting off a load of nonsense."

"Bingo."

"Who's going to believe all that?"

"Seriously?" Nate said. "You're seriously asking that? In this town?" He laughed. "Hoo, boy. This is gonna be *fu-u-un*."

"What did you do, Nate?"

"Oh, relax. I lit the match. You don't got to do nothin' but sit back and watch shit burn."

"Oh, God. Please."

"I ain't a total asshole. I'll take some mercy on you. Go ahead, change the channel. I know you wanna."

Nathanial picked up the remote and switched over to the weather. There was a blizzard in the Rockies. First major winter storm of the season. Nathanial watched for hours as the snowfall totals mounted, until he fell into comforting dreams of being buried in cold, white softness.

CHAPTER 27

6:53 PM

LANA SAT ON the edge of the toilet as Chelle soaked in the steaming, sudsy water. The bathroom adjoining their master bedroom only had a shower unit, but the downstairs bathroom contained this huge tub with the monster-claw feet. It was so deep Michelle could almost float, weightlessly suspended. The water contained enough aromatic bath salts for the lavender, eucalyptus and rosemary scent blend to counteract the Bakersfield tap-water funk.

Lana had tried to get close to Michelle as soon as she got her home, but she'd protested. "No, no. I stink. I smell like jail and afterbirth." This bath had been entered into as a cleansing preparation for their healing lovemaking, but it had become a restorative end unto itself. Michelle showed no signs of wanting to get out, content to luxuriate in the suds as Lana refilled the glass of Chianti (three times so far) precariously balanced on the edge of the tub. The Spotify Classic Jazz station pumped complex Dave Brubeck chords into the steamy air. Michelle drifted on the gentle waves, leaning back with a wet folded-over washcloth placed over her eyes.

Perhaps she dozed off for a second, because her right hand slipped into the water. Michelle sat up, wincing, sloshing the water as she shook off her hand. Lana hadn't noticed before, but Chelle had four red, inflamed scratches across her knuckles as well as the one on her cheek. They must have stung her when she'd dipped them in the hot, soapy water.

Lana took her wife's hand and examined the cuts. "How'd you get these?"

"Sandy's cat." Chelle said. She pulled the cloth from her eyes and wiped it over her neck and her chest. "Nasty fucking beast."

Lana kissed Chelle's knuckles, gently, like a mother would. "My poor baby."

Chelle looked up at her. "What's Ben doing?"

"In his room, watching TV."

"Is he all right?"

Ben had been unusually clingy towards his mother since her release from jail, hugging her tightly, not wanting to let go. He'd apologized over and over again for sneaking out the night before, promising that he would never do it again. He seemed to associate his transgression with his mother's arrest, as if one had somehow caused the other. Despite reassurances from both Michelle and Lana that they were not angry with him, that they were just happy that everyone was safely together, Ben wouldn't let it go until they arrived at a suitable punishment. At his own suggestion, he was grounded from his tablet and his X-Box for the next week. "And I'll only use the computer for school work," he'd promised.

Satisfied with this act of atonement, he'd gone into his room and shut the door, giving his implicit endorsement of their mommies-alone-together time.

"He'll be fine," Lana said.

Chelle gave Lana that smile of hers. "Get in with me?"

"There's no room for two people in there."

"Sure there is," Michelle said. "For now. There won't be in a couple months, Mama. We should enjoy it while we can."

"All right." Lana pulled off her clothes, folding them and putting them on the back of the toilet while Michelle watched intently.

"You're starting to show," Chelle said when Lana was undressed.

"Really?" Lana frowned, running her hand over her belly. It still felt flat to her. "You can tell already?"

"I wasn't talking about your tummy," Chelle said. Her eyes were focused a bit higher than that.

"Oh, the boobs," Lana said, gingerly touching her breasts. "I know, right? They look weird, don't they?" Noticeably bigger already, her nipples even darker than they used to be, the veins engorged and swollen.

"I like how they look," Chelle said. The naughty girl actually licked her lips.

"Yeah, well they're sore as hell, baby, so I'm declaring this a hands-off zone," Lana said, stepping over to the tub. "Scoot back."

"No." Michelle scooted forward instead, making waves in the tub. "Get in behind me. I want to be held."

Lana slid into the tub behind her wife. After a few awkward sloshing moments, getting all their knees and elbows aligned, Chelle slid comfortably back into her. They fit well together, they always had, like they'd been custom-molded for one another's curves. Lana ran her fingers through Chelle's long, soft, white girl's hair, a texture she never got tired of feeling.

"Is all the blood out of my hair?" Michelle asked.

"Yeah, baby. We washed it twice already."

"Ugh. That was the worst feeling. It made me want to cut it all off. What would you think if I had short hair? Like a pixie cut, like Mia Farrow in *Rosemary's*—"

"Ah," Lana cut her off. "I thought we agreed. We weren't going to even mention that movie for at least the next nine months."

"God, sorry," Michelle laughed. "You're right. That was *gruesomely* inappropriate."

"Anyway, I like it long."

Michelle leaned further back into her. Lana snaked her arms around the warm smooth skin of her wife's belly. She kissed her lightly, on the mouth.

"What are we going to do?" Chelle whispered. "I'm so scared."

"I'm scared too, baby," Lana said.

They'd watched the news together, in frank disbelief. Michelle's name and face broadcast to the world, though she was accused of no crime. Then that crazy fat man spouting his superstitious insanity. The town was already on edge, and that newscast might have been just the thing to push it over.

"Who's doing this to me?" Michelle asked. "Somebody put in an anonymous call to the police, but nobody even knew I was at Sandy's place except for you."

"Chelle," Lana said. "You know that I didn't—"

"God, baby." Michelle half-turned to face Lana. "No. I never thought that for a second. I trust you with my life. But somebody's pulling the strings here. I just can't grasp who or why."

"Bates, maybe?"

"Maybe. But the guy's cracking up, seriously. I think he's having a psychotic break. That's dangerous, but it doesn't really lend itself to organizing a conspiracy. And, looking back, there was something really strange about the Sandy situation from the start. She didn't seem to care about the baby, she wouldn't even quit smoking, so why did she hire me?"

"You're saying Sandy set you up?" Lana said.

"No, because that's nuts. She deliberately died in childbirth, to frame me? But then there's this whole business about the mysterious substance in the jar. Was that something she ingested, to purposely miscarry? I don't know what the hell to think. It all sounds so crazy and hysterical when I say it out loud. I feel like a paranoid nutcase."

"You're not crazy," Lana said. "The situation is. And paranoia's just plain good sense in this town."

"And I'm so worried about you," said Michelle. "And the baby. After going through that with Sandy, I don't know if I can…"

Chelle's body hitched in Lana's arms, and she thought for a second that she might be crying. But Michelle's eyes were dry when she turned to face Lana.

"I'm sorry I brought you here," Michelle said. "To this town. It was a mistake moving back. Bloody Bakersfield. Bad water, religious fanatics and racist farmers, Sheriff Psychobilly, goddamn Malovo. Jesus. I grew up here. You think I'd know better than to come back."

"It's all right, baby. Home is wherever you are, as far as I'm concerned."

"Then let's go somewhere else."

"What?" Lana said. "Where?"

"Anywhere. I mean it, Lana. I don't want to stay here another day if we can help it."

"I have a job. The school year just started."

"You're a good teacher, you can get a job anywhere," Michelle said.

"We don't have any money. We blew through all our savings moving out here."

"We'll sell the house," said Michelle. "Maybe my parents can lend us some money. I don't know. But we have to get out. Soon. Now."

"All right." Lana knew better than to suggest they sleep on it, or talk about it later. Michelle had made up her mind, and there was rarely any going back from that. Besides, Lana had got her fill of down-homey charm on about day two of living here. She had to admit that the thought of getting off Planet Cornfield held an undeniable appeal, even with all the complications. "How about a city?"

"God, yeah," Michelle said. "The bigger the better."

"Someplace where I might actually see another black person occasionally."

"Now you're talking."

"Okay, baby. We'll make it happen. We just have to figure out how."

Michelle nodded, and Lana could tell she was turning it over in her mind.

"Do you want to get out of the tub?" Lana asked.

"Not just yet," Michelle said. "This is nice, you holding me like this."

So Lana held her wife until the bathwater grew tepid. Then they stumbled out, their muscles having long gone lax, and toweled each other dry. After peeking out to make sure their son was still safely inside his room, they dashed naked together down the hall and fell laughing into their big warm bed. They did not speak further of the cataclysmic decision they'd made. First love, and then sleep. Tomorrow would come soon enough on its own.

CHAPTER 28

7:59 PM

FOR THE SECOND night in a row, Mark found himself drunk and heading back from Springfield on a dark country road with a strange woman. But where his mad motorcycle flight with Ellie the night before had been cold, arousing, and terrifying, riding in Sally's warm car was calm and relaxed. He liked her. She was easy to talk to. Jett's closed early on Sunday, so their dining options in Bakersfield had been limited to burgers at the Dairy Queen. Instead, they drove into Springfield and ate at a pretty decent Italian place downtown. They'd also shared a bottle of red wine, which seemed to amplify the effects of the beers Mark already downed at Wolfy's.

Their conversation had been laid-back and comfortable, and it got Mark to wondering. He knew it was common for straight women to have close friends who were gay men—that was practically a cliché. But the opposite configuration, a straight man and a lesbian, seemed unusual. He wondered why. There was a casual intimacy to his rapport with Sally that was lacking in Mark's friendships with other men, even with Sam Hansard and Bill Potter, who he met for beers at least once a week. There was some kind of barrier to emotional honesty in his male friendships, but though he and Sally had just met, they'd really opened up to one another. There had been none of the uncertainty of being on a "real" date, either. Mark had not been subject to constant speculations about Sally's motives, as he had with Ellie. There had not been the jittery obsession with the moment-to-moment fluctuations of his odds of getting laid. With Sally, that was off the table completely.

It was also illuminating to talk to someone who held a torch for Missy almost as big as his was.

He was trying formulate a way that he could ask Sally if she'd like to do this again, without sounding like he was coming on to her, when she turned to him and said: "Mark, I have kind of a confession to make."

"Uh-oh," he said. "What is it?"

"Well, I had kind of an ulterior motive in wanting to go out with you."

"Ulterior?"

"Maybe it would be easiest just to show you," she said, and then lifted up the side of her shirt a little. There, just above her right hip, was a tattoo. A woman astride a crescent moon.

"Holy shit," Mark said, goggling at the tat. "That's...so you're...one of them? In their club or whatever?"

"The proper term is 'coven,' Mark. We're witches. We call ourselves 'Bell's Angels.'"

"Whoa," Mark said, shaking his head. "I was not expecting you to say that."

"Ellie was supposed to recruit you, to help us with a project we're working on, but in case you didn't notice, she's kind of a flake."

"I was being *recruited*?"

"We figured sex would be the easiest way to get you on our side," Sally said. "Men are kind of predictable that way, no offense."

"None taken."

"Ellie's the only one of us who's straight and of an appropriate age, so she was the only one qualified to do it. You wouldn't think getting a horny divorced guy to sleep with you would be that complicated, but of course Ellie found a way to bungle it. She really is a basket case."

"Well, I'm screwed up enough to think that was part of her appeal," Mark said.

"I know what you mean. I almost went down that road myself, you know. I'm so glad I didn't end up making that mistake."

"You and Ellie?" Mark said.

"Yeah. Weird, isn't it? You and I have pretty much the same taste in women."

"This is a lot to process, Sally."

"Well, get your head wrapped around it," Sally said. "Because we're headed back over there now."

"To Roberta's house?"

"Yeah, I called her already and let her know we're coming. Tonight's the big gathering. It's all been leading up to this. That's why I couldn't believe it when you just walked into my dad's place. I honestly believe there's no such thing as coincidences, Mark. You were meant to help us with this."

"What do you want me to do?" Mark said.

"We'll talk about it when we get there. Just keep an open mind, okay?"

The clouds had all cleared away and the full moon was rising as they drove out to where the cornfields gave way to wooded timber. Sally crossed over the little river bridge Ellie had been so afraid of the night before. She turned down a road that was almost hidden by the trees, down a gravel drive into the deep woods. The house was completely concealed, invisible from the road. Mark had been a little too distracted to notice much on his approach the night before, but he saw now that it was a very modern-looking, faux-rustic house constructed from reclaimed barn-wood, with huge bay windows spilling golden light out into the woods. It was a beautiful home, like something he'd see in an architectural magazine.

Stepping onto the porch, Mark saw that the trellis he'd burst through the night before was still splintered and broken. There were rubber skid-marks on the hardwood planks of the porch.

Sally glanced over at the damage. "Yeah, we all had a pretty good laugh about your motorcycle skills."

She rang the bell and Roberta opened the door a few moments later. She was wearing clothes this time, a long black cloak covered with purple designs. Moons and pentagrams and Celtic-looking symbols.

"So glad you're with us, sister. We couldn't have asked for a more beautiful night for the invocation," Roberta said, beaming out at Sally. She turned to Mark, and grabbed both his hands. "And Mark, thank you so much for joining us. Please, come inside."

Stepping into the spacious front room, Mark saw that the mural had been finished. The life-sized woman astride the moon had been painted with a level of detail that was startling at this scale. Her skin was sheeny with sweat, and every bead of moisture was vivid and clear. Every hair on her head and every follicle on her body was a thin, distinct line. The woman's body was clearly that of Roberta's daughter Lizzy, but her face more resembled a Madonna from a Catholic icon—which lent the expression of ecstatic abandon she wore an almost sacrilegious charge. Mark was so transfixed by Roberta's artistry that it took him a moment to notice the other women in the room.

Lizzy was there, and Ellie, avoiding his eye. There was also a younger girl Mark didn't recognize, with dark brown eyes heavily lined with black make-up. All three women wore black cloaks like Roberta's. Theirs were plainer, though, edged with purple fringe but no ornamental designs.

"You remember Ellie and Lizzy," Roberta said. "This is Gemma, our youngest covener. Gemma, this is Mark Davies. He's a very well-respected author."

"Actually, I'm hardly respected at all," Mark said.

"I know who you are," Gemma said, looking up at him intently. "I'm friends with your nephew James and Alice Kiernan."

"Oh yeah," Mark said. "Alice is a great kid. She and James are inseparable now."

Gemma nodded. "I was going to have her join us here tonight, but Roberta wanted me to put her on another mission instead."

"Mission?"

"Gemma, Lizzie, Sally," Roberta called. "Why don't you three come with me into the kitchen to help prepare communion? I think Ellie and Mark need to talk."

The women cleared out of the room, leaving Mark and Ellie alone together. The long silence was about as awkward as Mark had feared.

"Look," he finally said. "I'm really sorry about how I left last night, it just..."

"Shut up," Ellie said.

"Okay, I was hoping we could at least be friendly with each other, but..."

"No." Ellie grabbed his arm and looked him in the eye. "I didn't mean to say, 'shut up.' I should have said, 'don't apologize.' It wasn't your fault. It was all me. I thought I could go through with it, but I was just too disgusted."

"Okay..." Mark sighed.

"No. You're not disgusting, Jesus. Just listen, okay? I'm not a whore. They wanted me to be a whore, to get you to go along with this. And I just...couldn't. There's nothing wrong with you. You're fine. You're just not my type."

"All right," Mark said. "I guess I can live with that."

"See, I like tall guys with muscles. If I was going to hook up with anybody from work, it would be Abe. Have you ever seen that guy without a shirt on? He's *ripped*. Seriously, he could be stripper or something."

Mark grinned bitterly and shook his head, laughing.

"He came by earlier," Ellie said. "I thought for a second maybe I was going to get lucky and he was going to ask me out, but he just came over to tell me I was fired."

"That sucks, doesn't it?"

"Yeah, it does. I liked that job."

"Me too," said Mark. "So, what is this, anyway? I mean, if you guys want my help with something, why not just ask instead of trying to seduce me into it?"

"Oh, you'll see," Ellie said, her eyes gleaming.

The other women emerged from the kitchen then. Gemma and Lizzy were carrying silver trays. One was laden with shot glasses, the other with crackers covered with what looked like a pesto spread.

"Will you join us on the patio for sacraments, Mark?" Roberta asked.

"Uh, sure," Mark said. "I left my wizard robes at home, though."

"Oh, the robes were only for the preamble," Roberta said. "We're done with that."

She dropped the robe from her shoulders and stood naked before him. Ellie, Lizzy and Gemma followed suit. Even Sally took off her t-shirt and jeans. Five nude women were now looking at Mark with various expressions of embarrassment or expectation.

"Get undressed and come out onto the patio with us," Roberta said. "The hot tub's ready and we have quite a story to tell."

CHAPTER 29

8:06 PM

J AMES AND ALICE sat together on metal folding chairs as the room filled with the younger Church of the Shepherd congregants, and quite a few curious newcomers. Alice wore a sort of dreamy smile as she waited, looking genial but determined in her studded eye-patch. Only the beads of sweat on her forehead and the mentholated vapors wafting off her gave any indication of her distress.

James had no idea how she could possibly be up and moving around. She'd been in bad shape earlier in the afternoon, as bad as James had ever seen her. He knew she should have stayed in bed, but Alice was so determined to do this. When she put her mind to something, James knew, a little thing like terminal cancer didn't have a chance of standing in her way.

Following her chat with Gemma Gordon, Alice had spent the afternoon girding herself with medication. She consumed pain pills like breath mints and had downed a staggering assortment of edible marijuana products. Then smoked two joints on top of that. And *then* raided her dad's secret emergency liquor stash for several shots of whiskey. That level of chemical intake would have left most people, James certainly included, utterly stupefied. Probably hospitalized. But Alice's pain was such a behemoth that it had absorbed everything she'd thrown at it, rendering her in a state close to what could be called sobriety in a normal metabolism.

Right before they'd left to come over here, she'd had James rub her down with some kind of prescription liniment. A powerful analgesic cream that had left his hands red and burning. That was kind of strange for him.

Alice had just handed James the tube and then, without warning, whipped her top off.

"What's your problem?" she challenged when he'd looked away, blushing. "I barely even *have* tits. And what would you care if I did?" Then she'd rolled over and offered up her naked back. James rubbed in the icy hot ointment, disturbed at how thin and fragile his friend felt beneath his hands. Her sharp bones felt like they might just snap if he pressed too hard.

All this medicinal preparation had been in service of getting them here, to the YIA Club's "emergency presentation and prayer meeting." It was being held in a downtown storefront that the church had rented and fashioned into a hangout spot for its younger members. They called it the "Underground Club."

James had never been here before, needless to say. The Church of the Shepherd, unsurprisingly, took an explicitly anti-gay stance. What was surprising to James was the strange deference the kids who went the church showed towards him. Since officially coming out earlier in the year, right after his mom died, James *had* suffered some homophobic bullying. Taunting, name-calling, shoves and half-hearted threats of further violence. Nothing he couldn't handle. Mainly it came from two specific members of the football team and a few of the more roughneck farm and ethanol plant kids. The Church of the Shepherd crowd took a different tack, though. They seemed to see in James a thrilling opportunity to save a soul in desperate need of redemption. It was like a competition with those people, to see who could reclaim James for the Lord first.

James had been given more than a dozen copies of a brochure, printed with the church's logo, titled "You Don't HAVE to be Gay, with Jesus' Healing Love." Some were handed to him in the hallways with meaningful nods, but most were anonymously slipped into his locker. The brochure was filled with useful tips for distracting oneself from "unnatural urges," ("Play a sport!" the brochure suggested. "Watch a wholesome movie!" "Get a hobby!") and contained several paragraphs about the effectiveness of "Christ-centric conversion therapy." James thought it somewhat ironic that the Jesus pictured on the front of the brochure looked like a long-haired, better-built Robert Pattinson, which was a less than ideal image to distract him from his unnatural urges.

In addition to the brochure, he'd been handed quite a few "prayer intention cards," which he gathered the Shepherd kids were required to fill out every week. These informed him that "_____ is saying a prayer for you this week for _____." The second blank was always filled in with "an end to your same-sex attraction." Sometimes they abbreviated it as "SSA," like it was some kind of rare blood disease.

James supposed he appreciated that they were motivated by genuine concern for his immortal soul and honestly thought they were helping. But if their goal was to make him less gay through the power of collective prayer, so far it seemed to be having the opposite effect.

James didn't know how they scored their "souls saved" game, but the gay kid and the terminal cancer girl had to garner them some kind of bonus points. That was probably the reason no one treated him and Alice like suspected interlopers when they stepped into the club, but rather bathed them with a communal "so glad you finally joined us" welcome. Alice's eye-patch was a tremendous hit. Several of the girls there called her "Christian Grace," for some reason.

Despite the warm reception, James felt distinctly uncomfortable here in the belly of the beast. There was a strange agitation to the young congregants who filled the room, a tinge of mania to their overheard whispers. He got the sense that the torches and pitchforks were stockpiled in the back room, just waiting to be distributed.

"Raspberry," Alice whispered beside him.

"What?"

"Oh, sorry." She looked surprised she'd spoken aloud. "I was just thinking about flavors of sherbet."

He looked at her sideways. Maybe she wasn't quite as sober as he'd thought.

"Doesn't that sound good? Sweet and creamy and cold. Do you call it sherbet or sher-bert?" she mused. "Or is it sher-*bay*? Raspberry sher-bay. Wasn't that a song?"

Then, to James's horror, she sang: "She ate some raspberry sher-bay." This did garner them some curious glances.

"Alice," he whispered. "We're trying to blend in here, so maybe you should..."

"Right," she said. "I'll be cool."

Fortunately, somebody flickered the lights then, signaling that the presentation was about to begin. Travis Chasen, the church's handsome youth leader (who bore, in James's opinion, at least a faint resemblance to the Robert Pattinson Jesus) stood up behind a podium in front of the group to applause and enthusiastic hooting. Alice gamely joined in, with a loud "woo-hoo!"

"Thanks," Travis grinned. There was a microphone on the podium, but the room was small enough he didn't need to use it. "Thank you so much for coming out here tonight. As I'm sure you all know, this is a very troubling time to be a Christian in Bakersfield. Last night, a lesbian named Michelle Delany performed an abortion on a woman who lived just a few blocks from here." Boos echoed through the room at this announcement. Travis tamped them down with his hands. "Something went terribly wrong, and this...*procedure* ended with not only the death of an innocent child, but with the death of the mother as well. Though she committed a terrible sin by seeking to have her baby killed, she deserves Jesus' mercy, as we all do. So before we go any further, I want us to take a moment and say a prayer for the souls of Sandy Aswell and that poor little baby."

Though he didn't like the accusatory tone leveled towards his Aunt Michelle, James did bow his head. He didn't know if the thoughts running through his mind could be considered a prayer, but they were devoted to mindful sympathy for the dead mother and child.

"This is something we talk about a lot, but it bears repeating," Travis said after the silent minute. "This town we live in is a very strange place, containing extremes of both goodness and evil. It's the birthplace of our beloved church, founded here way back in 1971. The community that's built up around it since then is an undeniable force for good in the world. There are seven other churches in town, too. We may not see eye-to-eye with them on every point, but you know those congregations are filled with good, decent people. When bad things happen, the people in this town come together, regardless of faith."

"And bad things do happen here. That's the other extreme. They happen here a lot. Why, though? Why here, in this beautiful town filled with God-fearing people? Well, that's why I called you here. There is a reason. Dave Muldoon and I put together this video presentation. We threw it together pretty quickly, didn't even have time to add the narration, so please don't judge us on the production values. Just focus on the message. It may be the most important video you've ever watched in your life."

Travis wheeled the podium out of the way and pulled down a projection screen from the ceiling. Dave Muldoon, a sophomore at BHS, rolled up an A/V cart with a laptop that had a video projector attached. Somebody in the back of the room dimmed the lights.

"Whoa." Alice had been slumping in her seat, but she sat bolt upright when the lights went out. "What's happening?"

"It's all right," James whispered, putting his hand on her shoulder. "They're just playing a video."

"Oh." Alice nodded slowly. "I like videos."

The video began with ominous music, the audio patched through the PA, over a montage of old newspaper headlines and vintage local news footage. It was a slick editing job. Dave Muldoon was pretty proficient with the Adobe Premiere. The headline "HOLIDAY KILLER CLAIMS ANOTHER" scrolled diagonally across the screen, superimposed over news footage showing the five kids who were killed back then. A flame effect was applied, causing the lower part of the frame to crackle with hell-fire.

"Twenty years ago," Travis narrated live into the microphone, reading with a flashlight from a printed script. "Before most people in this room were even born, a man they called the Holiday Killer murdered five children right here in Bakersfield. Also known as the Snowman, this depraved killer began his reign of terror on Halloween night, and killed his final victim exactly one year later."

Now the headline read "UNEXPLAINED SLEEPWALKING EPIDEMIC RAVAGES ILLINOIS TOWN," over some shots of the devastation the Sickness had left in the town. The video lingered on a shot of the defaced water tower, with the red spray-paint graffiti that had proclaimed the town "BLOODY BLOODY BAKERSFIELD."

"Then, just this past May, most of us here caught the sleepwalking sickness, which caused us to do terrible things. Jesus forgives us for sins we commit when we can't think clearly for ourselves, but I'm sure Satan had a good laugh about it anyway."

Though that was probably not meant as a punchline, Alice laughed loudly. Or *cackled*, to be more precise. People turned and looked, causing James to slump down in his chair.

"The Holiday Killer and the sleepwalking sickness are only two examples," Travis went on. The video cut to cascading screen shots culled from various websites, statistical information with the lines pertaining to Bakersfield highlighted. "In a list of communities with populations under twenty thousand with the highest murder rates, Bakersfield ranks *fifth* nation-wide. For a town this size, we also have disproportionately high rates of suicide, teen pregnancy and drug addiction. No wonder people call this place Bloody Bakersfield."

"Woo!" Alice hooted. Now people were actively shushing her. James noted the locations of the exit doors, tensing himself for their escape.

"Now it seems like things are getting even worse," Travis pressed on, ignoring her outburst. "We've got water you can't even drink." The video showed Travis holding up a glass of the cloudy water. "And even before Sandy Aswell's abortion, there were several tragic miscarriages in town. Many of the babies had tragic birth defects like this one."

The screen was filled with the notorious photo of the dead baby, in vivid, screaming high-definition. Even though everybody in the room had certainly seen the picture by now, there was a collective gasp. James felt it, too. Projected larger than life, the image was jolting.

"No," Alice moaned beside him. "I don't like that, James. Make them take it down."

But the still frame lingered on the screen. Travis stepped in front of the projector beam, and the horrific image superimposed his features with bloody light. Theatrically speaking, this was quite effective. For a straight Christian kid, Travis had a real flair for drama.

"Are all these things coincidences?" Travis asked, the baby's twisted, tortured visage overlaying his own. "Or are they connected? What is the curse that plagues this town? Why has Satan singled out Bakersfield as his personal playground?" He paused here. By design or by happy accident, the baby's horns were projected right onto Travis's forehead, lending him a diabolical aspect as he pronounced: "Because he was *invited*!"

The screen went black and the room was thrust into darkness. Gasps and screams filled the room, along with a few titters of nervous laughter. Alice clutched James tightly. She was shaking, letting out a low groan.

When the screen lit up again, Travis had stepped out of the way. The video now showed a night-vision view, a green monochrome of hooded figures gathered in a field.

"People don't like to talk about it, but Bakersfield has always been a center for occult activity. Satanic worship. Witchcraft. Dark rituals disguised as childish fun and games. Cult ceremonies in the woods outside of town. Black mass orgies and animal sacrifices and maybe even worse. There are those in this town who serve the devil as you and I serve the Lord. Who are these practitioners of the dark arts?"

"Some were born here," Travis said. To James's surprise, his Uncle Mark's author photo filled the screen, followed by shots of his lurid book covers. *Blood World*, *Blood World War* and *Blood World's End*. "This man, Mark Davies, left Bakersfield to educate himself in the secrets of the supernatural. He exploited this dark knowledge for fame and fortune, authoring several occult novels filled with perverse sex and depraved violence."

James had to chuckle to himself. Mark would love hearing about the reputation he had with these people. He turned to Alice, to see if she was getting this too, but her one eye was closed and she was shivering. She leaned close to James.

"Others are outsiders." Now there was a shot of Lana's photo from the faculty page in the yearbook. "This homosexual woman, Lana Blair, actually teaches at our high school. Educating teenagers, flaunting her lifestyle in our faces. Corrupting our values. Her partner—I won't use the word 'wife,' because though they may be married according the laws of our fallen nation, they will never be married in the eyes of God—is none other than Michelle Delany, the abortionist who murdered Sandy Aswell and her unborn child."

"No," Alice said, loudly. "James, this was a mistake. We shouldn't have come here. Get me out of here now, okay?"

"What's wrong?" Travis challenged. He stepped in front of the screen again, which was showing a flashing jack o'lantern graphic that James recognized as a loop from the "Silver Shamrock" commercial in *Halloween III*. Thankfully, there was no corresponding audio. "Hitting a little too close to home?"

Others were standing, surrounding them as James helped Alice to her feet.

"You don't have any idea what you're talking about," she said. "You're full of shit!"

"Why don't you enlighten us, then?" Travis said, bright orange and white strobes of light painting his face with maniacal pumpkin glee. "You want to tell us what you people are planning for tomorrow night?"

"Just let us go," James said. "She's sick."

The lights came back on. The projector was still running. The orange and white still flashed on Travis's face, but more subtly now.

"Yeah, sick in her soul," he said. "Halloween is your big day, isn't it? Well, we're not going to let you drag our town down to hell with you. We have plans, too."

The kids were crowding closer, pressing in on them. James didn't know what they were going to do, but then Alice doubled over, clutching her stomach. She hurled forth a huge splash of vomit. It sprang from her mouth, splattering the floor. The smell was ripe. The streaks of blood in her puke were clear and vivid red on the white tiles under the bright fluorescent lights.

This, at least, drove the pressing crowd back. People staggered from them in disgust, clearing a path to the door.

"Sorry," Alice gasped as James half-carried her to the exit.

"Just go!" Travis yelled. "Get out!"

James and Alice stepped into the night, the cold air outside a blessed relief after the stifling heat inside that room.

"Well, you know how to make an exit, at least," James said, chuckling weakly.

"I'm sorry, James." She leaned against him. "We shouldn't have gone in there. You told me that and I didn't listen."

"Doesn't matter," James said. "Are you all right?"

She shook her head. "Take me home, okay?"

"Of course."

"Will you stay with me?" she said. "Sleep at my house tonight? I don't want to be alone. Not after that."

"Sure, Alice."

She went utterly limp in his arms and let out a sob.

"I can't even stand up," she moaned.

"It's okay."

He bent over and picked her up, easily. She weighed next to nothing. James carried Alice over to his car and buckled her into the seat. They drove away, into the night.

CHAPTER 30

8:43 PM

THE WITCHES HAD built a roaring fire in the pit in the center of the stone patio, just below the elevated platform with the spacious hot-tub. The platform was half-encircled by tall standing mirror panels, arranged like a band-shell around the tub. The mirrors reflected and multiplied the flickering light of the flames, and also ensured there was nowhere Mark could glance where he did not see naked female flesh.

Being the only man in a churning hot tub with five nude women sounded on the surface like an erotic dream come true, but Mark felt no sexual desire at all. His libido might have been dampened by whatever had been in the "communion"—a foul-tasting combo of a "body of the goddess" wafer, spread with some kind of vile vegetable matter, and a bitter shot of "blood of the goddess" liquor. But there were also taboos in place that prevented him from seeing any of the women through the lens of sexual attraction. Roberta was too old, Gemma was too young. Sally was gay, Lizzy had the mind of a child. Ellie had stated her complete lack of physical interest in him, and that had rendered her likewise untouchable in his mind. Also, with the obvious exception of menopausal Roberta, Mark suspected that some or all of them were menstruating—synched as they were with the full round moon overhead. This was an ancient taboo, but in Mark's pulsing mind the prohibition against touching them had less to do with patriarchal religious notions of uncleanliness than it did an awe-filled respect for the impenetrable mystery of the female body.

"We are the daughters of Adaleen Bell," Roberta began.

The other four women echoed this invocation, chanting as one: "We are the daughters of Adaleen Bell."

That name struck a deep chord with Mark. He'd heard it somewhere before, but could not at that moment place where.

"We're Bell's Angels!" Lizzy cried, smiling with delight.

"That's right, honey," Roberta said. "Bell's Angels, honoring the legacy of a wise and powerful woman. Dedicating ourselves to continuing her struggle. Born into slavery in Louisiana, she escaped her captors and fled north, braving great peril and constant danger to come here, to Illinois. In fact, this house is built on the very site of Adaleen's cabin. I reclaimed some of her hand-hewn beams to use for my rafters, and there is a section of my basement that retains the original foundation stones. From her cabin, Adaleen offered her services to black and white alike. She was a fortune teller and a midwife, and also—"

"A hoodoo lady," Mark said, suddenly remembering where he had heard the name.

Roberta looked over at him, curiously. "You've heard of Adaleen?"

"When I was ten, I went with my friend Jess to see his great-grandmother at the nursing home where she lived. She told us about an old lady named Adaleen Bell who lived in the woods outside of town when she was a girl. She called her a 'hoodoo lady.'"

"Yes." Roberta beamed. "What else did this woman tell you about Adaleen?"

"A man they called the Scarecrow murdered several children in Bakersfield back around 1919 and 1920. Adaleen Bell taught Jess's great-grandmother how to make a monkey doll out of old black stockings. The monkey came to life, and stopped the Scarecrow killer. Jess's Grammy taught Jess how to make another Black Monkey, ninety years after the first one. That one stopped the Snowman killer."

"I knew I was right to choose you for this." Roberta laughed with delight. The other women were looking at Mark with new interest, tempered perhaps with a level of distrust. "Yes, Mark. Adaleen possessed knowledge of powerful magic, which she used to fight against the evil that has always pervaded this town."

"But her magic was evil, too," Mark said. "It killed Jess. It almost killed me."

"Evil is a relative term," Roberta said. "And sacrifice is always necessary. Always."

"It's not evil to defend yourself!" Gemma said, with sudden fierceness, half-standing in the water and thrusting a dripping finger in Mark's face. "It's not evil to kill a man who's murdering children."

"Calm, Gemma." Roberta placed her hand on Gemma's naked shoulder and eased her back down into the water.

"Why is he even here?" the teen girl demanded. "A *man*, in our sacred circle? He's been staring at my barely legal tits all night!"

"Mark is harmless as a eunuch right now," Roberta assured Gemma (though this wasn't very reassuring to Mark). "His only sin is ignorance. It's our job to educate him, because he does have a vital role to play. Sally, why don't you tell Mark what became of Adaleen Bell?"

"The fuckers killed her," Sally said, with real venom. Perhaps out of modesty before Mark's male gaze, she had slid her thin body almost all the way down into the water, until it came up to her neck. Her short black hair was plastered to her skull. "Six men broke into her house. They beat her and raped her and burned the house down with her still inside."

"Why?" Mark said.

"Because they couldn't stand for a woman, a *black* woman, to have any kind of power in their white cock world," Ellie said.

"I'm sure there's more reason than that."

Gemma, Sally, and Ellie all scoffed.

"Sure, blame the victim," Ellie said. "Typical male reaction."

"Mark is simply trying to understand," Roberta said. "And he's right, there was a justification, at least in their minds. Adaleen was murdered in 1933, thirteen years after the events Mark described."

"Wait," Mark said. "Jess's Grammy said Adaleen was more than a hundred years old when she taught her how to make the monkey in 1920."

Roberta smiled again. "You're beginning to understand the extraordinary power Adaleen possessed. Yes, I believe she was well into her hundred-and-twenties when this happened, which is part of what made people so suspicious of her. Don't forget, either, that this was the midst of the Depression. People were desperate, and desperate people are dangerous."

"In those days, there was an unincorporated African-American community just west of Bakersfield, composed of the children and grandchildren of former slaves who'd migrated north after the Civil War.

It was called Sweetbrook, though you'll never see that name on any map. By the thirties, little of the community remained, mostly due to racist opposition on the part of the white residents of Bakersfield. Still, a few tenacious families clung to their homesteads despite all attempts to drive them out. Then, in '33, an outbreak of encephalitis struck Bakersfield. Dozens of people became sick, at least ten died. Somehow, a rumor started that the disease was spread by mosquitos that had bred in a standing pond on the property of a black farmer named Clem Tucker. A 'posse' of men from town, led by the sheriff himself, confronted Mr. Tucker in what was most likely an attempt to steal his land. They beat him with clubs, fracturing his skull and leaving him unable to work. Tucker's family and a few other of the black farmers—again, out of desperation—went to Adaleen, either for protection or for justice. She walked onto the town square one sunny afternoon and announced, in a loud, clear voice for all to hear, that she was placing a curse on the town, until reparations were made to Clem Tucker. Well..."

Roberta's eyes gleamed, lost as she was in her storytelling. "...There's no telling how much of what happened over the next few months was due to the curse, and how much was plain bad luck, which was in no short supply in those days. It was a hot, dry summer. The day after Adaleen issued her curse, a parcel of hogs owned by a farmer named Quimby went mad from the heat. They drowned themselves in the lake, just like the passage in the New Testament where Jesus cast demons into a herd of swine."

"A few weeks later, a train derailed as it was passing through town, killing six people. The conductor swore that he saw a grotesquely deformed hunchbacked man in a long black coat standing on the tracks right before the crash, but no man fitting that description was ever found."

"There were other incidents. Unexplained fires. The birth of a two-headed calf. A tornado that blew down a grain elevator. The sound of a woman weeping that could only be heard at night. The drought wore on and on and it just kept getting hotter, but then the skies grew black with clouds. A rain did come, but it wasn't water."

"What was it, then?" Mark asked.

"Spiders. Millions of fat black spiders fell like hail, all over town." Roberta held her thumb and forefinger together, describing a circumference similar to that of a half dollar. "They blotted out the sun while they were falling, and piled up in writhing black drifts all over town. It took months to get rid of them all. The webs were so thick around town that they baled it like hay and rolled it into the lake."

"Oh, shit," Mark said. He tried to laugh at the absurdity of that but, due perhaps to the hallucinogenic properties of whatever was in the communion beginning to take effect, he could picture the spiders a little too clearly in his mind. The image made his skin crawl.

"That was the final insult," Roberta said. "The sheriff gathered his men together again, and they went out to Adaleen's home. As Sally already said, they beat her and raped her. An elderly woman, raped repeatedly by six men. She was still alive, though, when they burned her cabin down around her."

"My God," Mark said.

She finished her tale with a sardonic smile. "And, as you know, Bakersfield has not suffered a single day of bad luck since."

Bell's Angels applauded the story, and Mark joined in with sincere appreciation.

"My mother told me the story of Adaleen Bell," Roberta said. "It was told to her by her grandmother, who was very close to Adaleen. They may have been lovers, I don't know, but what's clear is that my great-grandmother Roberta, for whom I was named, was being groomed as Adaleen's apprentice. Which is how she came to be in possession of her spell-book. Which she bequeathed to my mother, who passed it down to me."

"No shit?" Mark said.

"Don't be vulgar, Mark," Roberta chided. "It's true. I've spent three decades studying the book, learning its secrets. And teaching them to other, worthy women. And tonight, we are finally ready to cast her most powerful spell."

"And what might that be?"

"Adaleen was able to extend her life far beyond that of a normal mortal span, but she went even further than that. She did not truly die. She left instructions, by which a devoted follower may one day resurrect her into this earthly plane."

"Whoa," Mark said. He was dizzy, though he wasn't sure if it was from the brew he'd drunk, or from the unbelievable things Roberta was saying.

"We've made one attempt, but it failed. That spell involved impregnating a host woman and inviting Adaleen's spirit to reside within the child's soul."

"Sandy Aswell," Mark said.

"The seed was tainted and the soil was impure," Roberta said. "Sandy reneged on the pact she made, and refused to fulfill vital requirements of the spell."

"And it killed her," Mark said.

"We offered to make her the mother of a new age," Roberta countered. "But instead she made the choice to turn her back on us. She broke my heart."

Roberta did not look broken-hearted at that moment, though. She looked jubilant.

"Now, tonight, we are ready to try again. And this is where you come in, Mark. We ask of you something only you can provide. Do you know what that might be?"

Mark looked around at the eyes of the witches who were watching him. His head was spinning. "You want me to impregnate one of you, right? That's what this is all about?"

Dead silence for a few seconds as Bell's Angels regarded him with horrifying blankness. Then they all burst out laughing.

"Oh my *God*," Ellie shrieked. "What is it with you? Why do you think everybody wants your sperm?"

"No, Mark," Roberta's smile was a bit gentler than the others', but she seemed equally amused. "We want you to be our...historian, I guess you'd say. A chronicler. Bear witness to what will happen in the next few days, and write an account of it for the world to read. Some people won't understand, but you can make them understand. I appreciated how you portrayed the Lillithites in your novel *Blood World's End*, a group of women whose goals and motivations are not so dissimilar to our own. You treated them with an uncommon empathy, for a male writer. In a way, you made them the heroines of that book."

"So you want me to be, what, your minister of propaganda?"

"Look at it like you're a journalist being given a very important exclusive. Trust me, after what we're going to accomplish tonight, the world will want to hear our story."

"This is going to happen tonight? Doesn't it take nine months?"

"Good. That's a question a journalist should ask. But, no. Adaleen left two possible methods for resurrecting her. The second one does not require the male essence, nor does it rely upon a potentially unreliable host. Obviously, I should have tried this method first, but it's a more complex spell, and it...comes at a higher cost. This spell is performed directly upon Adaleen's mortal remains."

"And how are you going to find those?"

"That's easy, Mark." She pointed over at a dark patch on her lawn, just outside the ring of light cast by the fire. "She's buried right over there."

CHAPTER 31

9:00–9:30 PM

Pastor Tom Peters drove out to the town square at around nine o'clock. Carrying a large box of candles from the church, he positioned himself in the dead center of the park, where cars driving past on any of the four bordering streets would be able to see him. He set the box on the grass and removed a single candle. Lighting it with a match, he bowed his head to pray.

He had not announced this vigil, had not sent out word for others to join him. He thought it would be a more powerful statement if he just led by silent example. The town square was the center of public life in Bakersfield. This was where people came, to seek comfort in community in times of tragedy and fear. Tom was very afraid right now, more afraid than he had been in years, afraid enough that he had sent Liz and the kids to stay at her Mom's house in Athens. He had chosen to respond to his fear by lighting a candle against the darkness. Others in town were afraid, too. They would come and stand together with him, united against this fear. He had faith in that.

It was a lonely watch to stand at first, though. Tom worried that maybe people driving past would not see the candle flame under the brightness of the full moon. He tried to concentrate on his prayer—listening for the still, small voice in his heart—but Tom's mind wandered. He was distracted by physical discomfort. His feet were cold and he wished he'd worn his woolen socks. Tom hadn't thought to bring drip protectors, and so had to keep tilting his candle so as not to get hot wax onto his hand.

Tom kept thinking, too, of Travis Chasen's report about James Delany and Alice Kiernan's disruption of the Underground meeting. Perhaps Tom should have been more vigilant against those two, knowing how close they were to the cabal of Mark Davies and Michelle Delany and Lana Blair. But he had instructed Travis and the other YIA kids to reach out to them, in the belief that no soul was beyond redemption and that James and Alice were still yet young enough to be saved. That had obviously been a mistake. Alice had befouled their sacred space like a scene out of *The Exorcist* (without a doubt the most terrifying film Tom had ever seen). Still, perhaps the disturbance they had caused was for the best. It had certainly got the Youth in Action club rallied to respond to the satanic threat. Tom had never seen them so worked up, so ready to live up to their name and take real action.

As for what form that action might take, Tom was still mulling over the possibilities. That was the direction his thoughts took as lonely vigil wore on.

As Tom considered how he might best lead his flock through this crisis, two young attendees of the already notorious Underground meeting huddled together, giggling in the dark in a princess-themed bedroom in a comfortable house not far from there. Tina Connelly was sleeping over at her very best friend Jackie Roger's house.

"Oh my gosh," Tina said, carefully avoiding the Lord's name. "That was, like, the grossest thing I have ever seen."

"Yeah, really," Jackie agreed, her braces gleaming faintly blue in the glow of her Elsa nightlight. "I don't believe she *barfed* like that. And it was all bloody and stuff. Gah. I almost barfed, too."

Both girls got to laughing even harder.

"I have heard some crazy stories about Alice Kiernan," Tina said. "Oh my gosh. I mean, I'm sorry she has cancer and everything. But she was like a really big slut and did all kinds of drugs and stuff, so she kind of brought it on herself."

"Does she have *AIDS?*" Jackie asked, whispering the dreaded word.

"I think so, yeah," Tina said. "And other stuff, too."

"Oh my God," Jackie said. "I think some of her bloody barf got on my shoe. What if I got some on my hands? And then I like touched my mouth or something?"

"Don't say the G-word like that. That's taking his name in vain and it's one of the Commandments and everything."

"Sorry."

"It's okay," Tina soothed. "Anyway, I don't think you can get AIDS like that. Not if you wash your hands really good."

Tina was a Church of the Shepherd regular, saved at a tent revival along with the rest of her family the summer before. Jackie was sort of on the fence about the whole issue. She believed in God and everything, but had only been to a few evening services with Tina. All that speaking in tongues and yelling about brimstone and damnation kind of freaked her out. Jackie was grateful that Tina never got pushy about getting her to join, like a lot of the other Shepherd kids did. Mostly they just hung out and talked about normal things. Tina had been insistent that Jackie come with her to the Underground club that night, but only because Tina had a serious crush on Travis Chasen. She'd gasped and grabbed Jackie's knee when Travis had stepped out on stage.

"Seriously, though," Jackie said. "Is all that stuff about devil worshipers true?"

Tina nodded solemnly. "Yeah. My brother was out hiking in the woods around Lake Kenney and he found an altar with a dog's head on it."

"No!" Jackie laughed nervously.

"I swear," Tina said. "He was so freaked out he locked himself in his room and prayed for like seven hours. They're out there, you better believe it."

"Who are they?" Jackie asked.

"Kids, mostly. Like the ones who dress all in black," Tina said, lecturing. She had seen a presentation at the church on the subject, so considered herself an expert. "But there are a few adults involved, too. They're the real ringleaders."

"I heard that Mark Davies guy is one of the main ones," Jackie said. "He used to be married to the lady who did that abortion, so I bet he had something to do with it, too."

Tina nodded in agreement. "Now she's gay-married to Ms. Blair-Delany at school."

"Why did she have a husband," Jackie wondered aloud. "If she's really a dyke?"

"Well, actually they're all bisexual," Tina said. "They get out there in the woods and take all kinds of drugs and they get all into the ceremony and they don't even care who they get with. Men get with men, women get with women, like it doesn't even matter to them. They even rape little kids."

"Gross," Jackie said.

"Yeah, and they drink blood," Tina said, "and they eat feces."

"That is *so* gross!" Jackie, laughing now.

"They sacrifice animals, too," Tina continued. "Cats are the best. Especially black cats."

"I can't believe that something like that happens here in Bakersfield."

"They're everywhere," Tina said. "That's what it said at this presentation I went to at the church. All over the country. All over the world. It's organized on the Internet. And I think they're planning something big for tomorrow night because it's Halloween. That's like their Christmas and Easter rolled into one."

"What are they going to do?"

"Well, nobody knows for sure," Tina said. "But I heard that they're going to kidnap a virgin and sacrifice her, so the devil will come and do their bidding."

"Oh my God."

"Don't say that, Jackie. I mean it. It's bad."

"Sorry. Can they really call up the devil?"

"Maybe not the actual devil himself, but maybe a demon," Tina said. "There are lots of demons out there."

"Oh my gosh."

The girls continued this discussion into the night, until neither of them could keep their eyes open. Their speculations grew wilder and more gruesome as they went on, embellished with details from half-remembered horror movies.

Finally, they slept. Jackie had not been asleep an hour when she fell into the blackest nightmare she'd ever had. In the dream, nine tall figures in black hooded robes dragged her into the dark woods. Their faces were invisible except for their glowing red eyes. They tore Jackie's clothes from her body and held her down naked on an altar made of cold stone. From beneath the black robes, each of the hooded figures pulled a long knife with a gnarled blade. The leader removed her hood, revealing herself to be none other than Ms. Blair-Delany from school. She raised her jagged dagger and slashed Jackie open from crotch to neck as her followers chanted and laughed. They bathed in Jackie's blood and gorged themselves on her bared intestines.

Jackie awoke screaming and Tina sat bolt upright in the sleeping bag beside her.

"What? What?" Tina cried

Jackie was hysterical, and it took several minutes for her friend to even calm her down enough to find out what had happened. Tina held Jackie in her arms and, between sobs, Jackie related the still-fresh dream.

"Now do you see why it's so important to let Jesus into your heart?" Tina said

"Yes."

"Will you come with me tomorrow and make a heart pledge to Pastor Peters?"

"Yes!"

"That's good, Jackie. I'm so happy. If you do that, Jesus will protect you."

"I'm so scared," Jackie let out a final, hiccupping sob.

"Me too." Tina crawled across the floor to her purse and pulled out her phone. The little screen lit her face with blue light as she peered down into it, her fingers nimbly working the touch-screen keys.

"What are you doing?"

"Texting some people about this," Tina said, intent upon the screen. "I don't think that was an ordinary dream."

She nodded, the upturned light of her phone casting grave shadows over her eyes.

"I think it was a warning."

CHAPTER 32

9:31 PM

MARK HAD INGESTED quite a few psychedelics in his life. He'd dropped acid at a Radiohead concert, eaten shroomies on a Colorado camping trip, taken mescaline on a snowy Christmas morning and watched a blank white wall for hours while Neiro projected crazy cartoon dreams from his twitching eyes. From these experiences, Mark had learned that sanity was more pliable than most people supposed. He was able to ride the ebb and flow of his mental tides, even when the ebbing verged on a Cronenbergian body horror nightmare.

The communion was kicking in, wicked hard. And through its kaleidoscopic distortion, the strangeness of the female bodies surrounding him in the hot, roiling water was magnified to a horrific level. Their flesh bulged and throbbed, one melting into another until it was impossible to discern where one woman ended and the next one began. Mark saw eyes and mouths and nipples and navels and patches of hair in places where these things did not belong. By the way the women gaped back at him, he was sure he was as grotesque to their eyes as they were to his.

Mark was very aware of his *maleness* amongst them, and tried not to discomfit them with his stare. He looked away, into his own reflection in the tall mirrors that half-surrounded the tub. But that was even worse, because for several moments he could not find himself there. Blinking his goggling, steam-blurred eyes with mounting alarm, he counted the women in the mirror. Six. Six women in the reflection, but only five before him in the tub. It was not until he noticed that one of them moved her arms and her head in perfect synchronization with his own movements that he realized that the sixth woman in the mirror was him.

Again, Mark's experience with the vagaries of his own perception prevented him from immediately panicking. Similar things had happened before. He'd once looked into a mirror with twisted eyes and been surprised to see the face of his mother staring back out at him. The woman in the mirror now did not resemble Gillian Hudson to any great degree, unless perhaps it was a young, carefree Gillian, before a busted marriage and a disappointing son and a soul-blighting career had leeched her girlish beauty away. The woman in Mark's reflection was about his own age, with short black hair and slightly rugged features. Mark smiled at her and she smiled back, with his familiar sardonic edge. There was a definite resemblance. She could have been his long-lost sister or a version of him from some alternate world where the chromosomal dice had rolled double X's.

When Mark ran his hands down his body while looking in the mirror, he felt soft breasts. Then, looking away from the mirror and down at himself, he felt only his own wiry chest hair. Helpless with curiosity, his hands moved further down, between his legs. Looking at himself, he felt the familiar and expected things down there. But looking into the mirror again, his hands slipped past dense hair into a slick fissure. Touching it sent shivery waves through his entire body. Or bodies.

"Oh God," Gemma cried out. "Now he's playing with himself!"

"Jesus, show some fucking restraint, Mark," Ellie chided.

Mark's hands guiltily withdrew from beneath the water, and he looked away from the mirror again. Roberta was nodding in his direction, with black, dilated, trip-crazed eyes.

"Mirrors are powerful instruments in a place like Bakersfield, where the borders between worlds are thin and blurred," she said. "But be careful, Mark. There is a danger of forgetting which side of the mirror you're on."

Roberta stood up dripping, sloshing the water in the tub. "I think, if we're all half as far along as Mark is, we're ready to begin. So, is everybody in?"

"Dude, I'm trippin' balls," Gemma said, which made the others laugh. There were general murmurs of assent.

"Good," Roberta said. "Then come see what I've prepared."

The others stood and toweled off. Mark followed them past the raging fire-pit, stepping off the patio onto the back lawn. His blood was still warmed from the hot water, perhaps the strange communion drugs had even induced a fever, and so the cold night air felt bracing and refreshing against his damp, naked skin. Ellie, Gemma and Sally walked in a slow, solemn procession before him, but Lizzy ran along with joyful skips.

Mark and the five angels half-surrounded a large dark patch of earth on Roberta's lawn. The perfect circle, about four feet in diameter, was covered in white designs that gleamed pale blue in the full moonlight. Strange twisting symbols formed a circular border around yet another iteration of the woman-astride-the-moon insignia, this one drawn in white powder upon the dark earth. The earth drawing was as geometrically complex as a Buddhist sand mandala, but figurative rather than abstract and completely devoid of color.

"I have drawn the symbols Adaleen has prescribed upon the earth, with a mix of ash and salt and sand and ground bone," Roberta said. "The earth beneath, which shrouds the mortal remains of our beloved mother Adaleen, has been saturated and nourished with our sacred blended menses—and I thank you all for your contributions. I have also seeded the earth with reminders of sensual living pleasures to entice Adaleen back into this realm. Tea leaves and tobacco and the white rum of which she was so fond. Also a bit of cocaine, in which she indulged from time to time. Lastly, I have contributed the most sacred of bodily fluids, the divine maternal gift of milk, drawn from my own breast after my first daughter was stolen from me. I've stored this holy milk in my freezer for decades, in anticipation of this event. Earlier tonight, I spilled the milk upon the ground, to nourish Adaleen on her journey back."

"This place," Roberta called, "Bakersfield, has long been under the rule of men. Violent men, racist men, sexist men, rapist men. I myself am the child of rape. My mother, Abigail Stevens, was raped by a man named Charlie Trott. I'm sure you all know the Trotts. They're the wealthiest family in town. And Charlie believed this gave him license to have his way with any young woman he desired, as long as they were poor, as my mother was. And she was far from the only one. Because she was an uncommonly generous, loving woman," here Roberta's voice cracked a little, "her love for me was undiminished by the hatred of my conception."

"Anger is a prime motivation in rousing Adaleen from her slumber. Thus, the spell now requires each of us to step forward and name a man who has transgressed against her and who is deserving of Adaleen's rage.

And, possibly, of her vengeance. I am tempted to name my father, but he is less than nothing to me, so I shall name my former husband, Gary Dowd."

Roberta nodded to Gemma, who stepped forward, her bare toes just touching the white sand on the edge of the mandala. "Just one?" she said. "Then I guess I'll have to go with my asshole therapist, Dr. Russell Carell."

Gemma stepped back and Ellie was the next to come forward. "My brother, Carson," Ellie whispered, looking down at the ground.

Sally stepped forward. Her voice shook a little as she said: "Benjamin Wolf, my father."

Lizzy was dancing in spinning circles around the earthen mandala, and offered up no name of her own. Mark understood that he was not welcome to contribute, either, but had he been, he would have also spoken the name of his father.

Roberta knelt and picked up a long dagger from the grass. She held it aloft, stabbing straight up into the sky, as if trying to draw blood from the moon. "Adaleen Bell, hear our plea. Return to us now, beloved mother, to this wounded earth that needs your healing power."

The other Angels—save for Lizzy, who continued her dance—repeated this line: "Return to us now, beloved mother, to this wounded earth that needs your healing power."

Roberta traced complex shapes in the air with the tip of the blade. "We have prepared a home for you, beloved mother. We have prepared a fire to warm you, and water to cleanse you, and food to sustain you. Return to us now, beloved mother, to restore balance and avenge the martyrs and to destroy the fucking men we have named."

"Fuck yeah!" Gemma called out. "Amen!"

"And now, Adaleen, we humbly await your sign."

Roberta and Ellie and Gemma and Sally bowed their heads. Lizzy continued her joyful dance. Mark, who would have bet his life nothing was going to happen, was the first to see the sign when it came. It was unmistakable.

Something small fell from the sky and landed directly in the center of the insignia—right at the intersection of the woman's legs and the moon's pleasuring tongue. Mark's buggered vision required him to blink several times before he saw what it was.

A tiny owl, no bigger than a kitten, had fallen into the circle, its small wings kicking up brown and white dust with its pathetic broken-winged flapping.

"Oh shit," he said out loud.

The angels looked down at the owl and then up at one another, their expressions a mix of fear and puzzlement and elation.

"Yes," Roberta said. "Yes, there it is."

Only Lizzy showed concern for the little bird.

"Oh, it's hurt," she said. She stepped into the circle, her bare feet smudging the fragile designs. She knelt to examine the bird, falling to her knees with her back to her mother, obliterating the designs in the dust.

"Yes," Roberta said again. Tears poured down her face. She looked up at the others, as if in apology. "A sacrifice is always necessary. Always."

With that, she bent and drove the dagger deep into the back of her daughter's skull.

CHAPTER 33

9:30–10:00 PM

GRACE FRANKLIN, LIKE many people in town, was very afraid. She was a middle-aged woman who lived alone right off Old Main, not far from where Sandy Aswell had died. Grace was what would have once been referred to as a 'spinster.' She'd never married, which in her case was the result of crippling social anxieties that had prevented her from ever forming close friendships with either men or women. Though devoutly religious, she belonged to no church because the social pressures of even small communities caused her to recoil in horror. In recent years, though, she had found a social outlet of sorts via Internet media, which allowed her to interact with others safely from home, with a buffering veil of anonymity.

Earlier in the day, she had posted a lengthy anti-abortion comment on the newspaper's Facebook page, under the story about Sandy Aswell and Michelle Blair-Delany. Grace had spent much of the afternoon since agonizing over the post, certain that it had been a mistake to be so outspoken. Some of the comments below hers had been rude, bordering on hostile. She worried that those people might trace her through the computer somehow, and find out where she lived. She'd been hearing strange noises coming from outside her house for weeks and the foul odor just outside her back door was just getting stronger.

Grace's anxiety worsened after she watched the five o'clock news. Thomas Gorman's words chilled her to the core. Her mind spun in agonizing loops for the rest of the evening, spurred by the alarming things she read online and by the constant promos on the television, which promised "startling new developments in the Bakersfield abortion case" to be revealed on the ten o'clock newscast. Her nerves and her stomach twisted into knots, Grace stewed in her anxiety, tormented by the rising smell of rot that had made her close all her windows. Shortly after 9:30, she finally brought herself to go out back with a flashlight. What she saw there confirmed her worst fears. There was a dead dog under her porch.

In reality, the dog had been hit by a car the week before and had simply crawled under there to die. Grace was certain, though, that the dog had been a satanic sacrifice. The cultists had left it there as a warning, because of her on-line comments. Grace made a panicked call to the one person she could talk to, her elderly mother.

Opal Franklin, as it happened, was one of the main hubs in Bakersfield's old-school land-line gossip network. This system predated social media by several decades and yet disseminated the news of Grace's alarming find very efficiently, reaching an audience that was not connected to the newer modes of transmission.

Back on the square, Tom's candle had burned down almost all the way when his patience was finally rewarded. A young couple came over to him, walking hand-in-hand across the park. Tom had seen them around town, but wasn't sure what their names were. He'd seen them with a baby, though there was no wedding ring on either of their fingers. The young man had long hair and a frayed denim jacket over a faded Grateful Dead t-shirt. A hippie type. Tom wasn't positive, but he thought he detected a faint marijuana smell coming off him.

"Why are you standing there with a candle?" the man asked.

"Better that than to curse the darkness," Tom replied.

The man laughed at that, but the girl frowned. She looked more clean-cut than her boyfriend, better dressed and groomed.

"Is this a protest kind of thing?" she asked. "About the sacrifice?"

"Sacrifice?" Tom said.

"Yeah, I saw this thing posted on-line where a group of Satanists said they're planning to sacrifice a virgin on Halloween in Bakersfield."

She had actually read a second—or third-hand reiteration of a post sent out by Tina Connelly, following her friend Jackie's slumber party nightmare. Via multiple retellings, what had begun as a teenage girl's hysterical dream had quickly mutated into a prophetic vision and, from there, into an established fact.

"I told her it was bullshit," the boyfriend said. "And, anyway, it's not like *she's* got anything to worry about."

Tom disregarded the boyfriend's vulgarity and looked the girl in the eye. It seemed like she might be reachable. "I don't know about a sacrifice," he said. "I haven't heard anything about that. But I can tell you that there is an organized cult operating in this town, and they are definitely planning something for tomorrow."

"So what good will it do to stand out here?" she asked.

Tom handed her a candle. "To show them that we're not afraid."

The girl nodded solemnly and lit her flame off his. The boyfriend rolled his eyes, but he accepted a candle, too. Tom lit a fresh candle and blew out the first one. He was pleased. His was no longer a lone vigil.

CHAPTER 34

9:36 PM

"No!" Mark screamed. "Jesus fuck! What the fuck did you do?" Roberta pulled the dagger from Liz's skull. The girl's body slumped over sideways in the dust. "Ellie, Sally," she said calmly. "Hold him back, please."

Each woman grabbed one of Mark's arms. He was too stunned with horror to try to get away. "You fucking killed her!"

Roberta flicked blood from the dagger in two quick, deliberate motions over the earthen circle, one vertical and one horizontal, making a spattered red cross in the dirt. Then she turned the blade towards Mark's face

"I set her free." Roberta indicated with her blade the little owl on the ground. "Look."

The owl stopped flopping in the dust. It stood on its legs and glanced around quizzically. The bird preened its feathers for a moment and then took off in flight, apparently unharmed.

Roberta watched the little owl disappear into the night, smiling fondly after it. "She always loved birds," she said. "She always dreamed of flying."

"You crazy fucking bitch!"

The dagger jabbed close to Mark's chin. "I won't tolerate hateful speech like that."

"Oh, God. I'm going to be sick."

"Kindly vomit *outside* the sacred circle, if you don't mind."

Ellie and Sally pulled Mark away from the dusty circle and let him fall to the ground. His stomach expelled a steaming mix of Italian food, alcohol and whatever the hell had been in those wafers. Mark remained on his hands and knees, naked in the cold grass, until the spasms passed.

"Mark?" Roberta said to him, with what sounded like a note of real concern. "Do you feel better now? Can you stand?"

Mark nodded. He stood on shaking legs and looked around. The three remaining angels looked almost as scared as he felt.

"I know you're shocked by what you've seen, but I need you to be a calm, rational observer of what's going to happen next. Can you be calm? Because if you can't be calm, you're of no use to us." With a gesture of her blade, she made clear the penalty for his uselessness.

"Calm," Mark managed to choke out. He gave a weak nod.

"Good."

Roberta rolled Lizzy's body over onto her belly and stretched her out so she was lying flat. She pulled the girl's long hair aside with one hand. With the other, she drew the blade in a slicing line from the fatal wound on the back of Lizzy's neck, straight down her spine to the cleft of her buttocks.

"Ah, Jesus, what're you doing?" Mark sobbed.

Roberta let out a heavy sigh. "That's *very* distracting, Mark. Gemma, there's a roll of duct tape in my bag on the porch. Will you run and grab it, please?"

Ellie and Sally grabbed Mark again. Roberta came back over and leaned in close. "This portion of the ritual requires quite a bit of concentration on my part, and the timing is essential. This is your last warning, Mark."

While the other two held him, Gemma slapped a long strip of duct tape across his mouth.

Roberta knelt back to her butchery, making quick, efficient incisions with the blade, and then began to flay the flesh away from the muscle. She was skinning Lizzy, like a wild hare.

Mark moaned into the tape over his mouth. He appealed with his eyes to the women holding him. Ellie just looked away, and Gemma was watching Roberta work with a fervent eagerness, but Sally returned Mark's look of terror. Tears were flowing from her eyes.

Roberta rolled Lizzy's half-flayed body onto her back. She reached behind her daughter's head and pulled the scalp free from her skull with a sickening wrenching sound. The girl's face peeled away in a single pull. Mark looked away before he could see what was underneath.

Roberta had slit Lizzy's body up the back like a hospital johnny, and sliced bracelets about her daughter's wrists and ankles. Most of the skin came off in one piece, shaped like hooded one-piece pajamas, except the hood was a human face. Roberta carefully stretched the piece out on the grass. She peeled the skin from Lizzy's hands and feet like gloves and socks and set these on the ground near the larger piece.

Roberta, bloodied to the elbows, stood above the flayed body on the ground. The blood, black as ink in the moonlight, was also splashed all over Roberta's belly and her breasts. She wiped sweat from her brow with the back of one hand, smearing black blood across her forehead as well.

"There," she said. Mark saw now that she was weeping. "I've done as you've required, beloved mother. Please, find my sacrifice acceptable. She was all I had to give. She was everything to me."

For several moments, nothing happened. Roberta stood there naked, swaying on her feet, looking old and haggard as the sobs wracked her entire body. The bracing cool of the night had turned uncomfortably cold. Both Sally and Ellie pressed closer to Mark, seeking human comfort in the face of this atrocity or maybe just a little warmth. Gemma sat on the grass, an unreadable expression frozen on her face. She still wore her zealous grin, but her eyes were as dead and hollow as a doll's.

Mark felt a rumbling from the earth beneath his feet, like a minor earth tremor. By the looks on the angels' faces, they felt it as well. The dirt surrounding the red skinned body rose in a mound, as if something was moving beneath it.

Numbed by this point to further terror, Mark watched with a clinical detachment as a hole opened in the earth, just above the dead girl's head. The yawning mouth in the dirt kissed the top of Lizzy's flayed skull, drawing the smooth bulging head into the earthen cavity. The sucking hollow opened wider to swallow Lizzy's corpse, pulling the glistening red mass of muscle and skeletal bone in, inch by inch with gumming motions, like a toothless crone slurping meat from a pork rib. The body twitched and jerked with the writhing mastication, as if penetrating the earth of its own volition. The ground stretched open to take in the shoulders, and then slid with a moist smack over the fatty skinless lumps that had once been Lizzy's breasts. The squeezing, grasping pressure extruded white fluid from the corpse as it continued to slowly slip into the consuming earth. Past the stomach, with its stringy muscles, and over the gluteal bulge of the buttocks, until just the thin pink legs protruded.

Lizzy's remains disappeared completely into the soft ground, swallowed by the grave, leaving only a slight mound of earth bisected by a muddy slit to show it had been there at all. It had been like watching a snake swallow its prey, or a breech birth in reverse.

"Thank you," Roberta whispered, smiling through her devastated tears. "Thank you thank you thank you."

Ellie and Sally held Mark close between them. Gemma got back to her feet, watching with dread expectation the flat earth where Lizzy's body had been a moment before.

There was motion beneath the earth, undeniably. Something big moving just under the surface, like worms beneath the skin.

An abomination burst forth into the moonlight, clawing out from the same hole that had swallowed Lizzy. If it had once been the body of Adaleen Bell, it now bore only the scarcest resemblance to human remains. The thing looked like somebody had torn a rotting corpse into little pieces, and then trusted a blind man to haphazardly reassemble it into a vaguely arachnid shape. It looked like a huge black widow spider scraped off the bottom of a shoe. The thing had thin black spider-like limbs, but far too many of them and no two were of equal length. Some were tiny severed stubs and others were long and multi-jointed. All the legs wriggled with broken spasms.

Nothing on it even remotely resembled a human head.

It was alive, though. The pathetic grasping thing scuttled across the circle of dirt in spastic, shuddering spurts, making awful wrenching noises with every move, as if mere locomotion caused its connecting tendons to rip and tear. It reeked, like moldering decay and rotten cabbage, and left a slug-trail of tarry black slime behind it as it crept towards Lizzy's discarded skin.

Roberta watched the thing's agonizing progress across the lawn, eyes wide and lit with mania. Like a devout Christian laying eyes upon the resurrected Christ. The women holding Mark released him now and took two cautious steps in the thing's direction. Gemma, stopping briefly to vomit in the grass, followed close behind. Mark hung back, watching.

Roberta grabbed Lizzy's skin and dragged it closer to the scuttling thing, though she was not quite brave enough to actually touch it. The thing, by its posture, seemed to sniff the skin like a dog would. Perhaps it was blind.

Then it crawled inside.

Mark didn't think it would work. The skin was too small, and the thing was not even close to the right shape. But it seemed to restructure itself as it pulled the skin on, folding and fracturing its limbs to make them fit, with wooden cracking sounds that made everyone cringe. The thing issued mewling, screaming sounds of agony as it conformed to the human shape.

Finally, it stood on shaky legs. The thing pulled Lizzy's face on, up over its empty black maw, and adjusted the skin there until it looked out with bloody red eyes. It stepped into Lizzy's skin footies and slipped on the gloves as daintily as any lady in a costume drama.

The fit still wasn't perfect. The skin sagged in some spots and stretched with odd bulges in others, but it would pass. The resurrected Adaleen Bell, her new skin flapping open in the back, staggered over to Roberta's patio and sat down hard on the bench next to the fire. She looked around, taking in the strange, new world.

Roberta went to her, beaming.

"Welcome," she said. "Beloved mother."

She knelt and kissed Adaleen on the mouth.

CHAPTER 35

10:00–10:30 PM

THE BAKERSFIELD LEAD on the five o'clock broadcast earlier in the day had generated more positive buzz than any story Channel 2 had run in years. The station's social media director noticed *#BloodyBakersfield* sharply trending on Twitter as early as 5:30. She moderated dozens of comments on the station's website and Facebook page and logged almost forty e-mails in just a few hours. Older, less tech-savvy, viewers inundated the phone lines with questions and concerns. Some of these messages, both written and spoken, verged on the hysterical, with strange reports of occult activity. The kooks really connected to stories like this. There were alleged animal sacrifices, lights seen in the sky, chanting heard in the woods. Rumors of poisoned water and arson plots. One very persistent man called back four times to report a "mist in the shape of a man" roaming around his house that, "smelled like a rutting goat."

At six o'clock, news director Josh Murray assembled his entire team for a hasty meeting, to determine the best ways to capitalize on the popularity of the story. The promo they'd already shot was scrapped and hurriedly re-cut to emphasize the Bakersfield story, with a sinister-looking, blood-splattered title card and ominous voice-over. It was inserted during commercial breaks throughout the evening's network feed.

The follow-up story was greatly expanded. A news van had been dispatched to make the thirty-mile drive up to Bakersfield to shoot some new B-roll, mostly interviews with frightened residents. Prominently featured was a sound-bite by Denise Kindely, owner of the recently opened Heavenly Treasures gift shop, who attested that, "There's always been satanic activity here, but in the past few weeks, it's been rising to levels I've never seen before."

To round out their coverage, Murray once again contacted occult expert Thomas Gorman, to see if he would be willing to expand on his earlier comments. Not known for his media reticence, Gorman happily obliged. He noted the increasing prevalence of infant sacrifice in occult rituals and expounded at length about ritual hematophagy. His comments were edited for broadcast length, but the full interview was made available on the station's website.

A few people joined Pastor Tom's impromptu vigil on the square while the sensational broadcast was airing. Once the news report ended, though, a flood of people arrived. Tom ran out of candles and called Travis to bring him more from the church. Hymns were sung and the crowd at large projected an air of calm defiance, though most people kept one eye on their phones for the updates that were still rolling in.

Someone tweeted pictures of vandalism at the old Ball Church Cemetery. A few headstones had been knocked over, and others had been defaced with red spray paint pentagrams and triple-sixes. This vandalism had actually occurred back in August, perpetrated by bored, destructive teenagers. As it was just now being discovered, the defacement was ascribed to the sinister satanic coven.

Another rumor making the rounds that night was that the cultists were planning to burn down a church. Self-appointed guardians of the peace made slow drive-by surveillance checks of all eight churches in town, as well as other potential trouble spots, such as the home of Lana and Michelle Blair-Delany, and the house shared by Mark Davies and James Delany. Men with guns patrolled the base of the water tower to prevent further poisoning of the water. There were some reports of suspicious activity, but every one of these was the result of one car of vigilante watchdogs noticing another car of vigilante watchdogs out on the same mission they were.

Janice Forby, who worked the dispatch desk at the Sheriff's Department in Lincoln, logged twenty-seven non-emergency calls that evening related to the satanic threat. Most were repeating the same rumors about virgin sacrifice or of people alleged to have contaminated the water. She took several calls about carloads of suspicious people driving slowly past churches. Janice was already on edge because of the photo of the baby that had somehow been sent out via the emergency notification service the night before, and all these crazy calls did nothing to soothe her nerves. She couldn't get ahold of the sheriff, he wasn't answering his phone, but she had reached out to the deputies on patrol tonight, asking them to be especially vigilant. On a normal Sunday night, Bakersfield would be covered by one deputy patrolling the entire southern part of the county. Tonight, Janice told both Deputy Brewer and Deputy Montaño to pull off their normal routes and stay close to the town.

Both deputies made slow passes around the square, to verify that Pastor Tom's vigil was a peaceful demonstration. The highly visible presence of police cars downtown did not soothe the people assembled there, but rather reinforced their fears that there was lawlessness afoot. Their presence also made for some dramatic footage for the news crew, who had stuck around to shoot additional material for the station's morning show tomorrow.

Before the half-hour newscast ended, Channel 2's station manager received a phone call from New York City. One of the producers of the network's morning news program expressed interest in picking up the story to go national. The timing, after all, was perfect. A real-life satanic menace was a custom fit for Halloween.

CHAPTER 36

10:13 PM

THE THING WEARING Lizzy's skin looked up at the four naked women and one naked man who were staring back at her with varying mixtures of adulation, disbelief, and horror. Her blood-filled eyes darted from one to another with animal distrust.

Only Roberta seemed unreservedly pleased. She fetched a large needle and thick black thread from her bag on the patio. "Let's get you stitched up, dear," she said.

She took a seat behind Adaleen and went to work closing up the flapping skin on her back, starting at the neck and working her way down.

"Si..." Adaleen said, Lizzy's lips not quite obeying her attempts to move them. "Si...Si..." A stuttering hiss.

"What is it, dear?" Roberta said. "What do you need?"

"Sig," she spoke with the dirt-choked rasp of a voice that had not uttered a word for more than eighty years. "Sig...Cigger."

"You want a cigarette? Oh, I didn't think to bring them outside." Roberta nodded up at Sally. "In my purse, on the kitchen counter. Go get them, quickly."

Sally nodded, wide-eyed, and hurried off. Her gratitude at getting away from this scene even briefly was all too obvious on her face.

Adaleen looked down at her new body. "Why?" she said. "Why?"

"Why what, dear?" Roberta asked, her eyes gleaming with tears as she stitched her way down Adaleen's back.

"White?" Adaleen croaked. "White girl?"

"Why, yes." Roberta nodded. "My daughter..." A sob escaped her throat. "Elizabeth. She graciously...donated...her flesh for you." She was

194

shaking so badly she had to stop sewing for a moment. "I'm sorry, I'm okay. I'm just...so full of joy."

"Colored...skin...better," Adaleen said.

"I'm sorry." Roberta's face looked like it might just collapse.

Sally returned then. Mark saw with pure envy that she'd put her black cloak back on. It seemed to be getting colder by the minute out here, even as close as they were to the fire.

Sally handed Roberta the pack of cigarettes and a lighter. Roberta shook a cigarette out and lit it in her own mouth with shaking hands. She passed the smoke to Adaleen, who put it between two slack lips and inhaled deeply. Her bloody eyes rolled up inside her head with ecstasy as she drew in the smoke.

"It's funny," Roberta made a sound that might have been an attempt to force laughter, but it came out like a cry of pain. "I almost didn't think to buy you cigarettes. Most people don't smoke now. It's unhealthy. Not that...not that that matters to you."

Adaleen released a funnel cloud of smoke into the night. She lifted one bloody finger up and pointed at the people standing before her.

"Who?" she said.

"Yes." Roberta nodded and wiped her eyes. "I suppose we should do the introductions. You know me. I'm Roberta. You've probably heard me praying to you every night for years. I'm the one who's called you here. I'm the leader of this group."

"Was," Adaleen corrected, with a harsh grating snarl.

"Yes," Roberta said. "Of course. You will lead us now. Thank you, beloved mother. Um, this is Sally. She's a skilled trance medium and can speak with crows."

Adaleen motioned for Sally to come close. Sally, her terror plain on her face, knelt close to Adaleen. Lizzy's glove-like fingers slid loose, just a bit, as Adaleen gently brushed them across Sally's cheek. Sally shuddered.

"Angry," Adaleen noted.

"Yes." Sally nodded, tears dripping from her eyes.

"Good." Adaleen may have been trying to smile, but the skin of Lizzy's face was still too loose. It came across as a baring of her teeth.

"This is Ellie, beloved mother," Roberta said. "She has prophetic dreams."

Now Ellie knelt before Adaleen, who touched her face as well.

"Afraid," Adaleen said.

"No," Ellie insisted, shaking her head. She looked pale, even in the warmth of the firelight. "I'm not afraid."

"Yes," Adaleen said. "You are. But that's good, too."

Ellie backed away and Gemma eagerly stepped forward.

"This is Gemma," Roberta said. "Our newest, and youngest member. She shows a remarkable aptitude for spell-casting."

"Hatred," Adaleen assessed by touching her face. "Desire. Lusssst." She hissed that word. "You're hungry for it, ain't you, girl?"

"Bet your ass," Gemma grinned.

"Heh heh," Adaleen chuckled. She looked around, though, and frowned. "That's it? Three white girls?"

"I'm sorry, Adaleen," Roberta said. "There aren't many African-Americans living in Bakersfield anymore. Sweetbrook is gone. Maybe that's one of the things you can change. Restore racial harmony and—"

Adaleen silenced Roberta with an upraised palm. She took a final drag of her cigarette and tossed it into the flames.

"Who's the *man*?" The word came across as a vile epithet.

Adaleen's bloody red eyes rounded on Mark. The gaze of the recently dead woman made him tremble with dread.

"This is Mark, beloved mother," Roberta said. "He's a writer. I've chosen him to tell our story to the world."

Adaleen's face was as responsive as a Beverly Hills housewife with her cheeks full of Botox, but Mark thought he detected pure disdain there. She looked him up and down with a dismissive appraisal. He didn't like where her eyes settled.

"Not much there," she noted.

Mark peeled the tape from his mouth, feeling compelled to explain that it was cold out here and he was terrified, two things that always caused him to shrivel. But as soon as he freed his stinging lips, Adaleen flicked her wrist and the piece of tape flew back over his mouth, as if suctioned there by a vacuum.

Adaleen motioned him over with a little scornful wave. Mark, though he was desperately afraid, found himself kneeling close to Adaleen, as the women had done. She touched his cheek. The rubbery feel of Lizzy's peeled-away fingers was one of the most nerve-creeping things he'd ever experienced.

"Heh," she said as she touched him. For a second, she tilted her head in what might have been a quizzical expression. "Something there," she said. "But it's weak. He's been touched, two times, but he didn't learn nothin' from it. He'll betray us. Best to kill him now."

Mark staggered to his feet, almost falling back on his ass right into the fire.

"But beloved mother," Roberta protested. "We...create. We do not destroy. We celebrate life, not death."

Adaleen got to her feet. "Stupid bitch, ain't ya? You know the shit I seen? I seen the glittery pearl gates of Heaven slammed in my face. I seen the black foothills of Hell ablaze with fire. I seen the gray mists of eternity and all the cold-ass stars. I seen these things while I was moored to my grave like a boat to a dock, waitin' on your dumb ass to pull me out. Eighty-some years in the ground, awake every minute of it, while my body rotted and my bones twisted all outta shape. Life ain't shit. Death ain't shit. These young 'uns you got here know what matters, even if you don't. Anger. Fear. Hatred. Desire. Lust. *Power.* These things can be ours to rule, but this white devil will fuck it all up if you let him. Kill the fucker now."

Roberta looked down and seemed surprised to find that the dagger was back in her hands. She raised it weakly, her hand shaking as she pointed it in Mark's direction.

"Ah, you're a weak old woman," Adaleen said with disgust, taking the dagger from Roberta. "Any of y'all wanna step up?"

"I'll do it," Gemma said. Her eyes were blazing.

Chuckling, Adaleen handed Gemma the dagger. Gemma rounded on Mark, grinning. He seemed to be frozen in place.

Then Sally tackled Gemma about the waist, almost toppling them both into the fire together. The dagger fell clattering to the patio floor.

"Run!" Sally yelled, beating out the flames that had caught on her sleeve.

Whatever spell had rooted him to the ground was broken. Mark ran naked into the cold dark woods.

CHAPTER 37

All that long dark night...

Pastor Tom's undeniably successful vigil broke up at a little past eleven, and the more than a hundred people who had gathered went their separate ways. Doors were locked and handguns were fetched down from high closet shelves. Bibles were opened and read aloud. Grave conversations passed between husbands and wives in well-lit kitchens over coffee or between men with shotguns on their laps on dark front porches, over sipped whiskey. Nearly the entire town passed the night with restless watchfulness. Only the youngest children slept unburdened by worry.

James Delany lay in bed, keeping watch over Alice, who was lying beside him. He was afraid to sleep. He remembered when he had succumbed to the Sickness, dragged into a heavy slumber that had kept him under for days. When he finally awoke from that, his mother was dead. His heart couldn't bear for that to happen again, not with this girl who was the best friend he'd ever had. Alice's breathing was ragged and shuddering and uneven. He had never seen her look so fragile. He put his arm around her and Alice snuggled back into his grasp without waking. Her thin body was cool to his touch and he warmed her the best he could. James made a vow to stay awake all night, with a childish certainty that she would not be stolen away if he kept watch over her. But he was weary and this vow did not keep. Even as James slept, he held his friend in a fierce protective grasp. Death, if it came, would have to pry her from his arms.

In another house not far away, Michelle's eyes were open to the dark bedroom. Scant inches away from her, with only a thin bunched sheet between them, Lana also lay awake. Each woman assumed the other was sleeping peacefully. Neither wanted to disturb her wife with her own troubles, though their troubles were essentially the same. Both fretted about the incomprehensible forces aligned against them and the decision they'd made to escape and the myriad complications arising from this decision. Both worried about their son, sleeping in the next room, and about the new life unfurling in Lana's womb. Each woman debated, and rejected, the idea of waking the other for physical comfort, maybe even another round of the intense lovemaking that each assumed had put the other into such a sound sleep. *Better to let her rest*, each thought. *She'll need it with what's coming.*

A few feet and one thin wall away, Ben also lay awake, restlessly turning, moonlit tree-branch shadows painting his walls with abstract motion. He had overheard some of the conversation between his mother and Lana, and had pieced together the rest through his keen intuition. They wanted to move away. He understood why. He knew they were scared, and they were right to be scared. A lot of people in town wanted to hurt them, because they were scared, too. But Ben didn't want to leave. Before his dad had moved back home, he'd felt like he was split in half. But everything was good now. Half the week with Mom and Lana, and the other half with Dad and James. Everybody he loved lived in the same place, and he saw them all almost every day. And then there was Emily, at school. He'd never had a friend like her before. He knew that he never would again, if they moved to some other place. There was even more to it than that, though. They were all here, in Bakersfield, for a reason. If they left, he didn't know what would happen.

Though her last appearance had caused him nothing but trouble, Ben found his eyes going to his bedroom window, wishing Emily would come again. He needed someone to talk to. Emily would know what to do.

At his house, Sheriff Nathanial Bates dozed heavily in his chair while the late-night Weather Channel meteorologists broke down the nation's overnight forecast region by region. Nate, with some effort, pried open his other self's heavy lids. Coming out while Nathanial slept was harder to do than appearing in a mirror. Nate had to fight against the burden of sleep paralysis. It was a real chore just to will the body's sleeping muscles to move. He had to concentrate hard on every tiny action. But Nate was getting stronger all the time, and Nathanial was getting weaker. First thing he did was change away from the skull-fuckingly boring Weather Channel. Some other station was showing an all-night *Sons of Anarchy* marathon and that was definitely more Nate's speed. Nate glanced around and his eyes lit on a black Sharpie marker resting on the coffee table. That was too perfect. Nate dragged Nathanial's heavy sleeping body forward and reached one arm out for the marker. Clutching it, Nate reached up and wrote something on Nathanial's forehead, backwards, so the shithead could read it in a mirror. Then, just for shits and giggles, he added a little Hitler mustache under Nathanial's nose. The Hitler 'stache was a classic. Worn out from this pleasant exertion, Nate let the marker drop to the floor and fell back into a deep, satisfied slumber.

He may have rested easier than anyone else in town.

CHAPTER 38

11:08 PM

I'M STILL ALIVE, Mark thought as he ran cold and naked through the timber. Then, on the heels of that: *Thank God.*

Since he'd willfully and consciously declared himself an agnostic when he was a teenager, Mark had self-censored all casual reference to the unknowable deity. He never said, "Thank God" or "Oh my God." He never even blessed people when they sneezed. But now a reflexive prayer of gratitude came to him easily.

Thank God I'm still alive.

Surprising himself, he spoke this prayer aloud.

"I'm still alive!" he cried out to the dark woods. "Thank God!"

Following that, a decidedly less reverent question:

"Where the fuck am I?"

At first, fleeing the horror of what he'd seen, Mark had only concerned himself with escape. He had to get away from the terrible moonlit ritual. His flight had been driven by the images branded in his mind's eye. Roberta's sharp knife peeling the skin from poor Lizzy's body. The insect-like thing birthed from the blood-soaked earth and crawling into Lizzy's skin. Adaleen's bloodied eyes as she was reborn.

"Jesus," Mark sobbed. Having invoked the Father, he may as well call upon the Son.

At some point as he fled, Mark gained enough presence of mind to at least attempt to run in the right direction. He wasn't entirely clear where Roberta's house lay in relation to Bakersfield, having never travelled to or from there sober or in daylight, but he was pretty sure it was south of town. So he tried to run north.

Thank God it's a clear night. The starry sky sprawled above him. The Big Dipper pointed towards the North Star, Polaris. A shining beacon, visible through the leafless trees. He ran towards the bright unreachable star, recalling the old spiritual "Follow the Drinking Gourd" from a book he'd read about Harriet Tubman. *Thank God for book learning.* He also remembered reading that moss only grows on the north side of trees, though Mark didn't relish the thought of getting down on his hands and knees to feel up the trunks.

Rocks and twigs cut his tender soles as he ran. *Thank God they're numb from the cold.* It was so cold, though. Mark hugged himself as he ran, rubbing his arms for the friction on his skin. Running generated some warmth, but Mark didn't know how much further he could go. His side ached with a brutal stitch of pain. His lungs felt like they were being pierced with sharp icicles.

He stumbled, and then he fell. Slid down a muddy ridge and landed on his knees in a cold stream. Mark cried out with shock and dismay. Ice cold clamped his balls. For a second, he just knelt there in the trickling water, crying. It was so hard to stand, but he knew that if he didn't, he would die there.

Mark scrambled up the mud-slicked bank on the other side and, unable to stand, crawled on cold scratched hands and frozen skinned knees. He was cold, *wet* and naked now. Aware, too, that death was a real possibility out here. Exposure, they called it. Dying of exposure. Mark had never felt more exposed in his life. His scrawny, hairy white ass would look blue in the moonlight if there was anyone to see except the night birds and whatever nocturnal beasts were lurking about. His penis and his testicles had shriveled to hard nubs, retracting close to his body for whatever negligible warmth to be found there.

Keep moving, he thought. *Jesus, just keep moving.*

Somehow, he managed to stand. Somehow he managed to stagger forward and stay on his feet. Somehow, his will to live still outweighed the cold crushing hopelessness. He wondered if he died, how long it would be before they would find his body. Maybe not until some hunter in the spring came across his animal-gnawed bones. He wondered if Missy would cry at his funeral.

Mark thought of Jess. He hadn't thought of his friend in a long time. It happened like that. Years would go by without him paying much thought to Jess's memory, only to have him come rushing back into Mark's mind like he'd only been gone a day or two.

What would Jess do? he wondered.

In books and films and TV shows, the departed spirit of a friend often appears to a character in desperate straits, to offer help or advice. Usually the writer leaves it ambiguous as to whether this is a supernatural visitation or simply a trick of the mind. Mark wanted nothing more than for Jess's spirit to appear to him now. Would Jess still be the age he'd been when he'd died, or would he have matured in the afterlife and now appear as the man he would have become? Whatever his age, the ghostly visitation would be welcome. Jess was like a walking encyclopedia. He would know some trick for building a shelter in the woods, or for making fire by rubbing twigs or striking stones.

Fire, Mark thought with a lustful yearning. *Shelter. Are there any two words in the English language sexier than those?*

He was getting delirious now, but apparently not so delirious as to summon Jess. Mark was still alone, still cold and exposed to the night.

God.... he thought. His earlier simple gratitude at being alive had faded. Now he was reduced to inarticulate appeals to the same arcane, unreachable deity. *God help me.* To the extent that he personified God at all, Mark thought of him as a writer, as he himself was. A writer whose pen determined the course of the plot of life. *Author of my fate,* Mark thought. *Intervene. Please. Please don't kill me off like a supporting character. I'm the goddamn hero here. Heroes don't die cold and naked in the forest.*

Mark no longer ran. He couldn't even be said to be walking, exactly. He just kept falling forward and yet managing to stay on his feet. He climbed over a slight rise and stumbled down the other side, eyes barely open. He didn't see the big animal in the clearing until he was nearly upon it. Even when he did see it, he couldn't be sure what the hell it was. Just a big dark shape, a black shadow mass in the moonlight, no more than twenty feet in front of him. Mark froze.

The thing was squatting, hunched over and shuddering. That's when Mark realized it was a bear. A bear, shitting in the woods.

At least that settles that question.

Mark's eyes adjusted and he could see the animal better. It was thin, almost skeletal. And it appeared to be sick. Mark was close enough to hear the liquid spurting of its bowels voiding, and smell the sharp foul reek of animal diarrhea. The watery stool it expelled steamed in the cold night. Still, even a diarrhetic bear was an astonishing sight. There were no wild bears around here anymore, hadn't been for at least a hundred years, as far as Mark knew.

He wasn't sure what to do. The bear hadn't noticed him yet, and it was probably best that it stayed that way. Mark stepped to the side, but the dry brush crunched under his feet.

The bear looked up at the sound. Its eyes locked with Mark. For a second, he thought he detected an imploring plea. The bear wanted him to help it, somehow. Mark threw his hands up to indicate his own helplessness.

The bear let out a snorting growl, spraying a cloud of breath and liquid snot from its nose that Mark saw as a wet moonlit flash from its muzzle. It turned and lurched towards him, a halfhearted charge that nonetheless sent Mark stumbling backwards. They must have been a pathetic sight, he thought. The sickly bear and the naked man. But he was by far the weaker of the two.

Mark turned and ran. Again, running. No longer north. He no longer had any idea which direction he was going. Just away from the fucking bear. He heard its bounding steps in the brush close behind him. He couldn't tell if it was closing in, or if he was pulling away. He was almost to the point of being too cold and tired to care.

Now he cursed his hypothetical author/ god. *Motherfucker*, he thought. *I asked for a Deus ex Machina and you sent me a goddamn shitting bear.*

He ran until he could run no more, until the bear's claws and teeth would be a mercy to him. He fell to his knees and looked back, but the bear was gone. He was alone again. Abandoned by both god and beast.

Mark stayed on his knees for a few minutes and gave hard, serious consideration to simply giving up. How long would it take for him to die? Would it be a few minutes, or would it be hours of cold hopelessness?

Then, as if he was a beast himself, he scented something on the wind. Organic rot mixed with a sharper, sulfurous reek. A very distinctive, foul odor that nonetheless got Mark to his feet with a fresh burst of hope.

Because he recognized the smell. He'd last smelled it just a couple weeks ago, when he and James had finally cleaned out the basement. They'd borrowed Sam Hansard's pickup truck and driven the load out to the county dump.

It couldn't be far from here. He followed his nose, the smell growing stronger and stronger until Mark came to edge of the woods and found the chain-link fence that must have marked the dump's southern boundary. Beyond it, warm-looking sodium arc lamps illuminated the mounds of garbage with enticingly artificial electric light. Now at least he knew where the hell he was. Of course, the dump was a good five miles south of town and he'd never make that distance on bare feet with no clothes on, but the metal fence was the first man-made thing Mark had seen since he'd begun his mad flight into the woods. He grasped the cold metal links in his hands with gratitude. They represented to his mind civilization at the edge of the wilderness. He had never been more grateful for man's intrusion into nature, even if it came in the form of a stinking landfill.

He walked along the edge of the fence, clinging to it for support, looking desperately inside. There was a little trailer where the dump's offices were, but it was dark. Would there be a guard on duty at night? That seemed more and more unlikely as he thought about it. Why the hell would the county bother to hire somebody to guard fucking garbage? Nobody was going to try to break in and steal it. Even if they did, who would care? It was literally garbage.

Mark's surge of hope withered, shriveling up like his coward genitals. He wondered if he should maybe try to climb the fence. Maybe he could break into the trailer and sleep inside. But the razor wire lining the top of the fence dissuaded him. He couldn't think of any way he could possibly get over that naked without tearing himself to shreds. Why the hell would they even bother with razor wire to protect their precious garbage?

Then Mark remembered something else from that trash run. He and James had driven past a small housing development on the way out. New, high-end homes, just where the blacktop ended. Cookie-cutter McMansions. Mark even remembered remarking to James that he hoped the homeowners got a good price break for having to live downwind from the dump.

Mark rounded the corner of the fence. The white gravel road glowed in the moonlight. Far up ahead, he could see the faint shine of the neighborhood streetlights. He could even almost make out the distant silhouettes of the new houses. How far was it? Half a mile of gravel road? Naked in the dark, it seemed a world away. But he'd come so far already.

Mark staggered forward, spurred on by a new hope. He just hoped he could find someone who would open their doors for a naked madman in the night.

CHAPTER 39

11:59 PM

Tom Peters came home from the candlelight vigil on the square feeling upbeat. It had gone even better than he'd hoped. The entire community—not just his church, but all of Bakersfield—had stood as one. No matter what tomorrow brought, no matter what the cultists had planned, the town would stand united against the threat. It was thrilling, really. It was so rare in life to have such clarity, such a well-defined distinction between good and evil. And he had to admit it was gratifying to have so many in the town looking up to him as a leader in this fight.

Letting himself into the dark, quiet house, though, some of his elation gave way to a creeping unease. He was glad that Liz and the kids were safely away from all this, but part of him still longed for their company. Even knowing that they were asleep in the house would have been a comfort to him.

Tom knew he should not be afraid, not of Satan nor of his earthly emissaries. He knew that he had been delivered from Satan's domain and transferred to Jesus' kingdom on the day he had accepted Christ. He knew that Jesus had given him authority to tread upon serpents and scorpions and over the all the power of the enemy, and that in Christ nothing could harm his spirit. Still, Tom made sure to turn on every light in every room he passed through.

He went upstairs, to his bedroom. He was tired. It had been a long day, and with the way things were shaping up, tomorrow might even be longer. A good night's sleep was essential. In recent years, Tom had gotten into the habit of showering before bed. It saved time in the morning and the warm water relaxed him after a stressful day. So he undressed now and stepped into bathroom adjoining his master bedroom.

For a moment after turning on the bathroom light, something about his reflection in the mirror troubled him. He didn't know what it was. It almost seemed like there was a slight lag, just a fraction of a second, between his movement and that of the reflection. The sight of his own nudity bothered him too, as it sometimes did. He remembered the feeling of Pastor Barry's hand sliding up his naked back to the back of his head, to press it down. This made a shiver run through his entire body and invoked a gagging feeling in the back of his throat. He felt a sensation of horror, as if he was in the presence of the devil, a presence that was as palpable as a scent in the air.

Tom pushed the feeling away, buried it deep. He took a deep breath and whispered a quick prayer, and then turned on the hot water. By the time he was under the stream, lathering his hair with shampoo, he'd forgotten it completely.

His thoughts turned again to his wife. After little Faye died, Liz had said that she wanted to conceive again as soon as possible. Though Katie wasn't even three months old, Liz was all over Tom every chance they got. To the point where Tom sometimes had to beg off for being too tired. He could go for some right now, though. His wife's love would be a comfort to him, would take the edge right off.

Drifting on this thought, Tom caught himself paying excessive attention to washing one particular part of his body. Couldn't have that, now. This was a minor sin, but Tom imagined Jesus watching from the other side of the curtain and turned the water cold for a few seconds. The feeling didn't exactly go away, but he was able to exercise self-control. There would be quite a homecoming when Liz came back on Tuesday, though.

Smiling at the thought, Tom was startled by a sudden light in the mirror, which reflected the window overlooking the back yard.

The motion detector floodlights had come on.

Tom's blood ran cold. He hurriedly rinsed off and shut off the water. Hopping out of the shower, he looked out through the window. The whole back yard was lit up. He couldn't see anything, though. Maybe it was nothing. Their house was right on the edge of the woods and sometimes animals set off the lights if they were big enough. Deer and coyotes, sometimes even big raccoons. He didn't see any animals, though. Tom strained to see. Nothing. But then...

Was that the shadow of a man, standing over behind the pool house? He just couldn't tell.

Tom shut off the bathroom light. If there was someone out there, they wouldn't be able to see him at least. He dashed into his bedroom without toweling off and pulled some clothes on. Jeans and a sweatshirt, not even bothering with underwear. He had a 9mm pistol in his sock drawer and he dug it out, loading it quickly.

Of course being so outspoken about the satanic threat had made him a target. He was probably number one on their kill list. He should have been prepared for that. But he wasn't afraid. Not now. The adrenaline was pumping and he had both the light of Christ in his heart and the comforting weight of the gun in his hand.

He ran barefoot down the stairs, almost silently. Through the big bay windows in the living room, he saw the front yard floods come on, too. And then, no way he was imagining it, a white figure dashed across his yard. A man, he told himself. Not a crouching devil, but a man. Finger on the trigger, arm tensed and ready, Tom walked towards the front door.

A timid knock came before he got there. Whoever was out there was bold enough to knock. Tom flipped off the lock and wrenched the door open.

None other than Mark Davies himself stood on the porch. The only thing that stopped Tom from shooting him on sight was the astounding fact that Mark was stark naked.

"Ah," Mark threw up his hands when he saw the gun, and he seemed doubly freaked out when he saw who was holding it. "Tom...Peters...it's you! Hi. I know it's late and I know this looks really strange, but I could really use some help right now. You are not going to believe the night I'm having."

HALLOWEEN

CHAPTER 40

8:13 AM

Waking up the next morning, Alice was immediately aware of two things. One, that she was feeling much better. Her old friends Pain and Nausea had receded back down to the just-below-intolerable baseline levels to which she'd grown accustomed. The second thing she was aware of was that there was something very hard poking up against her butt.

James was still asleep, curled up against her, and she had a definite theory about what the hard thing she was feeling might be. Reaching back, she confirmed this hypothesis.

"James," she said, rolling over and shaking him. "Wake up."

"What?" he said. His eyes fluttered open and he blinked around blearily. He seemed surprised to find himself in her bed. "Oh, hi."

"Hi," she said, glancing towards the unmistakable bulge. "Hey, I couldn't help noticing. You have a...I mean, you're *really*..."

"Oh, jeez." James looked down at himself. "I'm so sorry."

"It's all right," she said. "I just thought it was strange. Were you having a really good dream or something?"

"No. That just happens in the morning."

"Really? You wake up like that every morning?"

"Most mornings."

"Wow. That's weird. Why?"

"No one knows," he said.

"Huh. Listen, James. I'm going to ask you something, and I want to really think about it before you answer, okay?"

"Okay."

"Do you want to just...do it?"

"What?"

"You know what."

"No, I mean...really? We've...I mean, I told you, I'm..."

"I know you are, but listen." Alice swallowed, hard. "I know you don't like me to talk about it, but I'm not going to be around much longer. And I really want to know what that's like before I...you know. And I want it to be with someone I like, and I care about. I don't think I'm going to find anybody else, so it really has to be you, James. You or nobody. And I just thought, since you're...ready. And I'm...actually, at this moment, I'm ready too. I thought maybe we could just do it, just to see what it's like. It doesn't have to mean anything."

James was trembling beside her, his whole body. She felt it through the bedsprings.

"We don't have any, uh, condoms."

"That's okay, James. I don't have a uterus, so I think we're good there."

"But what about, you know, STDs?"

"We're both *virgins*," Alice said. "You know what, just forget it. It was a stupid..."

"No." James grabbed her arm. "I want to. I think we should."

"Really?" she smiled over at him.

"Yeah. How do we..."

"I've done extensive research," she said. "And I think the first step is, we should really take off our underwear."

"Yeah, that makes sense."

After a few moments of awkward wriggling, they were both naked below the waist.

"Do I just get on top of you?" James asked.

"Yeah."

He rolled over onto her.

"I'm not too heavy?"

"No."

"Do I just..."

"Yeah."

"Like that?"

"No, it's...up."

"There?"

"No."

"Where is it?"

Alice reached down and grabbed him, guided him towards where he needed to go.

"I can't..." he cried. "It's not going to work."

"It will, just..." And then it did. He was in. Inside her.

"Oh," she said.

"Oh God, I'm hurting you."

"No."

"Are you all right?"

"Yes."

"Does it feel good?"

"I don't know. Just...just move, James. Move."

He moved. Alice reached down and was surprised at how perfectly the curve of his buttocks fit into the palms of her hands. Like they'd been custom molded for her touch. She pulled him closer. A strange cry escaped her throat, unlike any sound she'd ever heard herself make before.

"This feels really good, Alice," James said.

"Yeah," she said. "Could you maybe...kiss me, though? It feels weird that you're not kissing me."

"I have really bad morning breath."

"So do I," she said. "Who cares?"

They kissed, for the first time, and Alice thought it strange that they'd done the other thing first, before they'd ever kissed. That seemed backwards. But then James finally caught on that he wasn't going to break her and his motion inside her grew bolder and for a few minutes she didn't think about anything at all.

CHAPTER 41

9:38 AM

LANA HAD BEEN on the computer all morning, doing job searches. It was a teacher's in-service day at school, but she'd called in sick and instead looked at open teaching positions in the Chicago area, the St. Louis area, Rockford, Cedar Rapids, and Indianapolis. Any sizable city within a two hundred mile radius. She filled out online applications and e-mailed her resume out for every position that sounded halfway suitable.

She had not expected to hear back from any of them so fast.

Her phone rang at a little past 9:30. A 314 area code, which she recognized as St. Louis.

"Lana Blair? This is Jackie Phillips. How the hell are you doing, girl?"

"Jackie? Really? That's you?" Lana laughed out loud. Jackie had been her freshman year dorm-mate at the University of Denver. Lana had noticed the name of the human resources director at one of the schools she'd applied to, but had assumed it was a coincidence. Jackie Phillips was not that unusual a name. "Oh my God."

They spent a good ten minutes just catching up—Jackie had been married and divorced, had two kids—before they even got around to talking about the job. It was at the Emerson Leadership Academy, an all-girl public charter school, covering grades six through twelve. The official title was "Instructional Support Specialist" and it involved coordinating the math and science departments. This included teaching a daily lab-style math class, co-planning math instruction with other science and math teachers, managing the technology program and pushing into specific classes as needed to provide targeted math instruction for students who needed extra help. It was a switch from English, but Lana had taught math back in Denver. It sounded like a dream job, and the salary was well above what she was making at BHS.

"You'd have to start right away," Jackie said. "Next week or two. Is that a problem?"

"That is *not* a problem."

"You can relocate that quickly?"

"That's what we're looking for," Lana said.

"Do you mind me asking why?"

"I don't want to get into it too much, but in a nutshell—I'm black, I'm gay, and this is a really small town."

"I've never even heard of Bakersfield, Illinois. How'd you end up in a place like that?"

"My wife, Michelle, is from here. We thought moving back home might be a good idea, but we were wrong. *Epically* wrong, in a way that's approaching crisis levels."

"All right, say no more. I have to run your name past the hiring board, but you have my whole-hearted recommendation. And I shouldn't tell you this, but they're desperate to hire. We had the position filled, but the lady flaked on us. She went off to India on some kind of *Eat, Pray, Love* midlife crisis vision quest or whatever."

"Well, thank God for those."

"Yeah," Jackie said. "You'll love it here, Lana. It's a great school and the girls are amazing. You'll be a perfect fit."

"Thank you, Jackie. Thank you so much. I can't even begin to tell you."

"Hey, can you come down?" Jackie said. "Let's say Wednesday morning. We'll do the official interview and, if you promise not to tell anybody, I'll take you out to lunch afterwards. I'd love to see you again."

"Wonderful."

After she hung up, Lana let out a screaming cheer. Michelle came running into the office.

"What? What?"

"How do you feel about St. Louis?"

"I love St. Louis. Why?"

"I got a job."

"What? No. Really?"

"Ninety-percent sure thing, I'd say. The hiring director is my old college roommate."

"That's..." Michelle shook her head. "That's unbelievable."

"How did the talk with your mom and dad go?"

"Oh." Michelle laughed out loud. "That. Yeah. They're giving us five thousand dollars."

"No shit?"

"Ever since Jen died, they've been wanting me to get out of here. They'd rather we move down to Florida with them, but I told them we didn't want to go too far, so Ben could be close to his Dad."

"Did you get a hold of Mark?"

"He's not answering his phone."

That was one potential roadblock. According to their custody agreement, Michelle couldn't move Ben out-of-state without Mark's permission. Even then, they'd have to sign a written agreement and have it approved by a judge.

"He'll agree to it," Michelle said. "I'm sure he'll understand. I'll *make* him understand."

"Yeah. I hope so."

"This is really happening, isn't it?"

"It's happening really damn fast."

Michelle laughed. "Do you want to start looking at apartments?"

They pulled another chair up in front of the computer and were checking out a few apartment-hunter sites when Ben appeared in the doorway.

"We're not really moving, are we?" he said, looking pale. His thumb went to his mouth and he actually sucked on it for a second, a habit he'd broken himself of before he started kindergarten. He seemed to remember this, and bit the nail instead.

"Oh, Benny," Michelle said. "Come here."

Ben went over and half-sat on Michelle's lap. She slid her arms around her son and kissed him on the side of the head.

"This town is no good for us anymore," she said. "It's dangerous. After what happened Saturday, Lana and I are both afraid to stay here."

"You can't just give up because of that," Ben said, pulling away from her. "We're supposed to be here now. If we're not, it's just going to get worse for everybody."

"That doesn't make any sense."

"You know what I'm talking about," Ben insisted. "I know you do."

"We've already decided," Michelle said. "Lana already got a job."

"She doesn't have to take it, though. She can change her mind."

"I know this isn't easy for you, Ben," Michelle said. "And I'm sorry. I know you have friends here, and I know you like being close to your dad, but I am literally afraid for my life in this town. Do you understand? There are people here who want to hurt me."

"I won't go," Ben said. "I'll stay with Dad and James. I'd rather stay here with them than go somewhere else with you guys."

"That's not your decision to make."

"*Why not?*" he screamed. Lana and Michelle both flinched back at this. Lana could not ever remember the boy raising his voice to his mother. Not even once. "I don't get a say? Does it even matter what I think? Do I just get moved around like a piece of furniture? You can't make me go if I don't want to! I'm staying with Dad! I give him *custody!*"

He ran out of the room and stomped away down the hall. His bedroom door slammed shut. Michelle gave Lana a look of pure astonishment. The outburst had been completely unlike Ben. He just wasn't an argumentative kid.

"I'm sorry, Chelle."

"No, I get it. This is really rough for him. I've got to talk to Mark, though. He can talk some sense into him."

Chelle texted her ex again, which she'd already done about ten times that morning.

"Where the hell is he?"

"Have you tried James?" Lana said. "Maybe he knows where Mark is."

"James isn't answering either." Michelle squinted down at her phone as if she could will it into ringing. "What the hell is everybody doing this morning?"

CHAPTER 42

10:10 AM

JAMES WOKE UP again, very badly needing to pee. He managed to extricate himself from the blankets without waking Alice, who just rolled over onto her back with a funny little half-smile on her face. They'd fallen asleep afterwards, which gave what had passed between them a disconnected, dream-like quality. James could not pretend that this earth-shattering thing had not happened, though. She was all over him still, lingering as a physical scent and also as what felt like a persistent electrical charge still buzzing in every nerve of his body. He located his pants on the floor and slipped them on, and then quietly walked down the hall to the bathroom.

He replayed the scene as he relieved himself. It seemed strange to him now how not-strange it had seemed then. Connecting with Alice in that way had felt at the time like the most natural thing in the world. Now, though, trying to put the event in the larger context of his idea of self, he couldn't make it fit. James was gay. That was one of the few things in his life he was reasonably certain of. He was into guys. Comparing the feeling of being with Alice to how he felt when he saw Jose in the locker room, just for example, seemed like two entirely different realms of experience. The thought of being with a man filled him with a breathless, heart-skittering yearning. What had passed between him and Alice hardly even seemed sexual, relative to that. And yet it was, undeniably. Even the bare minimum of touching himself involved in the act of urination reminded him of the electricity that had coursed through him into Alice.

It was very confusing. James washed his hands at the sink, and was surprised by how widely his reflection smiled back at him.

With appalling timing, James opened the bathroom door at the exact moment Alice's father was walking past in the hallway. The man seemed as surprised and unnerved by James's appearance as James was by his.

"Oh," he said. "Hello, James."

"Hi, Mr. Kiernan."

"I told you, call me Bob. Please."

"Okay, sorry."

"It's all right. Listen, I wanted to have a word with you, about what you and Alice are...ah, this awkward."

"Oh, no," James said. Getting busted by a girl's father was a problem he literally never thought he'd have to face. "We were just...I mean, I spent the night here, but we didn't..."

"I heard you, James," Bob said. "You weren't very quiet."

"God." James felt like his face was about to melt from the sudden rush of hot blood. "I'm so sorry, sir."

"No," Bob said. He was blushing a deep scarlet as well. "I'm not angry. In fact, I'm glad. It's hard for a father to think of his daughter as a, you know, as an adult woman. But she is. She's eighteen, and I was afraid she wouldn't get to experience that part of life. So I'm happy that she can, with someone like you. Someone who cares for her, and who will treat her with the respect she deserves. You will do that, won't you, James?"

"Of course I will."

"I know you will. Alice is very fond of you. I'm fond of you, too. If things were different, if there was more..." He choked up a little. "...time, I'd be proud to have you as a son-in-law. But, as it is, it's important that we make the time she has left as happy as possible. And you make her happy, James. I can tell by the way she looks at you whenever you're around."

Bob was tearing up, and James felt the water in his own eyes.

"Be careful," Bob said. "And I don't mean just with her. With yourself. The closer you get to her, the harder it's going to be when...She's all I have right now. Her mother left us three years ago and since then, I've been living just for her. I had a problem with drinking for a while, but I gave that up, so...now I don't know what I'll do."

"I..." James had no idea what to say.

"I'm sorry." Bob laughed and wiped his eyes. "I didn't mean to get so heavy on you. Go ahead, have fun. Thanks, James."

James slipped back into Alice's room. She was awake, propped up in bed with her lap-top open on her pillow desk, smoking a joint. She flashed James a laughing smile when he walked through the door.

"Oh my God," she whispered, leaking smoke. "I'm so sorry."

James carefully closed the door behind him. "You heard that?"

"Every word. I didn't realize how thin the walls are in this house. How awkward was that for you?"

"Scale of one to ten? I don't know, eighteen or nineteen, maybe."

He came over and sat down beside her, noticing to his slight alarm that under the blanket, she was still naked from the waist down. Her physical proximity, something which he had never precisely noticed before, now seemed palpable.

"What are you, ah," he deflected. "What are you looking at?"

"Well," she said. "A lot happened during our long night of unbridled passion. Our humble little town was on *The Today Show* and *Good Morning, America*."

She tapped her screen, on a headline reading "Tiny Illinois Town in National Spotlight as Concern Mounts over Occult Crimes," over a large, stirring photo of a candle-lit rally on the square last night. This was on cnn.com.

"What the fuh..."

"Careful, James, you almost dropped an f-bomb there."

He read the frankly unbelievable article, which at least seemed to have a somewhat skeptical bent to it. It reported on the media frenzy as if that was the story, rather than the so-called "crimes," which were literally non-existent as far as James could tell. The word "allegedly" was sprinkled liberally throughout the article. On the other hand, the story did feature several quotes from some guy named Thomas Gorman, who seemed completely off his nut. He noted that there was an "extremely rare concurrence" of a full moon on Halloween night, and that this was "irresistible from an occult standpoint." Also quoted was Sheriff Bates, who said that, "...we are investigating the possibility that the alleged abortion has connections to Wiccan-type cult activity" and Pastor Tom Peters, who said: "Our community stands united against the satanic threat. We are not afraid of them."

"People are going to go crazy over this," James said.

"Oh, they already are," said Alice, stubbing out the joint in the ashtray beside her bed. "The tweets coming out of this town sound like open-mike night at a mental hospital. Oh, plus I got this *fucked-up* message from Gemma."

-EVERYTHING changed last night Alice I wish u coulda been there 2 see almost don't believe it myself but Berta said u weren't ready 2 witness. This town's gonna b a diff place tonight no more sexist racist christian homophobe sheep shacker bullshit. There's a new bitch in charge & honey she won't stand for that shit. Oh my god I'm shaking I watched her get born. I kinda believed before but that's nothing like seeing it with yr own eyes. She's gonna fuck shit up & it's gonna b all fucking good from here on out. Remember what I said about yr cancer? I told Adaleen about u & she said if u promise 2 walk with us then that shit ain't nothin'. That's what she said—shit ain't nothin'. U have 2 meet her first though b4 shit hits the fan because after it's gonna be 2 crazy. Like hell night on earth crazy. Call me & I'll tell you where we're @. Don't bring James she's got a thing about men esp. white men—I don't think she understands about gayboys & how they're diff now. We can explain 2 her after & he'll b ok but right now we better keep him away 2 dangerous. Call me Alice please I'm bugging the fuck out & I could really talk 2 somebody from earth these bitches here are as crazy as I am.

"Is she on drugs?" James said when he'd read through that.

"I don't know. She sent that at around three this morning, and there are twenty-three follow-up messages since then."

She scrolled through them, they were all pretty similar.

-Where RU?!

-Where the fuck RU?!?!

-Cmon Alice please say yr not ignoring me I'm serious u need to be on the right side of this thing or I'm worried u might get hurt.

There was a final message, sent at 8:52, about an hour and a half ago.

- She doesn't like phones so she's making me ditch this so FIND ME. We're gonna be all over town. Trust me you'll know where. Talk 2 me 1ˢᵗ & I'll talk 2 her. & remember what I said about James, ok? Get him someplace safe even out of town would b good.

"Wow," James said. "What is all that about?"

"I don't know. I want to talk to her, though. Maybe you should do what she says and actually get out of town."

"I'm not leaving you alone."

"I kind of thought you were going to say that." Alice looked over at him and sighed. "James, do we need to talk about what happened?"

"Do you want to talk about it?"

"Not really. I just want to know how you feel. Do you think it was a mistake?"

"It wasn't a mistake," James said.

Alice smiled. "I don't think so either. But I don't want it to change things between us."

"I think it does change things, whether we want it to or not."

"In a good way?" Alice asked. "I know it's weird for you because I'm a girl and everything. I mean, you're still gay, right?"

"Last night I would have said yes, one hundred percent, without a doubt. Now I'm not that sure about anything."

"Sorry."

"The whole thing's really confusing for me. I don't know, I think maybe we should..."

Alice's eyes went wide, afraid of what he was going to say. "Maybe we should what?"

"Maybe we should...do it again."

"Really?"

"Just to be, you know, sure that it wasn't..."

Alice laughed. "Right now?"

"Yeah. Let's try to be quieter this time, though."

"Oh, James," Alice said. "You were the one making all the noise."

They turned to one another. All her electronic devices, with all their troubling communications from the chaotic world outside, tumbled forgotten to the floor.

CHAPTER 43

11:31 AM

Sheriff Nathanial Bates awoke late in the morning, his back and neck stiff from sleeping in his chair all night. He came awake slowly, wondering dully why that stupid *Big Bang Theory* show was on instead of the weather, until he happened to glance up and see the time. That got him up. Holy gee, it was after eleven-thirty. He was supposed to be up at headquarters by eight. He'd never slept in that late before, never in his life. No time to shower, he just brushed his teeth in his mirrorless bathroom and splashed some water on his face, then swiped on some deodorant so he wouldn't smell too bad. He was sure his uniform looked like he'd slept in it, because he had, but it would have to do.

He phoned in and told Deputy Anderson at reception he was feeling sick, but that he'd be in as soon as he could. Then Nathanial had to sit there and listen to a long litany of troubling developments that had occurred throughout the night and morning. A big demonstration on the square last night, armed vigilantes and news crews prowling around at all hours. Weird rumors about devil worshippers planning a virgin sacrifice under the full moon, or some such craziness. Bob punctuated his list of crises by reminding him that, "...we couldn't get hold of you," in case Nathanial might miss that point if it wasn't constantly reiterated. Now, this morning, Bakersfield on the national news as an example of small-town mass hysteria, and people seeing the news were getting even *more* hysterical. Bob said the phones had been ringing off the hook all morning and it was getting harder to sort out the pranks from the cranks.

Nathanial downed a fistful of Tylenol and hit the road. It was going to be a *long* day.

He drove up to Lincoln and people started to give him weird stink-eyes as soon as he walked in the door. He tipped his hat at a citizen lady who was sitting in the waiting room with her two kids. She bustled them away from him, like he was Count Dracula or something. Two deputies coming down the hall just gaped at him with barely concealed horror, like his nose had rotted off and they were just too polite to say anything about it.

Deputy Anderson had seen everything in the world pass in front of his desk at least twice, and had lost his ability to be shocked by any of it sometime in the mid-eighties. But even he gave Nathanial a sideways look.

"You fall asleep first at a slumber party last night, boss?" Bob deadpanned.

"What in the heck are people staring at, Bob?"

"You haven't looked in a mirror yet this morning, have you?"

"No. Why would I...oh, crap."

Nathanial went into the men's room. Nate grinned back out at him from the mirror.

"So," Nate said. "Whattaya think?"

The lousy so-and-so had written "I ate all them pussies," in magic marker plain as day across Nathanial's forehead. The words were backwards, of course, so it would be readable in the mirror. As if that wasn't bad enough, there was also a little Hitler mustache under his nose. Nathanial couldn't believe it. That was it. The final straw. Nate had crossed the line here.

"You son of a..." Nathanial gasped.

"Watch it there, partner," Nate leered. "I won't hear you saying nothin' about Mama."

Nathanial pumped a handful of the pink soap from the dispenser and scrubbed as hard as he could with paper towels. This lightened the marker slightly, but it was still clear and readable.

"You dirty, lousy monster. Why did you do that? I look like a dang fool."

"I just thought everybody ought to know what a goddamn carpet muncher you are."

"*Why can't you just leave me alone?*" Nathanial screamed into the mirror. "I'm trying to be a good man! I'm trying!"

"Whoa, you might want to keep it down there. This room ain't too sound-proof."

"I hate you!"

"You know how goddamn silly you look right now?"

Nathanial let out a screaming roar. Not even thinking anymore, he clenched his fist and swung with everything he had, into the glass mirror with the concrete wall behind it. The glass cracked into a glittering red star, but it did not shatter. The pain took a second to travel from Nathanial's fist up to his brain so he punched again, punched this phantom man that was the worst part of himself.

"There you go," Nate's fractured image, multiplied a hundred times, taunted in hellish chorus. "That's my boy."

And though Nathanial knew that he had been goaded into doing this very thing, that this was what Nate wanted, and though he was dripping blood from his shattered hand, he punched again and again and again. Obliterating the hated visage, grinding it to powder, a million tiny cutting slivers driving into his blood, into his bones. Nathanial knew that by doing this, he was setting Nate free. But there was only so much torment a decent man could endure. Surrender at least brought him relief.

The deliberate creation, the artificial construct, the noble experiment who had lived briefly, righteously as Nathanial Bates, receded back into a dark, shadowy corner of Nate Bates's mind. Nate came rushing forward. Had anyone been watching his eyes closely at that moment, they would have seen their hazel color abruptly shift several shades darker.

Nate looked around, dazed, hardly daring to believe it had been that easy. Shit, if he'd known that was going to work, he would have written stupid crap on the asshole's forehead on day one.

Nate's limbs were suffused with surging power and his head was filled with a reeling, rushing pleasure that made getting his rocks off feel like nothing. Even the searing pain in his hand was a sensual revelation. Being trapped in the mirror had been cold, numb nothingness. Almost like being dead. This was life right here, baby. He was *alive*. So fucking alive it burned like a nova inside his heart.

Shit, his hand though. He was going to have to deal with that.

Nate stuck his head out the bathroom door and wasn't too surprised to see a bunch of alarmed faces gaping at him all up and down the hall.

"Hey, would somebody mind bringing me the first aid kit?" Nate said mildly. "No big deal, but I had a little accident in here."

Deputy Bob showed up with the kit a couple minutes later.

"You all right, boss?" Anderson's sharp eyes took in the shattered glass and the blood all over the sink.

"This is going to sound crazy, Bob, but I've never felt better in my life. Give me a minute to get patched up here."

Bob withdrew and Nate went to work on his hand, picking the glass shards out the best he could with a pair of tweezers. Didn't look like he'd broken any bones, but he might have sprained it pretty bad. He'd probably have to see a doctor before the day was out, but right now he had too much to do.

Nate did a serviceable job cleaning and patching and wrapping his hand, considering he was working on his good hand with his left. He found some alcohol wipes in the kit, too. They worked pretty well in getting most of the marker shit off his face. If he kept his hat brim pulled down, nobody would even notice anything on his forehead. There was a faint ghost of the mustache left, like five o'clock shadow, but he could live with that. After all, everybody just called that a Charlie Chaplin mustache until old boy Adolf went and fucked it up for everybody else. Hell, maybe he could even reclaim the style for the good guys.

Nate smiled at himself in one of the unbroken mirrors. He thought maybe he would see Nathanial trapped inside there, like they'd just swapped places. But if that loser still even existed, he was hiding deep down in some hole. Right now it was all Nate, and that was *all* fucking good.

Deputy Bob showed up again a few minutes later, knocking on the men's room door before stepping inside.

"Sheriff, I'm asking you very seriously now. Are you sure you're all right?"

Nate chuckled. "Tip-top, Bobby."

"Okay, then you ought to know about this really strange call we just got."

"Thought you'd be used to those, the kind of morning you've been having."

"Yeah, well this one takes the cake even with all that."

"Let me guess," Nate said. "Bakersfield."

"Where else? It was Jim Jenkins, he runs that little egg farm over there."

"Yeah, sure. I know Jim."

"Well…" Bob shook his head, and Nate saw something he doubted he'd ever seen on the man's face before. Astonishment. "He had several of his eggs hatch. Now these eggs aren't roostered, understand? They're unfertilized."

"That's peculiar, sure," Nate said. "But why's he calling us? Doesn't the farm bureau have a hotline for shit like that?"

"Thing is, sheriff. It wasn't chickens that came out of those eggs. It was live snakes."

"The fuck?"

"Little black snakes, he said. Jim thought maybe they were cottonmouths, but he wasn't sure. He said he's had eight of them hatch like that so far. He's destroying the whole batch of eggs he's got, but thing is, he already sent a truckload to market this morning. He's afraid somebody's going to get bit while they're making their breakfast."

Nate stared at Bob for a second. The deputy was not renowned for his sense of humor, but surely this had to be a prank. Bob looked chilled to the bone, though. Finally, Nate shook his head, laughing.

"Holy Christ, you weren't kidding when you said, 'strange.'"

"There's one more thing, too. Dave Muldoon is a high school kid who works for Jim. He was actually the first one to see one of these snakes hatch out."

"Shepherd kid, right? One of Tom Peter's crew?"

"I think so. Anyway, after the snake hatched, he went into the bathroom. He looked out the window and he claims he saw five women dressed in black standing just outside the fence, staring in at the egg house. He said it looked like they were waving handfuls of roots or something in the direction of the building. Chanting, maybe."

"No shit." Bates chuckled. That was just too goddamn rich. "He get an ID on any of these alleged ladies in black?"

"He said they were too far away for him to get a good look, but he was pretty sure one of them was our girl Michelle Blair-Delany."

"Goddamn, this just keeps getting better, don't it? All right, I'll go check it out. I guess it's just the town's way of welcoming me back."

"Back, boss?"

"Never mind, Bob," Nate said. "Just keep me posted. I got a feeling this is going to be a Halloween to remember."

Even though Bob must have thought it pretty peculiar, Nate was still in such good spirits that he whistled his way out to his cruiser. Andy Griffith theme. Never thought he'd grow to like that one, but he had to admit it was a damn cheery tune.

CHAPTER 44

1:00 PM

THE ANNUAL No Tricks, All Treats Bash, now in its third year, was Bakersfield's only official Halloween event. For many years before the Bash's founding, the town had done nothing at all to recognize the holiday. Halloween was a rough season in Bakersfield, a reminder of the dark days of the holiday killings. So there were no haunted hay-rides or cornfield mazes, like in other towns. No pumpkin-carving or costume contests. Would-be trick-or-treaters were yearly flummoxed by restrictive curfews and street after street of darkened porch-lights.

Co-sponsored by the Jaycees and the volunteer fire department, and directed annually by local philanthropist David Trott, the Bash was an attempt to reclaim the holiday as a source of family fun. It was a decidedly kid-oriented event, with pumpkin painting, apple-bobbing and trunk-or-treating from cars parked around the square, all kicked off with a costume parade. The costumes on display here veered away from horror-movie staples like zombies and vampires, more towards miniature super-heroes and Nick Jr. characters. The smallest, stroller-bound children were dressed as adorable ladybugs, teddy bears and baby dinosaurs. The Bash produced more photo opportunities for grandmothers than any other event of similar scale throughout the entire year.

As innocuous as all this was, the previous two years had seen protests organized by the Church of the Shepherd, who saw *any* Halloween celebration as inherently diabolical in nature. The spirit of family fun was considerably dampened by demonstrators holding signs informing the attendees that they were all going to Hell. As a result, attracting a decent attendance had always been a struggle.

This year, though there were no protestors (the church had bigger fish to fry on this particular Halloween,) and the children were out of school for the day, only five families had been brave enough to show up. Happily, one of them was the large, devoutly Catholic Millard family. The Millard kids accounted for almost half of the thirteen total children who gamely marched around the square in perhaps the most pathetic parade ever. Still, the overall mood was light and festive, and the children were young enough to view the sparse attendance with "more candy for us" optimism.

Things didn't go wrong until the pumpkin egg hunt.

Borrowing a page from the more successful Easter festivities, David Trott had purchased a gross of plastic "eggs" in the shape of jack-o-lanterns. Volunteers had stuffed them with candy and strewn them about the square. Following the parade, the children were turned loose in a happy frenzy, to stuff their bags with as many as they could find. Even the kids too young to grasp the math understood that that many eggs, divided by their own small number, would equal a pretty decent haul.

Pete Millard, age five, was the first to notice something amiss. He found his first pumpkin egg at the base of the war memorial statue and, frowning, immediately brought it over to his mother.

"Mommy, my egg is *buzzing*."

Christie Millard held the little pumpkin up and was surprised by its angry droning vibration. She held the orange plastic up into the sun and made out a silhouette of a frenzied insect shape inside.

Then the screams began.

Impatient little hands, unable to wait until the hunt was over, opened eggs as soon as they were found. This released enraged hornets that had somehow replaced the candy the eggs had been stuffed with. Other eggs were dropped to the ground and stepped on by little fleeing feet, freeing more of the hornets. The furious black-and-yellow insects went berserk with attack pheromones. Parents rushed in from all sides to grab their little ones, slapping at the hornets covering the bodies and faces of their shrieking children. Suffering painful, searing stings of their own, the grown-ups picked their kids up and carried them howling over to the cars, pursued by black clouds of rage. The families weren't safe even inside their cars. The hornets had clung to hair and to clothing and had imbedded themselves in Halloween masks and just kept stinging and stinging. Several cars collided in the mad rush to escape their wrath.

David Trott had already suffered dozens of stings helping panicked parents carry their children to the relative safety of the cars. Now he collapsed huddled into a ball on the ground as the hornets wreaked furious vengeance upon his back and buttocks. He sobbed against the unbelievable pain, his swollen hands clasped behind his head and his arms folded to protect his face. In his agony, he moaned out a cry of surrender. The bastards had won. Let some other sap try to save Halloween.

Even in their panicked flight from the square, several of the parents noticed five women, dressed all in black, standing over on the opposite side of the square, near the swing sets. In the police reports filed later, most of the parents attested that the women had just stood there, impassively watching the terrible scene, but a few reported that the women were making odd gestures over at the children. Christie Millard swore she heard them chanting something.

Across the street from all this, Vic Frazier, a senior member in the Youth in Action club, was eating lunch with his dad at Jett's Diner. He noticed the commotion on the square, but couldn't really tell what was going on. From that distance, it just looked like everybody ran to their cars all at once. He did see the women, though. They walked right past the diner's front window as they filed away from the square, close enough for Vic to positively identify one of them as Gemma Gordon from school.

At the exact moment the women walked by, the strangest thing happened. His dad's glass of milk went sour. He'd just taken a sip a minute before and it had been fine, but now his glass was full of congealed chunks and smelled like it had been left out on the radiator overnight. Vic's dad, though alarmed, just called for another glass. The waitress, Iris Wilson, came back apologizing a few minutes later and told them that *all* the milk in their fridge was bad. She seemed baffled. The expiration was several days away, she said, and she'd been pouring the stuff all morning without any problems. But the milk had all gone bad, all at once.

Vic's dad recognized the presence of evil forces and insisted that they bow their heads and pray for deliverance. Vic readily agreed. He'd already been pretty freaked out even before the thing with the milk. Vic had awoken that morning bathed in sweat from a terrible nightmare. He couldn't remember the details, only that it had been a sex dream so dark and disturbing that he'd required cold shower flagellation to expiate the sleeping sin from his mind.

Then, while the family was saying their morning prayers in their living room, the big gold-plated cross on their wall had slipped a nail and flipped over so it was hanging upside down. Vic's dad had laughed that off, probably so as not to scare Vic's little brother and sisters, but Vic saw the fear in his father's eyes as he righted the cross.

Later on that morning, Vic had stopped by Casey's General to buy a nutritious breakfast of donuts, beef jerky and Mountain Dew. The total for his purchases came to $6.66. The number of the beast. This freaked him out so bad he had to add a pack of Twizzlers, even though he didn't really want them.

Some of these things might have been coincidences, but the cumulative evidence of the wickedness afoot could not be denied. As soon as lunch was over, Vic called Travis and told him everything. Then Travis filled Vic in on all the other diabolical things that were going on, like how Dave Muldoon was almost bitten by a serpent that had hatched from a chicken egg.

"This is so freaky, dude," Vic said.

"It's all right," Travis soothed. "We're not going to just sit by and let it happen. We call ourselves Youth in Action, so it's about time we *took* some action."

Vic nodded. He was reassured by how Travis was taking charge of this thing. It was no accident that he was their leader. Travis explained what he had in mind, and Vic felt himself grinning from ear to ear.

CHAPTER 45

2:34 PM

B EN DAVIES SAT in his bedroom, feeling trapped by the machinery that had been set into motion. He'd apologized to his Mom and Lana for his outburst that morning, but was still sick with worry about having to move. More than anything, he wanted to talk to his dad, but he still wasn't answering his phone. James wasn't picking up either. Ben had nobody to talk to except Mom and Lana, and they were both resolutely on the same side. They were excited to leave. Ben hadn't seen them this happy in a long time. He felt utterly powerless. It wasn't fair.

A *splat* from his bedroom window, loud enough to make him jump, shocked Ben out of his miserable loop of self-pity and helplessness. He looked up and saw yellowish slime dripping down the glass.

He went to the window to look outside. Three cars had pulled up to the curb in front of the house. Several teenaged boys stood on the lawn, a carton of eggs at their feet. The boys grabbed eggs from the carton and started lobbing them at the house. They shouted things, mean things. Angry hate-words. Ben heard the n-word and the d-word that rhymed with "bike." He heard the b-word and the c-word, hateful names that men used against women.

When the boys ran out of eggs, they started throwing rocks.

Downstairs, Lana and Michelle were in the kitchen making lunch. Chelle was warming soup up on the stove and Lana was spreading mayo onto bread to make sandwiches when they heard the shouting outside, followed by breaking glass. They ran into the living room and found the big bay window shattered. Again. They'd just replaced the glass a few months ago, after the sleepwalkers had burst through it. Now there was a big rock in the middle of the floor and broken glass everywhere.

"Motherfuckers," Lana spat.

Loud hammering bangs bombarded the front of the house. People were outside, throwing rocks and shouting obscenities.

"Ben!" Chelle screamed up the stairs. "Go into the bathroom! Lock the door!"

Lana ran back to their room and grabbed her Glock from the top dresser drawer. She burst outside just as one of the kids tossed a bottle onto the porch with a flaming rag stuffed into the neck. By sheer providence, the glass didn't break. Without even thinking, Lana stomped on the burning cloth wick, extinguishing the Molotov cocktail before it could ignite.

A hurled rock smashed into the siding beside the front door, missing Lana's head by inches. Snarling, she raised the gun and fired two shots into the air, just to show these shitheads she wasn't afraid to pull the trigger. Then she lowered the weapon, pointing it right at the face of the boy who had thrown the rock. She recognized him as the leader among the Church of the Shepherd kids at the high school.

"Travis Chasen!" she named him with a scream.

The cocky grin slid from Travis's face when he looked down the still-smoking barrel of Lana's gun. A second rock clutched in his hand fell to the grass with a thud. He took two stumbling steps backwards.

"Yeah, that's what I fucking thought." There were eight of them. The ones Lana recognized from school were all Shepherd kids. She called their names, pointing the barrel at each of them in turn. "Dave Muldoon, John Gearhart, Vic Frazier. Any of you other motherfuckers want to throw some more rocks at me?"

They scrambled away, pouring back into their cars. The vehicles peeled out with screams of burning rubber.

"Fucking *cowards*!" Lana shouted after them. She leveled her gun at one of the escaping cars and with deep, bitter regret restrained herself from shooting out the back windshield.

There was a bang and a shattering pop from across the lawn. One of the assholes had dropped another Molotov on the ground before running away, and it had detonated right at the base of their mailbox. The flames licked up the side of the wooden post and caught on the cross-beam, turning the mailbox stand into a little burning cross on her lawn.

"Chelle!" she screamed back into the house. "Grab the fire extinguisher!"

Lana doubted that the ignorant shitheads had intended the KKK symbolism, but it wasn't lost on her. She couldn't get out of this fucking town a minute too soon.

CHAPTER 46

4:06 PM

Emma Holmes saw the women in black when she pulled into the school parking lot for cheerleading practice at a little past four. They were standing by the fence over on the other side of the football field. She briefly wondered who they were and what they were up to, but didn't dwell on these thoughts. Emma was more concerned with the practice she was heading towards. regionals were coming up, and Coach Ruby was turning into a real hard-ass about it, riding them ragged as if they actually had a chance in hell of accomplishing anything there.

She went inside and got changed and then the team started out by doing some stretches. Standing up from a toe-touch, Emma's best friend Maxine Gardner turned to her with an expression like she was about to say something of great importance. Then she opened her mouth and meowed like a cat.

For some reason, this struck Emma as the funniest thing she'd ever heard in her life. She laughed, hysterically. And when Megan Phillips looked over to see what the hell was so funny, Emma meowed at her. That got Megan laughing, too, so hard that she gripped her sides. All three girls then started meowing, which got the other girls on the crew laughing. Then they started meowing too.

Coach Ruby blew her whistle to get them to cut it out, but this just made everybody laugh and meow even harder. Coach started screaming at them, "Stop! Stop!" but it was uncontrollable now. Emma couldn't stop laughing and meowing, it was coming from deep inside her. It was terrifying, but hilarious at the same time. All around her, girls were falling to the ground laughing. Some were crawling around, acting like kittens, romping and batting at imaginary balls of yarn. Maxine fainted cold and Megan started convulsing like she was having a seizure. A few girls even wet themselves, they were laughing so hard. Coach Ruby just stood there, jaw dropped in astonished horror.

The weird group fit, or whatever it was, only lasted a few minutes, but afterwards the girls were all worn out and terrified. A few of the girls seemed so weakened by the experience that they couldn't even get up off the floor. Coach Ruby called 911, and was shocked to hear that it would be an hour or more before an ambulance might arrive.

Bakersfield received ambulance service from Logan EMT Transport in Lincoln, which was overwhelmed by the more than twenty round-trips the company had already made to and from the little town on that Halloween afternoon. They were still transporting victims of the hornet attack when the call about the hysterical cheerleaders came in. The sheriff's department was likewise inundated with strange emergency calls, and had to request back-up assistance from the state police. By five o'clock, when the massive explosion happened, the area's emergency services were strained to the breaking point.

Halloween was just getting started.

CHAPTER 47

4:51 PM

IT TOOK NEARLY two hours for anyone to show up after Michelle called to report the incident with the stone-throwing Shepherd kids. A tall, fortyish deputy named Brewer finally came out to the house just before five. He offered a curt apology, citing the tremendous load of calls the department was dealing with today, then made a cursory examination of the damage. Brewer glanced over the burned mailbox post and the broken front window, and the cracked siding on the front of the house from the stones.

"Yeah, they got you good," Brewer chuckled, as if this had been nothing more than a harmless Halloween prank.

They sat down inside and he took their report. Ben told how he'd first seen the teenagers pulling up and throwing eggs at the house, and then Lana gave her account. Deputy Brewer stopped her when she reached the part about firing the warning shots.

"Wait," he said. "You shot into the air? Do you know how dangerous that is, ma'am? Those bullets have to come down somewhere. People have been killed that way."

"I know," Lana said. "But I felt like I had to show them that I wasn't afraid to..."

"Are you aware that reckless discharge of a firearm is a class four felony in this state?"

"What?"

"Were these boys armed?" Brewer asked.

"Yes, I told you. They had rocks and Molotov cocktails."

"But no guns."

"I don't know if they had guns or not," Lana said. "Maybe they did."

"So you discharged your weapon in the direction of unarmed minors?"

"They were attacking our home!" Michelle put in. "With our son inside. One of those rocks could have hit him in the head." She clenched her teeth. "Look, she told you their names. You know who they are. Why don't you go arrest them instead of giving her shit about her using her gun in self-defense?"

"This becomes an entirely different kind of incident when a weapon is involved," Brewer said. "Do you have firearm owner's identification?"

"You want to see my *FOID* card?"

"Yes, ma'am. Please."

"Jesus. Hold on."

Lana stood up and grabbed her purse from the stand beside the door. She dug out the little card and handed it to the deputy, who attached it to his clipboard as he wrote.

"If I was white and it was a bunch of black kids that drove up to my house throwing rocks, this would be a different conversation, wouldn't it?"

"Ma'am," Brewer said, his voice growing harder. "I don't think you realize—"

His words were cut short by a sound like a jet plane breaking the sound barrier off in the distance. It was loud enough that one of the cracked panes on the big window rattled off and fell to the floor.

"What the hell?" Brewer got to his feet and looked out the broken window.

Off to the north, just over the horizon, they all saw a massive fireball. A huge cloud of black smoke billowed into the dusking sky.

"Dispatch," Brewer spoke into the radio microphone strapped to his shoulder. "This is twenty-eight. I'm in Bakersfield right now, and I just saw what looks like a large explosion off to the north. Are you getting any reports?"

"Stand-by, twenty-eight," the radio crackled.

"What was that?" Ben asked.

"I don't know, Benny," Michelle said. "But I've got a really bad feeling about it."

For a few long minutes, they all stood in silence, watching the awe-inspiring sight. Several smaller aftershocks rippled through in quick succession, which they felt in the pits of their stomachs, like bass drumbeats.

"Be advised, twenty-eight," the reply came on Brewer's radio. "The switchboard's lighting up like a Christmas tree. We're thinking it's a possible train derailment north of the ethanol plant. You're the closest available unit. Can you respond?"

"Yeah, I'm done here. I'll check it out."

Brewer handed Lana her FOID card back. "Ma'am, on any other day I would cite you for reckless discharge, but given the circumstances and with everything else that's happening, I'm going to let it go."

"Let it go?" Michelle said. "What about the little punks who attacked our house? What are you going to do about them?"

"Look," Brewer said. "I know who you are. And I know what you did Friday night. So if I were you, I'd consider myself damn lucky to get off twice in one weekend. I'll give you a copy of my report so you can file a claim with your insurance company, but I'd advise you to let this go. I don't know what the hell is going on in this town, and I don't know what your involvement is. But next time we get a call about you, you can bet your ass you're not going to get off so goddamn easy."

He left with that. As soon as he was out the door, Lana looked Michelle in the eye and said: "We're leaving tonight."

"Goddamn right we are," Michelle replied.

CHAPTER 48

5:04 PM

EVERYONE IN TOWN heard the train explode.

The freight train had taken on seven tanker cars at the Malovo Renewable Bioenergy plant in Bakersfield, each containing thirty thousand gallons of ethanol. Less than five miles north of town, the engine and the front twenty-six cars, including the ethanol tanks, flew off the tracks. All seven tanker cars telescoped into the grain cars in front of them, rupturing the tanks and spilling thousands of tons of flammable fuel, which soon ignited.

The distant metallic wrenching noise of the crash, followed by a window-rattling sonic boom of the ethanol detonation, reverberated throughout the beleaguered town at a few minutes after five.

From all four sides of the downtown square, the shop owners representing Bakersfield's small business community stepped outside and looked north, where the blast had come from. There they saw an angry mass of flames, and plumes of fire and black smoke shooting into the air. The ground rumbled with a second and then a third explosion in quick succession.

Iris Wilson, closing up Jett's Diner for the night, was smoking a cigarette in the alley behind the restaurant when it happened. She'd officially quit years before, but still kept an emergency pack hidden in the back closet where the cleaning supplies were stored. (She doubted her daughter Alyssa, with her aversion to serious cleaning of any kind, even knew the closet was back there.) Iris only lit up after particularly stressful shifts, and the one today sure as hell qualified. The thing with all the milk going bad had shaken her, and then the news of those poor little kids stung by wasps when all they wanted was some candy and fun. She just didn't know what to think. She liked to keep a diplomatically neutral stance on the religious and political views of her diverse customer base, but the Shepherd folks seemed to be the only ones taking the right line on the day's deeply troubling events. Seeing the edge of the sky tinged with hellfire glow cemented this feeling. Though she was not particularly religious, the sight filled Iris with a deep dread she felt in her mortal soul.

Gerald Grady, of Grady's Feed Store, was likewise closing shop, counting down the till while his daughter Emily sat at his desk, drawing strange little comic strips in her notebook. Emily's school was out today and Leslie couldn't take the day off, so Emily had come into work with him. They both liked these occasional daddy-daughter days. Emily was good company, and she actually seemed to enjoy jawing with the old farmers who came into the store. Gerald knew they got a kick out of her, too. Such a bright, gregarious little girl, who'd actually listen with interest when they started rambling on about how much candy used to cost, or spin tales about blizzards and tornados they'd seen when they were her age.

Of course, today there was only one topic of old-timer conversation. Like everyone else in town, Gerald was troubled by the startling events of the day, though he didn't know how much of what he heard he could actually believe. Emily, though, took it all in with wide-eyed credulity. She'd transcribed some of the stories in her picture-book journal, and right now was drawing out a graphic comic-book depiction of the hornet attack on the square. Gerald sneaked a look when she went off to the bathroom, and was a little disturbed by how luridly she'd drawn the looks of terror on the little stick-figure children she'd drawn fleeing from the madly grinning hornets. He knew Emily was imaginative, but her imagination tended towards the morbid sometimes and he didn't know if this was something he should be concerned with.

When the blast shook the building, Emily looked up from her drawing and tilted her head curiously. She followed close behind when Gerald went outside to have a look.

"Holy wow!" Emily screamed when she saw the blast billowing into the sky. "What is that, Dad? A plane crash?"

"I don't think so, honey," Gerald said. He felt a sinking unease at the sight.

"Is it a *bomb*?" Emily cried. She was jumping up and down in her excitement. "Is this a real-life terrorist attack?"

He looked down with alarm at his daughter. Her eyes were gleaming, not with fear but with manic glee, like she'd never seen such a beautiful sight.

Wolfy's Tavern was right next door to Grady's Feed Store and, unlike most of the neighboring businesses, the bar was just opening for the evening. A few dedicated customers already had an early start on their Halloween inebriation, and they came rushing out of the bar to gesture and exclaim at the burning sky.

Ben Wolf, known to one and all as Wolfy, followed his customers out onto the sidewalk at the sound of the blast, keeping a vigilant eye on his beer mugs lest one of the idiots drop one on the pavement. He was out of sorts. Sally had never come home the night before. He might have taken this as an encouraging sign, except she didn't show up for work tonight, either. He hadn't made up his mind yet if he ought to be irritated with her or concerned. Strange thing though, when he looked at the bright orange flames to the north, he had a nagging, nonsensical feeling that Sally was somehow involved.

Over on the east side of the square, the owner of the newest downtown business hobbled out on her crutches when she heard the tremendous bang. Denise Kindely gazed upon the fiery sky, her face drawn as if she'd been stricken.

The past two days had been a trial for her. When she awoke yesterday morning, her knee had been throbbing with pain she hadn't known since Pastor Tuttle laid hands on her and removed her affliction in Jesus' name. Then she went to church and was dismayed to find that Alice, the girl with cancer to whom she'd given Christian Grace's eyepatch, had reneged on her promise and had not shown up to attend the services with her. By Sunday evening, Denise's pain was so bad she had to pull her hated crutches down from the shadow box behind the counter at her store. These two events, the return of her pain and being tricked by the girl, fit easily together in her mind.

Denise heard the rumors about Alice Kiernan. How she had disrupted the meeting at the Underground club, about how she was connected to the occultists, about all the bisexual sex and the drugs she was involved with. Denise had spent these last two troubling days brooding over thoughts of Alice Kiernan, fantasizing about confronting her. Every time she heard of a new atrocity perpetrated by the satanic witches, Denise wondered if Alice was directly involved. And now, witnessing the fiery light like the devil's rising just north of town, Denise knew in her heart that the sickness in Alice Kiernan's body was nothing to the sickness in her soul.

Mark Davies, on the far south edge of town, heard the distant explosion as a low rumbling, and noticed it mainly as curious ripples in his glass of water on the coffee table. He thought this was mildly strange, spent half a second wondering what it had been, and then forgot all about it.

Mark had spent the entire day, and most of the night before, locked in Tom Peter's basement. This was more comfortable than it might have sounded, as the basement was nicely finished, with plush carpeting, a comfortable overstuffed couch and a widescreen television. With literally nothing else to do, Mark had passed the time watching television. Tom didn't have cable in his basement, though. What he did have was a web connection and a streaming box with a subscription to FaithFlix, the all-Christian version of Netflix. Mark had spent the past eight hours or so skimming through old "Davey and Goliath" cartoons, feature-length polemics against atheist college professors, Rapture "thrillers" with sub-Syfy Channel effects budgets and the entire oeuvre of Kirk Cameron. Weirdest of all for him was a movie called *Fifty Shades of Grace*, which was exactly like *Fifty Shades of Gray*, except instead of kinky sex, the handsome, domineering millionaire (with a suave eyepatch) introduces the shy young wallflower to the joys of Evangelical Christianity. This made it somehow even creepier than the original.

Mark at first watched these entertainments with ironic amusement, and then with a clinical sociological interest. Eventually, though, the treacly messages, complete lack of nuance or true dramatic conflict, and shaky production values grew numbing. Turning it off was worse, though. With the television off, Mark had nothing to distract him from the visions that had been seared into his brain the night before. With the resurrection of Adaleen Bell in his head, he could begin to understand the vapid appeal of talking vegetables acting out Bible stories.

He'd told Tom everything that had happened at Roberta's house. Several times, in fact. Tom had come downstairs at multiple points throughout the day, sometimes bearing food for his prisoner. Each time, he'd had Mark go over the whole thing, start to finish, as if trying to catch him in a lie or inconsistency. Tom accepted the existence of a coven which had reanimated a two-hundred-year-old witch with surprising ease. That part apparently made perfect sense to him. What he couldn't seem to grasp was that neither Missy nor Lana had anything to do with it. And that Mark's involvement had been only as a horrified witness. In Tom's mind, he'd already cast the three of them as the heads of this unholy church, and he had a difficult time letting go of that presumption.

Being ensconced in Ned Flanders's basement as he'd been all day, Mark had little sense of the chaos that had once again consumed the town. He'd been able to gather a little bit from the snatches of phone calls and conversations he'd overheard through Tom's heating vents. There had been a particularly urgent call at just a few minutes before five, from somebody named Greg.

Mark knew his name because Tom kept saying it: "No, Greg. Please don't. Listen. Greg, please just pray first. That's all I'm asking, Greg. Pray to Jesus and ask him if this is really the right thing to do. No, don't hang up, Greg. Wait!"

Whatever that was about.

The "Greg" Tom was talking to was Greg Chasen, Travis's father. Chasen was halfway up the ladder on the side of the Bakersfield water tower at the time of the initial blast. This was already a precarious position, and the resounding shock wave nearly knocked him off the ladder. Greg, heart racing and adrenaline pumping, saw a huge fireball off to the north. The whole sky was lit up with orange and red, like a second sunset. Greg froze for a long moment, until he once again trusted his grasp on the still-humming metal rungs.

"What was that?" he called down to the ground.

His voice was lost in the rumbling sound of two more distant explosions, louder than thunder. The people down below were all gesturing off to the north. He heard their panicked appeals passing by him on their way to Heaven.

Greg said a quick prayer himself and then continued to climb, his resolve strengthened. Whatever that blast was, the witches were probably behind it, too. Greg moved up, rung by rung. The two lengths of rope attached to his belt hung below him like dangling tails.

They'd drawn straws to see who would climb the tower to string up the ropes, and Greg had drawn the short one. Lou Witzky had a flask on him, and though Greg seldom drank, he did accept a couple shots of whatever was inside, to give him courage. He hated heights, really, but somebody had to do this.

Lou owned a small construction company, and he'd contributed the scissor lift and two high-powered night-work lights. Though it was not quite proper twilight, the men on the ground fired up the generator and angled the big lamps up the side of the tower. Looking down, Greg was dazzled by the bright white light. When he looked away, his vision was covered with red and green spots. He knew they had to test the lights, but he wished they'd at least wait until he was decently back down on the ground.

Finally, Greg pulled himself up onto the platform encircling the massive reservoir tank. He stood there staggering in the open air for a few moments, catching his breath and gathering his courage, willfully ignoring the altitude beneath him and the distant fire on the northern horizon. Once he'd recovered himself, his hands set to work forming the knots that would secure the ropes to the metal railing. Once they were fixed, he pushed the ropes off the side of the tank.

Two nooses now dangled side-by-side beneath the tower, swaying gently in the breeze. When they dropped, the cheer that went up from the crowd below was loud enough that Greg could hear it even from his perch in the sky.

CHAPTER 49

5:50 PM

They couldn't wait any more. Lana and Michelle had booked a double room at the Marriott Courtyard in Springfield. They packed three suitcases with clothes and toiletries to last a few days. Books and games for Ben, their photo albums, anything essential that they couldn't bear to part with in case things went seriously bad and they weren't ever able to come back here.

Lana put the odds of that happening at about fifty-fifty.

They still couldn't reach Mark, which had Chelle worried and Ben nearly frantic. James had finally answered his phone, at least. He was with Alice Kiernan. James hadn't heard from Mark either. Michelle asked James if he and Alice wanted to come with them to Springfield, she even offered to get another room for them, but he assured her that the two of them were safe.

Leaving a car behind would present some problems. They didn't know when or if they'd be able to come back and get the other one. Lana and Michelle didn't want to split up, though, so they decided to take Lana's new Prius rather than Michelle's older Civic. Ben cast a last look back up at his bedroom window before he got into the back seat. His eyes welled with tears.

"It's going to be okay, Benny," Michelle said, pulling him close to her for a second. "We just have to get someplace safe."

"I know." He nodded, the tears falling. "I just want to see my dad."

They all got into the car. Lana backed out of the drive and pulled away from the house where they'd made their home for more than a year.

Twilight was falling on Bakersfield when Lana turned left at the square and headed south, out of town. There were quite a few people out on the square, watching the massive black column of smoke from the burning train fire pouring up into the sky. The lights of the fire crews flashed just over the horizon, reflecting off the smoke like flickering red lightning. This only added to the surreal doomsday feeling.

They almost made it. Lana cruised past the big pink water tower on the edge of town. There was some kind of commotion there too, a throng of people gathered at the base. Bright spotlights shone up on the tower, illuminating the crowned cow chip painted on the side.

If I never lay eyes on that stupid piece of shit again, Lana thought. *I'll die happy.*

She tapped the gas a little to propel them out of town. At that exact moment, the rear view mirror was filled with flashing red and blue light.

"Shit," Michelle swore.

"Don't pull over," Ben said anxiously from the back seat. "Just keep going."

For half a second, Lana actually considered that. But she'd seen enough police chases on the news to know they never ended well, especially for people of color. Taking a deep breath, she pulled over to the curb.

"Everybody be cool," she said, perhaps more for her own benefit than for Michelle's or Ben's. "Everybody be calm."

After an agonizingly long minute, a deputy walked up to the driver's side door and shined a bright flashlight into Lana's face. It wasn't Deputy Brewer, it was a man she'd never seen before. She noted with grim, inevitable foreboding that he wasn't wearing a name badge. Lana rolled down her window and attempted a smile.

"Good evening, deputy," she said. "I wasn't speeding, was I?"

"Shut up."

Two more vehicles pulled up in quick succession. Civilian, not police. A pick-up truck spun around on the road to pull in front of them and block their exit, its bright headlights further dazzling Lana's eyes. An old Chevy jumped the curb to pull up close to Michelle's passenger side door, pinning it closed, close enough to make a metallic scrape.

They were completely boxed in.

"Watch out, the black one's got a gun," somebody standing behind the deputy said. Lana couldn't be sure with all the lights in her face, but she sensed there were at least six or seven men surrounding their car. "She pulled it on my son earlier."

"Do you have a weapon?" the deputy demanded, clipping the flashlight back to his belt and trading it for his gun.

"Yes," Lana said, eyes going wider as she stared down the barrel. "In the glovebox. I have a concealed carry permit, though, so it's—"

"Shut your black trap, bitch!"

Lana flinched back as if she'd been slapped. Her whole body was shaking. She'd never been so afraid in her life.

"You." The deputy leaned into the car and pointed his gun across the front seat, over at Michelle. "Open the glovebox and hand the weapon over. *Slowly.*"

"Yes," Michelle said. She opened the glovebox. "I just want to make sure you're aware that there's a child in the car, in the back seat. He's eleven years—"

"Shut your fucking mouth!"

Nodding, Michelle reached in for the gun.

"Grab it by the barrel," the deputy said. "Good. Hand it over."

Michelle passed the gun over to the deputy. He handed it back to someone standing behind him.

"Okay," Lana said, willing herself *calm calm calm*. "You have our gun. We're unarmed. Can we talk now? Why did you pull us—"

"Get out of the car."

"I don't know if I'm comfortable—"

Something struck the rear window with a tremendous blunt clunk that left a cracked silver star on the glass. In the back seat, Ben shrieked. An alarming cry of childish terror that sent sharp bolts of maternal adrenaline spiking through Lana's brain. Outrage flushed her blood. It was one thing to terrorize grown women, but to scare a kid like that? Especially *her* kid.

"Get outta the fuckin' car!"

"Okay, okay," Lana said. She undid her seatbelt. "I'm coming. You want to take the gun out of my face now?"

"Shut up. You two behave and we'll let the kid go."

Lana's door was wrenched open. The deputy grabbed her roughly by the arm and yanked her out of the driver's seat. He tossed her over and slammed her down on the hood of the car.

"You got another weapon on you?" the deputy demanded.

Lana felt rough hands on her body. Not just the deputy's, but other men's hands as well. Patting her down, groping her buttocks, sliding up between her legs. She still couldn't see any of their faces. They were just shadows in the light.

Behind her, another of the men dragged Michelle out of the car. He gave her a pat-down just as invasive as Lana's had been. Unless he honestly believed she might have a gun hidden in her bra.

"Get your hands off me," Chelle protested, trying to pull away. "We didn't do anything!"

"Shut up, witch!" called the man who had groped her.

"Witch?" Michelle cried. "That's what this is about? Are you fucking kidding me?"

The man slapped Michelle across the face.

They're going to lynch us, Lana realized. *That's what this is. A lynching. They're going to hang us from a tree or burn us alive. Probably rape us first.* She felt a flush of pure hatred for these men and their deadly ignorance.

Then Ben was climbing out of the car, crying: "Leave my moms alone!"

"Ben, no!" Lana screamed.

"Get back in the car!" Michelle yelled at him, her voice edged with anguish.

"Listen to your mother," the unnamed deputy said to Ben, with a strained benevolence. "Get back into the car right now, son."

"No!" Ben shouted. He rushed forward and was grabbed by rough hands. "Let us go!"

"Get that goddamn kid back in the car or he's going to get hurt," the deputy said to Lana, pressing his gun hard between her shoulder blades. He pushed her off balance, so all her weight was on her face.

"Ben!" Lana screamed into the hood of the car. Her lips were mashed against her teeth by the metal, hard enough to draw blood. "Get back in the car!"

But Ben struggled to break free from the men holding him. He kicked one of the men in the shins, screaming: "Let my moms go!"

CHAPTER 50

5:54 PM

JUST A FEW blocks away, Sam Hansard was in his truck, driving out to Tom Peters's house to pick Mark up. Tom had called him at home just a little bit ago.

"Your friend Mark," Tom had said. "I need you to tell me the truth. Is he involved in witchcraft or devil worship at all?"

"Mark?" Sam had to laugh. "Hell, no."

Tom could be a little intense sometimes, but Sam liked him. Sam's grandma had been a member of the Church of the Shepherd. After she died back in August, Tom was a huge help in organizing the funeral. They'd become friendly after that. Not hanging out or anything, but stopping to chat whenever they ran into each other around town. Tom was a good guy, but he had a hard time seeing things except through the narrow focus of his religion.

"But those books he writes," Tom said. "They're full of demons and hatred against Christianity. Bizarre sex and gory violence and foul language. How can somebody write that stuff unless he's got an evil mind?"

"Dude, they're horror books," Sam said. "What, you think Stephen King is some kind of satanic priest, too?"

"Well, actually, yeah I do," Tom said. "He gained earthly wealth and fame by glorifying the occult."

"Have you ever read any horror books?"

"Of course not."

"Well, then how can you say that?" Sam said. "They're fun, that's all. It's fun to be scared. They're not real, you know. It's just make-believe."

Brief silence on the other end of the line as Tom mulled that over. "What about his ex, and the other lady? Michelle and Lana. Are they witches?"

"No," Sam said. "They're really cool ladies."

"But they're lesbians."

"You know lesbians and witches aren't the same thing, right?" Sam said. That seemed obvious enough to Sam, but sometimes you had to spell things like that out for Tom. "They're just people. Trying to raise their kid and get through life, same as you. Why are you asking me about them, anyway?"

"Mark showed up at my house late last night," Tom said. "He was out running around the woods, naked."

"What?" Sam laughed. That was pretty out there, even for Mark.

"He told me a crazy story, about a coven sacrificing a girl. He said they resurrected a dead witch, who crawled into the murdered girl's skin."

"Mark said that? Mark *Davies*?" Sam said. "Was he high or something?"

"I think so, maybe," Tom said. "But I believe him. He saw something out there that scared him bad. And it fits in with everything else that's happening. I just don't know whether to trust him when he says that his ex and her girlfriend had nothing to do with it."

"I'll tell you right now, Lana and Michelle are *not* witches. Okay? That's ridiculous."

"Okay." Sam heard Tom take a deep breath. "Then can you come over to my house and pick Mark up?"

"He's still at your place?"

"Yeah, I thought I should keep him here until I was sure that he wasn't, you know, organizing things."

"Dude, Mark has a hard time organizing his bank balance," Sam said. "He's not some kind of criminal mastermind. He's a good guy. Lana and Michelle are good people, too. Whatever the hell's going on, it's got nothing to with them."

Tom sighed, deeply. "I'm starting to think maybe you're right about that. Just come pick him up, okay? Maybe get him out of town. Things are getting...out of hand."

Tom hung up with that ominous statement. Sam immediately grabbed his keys and went out to his truck. He was a little concerned for Mark, who was his best friend. What if he'd got into some bad acid or something?

Sam was out of touch with the panic that had gripped the rest of the town. He'd spent most of the morning over in Decatur, finalizing the real estate sale. The Malovo people were purchasing his grandmother's property, including her house. Sam had inherited the whole parcel when she died, and all he wanted to do was get rid of it. Malovo made him an offer before he could even put it on the market, for almost double what Sam and his realtor had been planning to list the property for. He couldn't say no to that. Walking out of the meeting, he'd realized with dawning wonder that he was, by local standards anyway, a wealthy man. Rather than obsess about the rumors swirling around town, like nearly everybody else in Bakersfield, Sam had spent the rest of the afternoon in contemplative solitude at home, trying to figure out exactly what he was going to do with the rest of his life, now that he didn't have to worry about money.

If someone would have asked him that question six months ago, the answer would have been simple. He would have said that he wanted to buy some beachfront property someplace warm and spend the rest of his days getting baked and watching the waves roll in. But so much had changed in the past few months, since the Sickness. He didn't smoke even weed anymore, for one thing. Mark didn't smoke, and Bill had quit after he got back together with his ex-wife. Getting high by himself was just too lonely.

Sam's grandmother's death had affected him more deeply than he'd thought it would, too. She'd raised him after his folks died, after all. He and Gram had been somewhat estranged for years, but they became close again after their sleepwalking experiences. Her sudden heart attack had been a real shock to him. A real call to put childish shit behind him.

So now he was giving serious thought to investments he could make, and making plans to pay some back child support so he could maybe get visitation rights with his daughter. He hadn't seen Phoebe since she was a baby, when Lydia had moved her out to Oklahoma. Phoebe would be almost five now, almost ready to start kindergarten, and Sam hadn't even seen a picture of her in years. He hadn't been ready to be a father when he got Lydia pregnant, but now maybe he was. If it wasn't too late.

Sam was almost grateful when Tom had called. This drama with Mark, whatever it was about, served as a welcome distraction from Sam's sudden shattering realization that, holy shit, he was a grown-up now.

Sam was cruising past the water tower on his way out of town, when he saw something strange. A deputy had pulled somebody over, not that out of the ordinary, but there was also a civilian truck pulled in front of the car, blocking it in. Maybe half a dozen men were swarming around, none of them cops. Then, pulling up close, Sam recognized the car. It was Lana and Michelle's little hybrid thing. He hardly believed his eyes when he saw Lana, pushed down on the hood of the car while Mike Montaño pressed a gun into her back. Michelle was being held by two other guys, and a third guy had grabbed their son Ben.

What the hell was this?

Sam stomped the brakes, right in the middle of the road.

"What the hell are you guys doing?" he called, opening his door. "Let those ladies go!"

"Just keep moving, Sam," one of the men called. Sam saw that it was Hank Patton, a shift manager over at the ethanol plant. "This don't concern you."

"Those are my friends you have there, so it does concern me." Sam stepped down from the cab and walked around the front of his truck. "Now, come on. What the hell is this?"

"We're taking these women." Deputy Mike pulled his gun away from Lana and pointed it at Sam. "They're witches. You don't want to get involved with this."

"Witches?" Sam shook his head, hardly believing what he was hearing, hardly believing that Mike, who he'd considered a friend, actually had a gun pointed at him. "You crazy? You can't do shit like this. You're a cop. Dude, this is *America*."

"Take the kid, get him the hell out of here," Mike said, gun steady on Sam. "But we're going to deal with these bitches. Don't you see what they're doing to this town?"

"Get in my truck, Ben," Sam said. The kid looked terrified. More, Sam realized, for his two moms than for himself.

"But Sam," Ben protested.

"Go!" both Lana and Michelle shouted.

Lou Witzky, the guy holding Ben, let him go. Ben ran over to Sam's truck and climbed up into the cab.

"Okay." Sam gulped. "Now let Lana and Michelle come with me too."

"Ain't going to happen, Sam," said Deputy Mike. His gun arm tensed. "There's other witches out there. We have to show them we mean business. Move along now."

"You're not going to shoot me, Mike," Sam said, hoping to God he was right about that. "We used to play poker together."

"I don't want to do it, Sam, but I—"

"Lana, go!" Sam yelled.

Not stopping to think about what he was doing, Sam lunged forward. Throwing all his considerable weight into his shoulder, he bowled Deputy Mike over and knocked him back against Lana's car. Some of the other men came rushing in to join the fray. Lana managed to jump out of their way. She dove into the cab of Sam's truck, crawled in beside Ben, and slammed the door closed.

Mike got to his feet and raised his gun again. Sam backed away, knocking two other guys over as he retreated towards his truck. Deputy Mike grabbed Sam by the collar and Sam, who had never punched anyone in his life, took a swing at him. Mike fell back again, dodging the blow. Sam scrambled around the front of his truck, Mike hot on his heels.

"We can't leave Michelle!" Lana yelled as Sam slid in behind the wheel. Her cry of protest was half-drowned by gunfire. Two shots rang out. A hole appeared in the roof of the cab. Sam saw the spray of blood before he felt the hot jab of pain in his left arm.

Sam cried out and floored the gas. The big truck leapt forward, the driver's side door flapping closed with the forward motion. A couple of guys had stepped in front of the truck to block their exit, but they leapt out of the way when Sam peeled out onto the road.

"He shot me!" he called, outraged. His arm was sending throbs of alarm to his brain and what felt like gallons of hot blood was pouring down his sleeve. "I didn't think he'd really fuckin' do it!"

"Are you all right?" Lana said.

"No, I'm not all right. He shot me in the arm! Fuckin' asshole!"

Ben sat up and turned around in his seat. "*Mom!*" he screamed, his voice cracking with anguish. Wild and agitated, he clawed the back window open and would have climbed back out onto the truck bed had Lana not physically restrained him. "They took my mom!"

They roared away from the scene. Behind them, Sam heard the receding pop pop pop of men he knew, shooting blindly after his truck.

CHAPTER 51

6:11 PM

MARK WAS BORED out of his mind. He'd spent the past hour or so toggling back and forth between the Nicholas Cage version of *Left Behind* and the Kirk Cameron one, vainly trying to meld them into one coherent narrative. He'd just about given up on this fool's project when he heard Tom's doorbell ring upstairs, followed by loud, shouted voices. One of them sounded like Sam Hansard and—Mark thought he must have been imagining this—another was a woman's voice that sounded like Lana when she was really worked up.

Mark ran up Tom's basement stairs and made it to the top just as Tom opened the door. Mark was astonished and grateful to see Ben standing there.

"Dad!" Ben screamed when Mark emerged. He threw his arms around his father, in his excitement almost knocking him back down the stairs.

"Ben," Mark said, hugging his son tightly. "What are you doing here?"

"They took Mom, Dad! They took her!"

"What?" Mark said. "Who?"

Sam was standing in Tom's entryway, an old bloody t-shirt wrapped around one arm. Lana was there, too, looking utterly shell-shocked. Tom stood between them, his trademark dull scowl tinged with alarm, as if he couldn't understand how so many of his enemies could have gathered in his house at once.

"A bunch of goddamn Sheep Shackers ambushed us," Lana said. "A deputy pulled us over, and it was a trap. They grabbed Chelle and would have got me, too, but Sam came along. He saved our lives. We had to get out of there, though. The fucking Jesus shitheads were shooting at us!"

"Hey!" Tom said. "I won't have that kind of talk in my house, lady."

Lana rounded on Tom and probably would have pounced on him had Sam not stepped between them.

"Come on, guys. Stop," he said. "To be fair, they weren't *all* Shepherd people. Most of them were, but the deputy was Mike Montaño, and he's a Catholic. The asshole shot me!"

"Jesus, Sam," Mark said. "Are you all right?"

"I had a look," Lana said. "The bullet just grazed his arm. He'll need stitches, but he'll be all right."

"Are you sure?" Sam cried. "I'm bleeding like a stuck pig over here."

"We have to go back, Mark," Lana said. "We have to get Chelle. I'm afraid of what they're going to do to her."

"Why would they do take her like that?" said Mark.

"Because they're a bunch of ignorant, hate-filled—"

"No!" Tom said. "They're scared, and they have every reason to be. There are evil forces at work here, in this town."

"Evil forces," Lana scoffed. "It's just goddamn religious hysteria."

"Actually," Mark said. "You're both right."

"What?" Lana turned towards him. "What are you talking about?"

"I have seen some shit, Lana," Mark said. "You would not *believe* the shit I've seen. But Tom, your people are pointed in completely the wrong direction. Can't you talk to them? Tell them they're barking up the wrong tree?"

"I've tried," Tom said. "I've counseled calm. I've asked them to allow the authorities to handle the situation, and I was told that I should stay out of it. They said they didn't want me to get my hands dirty."

"Get your hands dirty?" Lana barked. "Your goddamn rabid lemmings are going to fucking lynch my wife!"

"I'm sorry," Tom said, and he actually looked it. "Things got out of control. We need to call the police. I'm good friends with the sheriff. I'll give him a call and maybe he can—"

"Bates?" Lana shrieked. "No. No fucking way. This whole thing is his fault. And did you miss the part where we said it was one of his goddamn deputies that pulled us over? You call him and Michelle's good as dead."

"You don't understand," Tom said. "He's changed."

"No fucking cops!" Lana's voice hit Tom like a slap, striking him silent.

She took a deep breath and rapped her head back against the wall two times, as if hitting some kind of reset button on the back of her skull. When she spoke again, her voice was calm: "Here's what's going to happen. Sam, go to the hospital in Lincoln, get your arm looked at. Take Ben with you."

"I want to stay with you guys!" Ben protested.

"Don't argue, Ben. It's too dangerous. If you want us to help your mom, you have go with Sam where you'll be safe, so we don't have to worry about protecting you."

Ben seemed to accept this. He gave a little nod and looked to the floor.

"If I go to the emergency room with a gunshot wound, they're going to call the police," Sam said.

"You're right." Lana said. "Just tell them not to call the sheriff's department. Have them call the state police instead. No, wait. Shit. One of those troopers arrested Michelle, he really had it out for her. The Lincoln City Police, maybe? Goddamn, I don't even know who to trust."

"Don't worry," Sam said. "I'll handle that part."

"Thanks, Sam. For everything. You saved my life, and Ben's. I'll never forget that. No matter what happens."

"Ah, man, don't talk like that. You'll get her back. She'll be fine." He walked over and gave her a one-armed hug.

Lana nodded, and swallowed her tears before they could fall. She pointed at Tom. "You. You're going to give me and Mark a car and a gun, and we're going to go get Michelle."

"I'm not comfortable giving you a gun," Tom said.

"Yeah, well I'm not comfortable with my wife getting burned at the stake, motherfucker," Lana snarled.

"Stop, Lana," Mark said. He looked Tom in the eye. "Then come with us."

"No," Lana said. "No way."

"He can help," Mark said. "These are his people. Maybe he can talk them down."

Tom shook his head. "I don't know. You and I, we don't share the same values."

"We share *some* of the same values," Mark said. "Like not wanting to see an innocent woman lynched. Wouldn't you say that's a value we share?"

"Of course." Tom nodded. "Of course it is."

"Then help us, Tom. Please. I mean, what would Jesus do, right?"

Tom bowed his head and closed his eyes for a moment. "Okay."

"Great." Mark smiled. "Now do you have *any* idea where they've taken her?"

"I know exactly where," Tom said. A shadow passed over his face, as if he was realizing for the first time the true implication of the location. "They took her to the water tower."

CHAPTER 52

6:13 PM

Is THIS LOVE? James wondered as he walked along the square with Alice. *Is that what I'm feeling right now?*

The southern horizon was dominated by a black cloud, darker than the freshly fallen night, lit by flashes of red emergency light and occasional orange flickers of the rising flames from the still-burning fuel. To the east, an impossibly huge hunter's moon was on the rise, stained a portentous blood red by all the smoke in the air. All around Alice and James, Bakersfield hummed with trepidation. People were either huddled in their homes with all the lights blazing, or darting about on furtive little missions. Everything was crazy. Lana and Michelle were skipping town with Ben, and nobody knew where Mark was. And still, despite all this, James could only think about how nice Alice's hand felt in his.

Alice stepped on something on the sidewalk that crunched under her shoe. Looking down, she saw it was a little plastic egg in the shape of a jack o'lantern, the detritus of some holiday festivity.

"Wow, I totally forgot it was Halloween," she said, kicking the shattered plastic aside. She stopped walking and looked up at him, rakish in her eyepatch. "Trick or treat."

James bent down and kissed her, an act which had lost none of its electric novelty, even after hundreds of repetitions.

"Mmm," she said, pressing herself close to him. "Treat."

"What, now?" James joked. "Here?"

Alice laughed, deep in her throat, and kissed him back.

They'd made love four times already. Or three and a half, really, the fourth attempt abandoned by mutual agreement halfway through when it became clear that their young bodies needed some time in between to recover. Kissing her now in the crimson moonlight, James felt ready for another go.

They had left the blessed sanctuary of her bedroom because they'd received another strange message from Gemma, who must have recovered her cell phone at some point.

-Hey so I'm sure by now u heard about all the shit we're doing in town. Its fuckin amazing feels like dynamite sex & drugs rolled into 1 but a million x better than any of that boring shit. A's an amazing woman a goddess come 2 earth. Please Alice come be with us before shit gets 2 crazy. I explained to her about James & I think she gets it now so if that's what's stopping u bring him 2.

When Alice, distracted as she was, didn't respond to that right away, Gemma sent a text to James's phone.

-James if you're with Alice have her TEXT me 4 fux sake.

And then, to Alice again:

-God if I didn't know better I'd swear u 2 were fucking.

Finally, Alice had replied:

-All right, freak. We'll come. Where are you now?

-FINALLY, bitch! ☺ Thank goddess. I can't tell u where we're @ right now but we'll be downtown later prob around 6. B there!!!

It was a little past that now, and there was no sign of Gemma or her cohorts, whoever they were.

"What do you think all this is about?" James said.

"I think Gemma's in a cult or something, and she wants us to join," Alice said. "My cousin Kerry found Jesus at summer camp when we were in the eighth grade. All her e-mails to me for a whole year after that sounded just like Gemma's crazy shit."

"She said..." James wasn't even sure if he should say this aloud, it was too fragile a hope. "She said they could cure your cancer."

"Well, it's probably the same kind of deal the Shepherd people have. 'Sure, you can have eternal life. You still have to die first, but after that it's all good.'"

"You're probably right." James let go of her hand and slipped his arm around her waist instead, pulling her close as they walked.

"Oh, shit," she said, stopping suddenly.

"What?"

Alice looked up ahead on the sidewalk. A short, heavyset woman was quickly hobbling towards them on a pair of crutches. She was flanked by two younger boys.

"That's her!" the woman screamed. "She's one of them! Grab her!"

The boys sprinted towards them. As they dashed beneath a streetlight, James saw that one of them was John Gearhart, a Shepherd kid. The other was Jose Collier.

"Hey, faggot," Jose said when he came close, grinning at James.

"You are such an idiot, Jose," James said.

John caught up to Jose a second later, and he grabbed Alice roughly by the arm.

"Let her go!" James cried.

Jose stepped in front of James with the same kind of block he'd use on an opponent on the basketball court, standing in between him and Alice. Two more boys came running up then, seemingly out of nowhere. Vic Frazier and a boy James didn't recognize. Vic grabbed Alice's other arm. The other boy stepped behind James and threw an arm across his throat.

The woman on the crutches reached them, her face twisted into an ugly hateful grimace.

"You lied to me," she accused. "Give that back. It's mine!" She reached out with a clawed hand and snatched Alice's eyepatch off.

Alice wasn't wearing her glass eye underneath. Her pink socket looked naked and exposed beneath the streetlight. Alice's good eye darted around, panicked, rolling towards James with fear and mortification.

"Leave her alone!" James screamed. He tried to squirm out of the chokehold the boy had him in, but it was too tight. "You bitch!"

Sneering with glee, the woman reached out and pulled the wig from Alice's head. Alice's cry of humiliated anguish tore through James's heart.

"There!" the woman cried. "There! Now they all see you for what you are! An ugly, bald, one-eyed *witch*!"

There was a whistle around her neck and she blew it for all it was worth, the shrill sound echoing around all the buildings on the square.

"Tell them to hold up on the hanging," she called. "We got another one!"

CHAPTER 53

6:17 PM

THE SCISSOR LIFT rose more than forty feet into the air when it was fully extended. When Michelle had been standing on the platform at that height, the rope was slack and the noose around her neck was not yet taut. But the sweaty little man beside her on the platform, named Lou something, kept pumping the pneumatic release lever. Every time he did this, the platform dropped a few jerking feet with a hiss of air. Now Michelle, her hands tied behind her back, had to stand on her tip-toes in order to breathe. He was tormenting her with these short drops, and at the same time putting on a show for the crowd below. Building suspense. Making it more of a climax when the big, final drop finally happened.

Michelle was strangely calm. It was strange to her, anyway, how calm she was. She supposed the reason for this was the second, empty, noose dangling beside hers. The one that had been meant for Lana. She was grateful that Lana was safe, and that Ben was safe. God bless Sam Hansard for that. Michelle was grateful that Lana and Ben would have each other for the rest of their long lives, which they would hopefully live far, far away from bloody Bakersfield, Illinois.

It was a beautiful night. The moon was full and red, maybe bigger than she'd ever seen it before. The stars were just beginning to shine. Not too cold, either. If she had to pick a night to die, she'd be hard pressed to find a prettier one than this.

Michelle couldn't tilt her head down anymore, but even when she'd been able to, the bright lights shining up in her face had made it impossible to see the crowd gathered on the ground below. She could hear them, though. An excited murmur, like the buzz before a concert, audible even above the roar of the generators powering the lights. She could sense their eagerness, their hunger to see her die. As much as she'd love to disappoint them, she didn't think that was going to happen.

She wondered what it was going to be like. Wondered what was on the other side.

Lou's walkie squelched. "Hey, Lou," a male voice crackled through.

"Yeah?" Lou brought the little device to his mouth and pressed the little button. "You ready for me to drop her?"

"Hold up just a minute. We got another one."

"No," Michelle moaned, something inside of her breaking. "Oh no, no."

Lou winked at her and flashed a gruesome smile.

"Is it the black bitch?" he asked.

"Negative," came the reply, and though Michelle knew this meant another innocent woman was going to die alongside her, she nonetheless thanked God that it wasn't Lana. "It's some younger chick. Bald, only got one eye. Ugly as sin."

"Oh, Jesus," Michelle cried. "Alice."

Lou glanced up at her. "You want me to drop this one now, and then come down and get the other one, or should we swing 'em together?"

"I'm inclined to think two at once is better," the other man answered. "Let's hang 'em side by side."

"Roger that," Lou said. He raised the platform a couple of feet. Michelle felt the pressure ease on her throat.

"You got a little reprieve there, honey," Lou said, slipping the noose from her neck.

From the ground below, the crowd booed and jeered with disappointment.

Lou hit the lever and the platform sank smoothly to the ground.

"Michelle Delany," a bullhorn-amplified voice called up to her as they descended. "We've captured one of your disciples. A young girl. Maybe she's an innocent you led astray. So I'll make a deal with you. If you confess everything, confess to being a witch who has consorted with Satan, we'll let this girl go. Otherwise you two will hang together and so will every other witch we find."

"Don't do it!" Alice screamed from below. Michelle couldn't see her yet. The platform had descended past where the bright lights were focused, but Michelle's eyes were still dazzled, and she was night-blind.

"Don't you dare make some bullshit confession, Michelle!" Alice yelled. "Don't give these fucks the satisfaction. I'm ready to die, I've been ready for months. Goddamn ropes don't scare me, I've got fucking cancer!"

Michelle blinked the bright splotches away. The crowd was not as big as she had supposed. There were fewer than twenty men and women out there eager to see her die. She could see Alice now, squirming wildly against the tall teen boy who was holding her. She looked so small and fragile with no wig, and her naked eye socket exposed. James was right behind her, pale and defeated, grasped tightly by two other boys.

The lift had collapsed completely and they were on the ground. Michelle saw that the man with the bullhorn was a big, burly guy with a mustache. She'd seen him around town, but didn't know his name.

"What's your answer, witch?" he screamed through the horn into her face, the amplification only for the benefit of the crowd. "Will you confess?"

Michelle was afraid that her mouth was too dry, and that her voice would be too weak, but her words came out loud and clear and strong.

"Suck my dick," she said.

Loud jeers, tinged with bloodlust, welled forth from the assembly.

"Yes!" Alice cheered, grinning wildly.

"All right, we gave you a chance to save this girl, at least," the guy screamed into the bullhorn. "Now her death's on your head, too."

The boy holding Alice dragged her up onto the platform beside Michelle. He stood behind her, grasping her tight.

"As our Lord commanded in the book of Exodus, we shall not suffer these witches to live!" bullhorn guy pronounced, to the cheers of the small crowd.

The scissor lift gave a lurch and began to rise.

"I'm sorry, Alice," Michelle said.

"Don't be," Alice said. She was actually smiling. "This beats the hell out of dying in bed in some cancer ward. I get to go out on the happiest day in my life."

"I love you, James!" she shouted.

Down below, James was looking up at them with horrified impotence. But as soon as Alice spoke those words, his face changed. It grew harder, seemed to age ten years in the space of seconds. He snarled and spun around, pulling free of one of the boys holding him. He turned to the other one and butted his forehead into the guy's face.

James bounded towards the lift and scrambled up the scissor arms as they unfolded. He threw one arm up onto the platform, dangling from the side as it rose towards the makeshift gallows above.

CHAPTER 54

6:21 PM

"HONESTLY, MARK," LANA said, turning in her seat to face him. "How much of that shit do you think you hallucinated?"

"I don't know," Mark said. "It all seemed pretty real to me."

"You said yourself they dosed you with some kind of drug. Maybe they put on a production for you, and you were tripping so hard your mind made it real."

"I guess that's possible, yeah, but..."

"I mean, you can't just skin a person like that," said Lana. "And then some dead lady comes out of the ground and slips the skin on like a jumpsuit? That sounds like the kind of shit you'd make up for one of your books."

"I know it does, okay? But *something* happened. Something is *still* happening. What about all the craziness in town Tom was talking about?"

Tom glanced up into the rear-view mirror, catching Mark's eye. His expression was dull and unreadable.

"Religious superstition," Lana said. "Mass hysteria, snowballing out of control."

They were coming into town now, the water tower visible just ahead, lit up from beneath by some kind of spotlight. Strange fluttering shadows crawled up the side.

"I'd love nothing more than for you to be right about that, Lana. All I'm saying is, be prepared in case you're wrong and...oh shit."

"What?'

A sheriff's department cruiser was pulled off to the side of the road. As soon as Tom blew past it, the car flashed its red-and-blues and gave a quick blast of the siren.

Tom glanced up in the mirror, and a weight seemed to lift from his face. He immediately pulled over.

"What the fuck are you doing?" Lana barked. "Keep going!"

"It's the sheriff," Tom said. "I told you, he's a friend of mine. He can help us."

"Jesus, you're stupid."

"Lady, I warned you about taking his name in vain."

"Oh my fucking God!"

Mark shriveled down in the backseat, trying to make himself as small and inconspicuous as possible. Bates stepped up to the driver's side and Tom rolled down the window.

"Hey, Tom," the sheriff said mildly, glancing curiously into the car. "What'd you bring me? Holy cripes, Mark goddamn Davies *and* Lana Delany? Jesus, Tom. It ain't even close to Christmas yet. Damn, I'm going to have to get you something *nice* this year."

"Sheriff, there are people up there at the water tower," Tom said. "They're lynching Michelle Delany. They're going to hang her."

"Yep, I know all about it," Bates said, waving his bandaged right hand towards the tower. "I've been watching them through my binoculars for the past twenty minutes or so. Actually, they got a second little lady now. Looks like they're goin' for a twofer."

"Aren't you going to stop them?"

"I reckon I'll have to bust up that necktie party. But I'm going to let 'em finish up first. Simpler that way. Murder's an easier case to make than attempted murder any day."

"No!" Lana screamed from the passenger seat.

Bates leaned in and tipped his hat at her. "Howdy, ma'am. You mind stepping out of the car? You and your friend there in the back seat, too."

"What are you going to do?" Tom said.

"Well," the sheriff said. "I was thinking about driving them way out into the country, putting a couple bullets in each of their heads and burying them in a ditch someplace. Unless you got a better idea."

"Why would you say something like that, Nathanial?"

"Nathanial? Yeah, about that." Bates chuckled. "Nathanial's dead as fuckin' dirt, Tom. Nate's back. Big time, baby. And you and I need to have a long conversation about getting our business up and running again. So why don't you help me get these two shitheads into my car and we'll talk?"

"No," Tom said. "I'm not going to let you kill them."

"It ain't a matter of you letting me do anything. It's gonna happen, and I'm sure you don't want me shooting a bunch of holes in your nice new car. Getting blood and brains and shit all over your seats. That stuff's a mad bitch to clean up. Trust me, I know."

"I don't want to go back to the way things were," Tom said, almost a whisper.

"Well, that's a shame, Tom," Bates said. "It really is."

The sheriff tore open the back door. Mark scrambled back, but Bates grabbed one kicking leg and dragged him out, spilling him onto the hard ground.

"Get up," he growled.

Mark struggled to his feet, holding his hands up, his mind grasping for any possible scenario where he wasn't about to die.

The sheriff drew his gun with his right, bandaged, hand. This obviously caused him some pain, because he switched the weapon to his left hand. He looked over at Mark, squinting.

"What the hell are you wearing, boy?"

Mark glanced down at himself. He still had on the t-shirt Tom had lent him the night before. A big grinning monkey in the middle of a Ghostbusters-style red-slash logo, over the slogan "Don't monkey around with evolution."

"That is a stupid shirt," the sheriff said. "Get over there by my car."

"Okay," Mark said, his hands still up. He stepped backwards towards the police cruiser, not wanting to turn his back on Bates.

"Look," Mark said. "I know you and I have had some issues in the past, but..."

"You pulled a gun on me," Bates said. "Twice. You know how many other motherfuckers have done that even once and lived?"

"I'm sorry about that. I really am. And I'll do whatever you say, but first can you please go help Michelle?" Mark had backed into the police car.

"Do you know what your mom and her fuckin' Malovo buddies did to me?"

"No."

"They *fucked my head*!" Bates screamed. He jabbed the gun in Mark's direction, and for a second, Mark was sure he was going to fire. "They went in there and rewired shit, and turned me into some kinda walking pussy for five months."

"I'm sorry about that, too."

"Not yet you ain't. Turn around."

Mark did as he was told. Bates shoved him forward, bending him over the hood of the car. Behind his back, the sheriff struggled to cuff him. He was having a hard time doing it with his wounded hand, though, while still holding the gun on Mark with his left. Mark heard the cuffs fall to the pavement with metallic clanking.

"God damn it," Bates swore.

"Sheriff!" Tom shouted from behind them. He had stepped out of his car and was walking towards them, his gun clenched in one outstretched arm. "Let him go!"

"What the fuck are you doing, Tom?" Bates said. "Get back in your car."

At that moment, Tom's car peeled away up the road, making it impossible for him to comply. Lana was at the wheel, of course. Mark couldn't really blame her for abandoning him. In fact, he was glad she was going to help Michelle. But still, this left him in a pretty bad spot.

Bates pulled open the back of his cruiser and shoved Mark inside. He slammed the door, then turned his gun on Tom.

"Put it down, son," Bates called. He took a few steps in Tom's direction. "You don't want to do this. We had a good thing going and we can get it back."

"No, Nathanial."

"Don't call me that."

"I know you're still in there, Nathanial," Tom said. "Don't let him win. You were a good man. You can still be a good man."

"Shut the fuck up, Tom."

Mark wasn't sure which of them fired first, the shots were nearly simultaneous. Two loud bangs, two bright flashes of light, and both Tom and Sheriff Bates fell in the street.

"Shit!" Mark screamed.

He blindly grasped for the door handle, but there were of course none in the back of the cruiser. The front seat was partitioned off from the back with bulletproof glass, reinforced with heavy-duty metal mesh. He was trapped.

On the road up ahead, the fallen lump in the street that had been Sheriff Bates began to stir. He was still alive, struggling to his feet.

"Shit!" Mark screamed again. Bracing his back against the seat, he kicked out with all the strength in his legs, trying to break through the partition. It was solid as a brick wall.

Then the driver's door opened. Somebody dressed all in black slid in behind the wheel.

"Hi, Mark." Ellie Tarwater turned and flashed him a strange, uneasy smile. "You want to go someplace and get a drink with me."

That wasn't a question. Ellie put the police car into gear and floored it, hitting the lights and the sirens. She tore away up the street, swerving and narrowly missing the sheriff, who was slowly rising to his knees.

CHAPTER 55

6:26 PM

J AMES PULLED HIMSELF onto the platform as it rose to perhaps half its full
height. The balding man working the lift controls kicked out at James,
stomping his heavy work boot down on his arm. James almost lost his grip,
almost fell, but Michelle threw her weight sideways. Her hands were still
tied behind her back, but she managed to knock the sweaty guy aside with
her hip. He was already off balance, and Michelle sent him screaming over
the edge, headfirst into the ground twenty feet below.

James struggled to his feet. Jose backed away against the far railing,
his arm locked hard across Alice's throat.

"Get any closer and I'll throw her off," Jose cried, eyes darting back
and forth between James and Michelle.

James saw that Jose could do it, easily. Alice was so light, he could just
pick her up and toss her off the side with hardly any effort. James tensed,
his teeth clenched and his heart pounding. For a second, the four people
on the platform stood there, frozen. Below them, the people on the ground
howled with rage, their words devolving into a rabid, incoherent babble.

Alice's lips were turning blue and her good eye was bulging. Jose was
choking her. James doubted he even realized he was holding her so tight.
Jose was scared, maybe even more scared than James was. He might choke
her to death out of pure panic.

Alice clenched her fist. She flashed James, for what reason he could
not in the moment fathom, a thumbs-up. Then she jabbed her thumb up
and back, gouging Jose in his right eye.

Jose cried out and released Alice, his hand going by reflex to his
wounded eye. Alice, off balance, fell against him, knocking him backwards.

For a second, James thought they were both going to go over. He dove forward, clutched Alice by the arm, and pulled her towards him.

Jose stumbled back, reaching blindly out, but his fingers found nothing to grasp. He flipped over the thin railing and toppled off the side of the platform. A long, terrible second later, James heard the thud as Jose hit the ground.

Alice threw her arms around James and held him tight.

"God," she choked. "I can't believe you used to have a crush on that guy."

"Is he all right?" Michelle asked.

James hazarded a glance down at the ground. Jose was moving, but James didn't like the odd, twisted angles of his limbs. On the other side, two women knelt beside the man Michelle had knocked over. He was on his back, either unconscious or dead, with a smear of blood around his mouth.

Looking down, James saw another man crawling over to the base of the lift. The man was reaching for a big red button, labeled with letters that James could make out even from this height. EMERGENCY RELEASE.

The man slammed the button and with a loud hiss of air, the platform sank to the ground again. The crowd pressed in, eager for the three of them to be delivered into their grasp.

From across the gravel lot came the sound of a roaring engine and someone laying on a horn. A car barreled towards them, heedless of the thronging mob. People scrambled to get out of the way, but not everyone made it. James saw at least two people side-swiped and knocked over, and one woman was mowed completely down. The car pulled to a stop right beside the scissor lift. The passenger door popped open.

"Get in!" Lana screamed from inside.

The three of them scrambled off the platform and into the waiting car. James was the last one in, climbing in behind Michelle and slamming the door closed behind him.

The people immediately fell on the car. A brick hurled at the windshield lodged halfway in the safety glass, obliterating the view with starry cracks. On both sides of the car, men swung baseball bats, breaking out the side windows. Glass flew about the interior in explosive meteor showers of flying shards.

"Go!" Michelle screamed to Lana. "Drive!"

Though blind, Lana hit the gas. The car leapt forward a few hopeful yards, and then slammed into the scissor lift.

Screaming curses, Lana threw the car into reverse. Another car had pulled behind them, though, blocking them in.

They were trapped.

CHAPTER 56

6:28 PM

Ｅｌｌｉｅ ｆｌｅｗ ｔｈｅ sheriff's car, lights and sirens screaming, past the water tower on her way into town. The tower was illuminated from below by two big spotlights, but Mark couldn't tell what was going on over there. He just saw a mass of people and, as Ellie drove close, two long ropes dangling from the side of the tower, looped at the bottom with what looked to be nooses. That was certainly ominous, but at least no one was hanging from them. Yet.

"Missy and Lana are over there," Mark said. "We have to help them."

"Don't worry," Ellie said, eyes steady on the road ahead. She sounded calm and happy. "It's being taken care of."

"Taken care of? What does that mean?"

"You'll see."

"Where are you taking me?" he asked.

"We have a temporary headquarters set up," Ellie said.

"Are you going to try to kill me again?"

"No." Ellie laughed, as if that was in any way funny. "Adaleen is reconsidering your place in our circle. She is a reasonable woman, you know. We've been talking to her about you. We even read her some of your book."

"What did she..." Mark, even with the million dire things on his mind, couldn't help but wonder what kind of opinion a two-hundred-year-old witch might have of his writing. "Did she like it?"

"Oh, she thought it was hilarious," Ellie said. "She laughed so hard we thought she was going to split her stitches."

278

"Glad I could amuse her." Comedy wasn't been exactly what he'd been going for, but Mark supposed any reaction short of murderous rage had to count as a positive review.

Ellie killed the lights and sirens as she came up on the square. She pulled into a parking space in front of Wolfy's Tavern. The bar's front window was fogged over, so it was impossible to see inside. The neon signs advertising Budweiser and video gaming had been rendered into smears of vivid color that swirled and pulsed beneath the blurring frosted glass.

"Temporary headquarters?" Mark said. "This doesn't seem like your kind of joint."

"We've done some remodeling." Ellie turned to face him. "So if I let you out, you're going to be cool. You won't try anything stupid. You'll just come inside and talk to everybody."

"Sure," Mark said, answering her non-questions.

Ellie let him out of the back seat and he followed her into the tavern. She'd been right about the remodeling. The interior of Wolfy's had been transformed. The smell was the first thing Mark noticed. The stale beer and urinal cake had been replaced by a misty spice scent, like ancient incense wafting in on an ocean breeze. The room was also darker than it had been the last time Mark had been inside, lit now by the hundreds of candles, which lined every flat surface in the room.

The confederate flag had been pulled down from the wall, replaced by Roberta's moon mural. The painting was clear and vivid even in the dim room, as if lit from within. Mark saw now that the woman with her naked thighs wrapped so shamelessly around the moon's face was clearly meant to be Adaleen.

Roberta, Sally and Gemma sat on stools at the bar. All three were dressed in sheer and shimmering robes of pearly white silk. Wolfy stood behind the bar, still and impassive, staring into space. Mark didn't see Adaleen anywhere.

"Mark!" Roberta walked over and took both his hands. "I'm so glad you came back."

"It wasn't really by choice," he said.

"That's all right," Roberta beamed. "I'm sure you'll decide to stay with us when you hear of all the wondrous things we've done, and still plan to do."

"Hey." Ellie tugged on the sleeve of Roberta's robe. "Why didn't anybody tell me we're doing the white robes already?"

"We're about to begin," Roberta said. "Go get changed, dear."

Ellie, frowning, hurried off into a back room. Roberta led Mark over to the bar.

"Gemma has something to say to you, Mark," Roberta said.

The teen girl flashed her dark eyes up at Mark, then nervously looked away.

"I'm sorry I tried to stab you," she whispered.

"What's a little dagger in the heart between friends, right?"

Gemma didn't seem to catch the sarcasm. "Hey, have you heard from James, or Alice?" she said, looking back up at him. "They were supposed to meet us on the square, but now neither one's answering their texts. I'm a little worried."

"I've been locked in a basement all day," Mark said. "I don't know anything. Do you think they're okay?"

"I don't know," Gemma said, looking genuinely concerned.

"Jesus," Mark hissed. It seemed everyone he loved or cared about was now in mortal danger. All because of whatever game these women were playing. At least Ben was safe. Mark hoped so, anyway.

"Nice shirt," Sally said to him. "So you're not into monkeying with evolution?"

"Yeah, well, beggars running naked through the woods can't really be choosers with their t-shirt messages," Mark said. "Tom Peters gave me this shirt. I always thought the guy was kind of an asshole, but you know what? He clothed and sheltered me in my most desperate hour. Then, just a couple minutes ago, he saved my life *again*. And as a reward for all his Christian decency, Tom got shot down in the street like a mad dog. He's probably dead."

"I'm sorry, Mark." Sally grabbed his arm "I really am."

He looked her in the eye. Sally had been transformed. The woman he'd eaten dinner with the night before had been nervy and withdrawn, turned within herself under protective layers of irony and self-deprecation that had been built up so long they'd calcified into a mask. Sally looked taller without her defensive slouch, but there was more to it than that. She exuded a new confidence, an awareness of her power. Mark didn't want to say prettier, because that was reductive, but Sally had become more fully herself. It radiated from her like a glow. Her newfound self-assurance suited her well, Mark thought, if you didn't think too hard about where it came from.

"What's with your dad?" he asked.

Wolfy stood like a redneck waxwork behind the bar, arms hanging loose at his side. His face was blank and emotionless, except for his sharp blue eyes, which blinked and watered and darted around with horror.

"Entranced," Sally said. "It was a simple spell."

"You did that to your own father?"

"Come on," Sally gave him a look. "I don't have to tell you what he did to me. Just assume the worst, and you'll be right. Fucker deserves everything that's coming to him."

"He'll make you any drink you want," Ellie said. She'd just returned from the back, changed into the same pearly white robe the others wore. Like the rest of them, Ellie was resplendent with beauty now, glowing with power. "Hey, Wolfy, make me a piña colada."

Wolfy went to work, mixing and pouring like a bartending automaton, his motions precise and mechanical. His expression was slack as a zombie's, but with terror in his frozen blue eyes. A minute later, he set a frosted white glass on the bar in front of Ellie.

She took a sip and frowned. "I guess it was too much to ask to hypnotize him into being a *good* bartender. I don't even think that's coconut."

Mark turned to Roberta. "So where's your boss lady?"

"Preparing for our next invocation," she answered. "It's a particularly complex one."

"Is this the one that's going to help Missy and Lana?" Mark said. "Ellie said you have a plan for that."

"As a matter of fact, Mark, yes it is."

"Good. But tell me the truth, all right? Missy was always a part of this, wasn't she? You set her up from the beginning."

"We have the utmost respect for Michelle. Midwifery is womankind's oldest and most noble calling. So, yes. I gave Sandy the money to pay for Michelle's services," Roberta said. "Even after it became clear Sandy was unwilling to bear the vessel for Adaleen's rebirth, I didn't want to cast her off with no one to help."

"So what happened there?" Mark asked. "Sandy decided she wanted her baby to be a normal baby and not a reincarnated witch?"

"In the simplest terms, yes. The maternal instinct is very strong, after all. But, unfortunately, the spell was already partially complete. We had induced changes to the fetus's physical form, to make it a more conducive host."

"You mean a deformed little mutant."

"Sandy went to a doctor and obtained an ultrasound," Roberta said, ignoring Mark's comment. "She learned that the baby would be unlikely to survive. So we offered her a way out. I supplied her with a simple brew that would expel the child, and she summoned Michelle to oversee the purging. Regretfully, it went badly."

"Yeah, it fuckin' did," Mark said. "But that was part of the plan, too. Wasn't it? 'A sacrifice is always necessary.' Your own daughter wasn't enough. You had to offer up Sandy and Missy, too."

"Think of it this way, Mark," Roberta said, growing visibly frustrated. "What we wish to accomplish requires a tremendous amount of energy. The rage and fear these people have is only that. Energy. Which we can harness and channel and turn back against them. So, yes, it became necessary to supply a martyr."

"Aren't martyrs usually willing?"

"You don't understand," Roberta said. "Maybe you're not capable of understanding."

"I understand perfectly," Mark said. "But what I want to know is, where's it all going to end? What's this grand thing you're going to accomplish that will justify all the death and destruction you've caused?"

"I'm glad you asked me that," Roberta said, regaining her composure. "That's the question we need to answer when we tell the world what we've done here." She closed her eyes for a moment, choosing her words carefully. "In nature, female and male energy is perfectly balanced. But society is out of step with nature. The scales are tipped entirely towards masculine energy. Men rule the world, with their killing guns and their raping cocks and their fucking murderous God-the-father. They're choking the planet with their corporate greed and their constant wars, which are all just expressions of a patriarchal need for domination. This town, Bakersfield, is a perfect microcosm of all of that. With our idiot mayor and our murdering sheriff and the blind ignorance of the male-led churches. And Malovo, the ultimate expression of male, white corporate greed and destruction. Poisoning our water, our food, the air we breathe. Turning our sacred places into golf courses. Holding the people of this town in economic slavery. Using them as guinea pigs for their experiments. The life, health and safety of this town and her people are secondary to Malovo's insatiable hunger for profit."

"Maybe it's just a personal bias," Mark said. "But I've always viewed Malovo as a matriarchal organization."

"Don't make the mistake of believing that your mother is anything more than a servant."

"Whatever." Mark shrugged. "You still haven't told me what the point of all this is."

"To tear down these male institutions, and replace them with true feminine wisdom and power. To turn Bakersfield into a counterweight to the masculine violence and hatred of the rest of the world. A shining beacon for powerful women everywhere. A seed planted that will grow into a forest of—"

"Ain't that a load of happy horseshit?"

They all turned. Adaleen had stepped from the back room, dressed in the same lustrous white robes the rest of them wore. The gossamer silk clung like mist to the curves of her stolen body. Lizzy's skin had been loose and ill-fitting when Mark had last seen Adaleen, right after she was reborn, but she fully inhabited the flesh now. She had been transfigured into the most beautiful woman Mark had ever seen, without question. Her beauty was fearsome, though, and terrible, like an evil queen who would demand the blinding of any of her subjects who dared lay eyes upon her.

She stalked across the candle-lit room like a predatory cat.

"What'd I tell you about spoutin' that crap?" she said, her old woman's croak jarringly at odds with the youthful splendor of her body.

"I'm sorry, beloved mother." Roberta, chagrined, cast her eyes down.

Mark noticed that all of Bell's Angels were only paying quick, furtive glances at their mistress. As if Adaleen blazed with an irresistibly beautiful light that hurt their eyes if they looked for more than a second.

"You have that bowl I told you to bring?"

"Yes, beloved mother."

"Fetch it," Adaleen demanded.

"Yes."

Roberta hurried off. Adaleen stepped behind Mark's bar stool and rested one hand on his shoulder. Every cell in his body went on high alert at the contact. His body and mind flushed with heated arousal and icy revulsion at the same time.

"Did you bring what I asked you to bring, Sally?" Adaleen asked, her voice a bit warmer than it had been when she'd addressed Roberta.

"Yes." Sally gulped. "Beloved mother."

"Fetch it too, then."

Sally stepped behind the bar and picked up what looked like a spigot attached to a hollow spike, like something used to tap a maple tree.

"Do you want me to do it?" Sally asked.

"Yes, Sally," Adaleen hissed, close to Mark's ear. Her hand slipped inside his collar, fingers tracing the nape of his neck, her thumb caressing his ear lobe. Mark shuddered helplessly. "It has to be you."

Sally nodded. She unbuttoned her father's denim shirt. Wolfy remained expressionless as his daughter pulled his shirt open. Just above Wolfy's heart, nearly obscured by the dense curly white hair, was a faded tattoo of a howling wolf. Sally pressed the sharp hollow point of the tap against the wolf's throat. From beneath the bar, she found a hammer.

"Drive it deep," Adaleen said. "Gotta penetrate his heart. Just like he done to you."

Sally nodded. She was grim, determined. Her eyes watered only slightly.

"It's for your own good," she whispered, in a voice that perhaps only her father was meant to hear. "I'll make a real woman out of you."

Sally struck the tap hard with the hammer and drove it through her father's rib cage with one clanging strike. Wolfy's sky blue eyes froze a wintry gray when the spike pierced his heart.

Mark looked away, over at his own terrified reflection in the back bar mirror. Strangely, he couldn't see Adaleen in the reflection. Instead of an imposingly beautiful woman standing behind him, he saw only a dark shadow, wrapped about his shoulders like a black cloak. Though the shadow was only vaguely human-shaped, it had gleaming blood-red eyes and a grinning toothy mouth. Adaleen's dark reflection flashed Mark a knowing wink.

Sally picked up a shot glass from the back bar and raised it to the tap at her father's breast. She turned the knob to open the valve, and filled the glass with her father's heart-blood.

"Don't spill none now," Adaleen implored, her breath close and hot in Mark's ear.

Very carefully, Sally filled four more glasses with blood from the tap. She set them all on a tray.

Adaleen chuckled. "Good, girl," she said. "All right, we're done with that old fucker."

Sally turned back to her father.

"Lie down, Daddy," she said. "You can die now."

Wolfy obediently fell to the floor.

Adaleen took her hand off of Mark and stepped away. He took a deep gasp of air. He hadn't even realized he'd been holding his breath the entire time she'd been touching him.

On the floor across the room, Roberta had placed a large metal bowl, perhaps twelve inches in diameter and just as tall. The bowl had been painted a pale pink. Plain block lettering spelled out "Bakersfield" around the side. Right next to the name of the town was a reproduction of King Chip, the town's crowned cow turd mascot. The bowl looked exactly like a smaller, lidless version of the water tower's reservoir tank.

"Gather 'round," Adaleen called.

The angels knelt in a semi-circle around the metal bowl. Mark stood a small distance away, watching curiously.

Adaleen struck the side of the bowl with a wooden gong, grasping it by a leather-wrapped handle. The bowl rang out with a deep toll. Adaleen ran the wooden mallet in counter-clockwise circles around the outer rim of the bowl, producing a ringing harmonic tone. Each of the women sang along, deep in her throat, with steady moaning hums. The chorus of human voice and resounding metal filled the room with resonating vibrations that caused every mug and glass bottle on the bar to rattle and shake. Mark felt the ambient ringing in the pit of his stomach.

The empty bowl seemed to fill with churning black mist, like roiling storm clouds. Lightning flashed deep inside and the strange reverberating frequencies took on a rumbling undertone, like rolling thunder.

"Now," Adaleen said.

Each of the angels picked up a glass and knocked back a shot of Wolfy's blood. They leaned forward and each sprayed her mouthful, expelling crimson mist into the swirling clouds within the bowl.

Adaleen grasped the rim of the bowl in her hand, silencing the tone at once. She licked her bloody lips with a lascivious relish, but the other angels used cloth napkins to daintily wipe their mouths.

Mark glanced into the bowl. The clouds were gone. The inside was clean, the shiny polished brass gleaming with reflected candle-light.

"Where did the blood go?" he asked.

CHAPTER 57

6:33 PM

A LICE HUDDLED IN the back seat. James had his arms around her, shielding her from the flying glass and the angry jabbing prods of the baseball bats. Men were reaching into the front seat, grabbing at Lana and Michelle, who fended them off the best they could with punches and bites and scratches.

Dave Muldoon reached in through the shattered window and unlocked the back door. He wrenched the door open and crawled halfway inside, grabbing James by the hair. From the other side, Vic Frazier snatched Alice. The two boys tore Alice and James apart, pulling them each out through opposite doors.

Vic tossed Alice to the ground and pinned her there, pressing her down with all his weight. He was on the wrestling team, solid and muscular.

"Ugly fuckin' witch!" he growled into her face.

Alice hawked and spat, a glob of phlegm striking Vic just below his right eye. He let out an enraged roar and wrapped his hands around Alice's throat.

If that turns out to be my last breath, Alice thought, *then I spent it well.*

A strange ringing sound filled the air. At first Alice thought it was just inside her head, some effect of oxygen starvation, but as it grew louder, it was clear that Vic was hearing it too. He rolled off her, throwing his hands over his ears. The high-pitched ringing peal sounded like somebody running a finger along the rim of a crystal wine glass, only amplified a million times.

Alice sat up, gasping air. The sound reverberated through her, every bone in her body oscillating with sympathetic vibrations. All around her, the members of the lynch mob were staggering around, clutching their skulls. The sound kept getting louder. The vibrations caused the cracked windows of the car to shatter completely, raining to the ground with a million glittering shards.

Looking up, Alice saw one of the strangest sights she'd ever seen. The water tower was ringing like a massive bell. The tower was the source of the sound, somehow, the entire metal structure resonating at a high frequency.

"James!" she tried to cry, but her voice was muffled by the pervasive tone.

She saw him on the other side of the car and ran to him. Lana and Michelle had climbed out of the car, too. The four of them exchanged glances, the sound too all-encompassing for words. No one seemed to notice them escaping. All their persecutors were staring in horror up at the pulsating tower, screaming in vain against the deafening reverberations.

In the sky above the tower, the full rising moon was blurred, as if it too was vibrating at the same infernal frequency. It took a second for Alice to realize that it was not the moon that was ringing, it was her eye quivering in its buzzing socket, all the bones of her skull rattling along the radiating clang.

An ear-wrenching metallic screech rose up beneath the steady ring, as the reservoir cracked from the stress of the unnatural vibrations. The thin fissure extended from the grinning turd's arm, as if he was casting lightning from his shitty little fingertips.

The leak began as dripping seepage from the thin slash, but the massive pressure soon burst through the metallic skin. Liquid sprayed out in a spurting torrent over the people below, but it wasn't water that erupted from the side of the tower.

It was blood.

Red rain poured down upon the already fearful crowd, sending them into paroxysms of terror as they were drenched in the warm crimson fluid. The ringing bell tone came to a sudden halt, and their screams rose up to fill the silent void. The ghastly downpour was inky black in the moonlight, filling the air with a coppery stink, dripping thick and salty into their wide-open screaming mouths.

Blood filled Alice's one eye, turning her vision into blurred red shadows. Disgusted, she wiped it away.

Denise, the woman from the gift shop who'd torn away Alice's eyepatch and her wig, was hobbling around on her crutches right in front of her. Blood dripped from Denise's stringy hair. Her glasses were coated with gore.

"No!" she screamed to the heavens as she blindly tried to stagger away from the blood-gushing tower. "No! No!"

Denise's rubber-tipped crutches slipped in a gory mud puddle and she fell gracelessly face-first into the red muck, still gurgling bubbly denials into the blood-soaked ground.

"Come on," James yelled.

He grabbed Alice's hand. The two of them ran away from the terrible bloody scene, following Lana and Michelle, who were already sprinting across the lot.

CHAPTER 58

6:38 PM

"So that's it?" Mark said. "You spit some blood into a bowl and they're safe?"

"Oh, your people are safe, white boy," Adaleen said. "Don't worry none about that."

She stood, rising gracefully from her knees. The other angels followed suit. Adaleen smiled, with the cool, regal forbearance of a queen well pleased with her subjects.

"How you doin', daughters?" she said. "Tired of this shit yet?"

"No, beloved mother." Sally, Ellie and Gemma each offered up denials.

Roberta, though, said: "I am growing weary, beloved mother. Not in spirit, but in body. It's been a long day."

Adaleen's smile fell away. "And it's gonna be a longer night still," she snapped. "We got lots to do 'fore we see the sun. Folks gonna wake up tomorrow in a whole new town. What's the matter, old woman? You sayin' you can't keep up with these young girls?"

"No, beloved mother." Roberta cast her eyes down. "I'm sorry. I'll be fine."

"Come here."

Adaleen grasped both of Roberta's hands in hers. A strange, ozone smell wafted up from the contact, as if an electrical charge had passed between the two women.

Roberta's eyes went wide. A look of staggering ecstasy passed over her face, like she'd been simultaneously granted a massive orgasm and an injection of medical-grade cocaine.

"Weary now, are ya?" Adaleen said.

"No, beloved mother," Roberta said, with a beatific smile. "Thank you. Thank you so much. I feel twenty years younger."

"Heh," Roberta croaked. "That still makes you the oldest bitch up in here. Any of you young 'uns want a shot of that?"

The other three gathered eagerly into a circle, Sally and Ellie each taking one of Adaleen's hands, with Gemma between them. There was the same crackling, smoking jolt, and the three angels let out simultaneous gasps.

"Shit, that felt good," Gemma said. "Oh, God. Thank you, beloved mother. So much."

Sally and Ellie gushed their thanks as well, each of them looking flushed and sweaty.

"That should keep you going for a while," Adaleen said. "Our next incant's gonna be a good one. This is gonna be the one that takes over that factory y'all were telling me about, where they make corn into gasoline." She shook her head at this marvel of the modern world. "I'm gonna need a token to work it, though. Four Christian tongues."

"What?" Roberta cried.

"Find somebody you know to be a Christian," Adaleen said, annoyed at having to explain herself. "Cut their Christin' tongue out of their head, and bring it to me."

"But, beloved mother..."

"They ain't hard to find," Adaleen said. "Hell, you can't take a piss in this town without splashin' it on some Christian's shoes."

"It's not that, beloved mother. It's just—"

"It's just you ain't got a taste for blood," Adaleen said. "And you're startin' to think you bit off more'n you can chew when you woke my ass up. You thought it would be all crystals and candles and drawin' down the moon and all that white witch bullshit. That ain't me. This bitch wants power, and if you side with me, you can bask in all the glory I got to share. Otherwise, you can hang with the rest of 'em. So I expect you back here in one hour and if you ain't got a Christian tongue for me, I'll take yours instead."

"Yes, beloved mother," Roberta whispered.

"Any of you young 'uns got a problem fetchin' me what I require?"

No one answered her or met her eye.

"Good," Adaleen said. "Then go. I'm gonna stay here and have a chat with white boy. Unless..." She tilted her head curiously up at Mark. "You a Christian, honey?"

"No," Mark said.

"Thought I could save one of y'all a trip, but it looks like white boy's got at least a little bit of sense in his head. Go on now, daughters. Hurry back soon."

The four angels hesitantly filed out of the bar, leaving Mark alone with Adaleen.

"Come back here, boy," she said. "I got something I want to show you."

Mark, though he was very afraid, followed Adaleen into the back. Down a short hallway, past the bar, was a small office with a desk, probably where Wolfy did his books. A computer monitor lay cracked and broken on the floor, no doubt swept aside by Adaleen, who would have no use for such a device. The Confederate flag that had been hanging on the wall in the other room now covered most of the desk, along with a pair of scissors. Several strips had already been cut from the flag.

"I hate the sight of that goddamn flag," Adaleen explained. "So I'm cutting it up for our moon-rags."

"Very poetic," Mark said. "Is that what you wanted to show me?"

"No." Adaleen knelt in a corner of the room and picked something up from near the floor. "Looky what I found."

She stood up and showed Mark what was in her hand. A largish black spider, with thin legs and a round, shiny body. She grasped it lightly between her fingers, turning it over so he could see the red hourglass on its belly. "You know what this is?"

"Black widow," Mark said, flinching back when she held it close to his face.

"That's right," Adaleen said, releasing the venomous thing and watching with affection as it crawled lazily over her hand. "These are the best spiders."

"If you say so." Mark felt a mild, creeping arachnophobia. Considering all the other horrors he'd witnessed in the past couple days, the spider didn't freak him out nearly as badly as it might have.

"The first spell I ever cast was with widow spiders," Adaleen said. "I was eight years old. You know I was born a slave, down in Louisiana?"

"Roberta told me that," Mark said. "I'm sorry."

"What the hell you sorry for? Just 'cuz you're white don't make that your fault." Adaleen held her arm up, watching the black spider walk a bracelet path around her wrist. "That was a long time ago, anyway. *Long* time. It was a sugar plantation, just south of Baton Rouge. My mama was a housemaid. House slaves had it a little easier than those that worked the fields, but it also meant we lived closer to the white folks. That caused its own problems."

"The plantation was owned by a man named Jack Bell. He had a son by the same name. We all had to call him Young Master Jackie." Adaleen made a face, like the name left a bad taste in her mouth. "Young Master Jackie seemed to think the little girls what belonged to his daddy were his to do with as he pleased. I don't got to tell you what that means, do I?"

"I can imagine," Mark said.

"No, you can't." Adaleen shook her head with disgust. "Anyway, he done those things to all the little girls, in the house and in the fields, but I was his favorite one. Lord knows why. I was eight, like I said, and he was fifteen or sixteen. He came to me every day while my mama was workin'. Said he'd kill me if I told anybody. I believed him, too. He made me watch him kill a kitten once, just twisted its head and snapped its little neck. Said he'd to the same to me if I ever said anything. I was so scared of that boy."

"Then one day, I found a widow web in the corner of the room I shared with my mama. With an egg sac."

Adaleen chuckled. "I put that sac in the bureau drawer where Young Master Jackie kept his britches. Hundreds of baby spiders hatched all over that boy's pants. Heh heh. Baby widows got poison from the day they's born and they bit Little Master Jackie all over his tenders. That boy's scrote swole up like a honeydew and turned black as my own ass. Heh heh heh. I heard it say they lanced it with a hot needle to get the poison out, but all his nasty bits just rotted clean off. He never poked another black girl from that day on. No white girls, neither. That boy's pokin' days was clean behind him."

Adaleen laughed at the delightful memory for several long seconds, playing with the spider on her hand.

"Some folks would say that wasn't a proper spell, because there was no magic to it. But all I mean when I say 'spell' is a way of gettin' nature to your bidding to give you power. I got my first taste of it day and I mean to tell you, it tasted *sweet*."

With that, Adaleen popped the black widow spider into her mouth. She chewed it up and swallowed it down. Mark looked away, gagging a little.

"Widow spiders have powerful magic to 'em," Adaleen said, picking a skinny black leg from her teeth. "They're damn useful for a wide range of spells. I used to make goofer dust from six dried up widows ground into powder, mixed with grave dirt, a little anvil dust and a few other things. Lay a line of that over a man's doorway and he'd be dead inside a week. No doctor in the world would ever know he was poisoned, neither. You know why they work so good?"

"Why?" Mark said.

"What're widows famous for? How'd they get that name?"

"Because the female eats the male after mating."

"Right." Adaleen grinned. "Them little man spiders know they gonna get ate, too, but they *still* can't help themselves. Just think how good that widow spider pussy must be that they're willing to die just to get some."

Adaleen laughed hard at that. Mark looked away. He didn't like where this was heading.

"See, most times fuckin' is an expression of a man's power," Adaleen said. "A way of dominating a female. Like Young Master Jackie done to me. But widows turn all that on its head. It's woman's sex power, pure and cold." She looked Mark up and down with the expression of a hungry woman eyeing a steak dinner. "You got something I want, white boy."

"Really?" Mark said, backing away. "What?"

"You know what," Adaleen said, biting her lip as she advanced on him. "When that bad boy raped me, he broke something inside so that I never could have no babies. I tried every healing conjuration I knew, but I never could fix it. But that that was my old body. I think this new one *could* make me some babies. That's all I ever wanted, some daughters of my own."

Adaleen loosened her robe. The silk slid free of one naked shoulder, whispering against her skin.

"That's the one trick, and I mean the only one, I need a man for."

Her smell was heavy in the room, sharp and musky, a salty tang with notes of sweetness and faint decay. The strange, alluring scent brought

Mark to an unknown realm of olfactory experience, affecting his brain like a mind-altering vapor. His erection was keen as a blade, painfully acute.

"I couldn't abide a man makin' a claim of dominion over me or my child, though." She had him backed up against the wall now. "So after I get what I need, I'll have to kill you."

One of Adaleen's exquisite breasts slipped completely free of the thin fabric containing it. Mark offered no resistance when she cupped his right hand in hers, and brought it up to grasp her. The warm soft weight was gratifying on a primal level. Her nipple was fat and swollen, an inflamed coppery red that felt hard enough to pierce his palm.

"But we can have some fun before that," she whispered, kissing his throat. Mark felt an ecstatic charge at the touch of her lips, the same invigorating jolt which she had granted to her angels. Every nerve in his body hummed like a struck piano key, the vibrations radiating in opiated waves outward from the spot where she'd kissed him. "I'll fuck you like you never been fucked before. You'll die smilin', I tell you that."

Her teeth grazed the skin of his neck. She granted him another suckling little kiss, right on his Adam's apple.

"Put some babies up inside me," she commanded with a whisper. "I can make 'em come out triplets, easy. It's a simple spell to make 'em all girls, too. I'll raise up my daughters to be powerful witches, and I'll tell 'em what a funny little white boy their daddy was."

She kissed Mark on the mouth. Her lips tasted of sweet liqueur and smoke, blood and venom, rotten meat, and sugar, but mostly her lips carried the salty, musky taste of sex. Adaleen's tongue fluttered against his like a snake tasting the air.

The robe slid all the way off and fell to the floor. She pressed naked against him, her hot groin writhing against his. The air was redolent with her arousal, penetrating Mark's nostrils. The scent was as thick as smoke, invading his lungs and slipping into his bloodstream.

"It won't barely hurt," she promised between kisses. "I'll bite through your throat quick and clean. Put your spurting vein in my mouth and suck your essence out, like one of them Draculas in that silly book of yours."

Mark returned Adaleen's kiss, losing himself to his mortal desire. He couldn't help himself. The scales weighing his drives for sex and for survival were grossly imbalanced. He wanted her so badly the promise of his death was almost beneath consideration.

He pulled her close, sliding his hands up her flawless naked back. The black thread binding Lizzy's skin to Adaleen had been absorbed into her healing flesh, leaving no trace of a seam or a blemish that his fingers could find. Until he touched the base of her skull, where Roberta had first driven the dagger into her daughter's head. Coarse stitches still bristled from Adaleen's skin there, like black spider's legs.

"You gotta ask for it, though," she said. "I ain't no rapin' man, takin' what ain't freely offered. You gotta say 'fuck me, sweet Adaleen.'"

"Fuck me." Mark said wrapped the wiry thread around one finger, wondering if he dared to do it. Wondering if it would even work. Wondering if it wouldn't be a better and easier thing to just surrender to the lethal ecstasy she promised. "Sweet Adaleen."

She laughed. "Good boy. Now say 'kill me, sweet Adaleen.'"

Mark knelt to kiss her throat.

"Kill me," Mark said. She arched her neck, receiving the nibbling flutters of his lips. "Sweet Adaleen."

Mark pulled the black thread into his mouth and clenched it between his teeth. Jerking his head back, he popped the top two stitches free of her skin.

"Ow!" Adaleen cried. "Shit, boy. What the fuck are you doing?"

Mark tugged hard with his teeth, pulling enough of the thread free that he could grasp it in one fist. Then more, so that he could grab it with both hands. Adaleen spun around, the stitches ripping a jagged line down her spine, tearing open like the pull tab on an envelope. The stitches ran all the way down Adaleen's back, to the base of her spine, just above the cleft of her perfect, heart-shaped buttocks. Mark pulled the bloody thread free and tossed it to the floor.

"You fucked up my pretty skin, peckerwood!" she screamed, enraged.

Adaleen reached back, trying to pull closed the flapping skin of her back. It was sliding right off her.

Mark grabbed her by the hair. He gave a mighty pull and yanked her scalp off. With another tug, he ripped Lizzy's face free from Adaleen's skull.

The black shape beneath the mask had no mouth with which to speak, but its glowing red eyes narrowed on Mark with rage. The thing let out a hissing scream from its gaping maw.

Mark tore the skin completely away, letting the beautiful woman's flesh fall into a heap on the floor. The spidery thing that was Adaleen's true form began to unfurl almost immediately, losing its shape without the skin to mold it. It fell to the floor on its back, convulsing. The black membrane covering its body was so thin Mark could see the organs inside. Something beat just below the surface, with frantic irregular flutters. He took this to be the witch's heart.

Mark grabbed the scissors from the desk, from where they rested atop the strips of flag. Grasping them in one hand, he drove the sharp end deep into the pulsing mass.

The witch-thing let out a nerve-raking screech of pain when Mark stabbed it. The black limbs twitched helplessly, too weak to push Mark off. He pulled the scissors out and tossed them aside. The heart, if it was a heart, spurted fluid that was not blood, but something more akin to bile. Pale greenish-yellow in color, with a curdled texture like thick cottage cheese. The stuff had the foul acidic odor of fresh vomit. Mark staggered back with his hand over his face.

The thick, stinking pus gushed out with spurting pressure, spraying everywhere. There was so much of it, more than the fist-sized organ could seemingly contain. The dying witch-thing shuddered in a pool of its own mucous-like discharge.

Its cries were now just pathetic gasping mewls and its motions were listless death spasms. Mark staggered out of the office, leaving it to die on the floor.

He ran out the tavern's back door, out into the alley, and greedily gasped the cold, fresh air. The night smelled of distant blood and smoke, but was still cleaner that the hot, sickroom stench of that back office. The scent still burnt into his nostrils, the sight of the black writhing abomination still etched onto his eyes, the sound of its death cries still echoing in his ears, Mark knelt onto the asphalt next to the dumpster behind the bar. He puked his guts out.

This purging took a few seconds, but Mark felt undeniably better when it was all out of him. He got to his feet and leaned back against the brick wall with his eyes closed, letting it sink in for just a minute that he was still alive.

He heard a pained voice call out "shit" from somewhere close by, and then the sound of something metallic falling to the pavement.

Mark opened his eyes and saw Sheriff Bates bending down in the alley not twenty feet away, picking something up off the ground. When he stood up again, Bates had his gun clutched in his left hand.

CHAPTER 59

6:49 PM

NATE WAS HURT, bad. Gut shot, maybe, though it felt lower than that. Maybe in his hip. He couldn't tell, and he was afraid to look. Hurt like a son of a bitch, though, and bled like one too. He was leaving a trail behind him. That Nate was still on his feet surprised even himself. He knew it was a testament to his determination and his bad-assery.

He had not expected Tom Peters to shoot him, had not believed that the boy had it in him. And for what? To defend Mark goddamn Davies, who Tom hated as much as Nate did. The betrayal stung Nate as badly as the bullet. He and Tom had a good thing going once. Well, shit. That was done. Nate hadn't checked to be sure, but Tom wasn't moving on the street where he'd left him, and that sure as hell was a big puddle of blood underneath him.

That's what double-crossing fuckers get.

Then Lana Delany stole Tom's car and some bitch dressed all in black had appeared out of nowhere and drove off in Nate's cruiser with the Davies fucker still inside. Nate was left alone to die in the street like a run-over possum. He'd shown them, though. He just flat-out refused to fuckin' die.

Nate shuffled back into town, a journey of a few blocks that took him half a goddamn hour in his weakened state. Unsteady forward motion, not wanting to stop and rest for fear he'd never get back up again. He was delirious with pain and blood loss. Hallucinating, even. He thought he saw the water tower vibrating like a tuning fork, making the most god-awful sound. Then it split across the side and sprayed blood all over the people below. The townsfolk dancing beneath in the bloody rain looked to Nate like sinners writhing in some deep pit of hell.

That worried him. What if it wasn't a hallucination? What if he was dead after all, and this was the form Hell had taken to punish his soul? Nothing could be worse than being condemned to forever wander through godforsaken Bakersfield, with pain deep in his body and no hope for rest or respite. The distant smoke and occasional flickers of fire off on the horizon did not reassure him that this was not the case.

Nate had been raised to believe in Hell like the rest of this goddamn sheep in this town, but he'd rejected that simple-minded bullshit when he was a young man. He'd tossed God in the same garbage bin as Santa Claus and the Easter Bunny, kiddie stories he was embarrassed to admit he'd ever swallowed. And if there was no God, the opposite side of the coin was just as big a lie.

But what if he was wrong?

If anyone deserved hell, Nate knew, it was him. The things he'd done. If all the shit Tom Peters was always spouting was true, then Nate's soul was burdened by the weight of a thousand sins that would sink him down to the very depths. Maybe that's where he was right now.

Nate shook this off. That was the pain and the creeping hopelessness talking. He just needed a doctor, to get himself fixed up. Then he'd be right as rain. He put his head down and watched his feet to make sure he was still putting one in front of another. He couldn't really feel them anymore.

He was coming up on the square now. A block up ahead, he saw a curious sight. His police cruiser was parked right out in front of Wolfy's Tavern. Like an omen or a beacon or whatever you'd call it. Nate smiled despite everything. Now at least he knew where he was headed. Wolfy was a good old boy. He'd have some medicine for Nate. He could call him an ambulance and then line up seven or eight shots of good whiskey along the bar, so Nate could knock 'em back one by one while he waited for the paramedics to show.

Nate's mouth watered at the thought. He picked up the pace of his zombie shuffle.

It took him a long time to cross the deserted square, and when he finally reached Wolfy's, he found the door locked. What the fuck? Nate had no idea of the time, but he knew it was early yet. Too early for the bars to close, even in this shitty one-horse town.

In Hell, the bars are always closed, a voice whispered inside him.

"Fuck that noise," Nate croaked out loud. Speaking triggered an acid burp that left the lingering taste of blood in the back of his throat. That couldn't be good.

He tried to look into the front window, but it was frosted over like this was the dead middle of winter. All he could see was some neon color through the fog, which seemed to throb with the tortured pulse of the veins beating in his eyes.

Nate beat on the door, but his fists were too weak to even knock very loud. Leaning against the brick building for support, he staggered up the sidewalk. There was a gap between Wolfy's place and the building that housed Grady's Feed Store next door. The narrow gangway was about two feet wide, choked with weeds and spider webs, smelling strongly of urine because of the nasty old drunks who liked to piss in there. Somehow, this dank and forbidding passage called to Nate.

He squeezed through the gap, shuffling sideways now, thinking that this would be an entirely appropriate place to just keel over and die. He didn't, though. He hobbled through the dark chute, which led out into the alley in the back.

Nate heard the unmistakable sound of retching, and the liquid splash of vomit hitting the pavement. Somebody puking out in back of the bar. Nate didn't doubt that Wolfy probably had to hose down the alley on a regular basis, but it struck him as strange now, and not just because the bar was apparently closed.

Nate crept around the side of the dumpster and all his intuition was rewarded, because the man barfing in the alley was none other than Mark Davies.

A sense of déjà vu washed over Nate. He had been in this same position so many times before, it felt like he was on some kind of infernal loop. This little punk-ass right in his sights, close enough to kill with nothing standing in his way, only for it to get fucked up somehow. And now fate, or whatever, had placed Nate and his nemesis in this same position yet again. Taunting him. Well, he wasn't going to squander it this time.

Mark stood up and fell back against the side of the building, his eyes closed. He hadn't seen Nate standing there yet. Very quietly, Nate reached down to pull his piece from his holster. From long-engrained habit, he used his right hand, forgetting in the moment how messed up it was. He grabbed the gun, but the weight of the weapon sent a sharp jolt of pain all up his arm. Even with the all the other pain he was in, the twinge in Nate's hand was bad enough that he let out an involuntary cry of alarm and dropped his gun to the ground.

Nate quickly bent down and picked up the gun, in his left hand this time.

Mark looked up at him. He didn't seem scared, or even really surprised, but instead regarded Nate with a weary expression of compounded misery. Like a man stepping out of a dentist's office after a double root canal to find that his car had a flat tire.

"Oh, great," Davies said. "*You.*"

Nate was a little taken aback by Mark's reaction, but he wasn't about to waste another opportunity. He lifted his gun up and tried to pull the trigger.

He couldn't do it.

He wanted to, so very badly, but it was like there was something between his brain and his finger, blocking the simple muscular command.

"Thou shalt not kill Mark Davies," Nathanial spoke from Nate's mouth.

Nate remembered now. In that hated chamber where the brain butchers had rewired his mind, they'd etched this indelible commandment above all others. Mark Davies was untouchable, his name and his image programmed into Nate's psyche with a big red STOP sign. Just the attempt, just the acknowledged intent, to harm this stupid motherfucker had made this deeply embedded conditioning kick in. Nate was restrained from doing what he needed to do.

He knew he could get around it. He knew he could will himself to overcome this ingrained prohibition, if he just focus on the problem for a minute. But, in that moment of weakness, Nathanial had managed to break free of the smothering weight Nate had buried that pussy-ass motherfucker under. He was scrabbling out, trying to take control again.

Nate's bandaged right hand reached out and, though it caused lightning bolts of pain, swatted the gun from his left hand. It clattered to the ground again. Nate went to pick it up, but again something was holding him back. His left leg pivoted out and left arm reached, but his whole right side was anchored where he stood.

Nate/Nathanial was split in two. Nathanial now controlled the right half of his body, and Nate the left, and these two hemispheres were at fundamental odds.

"I'm going to kill you, motherfucker," Nate tried to say from the left side of his mouth, while Nathanial tried to warn, "You better get out of here, Mr. Davies," from the right. What emerged was a schizoid mush-mouthed gabble that made Mark look at them with bafflement, and even a little bit of concern.

"You okay there, sheriff?" Davies said.

Nate's vision was all out of whack because his two eyes weren't tracking together the way they were supposed to. He saw two Mark Davies standing before him, both looking at him with identical expressions of curiosity and alarm. Nate tried to lunge for at least one of them, tried to pull the leaden weight of the right half of himself forward by sheer muscular power. But, at the same moment, Nathanial stepped back with his right leg.

Nate/Nathanial performed an awkward half-spin and keeled over sideways, landing on their left hip, where the bullet was lodged. This sent a crushing wave of pain throughout their entire body.

The two men in the single devastated body managed to roll over onto their back. Each was so desperate to rid himself of the other that each hand grabbed a handful of hair and pulled hard, as if they could tear themselves in half.

CHAPTER 60

6:54 PM

MARK WATCHED, ASTONISHED, as Bates writhed on the ground. The sheriff looked like he was trying to rip himself apart, but his struggles were growing rapidly weaker. The man was almost completely depleted.

Mark heard more running footsteps coming towards him in the alley. He looked up with resigned fatalism, to see who was coming to kill him now, and was gratified to see Missy, Lana, James, and Alice running towards him.

"Oh, God. I'm glad to see you guys," he said, and only then did he notice that they were all covered in blood. "Are you all right?"

"We're fine," Missy said, smiling at him. "Long story about the blood. Are you okay?"

Mark had to think about that for a second, but he nodded. "More or less, yeah."

Surprising him, Missy threw her arms around him and gave him a big hug. He embraced her back, gratefully, even though she was still dripping wet with blood.

Lana cast a look down at Bates, whose arms and legs were splayed out in an "X" shape, the two halves of him each trying to weakly crawl away from the other. "What the hell's going on with him?"

"I don't know," Mark said. He let go of his ex-wife, and hugged his nephew. "But, honestly, that's only the third or fourth most fucked-up thing I've seen tonight."

"I'm sorry I left you back there, after he threw you into his car," Lana said.

Mark waved this away. "It's fine. I'm glad you were able to help these guys get away. How'd you find me?"

"We went back to where the cars were," James said. He pointed down at the sheriff, who had descended into listless shudders and jagged breathing. "This guy was leaving a trail of blood behind him. We just followed it back here."

"What about Tom?"

"He's dead," Missy answered. "We pulled his body off the road at least, but we had to leave him..." She looked away.

"Jesus," Mark said. "He has a wife and kids."

Mark looked down at the man who had murdered Tom Peters, but it was hard to feel much anger towards the pathetic bloody heap on the ground. He saw the sheriff's gun lying on the ground a few feet away. Mark didn't think Bates was going to come to, but he picked the weapon up by the barrel and tossed it into the dumpster anyway. Just in case.

There were sirens in the distance now, a lot of them, growing closer.

"Is it over?" Alice asked, looking frail and weak with no wig and no glass eye. She had to lean against James for support.

"It's over," Lana said. "Come on. My car's parked out front. Let's get out of here. We'll go to Lincoln, meet up with Sam and Ben at the hospital."

"Yeah," Mark said. "That is a great idea. But I want you guys to see something first. I just have to make sure I'm not totally out of my fucking mind."

He was thinking of Adaleen, of course. Now that the adrenaline was wearing off, his final encounter with the old witch was taking on the quality of a half-remembered fever dream. He had to have some confirmation that he hadn't hallucinated it.

"What are you talking about?" Missy said.

"Follow me."

Mark led them into the candlelit bar through the back door. He pointed over at the little office. He didn't look inside himself, he couldn't bring himself to, but both Missy and Lana stepped into the little room.

"Jesus!" he heard Lana shout. "What the fuck is *that*?"

Good, Mark thought. *That is the appropriate response.*

Missy and Lana stepped out of the office, both looking pale and shocked.

"What is that *thing* on the floor, Mark?" Missy demanded.

"A witch," he said. "A *dead* witch. I killed her."

"So it was all real?" Lana said. "The resurrection ceremony and all the rest of the crazy shit you told me about?"

"Apparently so."

"But the witch is dead?"

"Ding dong," Mark said. "Hey, James. Do me a favor and look behind the bar over there. Tell me if you see a dead guy with a maple syrup spigot stuck in his ribs."

James, frowning at the odd request, walked around the bar to have a look.

"Oh my God, Uncle Mark," he cried.

"So I didn't imagine that part, either," Mark said with relief. "I'm going to assume that the rest of it was real, too."

Missy looked him in the eye. "Will you please explain this to me so it all makes sense?"

"That's a tall order," Mark said. "But I'll try. On the drive up to Lincoln, though. I think we should leave before every cop in this half of the state shows up. I don't really look forward to trying to explain all this to the authorities."

"Good idea," Missy said.

Before they could head out the front, though, the back door opened and closed. Sally Wolf stepped into the bar. She looked dazed, as pale and distraught as the rest of them, as she rounded on Mark

"What did you do?" she demanded.

"Sally," Mark said. "Hi. Why don't you sit down? We really should talk."

She glanced over at the office door.

"You don't want to go in there," Mark said.

It was too late, though. She pushed the door open and glanced inside.

"No!" she shrieked. She turned back to Mark. "You killed her!"

"Yeah, okay. But listen..."

"We knew," Sally cried. "We all felt her die. All the light inside us died with her!"

"Sorry, but she was going to..."

"You fucking idiot!" Sally screamed. "You fucked it all up!"

"Calm down, lady," Lana said.

Sally ignored her. She didn't seem to be aware there was anyone in the bar except her and Mark. "She was going to make things better," she sobbed. "She was going to make things *right*. I killed my dad for her. Now it's for nothing!"

"Sally..."

Sally reached behind her. From her back pocket, she pulled Bates's gun. She must have pulled it out of the dumpster. Mark stepped away from her, backing up against the bar.

"Hey, put that down, okay?" Missy said, with a forced calm. "We can talk about—"

Sally pulled the trigger twice. Two deafening shots rang out. Mark heard the back-bar mirror explode behind him and thought *Thank God, she missed*.

James, bless his heart, leapt at Sally from the side, tackling her to the ground. The gun went spinning across the worn wooden floorboards.

Mark looked up and wondered why everyone was looking at him with such horrified expressions when the shot had clearly gone wild. But then he tried to take a breath and felt a pain in his chest like someone had thrown a bowling ball into his ribs.

He looked down and saw a ragged black hole in the "Don't Monkey with Evolution" t-shirt. The hole was right over the monkey's waving hand, just below Mark's left armpit. As Mark frowned down at the hole, trying to figure out how it had come to be there, a red stain started to spread on the cotton fabric.

"Well, shit," he said. "This is Tom Peter's shirt."

Then he fell to the floor.

CHAPTER 61

6:58 PM

LANA SAW SOMETHING very strange in the moment right before the skinny girl in the silky white robes shot Mark. The girl had just pulled the gun out when Lana saw motion out of the corner of her eye, in the long mirror behind the bar. She glanced over, and though later she would discount this as her imagination, she thought she saw a shadowy figure standing directly behind her in the reflection. It was little more than a black silhouette, with long, stringy hair, though Lana received the impression of red eyes and grinning white teeth.

Then the girl fired the gun and everything began to move in a hyper-real, super slow motion. The mirror exploded and flying shards of glass blew back into the air. By reflex, Lana reached up to shield her eyes. Good thing, too, because she felt a sharp slice across the top of her wrist that might have gone into her eye. She looked down at her arm and saw a chunk of mirror, maybe half an inch long, imbedded in her skin. Her watch would have deflected it, had she been wearing her watch.

Lana pulled the silver splinter out. For a second, she seemed to see the same black shape in the tiny glass chip. A shadowy face, gleaming red eyes, a knowing smile. Then she tossed the shard to the ground and forgot what she'd seen because Mark was hit.

James tackled the thin girl to the ground, sending the gun flying. It came to rest on the floor at Lana's feet. She kicked it aside.

Mark looked down at the hole in his chest, and then over at Michelle. He appeared more confused than hurt. He gave her a quizzical look, as if imploring her to explain. Then he mumbled something about Tom Peters and fell to the ground.

"Mark!" Michelle screamed. She ran to him, knelt beside him, tore open his shirt and pressed her hand over the wound. "Phone!" she screamed. "Who has a phone?"

Across the room, Alice pulled her cell from her pocket and dialed 911.

"Oh God, Mark," Michelle said. She lifted his head up and rested it on her lap. He was pale as a ghost. "Just hang in there, okay? We're getting help."

Seeing them, Lana was struck by a curious thought. Since she and Chelle had been married, Lana had often wondered about her wife's previous marriage. As much as she'd tried, she could never imagine Mark and Michelle together. They seemed utterly incompatible. Lana had never even heard Michelle speak of Mark with warmth, only with cold disdain or, at best, an amused chagrin. But now, watching Michelle cradle Mark's head with such tenderness, Lana for the first time was able to imagine how they might have been when they were young and in love. The new awareness didn't fill her with jealousy, but rather a kind of wistfulness. Lana had told Michelle all the stories of her old lovers. These shared experiences had become part of the communal property of their marriage. But Michelle had always kept her time with Mark sealed off, behind a wall of bitterness. Lana was finally getting a glimpse behind that wall, but it came in what were perhaps Mark's final moments.

"It just keeps ringing!" Alice cried out.

James let the girl on the floor go and went to his uncle. The girl, all the fight gone out of her, just crawled behind the bar and curled up beside the dead man with the tap in his chest.

"I'm sorry, Daddy," she sobbed. "I'm so sorry."

Lana surveyed the awful scene. The girl crying behind the bar. James and Michelle doing what little they could to comfort Mark. Alice banging her cell phone against her forehead, as if by doing so she could force it to ring through.

The sirens outside were getting louder. It sounded like ambulances rather than police cars, though in the moment Lana had no idea how she could know the difference between the two. She unlocked the front door and ran outside.

Two ambulances were screaming into town, heading south down Mulberry Street, red and white lights flashing. Lana stepped halfway into the road, trying to wave them down, but they both just swerved past her.

They were headed south, towards the water tower. It struck her as a gross injustice that the men who had tried to lynch Michelle were receiving medical attention while Mark lay dying.

"Help!" she screamed into the night. "Somebody help!"

And then, as if from heaven above, her appeal was answered. A cluster of lights directly overhead began to descend, scanning the ground with beams of white. The roar and whine of the rotors became deafening as the helicopter lowered onto the square, sending dust and debris flying in swirling clouds.

The copter was completely black, except for the familiar lime green monolith logo painted on the back. Just below the plain green rectangle, a bold font spelled out the words Malovo Agricultural Development.

A side door opened. Two men in black jumpsuits and white helmets jumped out of the chopper, while the pilot remained behind the wheel. One of the men ran around to pull a wheeled stretcher from the hatch on the back of the helicopter. The other man ran over to Lana.

"Where is he?" the man shouted over the chopper noise.

"Inside the bar," Lana yelled, waving over at Wolfy's in case her voice was completely inaudible. "Over there."

The man nodded. He helped the other man with the stretcher and they pushed it at a run in through the tavern's front doors. Lana stood there, the chopping pressure of the air beating like a second heartbeat against her chest. After a few agonizingly long minutes, the door opened again and the men reemerged with Mark on the stretcher. He had an oxygen mask on and an IV attached to one arm, with some kind of dressing over his chest wound. He didn't appear to be conscious as the men loaded the stretcher into the back of the helicopter.

Michelle ran out behind them, along with James and Alice.

"Is he going to be all right?" Lana yelled.

"They don't know!" Michelle cried. "They think he has a collapsed lung!"

Lana embraced her wife, the air whipping about them with a hurricane intensity.

"I should go with him!" Michelle yelled.

"Go!"

"Get Ben, okay?" Michelle yelled. "Get Ben and tell him...tell him his dad's going to be all right!"

"I will! I love you!"

"Love you!"

Michelle kissed her and climbed into the helicopter. James and Alice huddled close beside Lana. The three of them watched the craft rise. They kept their eyes fixed on the receding light until it disappeared into the distant night sky.

CHAPTER 62

8:45 PM

ROBERTA STEVENS WEPT as she walked along the country road, past the dark sacred woods she had once loved, but which now held for her only terrors and regret. She didn't know where she was going. She couldn't go home. Roberta had already been back to her house. She'd parked a couple miles away, just to be safe, and hiked back to the house along paths she knew in the woods. This had proven to be a wise precaution. The place had been crawling with police, their red and blue lights casting penetrating flashes of color into the woods. She saw them walking in and out of the house, invading her home. More troubling, she had seen them in the back yard. With dogs and shovels.

Roberta quietly fled back through the timber, got back into her car and sped away. Again, to what destination she couldn't possibly say. But just a few country miles up the road, her old Ford had finally given up the ghost, smoke pouring from beneath the hood. For a few years now, Roberta had been casting spells and protective charms over every clanging of the engine or grinding of the brakes. Conjuring away every distressing dashboard light. One advantage of witchcraft at the level she was practicing it was that it saved a fortune in mechanic's bills. But all her magic was dying, because its source was gone. So she'd gotten out, pushed the faithful old car into a ditch, and continued on to nowhere on foot.

Walking gave her plenty of time to reflect upon her many failures. The dark quiet of the woods allowed the hectoring voices, which on good days she was able to suppress, free rein inside her head.

She was a failed student, dropping out of college after one semester noteworthy only for her discoveries of binge drinking and indiscriminate sex.

Lazy ungrateful little brat, her mother said. *I ain't surprised you flunked out. You were always so stupid.*

She was a failed wife, Gary walking out on her after nine middling years.

You stupid bitch, her husband said. *You let yourself turn into such a fat, frigid slob I* had *to go looking for it somewhere else.*

She was a failed mother, nosy neighbors calling child services on her just because she lost her temper that one time, and then little Charlotte being taken away from her forever.

If you want to kill yourself with drinking, that's your own damn business, said the social worker. *But if you have any love for your daughter at all, you'll let her go to someone who can give her the life she deserves.*

She was a failed artist, having never made a dime from her painting.

Flat, trite, uninspired, said the agent Roberta had talked into looking at her portfolio. *You just recycle every hoary 'women who run with the wolves' cliché in the book.*

And now she'd failed at this, her life's greatest ambition. Her final gambit. Her boldest and most daring attempt to make her mark on the world. She'd fucked it up, just like she'd fucked up everything else in her life.

Stupid bitch, ain't ya? her beloved mother Adaleen said. *What's the matter, old woman? If you can't bring me a Christian tongue, I'll take yours instead.*

That's where it had all begun to go wrong. After Adaleen had sent them away, Roberta had gathered her angels around her in the square across from the tavern.

"We can't do this," she'd said. Roberta understood the power of sacrifice, and was not above taking retribution against those who deserved it. But she was afraid that Adaleen's lust for power was blinding them all to brutality. It would be too easy, she saw, to fall onto a dark path where innocent life lost its meaning in the pursuit of their goals. "We have to be firm in our resolve. We must stand up to her and say that we will not spill the blood of innocents."

"Speak for yourself, old woman," Gemma had said. She had Roberta's sacred dagger in a scabbard on her belt, and it was obvious she was itching to use it. Gemma had already tipped over into pure blood lust. Roberta had to claim responsibility for that as well. "I already got a couple Christians in mind who could stand to lose a tongue."

Sally and Ellie did not relish the thought of slicing out someone's tongue, but they were afraid to defy the beloved mother. They were all still debating the matter when an icy pain slashed through their hearts. The ecstatic power that had been surging through them died away all at once, leaving only cold sadness and weary failure. They knew beyond any doubt that Adaleen was dead, that Mark had killed her, and for these things too Roberta was to blame. She was the one who had wanted to bring him into the circle. She'd thought from reading his books that he might be sympathetic to their cause, but now Roberta saw that she had been foolish to trust any man. That was just one of her many failings.

Her beloved coven, Bell's Angels, who had once sworn a blood oath to never let their circle be broken, had fled in four directions. Each of them running away in fear, thinking only of her own self-preservation.

Roberta had given literally everything up to bring her beloved mother back into the world, and now it had come to exactly nothing.

You're a murderer, too, don't forget that, a chorus spoke in her head, comprised of all the voices at once: her mother, her husband, the social worker, the agent and, loudest of all, Adaleen herself. All speaking in hellish harmony.

"No," Roberta said aloud as she sobbed along the dark road beneath the bright full moon. "I set Lizzy free."

Set her free? the voices chided. *You trapped her soul in the body of a bird that won't live through the night.*

"No." Roberta thought of her pretty, simple, loving, exasperating, and completely trusting adopted daughter. Thought of Lizzy's smile, which she would never see again.

You never loved her, the voices challenged. *You raised her up like a lamb to the slaughter. And for nothin'. You murdered that innocent child for nothin'.*

"No," Roberta moaned again. "Oh, Lizzy. I'm so sorry."

Her tears blurred her vision and her own weeping filled her ears so much that she did see the headlights or hear the car until it was almost upon her. When she became aware of the vehicle slowing down and pulling up alongside her, her first thought was that it was the police. This was a relief, in a way. She would surrender willingly, would confess to everything, and would hang herself in her cell the first chance she got.

But it wasn't a police car that pulled to the curb in front of her. It was a long, black car somewhere in between a limousine and a hearse.

The rear window rolled down and a grating snarl of a voice came from the darkness inside: "Get in, Roberta. We have much to discuss."

Roberta felt a stab of apprehension, but she was so numb and hopeless that she slid into the car. The woman sitting in the back seat wore a sheer white blouse through which a bright red bra was clearly visible. From the neck down, she had the body of a tremendously beautiful young woman. But her face and bald head were covered with horrible burn scars, the skin shiny and waxy-looking, like candle drippings molded to a skull.

"Sit down," the burned woman beckoned, with a cancerous rasp. "Close the door."

"Who are you?" Roberta asked, hesitantly doing as she was bid.

"My name is Shana," the woman said. "That's my assistant, Cassandra, driving the car."

The driver, a raven-haired woman with pale white skin and blood-red lipstick, turned and gave Roberta a nod through the partition. Then she pulled back onto the road.

"How did you know my name?" Roberta asked.

"We've been watching you, with great interest."

"Watching? How?"

"There are eyes everywhere, in Bakersfield," Shana croaked. "If one knows how to look through them. I've seen what you've accomplished these past few days. Very impressive."

"I've accomplished nothing," Roberta said, looking away.

"On the contrary," Shana insisted. "You did suffer a setback, but you did so many remarkable things. I'm quite impressed. You see, I have a... stake in the town of Bakersfield. A start-up enterprise, you could say. And there is a position available for a woman of your knowledge and talents."

"I don't understand," Roberta said.

"I have something for you." Shana reached beneath her seat, and pulled out a leather satchel. Inside was a very familiar bound book, which she handed over to Roberta.

"Adaleen's spell book," Roberta said. "How did you get this?"

"I took the liberty of removing it from your house before the police arrived." Shana gave a lipless grin. "We wouldn't want that falling into the wrong hands. It's such a fascinating read."

"But the magic is gone," Roberta said. "Adaleen is dead."

"Wrong," Shana said. "On both counts. What you call 'magic,' I prefer to call 'energy.' Adaleen Bell was not the source of this energy, but merely a conduit for it. Very powerful, but by no means the only one. There are others, which I can help you to channel."

"You said Adaleen's not dead?" Roberta asked, the stirring in her heart containing equal measures of hope and fear.

"Not quite. She is in a weakened state, but she's a very persistent entity," Shana said.

Roberta looked down at the spell book in her hand. "I'm sorry," she said. "I don't really understand what you're telling me."

"You will," Shana said in her gasping voice. "How's the line from the old movie go? This is the start of a beautiful friendship."

EPILOGUE:
THE DAY AFTER
HALLOWEEN

CHAPTER 63

11:47 AM

GETTING SHOT SUCKED. Mark sat propped up in the hospital bed. Dry, fiery pain filled his left lung with every breath he took. There was a button he could press every so often to pump morphine from the IV directly into his veins. "So you can control the dose," the doctor had said, which was complete bullshit because if Mark was actually controlling the dose, he'd give himself twice as much, twice as often as the miserly pump dispensed. The meager stream of opiates only dulled the pain a little. Mark couldn't even get a decent buzz going.

All that bed-ridden morning, he tried to put the events of the previous night into some kind of coherent order. Everything surrounding the moment when Sally had shot him was foggy and jumbled. Adaleen, pressing naked against him. Piercing the witch's black spider heart with scissors. Bates, trying to tear himself in two. All of it was strange and disjointed. And strangest of all was what had happened after. Rising into the sky, Missy touching him with such tenderness, smiling angelically down at him with tears in her eyes. Mark had been certain then that he was dead and passing over into an afterlife ill-deserved by a cynical, unbelieving and unredeemed sinner like himself.

Then he awoke here, in this mechanical bed in this plain white room, with a catheter stuck in his dick and a feeling like a construction crew had taken turns on his chest with a jackhammer. Missy was gone, and no one seemed willing to tell him what the hell was going on.

Bakersfield was all over the news, which Mark watched from the little television bolted to the wall across the room, the sound coming from a little remote speaker resting beside his pillow. With the national attention the witch panic had garnered the day before serving as build-up, the town's wild Halloween night made for prime "if it bleeds, it leads" material. The anchors on the national cable news channel Mark watched actually invoked the phrase "Bloody Bakersfield," and recounted the riots, the train derailment and the water tower explosion (satanic sabotage the presumed cause of the latter two) with gleeful doom-crier's relish. From the news, Mark learned that four people had died. Or, as Wolf Blitzer put it: "The Halloween death toll stands at four, with dozens more injured and potentially millions of dollars in property damage, in a wild night of terror that residents of this sleepy town will not soon forget."

He was watching the umpteenth reiteration of the story on the news, sandwiched between election updates and people shouting at one another about what was to blame for the latest mass shooting, when his mother walked into his room.

"Hi, Mark," she smiled. "How are you feeling?"

"Pretty much like somebody shot me in the lung."

"James wanted me to give this to you, he said it would help you pass the time." She handed him his laptop computer.

"Thanks," Mark said, setting the device on the swiveling overbed table. Now he would be able to obsess over the Internet coverage of the tragedy as well as the television news.

"He said he'd be by later this afternoon to visit," Gillian said. "He's helping to take care of his girlfriend, I take it she's not feeling well after all that she was through the past few days."

"She's not his girlfriend, Mom," Mark said. The pain was making him irritable. "James is gay, remember?"

His mom just raised her eyebrow at that. "I spoke to Michelle, too," she said. "She said she'd be by later, with Ben."

"Good." He took a couple of deep breaths. His little machine beeped, letting him know that he was finally entitled to another dollop of morphine. That helped a little. He looked up at his mother. "Why do these things always end with you talking to me in a hospital bed?"

"I was going to ask you the same thing, Mark," Gillian said, patting his leg through the thin sheet.

"Four people dead," the television blatted. "Scores of injuries, multiple arrests and millions of dollars in damage after Halloween riots tear through a small Illinois town that's becoming widely known by the nickname 'Bloody—"

Mark muted the television before he had to hear that stupid phrase again.

"Four dead," he said to his mother. "Who?" He knew she would know. Malovo's eyes in the sky no doubt had the whole thing recorded.

"You already know about Tom Peters and Benjamin Wolf," she said. "A man named Lou Witzky, a local building contractor, fell off a scissor lift platform while he was attempting to lynch Michelle at the water tower. Then there was a teenage boy named Teddy Johnson, who was out running around with a friend. The two boys thought it would be a good idea to prank their neighbor, a woman named Grace Franklin, by running around her house, knocking on her windows and doors, shouting out satanic-sounding slogans. Ms. Franklin panicked and fired her shotgun right through her front door, shooting Teddy and killing him instantly."

"Jesus," Mark said. "Not Bates? That guy actually survived?"

"Sheriff Bates is recovering in a specialized facility, under our supervision."

"I'm so relieved. What did your people do to him, anyway?"

"Nathanial Bates was an experiment in personality modification," Gillian said.

"*Clockwork Orange* shit."

"It was a little more sophisticated than that. We weren't just curbing unwanted behaviors. We used a combination of conditioning, surgery and drug therapies to actually construct a morally balanced persona."

"Worked like a charm, too."

Gillian shrugged. "Other individuals in the same trial have shown much more promising results, but the sheriff's underlying personality was unusually...tenacious. The break he suffered was quite severe. I'm not sure we'll ever be able to reintegrate him."

Mark somehow didn't feel too bad for the guy.

"What about Lizzy Stevens?" he said. "Did they find her body yet?"

"What's left of it," Gillian said. "But the police haven't released that information to the press yet. They're still trying to determine what the hell happened there."

"Have they arrested Roberta?"

"She's missing," Gillian said. "They found her car abandoned in a ditch a few miles from her house, but no trace of her. She couldn't have got very far on foot, so unless she has another accomplice, I'm sure they'll find her soon."

"What about the other..." Mark hesitated. He didn't know whether to call them "angels" or "witches," so he finally settled on: "...women?"

"Sally Wolf, Ellie Tarwater, and Gemma Gordon are all in police custody. Gemma's mother Joyce is one of our best lawyers, so I doubt her daughter will be in jail very long. It's also unclear what they could charge Ellie with. But Sally has admitted to not only shooting you, but also to killing her father. I'm sure she'll be going to prison for a long time."

Mark sighed. Despite the hot stabbing pain this sent through his rib cage, he felt more sadness than anger towards Sally.

"Couldn't you have done...something, before this got so out of control?"

"What could we have done, Mark? I know you think we have some kind of omnipotent power over this town, but we don't. We're still trying to understand the underlying forces at work. And you have to know that most of what happened was just due to ordinary human reactions to fear. We can't control that."

"Not yet," Mark said.

"If it's any consolation for you, this is going to be another very expensive weekend for my company, thanks to your friends. We'll have to replace the water tower."

"Not to mention the train wreck."

"Yes, well." Gillian gave a wry smile. "Your witches had nothing to do with that."

"They didn't?"

"Because fuel prices are so low, the ethanol plant has stepped up production in recent months. As a result, we've had to run the trains faster. But the necessary upgrades to the railroad tracks weren't in the budget until the next fiscal year. The derailment was the result of mechanical failure. The timing was just a spectacular coincidence."

"Well, at least they've got a handy scapegoat now," Mark said.

"Now you're thinking like one of our people," Gillian said. She looked down at her son. Gave him a long, serious consideration. "Speaking of that, have you given any thought to the offer we made you the last time we were in this position?"

"You mean how you want me to work for Malovo as a supernatural tour guide, or whatever?" said Mark.

"Three times now," Gillian said. "You've come in direct contact with the forces at work in this town. You probably have more of an understanding of these energy sources than the people on our dedicated Bakersfield team. Our people have researched these phenomena, extensively, but have never experienced them firsthand the way you have. I know they'd love to take you on as a consultant. You could make a real career out of this, Mark."

"I'm not working for Malovo," Mark said. "You may have sold your soul already, but I'm not prepared to do that."

"You're thirty-one years old, Mark. I know you enjoyed your little stint pretending to be a blacksmith, but that's over. What are you going to do now?"

"I don't know," Mark said. "Maybe I'll write another book."

"No offense, son, but you tried that. You have some talent, but I think you've proven that that's not an economically viable career path. You're an adult. A father. You need to find something that will give you and your family security. I know you've experienced terrible things in your life, but I'm giving you an opportunity here, to put those experiences to a good use."

"You mean work for a company that wants to do what Roberta Stevens did to this town, only on a global scale?" Mark shook his head. "She thought she could harness and control this 'energy source' too, you know. You're just as goddamn deluded as she was."

Gillian gave Mark a long, undecipherable look. He had no idea what was going on behind her eyes.

"I'm sorry you feel that way, Mark," she finally said. "I'll check in on you a little later."

She left Mark alone. For a few minutes, he just sat there stewing, but then something his mother had said came back to him, though almost certainly not in the way she'd intended.

She'd said he could put his terrible experiences to a good use

Mark swung the swiveling table over his lap and flipped open his computer. He opened up a blank Word document and started typing.

The Black Monkey, he typed. *By Mark Davies.*

He bit his lip, thoughtfully, and then typed: *Chapter One: The Gray Monkey.*

His morphine dispenser beeped, but he didn't hear it.

The first time I saw them bury the monkey, Mark typed. *I didn't know what it meant.*

CHAPTER 64

2:06 PM

Lana awoke again, listlessly. She lay on top of the sweaty sheets, drifting in and out as she'd done for hours. She had no energy at all. No will to rise. "First trimester lethargy," Chelle had called it. Then the stress and the fear and the running for their lives of the past few days on top of that. Lana had dozed restlessly through the night, through the morning, and now well into the afternoon. No dreams, but no real sense of having slept either. Just this sapping weariness and strange gaps in time. She glanced at the clock what felt like every few minutes, only to find that hours had passed.

All the windows in the house were open. The sky outside was hazy, the sunlight spilling through her bedroom window a dusky orange. After the deathly chill of the night before, the temperature had risen to an unseasonably warm mid-seventies. No breeze to speak of, either. The air was too still to dissipate the smoke of the train fire north of town. When Lana was a girl, they'd called warm, listless autumn days like this an "Indian Summer." God knows why. She doubted it was called that anymore. Just like how the kids at school didn't sit "Indian style" anymore, but "crisscross applesauce" instead.

Michelle was downstairs packing. Working, Lana was sure, with a detached efficiency. Filling boxes and taping them closed, stacking them by the door for the movers who would come tomorrow to pick them up. Michelle would not pause, as Lana was sure she herself would, to consider the reasons why they had to leave their home. Michelle would not allow herself the luxury of tears or anger.

Lana felt guilty for not helping, but even getting up to use the bathroom exhausted her. Michelle was understanding. She came upstairs every so often to check in on her. To talk, if Lana was awake enough to do so. Or just to touch her lightly or kiss her forehead if she didn't have the energy to speak.

Through the thin wall separating her room from Ben's, Lana heard the boy crying. Doing it quietly, so his mother downstairs wouldn't hear. In the last twenty-four hours, Ben had experienced his father getting shot and his mother almost getting hanged. And now he would have to move, to leave behind everything he knew. Again. It had been hard on Ben when they'd moved from Denver in the summer following his fourth grade year, and this would be even harder. This time he would have to leave his father and his cousin and his best friend Emily. Ben did not make friends easily, but the friendships he formed were intensely close. The boy had an almost limitless capacity to love. For the past few months, when he everyone he loved had been living close together, Ben had been happier than Lana had ever seen him. Now that uneasy happiness would be shattered.

Thinking of the injustice of this was enough to bring Lana to tears herself. She didn't have the strength to weep, though, and instead slipped into another fitful nap.

"Baby?" Chelle said sometime later, sitting on the edge of the bed and resting one hand lightly on Lana's hip.

"Huh, what?" she came to, startled by her wife's sudden presence in the room. It seemed that she hadn't been there just a moment before. The angle of the sunlight from her window had undergone another disorienting shift, too. Lana must have been out for a few hours that time.

"I'm going to take Ben to the hospital to see Mark," Michelle said. "I just wanted to let you know."

"Mark?" Lana said, still groggy and confused. It took her a second to remember exactly who Mark was. "How is Mark?"

"He sounded fine on the phone," Michelle gave the same bitter smile she often employed when talking about her ex. "A little doped up, but for him that was probably worth getting shot. We'll just be gone a couple hours."

The thought of being alone in the house filled Lana with a dull kind of dread, as if she might drown in the shallow waters of sleep if Michelle was not there to pull her out.

She sat up. "I want to go with you."

"You sure?"

"Yeah. I have to get out this bed sometime. Just let me get cleaned up a little, okay?"

"Okay, hon." Michelle gave her a quick kiss, and then frowned. "You should probably brush your teeth."

Lana grinned, covered her mouth. "That bad?"

"You've been asleep for eighteen hours, so yeah."

Lana chuckled as she swung her legs over the side of the bed. She just sat there for a moment until Michelle helped her get to her feet, then she walked unsteadily to the bathroom.

Once inside, she peeled off her tank-top and sweat pants. After a brief consideration of how long they'd been worn, she slid out of her panties as well. The bathroom had a full-length mirror and Lana caught a glimpse of her naked reflection.

Mmm, nice, she thought. *I do prefer a colored girl's skin.*

Lana wasn't sure where that thought had come from. It didn't exactly sound like her own voice in her head. Still, there was something undeniably novel and enticing about the sight of her own nude body. She paused for a moment to look at herself.

My my, look at them nice titties.

That *definitely* wasn't her voice. It didn't seem to be coming from her head, either, but from someplace lower. Inside her body. She wasn't scared, though. She still felt half-asleep and dreamy. She met her own brown eyes in the mirror, the lids heavy and drooping. Half-turned in the mirror so she could get a good look at herself all around, while that strange voice in the pit of her stomach voiced its appreciation.

Ain't you a pretty mama? it said. *I cannot wait.*

It was a woman's voice, familiar somehow, though Lana couldn't say where she might have heard it before. There was something very seductive about it. Lana ran her hands down the curves of her own body. Showing off. Enjoying the feel of her skin and touch of her hands and the gaze on her flesh that was not entirely her own. She cupped her left breast in her right hand, squeezing the nipple into stiffness. She moaned out loud, the sound in her throat echoed from down below by the voice of the other.

Mmm, yes, it said. *We is gonna have some fuuun.*

Lana slid her hand further down, over her belly. Here she found a strange hard lump under the skin, just below her navel. She pressed against it, and felt it move. There was something alive under there.

Still feeling no alarm, just a dream-like inevitability, Lana turned and stepped closer to the mirror. She looked down at her stomach in the reflection and saw, very distinctly, a handprint. Five little fingers, pressing through the skin, out from inside her abdomen. From inside her womb. The fingers wiggled slowly back and forth, waving at her. She felt it as a strange fluttering tickle, as if she'd swallowed a hummingbird.

Hey, Mama, the voice called. *Be seein' you real soon.*

Then the hand withdrew back inside her and a little face pressed against the pliant skin. Lana made out the nubby protuberance of a tiny nose. Just the hint of a brow and of a smiling mouth. The lips puckered as if blowing her a kiss from inside.

Lana turned from the reflection and looked down at her stomach directly, not through the glass. Strangely, she could not see the face when she looked at herself this way, but when she looked back in the mirror, it was clear as day.

On impulse, Lana reached over and turned off the overhead light. The room was now only lit with the soft golden glow of a nightlight plugged into the wall. When Lana looked at her belly in the mirror in the near-darkness, she saw two red points of light just above the bulge of the nose. Glowing eyes, shining through her skin. The eyes seemed to smile with the lips, wicked and knowing.

Lana finally felt a sense of dread at this sight. A rising alarm. An awareness that she was not asleep and that this was no dream. There was something alive inside her. It was not her unborn child. It was something that had swallowed her child's unformed soul.

She cried out and stepped back from the mirror. She pressed her hand over her belly, to remove the awful visage from her sight or to try to smother it, she didn't know which. She felt the mouth inside her stomach gumming at her hand through her skin.

If it had teeth, it would bite me, she thought with horror. *If it had teeth, it would just chew its way out.*

I wouldn't do no such thing, Mama, the thing inside her countered. *I ain't even done cookin' in here yet.*

Then Lana felt the thing reach up from the pit of her gut and grab a cord within her throat. The thing inside her tugged the cord, like ringing a bell or turning off a chain-pull lamp. Lana receded to the back of her head. She could still look out through her eyes and see what they were seeing, but her body was no longer hers to control.

Adaleen Bell stepped up into the mama-lady's head. She reached over and flipped on the electric lights so she could see what kind of fancy privy these folks kept. Everything was so *shiny*. Gleaming chrome and white porcelain. Even the commode was clean and shining white. Nothing like the dark stinking outhouses of her day, which had been just wooden seats over a shithole in the ground. Damn if *some* things didn't change for the better.

Curiously, she started pulling open cabinets to see what was in inside. She couldn't stay out for long. Not yet. Her soul was still too weak to drive this body for more than a few minutes at a time. But she would grow stronger. She had months and months to go. Then, she'd be born into a fresh new body. Just a little baby girl. A pure new life, with years and years ahead of her.

She found little orange bottles with pills inside. Medicines, she supposed, though the labels seemed almost to be written in some foreign language. She knew that if she thought hard enough, she'd find within the mama-lady's mind what these strange things were used for. Like the *toothbrushes* and *toothpaste* in its strange squishy tube. In her day she'd just used a cloth with some saltwater and little pick. Chewed spearmint leaves to freshen up her breath. Adaleen snarled in the mirror and saw that mama-lady's teeth that were as white and straight as a picket fence, while Adaleen had spent the last half of her long life without a tooth in her head.

My my, what wonders. What else you got up in here?

Adaleen felt her grip loosening just a bit, but she was so curious. The cabinets were crammed with marvels.

What are these little pink things? Razors? What you need razors for?

The answer came slowly, and Adaleen shook mama-lady's head in wonder.

Cut the hairs off your legs and under your arms and up around your pussy too? So you look like a little girl? Good Lord. There was a box full of what looked like little wrapped-up cigars. *What're these for? Tamp-Ons?* Adaleen laughed out loud when she found the answer. *Old rags ain't good enough no more?*

She pulled open a drawer and found the mama-lady's face-paints. Such an array! Café au lait foundation and mascaras and liners and shadows. How'd this bitch even decide which face to put on in the morning with so many to choose from? Adaleen picked up a tube of something that said "Tawny Port Lipstick" on the side. Experimentally she smeared some on her lips.

Damn if that ain't pretty.

Curiously, Adaleen took a bite from the stick. It tasted like clean dirt, or clay. Enticing, in a way. She took another bite and grinned into the mirror. The chunks of burgundy goop stuck in the mama-lady's teeth made her want to laugh.

There was a knock on the door and Adaleen gave a guilty start before she remembered that she was inside the mama-lady's skin. That other bulldagger gal wouldn't know the difference no-how.

"Lana?" Michelle called through the door. "You almost ready?"

"Just gettin' gussied up," Adaleen called with Lana's voice. She liked how it sounded, low and smooth in the throat. She looked into the mirror and saw mama-lady's eyes go wide with fear in the reflection. Adaleen grinned to reassure her, but her lips and teeth and tongue were smeared with the greasy wine-red color. That was funny as hell. Cracked her ass up.

"That's right," she called, a delighted cackling laugh rising up from inside. "I'm gettin' good and gussied in here!"

Adaleen laughed and laughed. Lord, did she love being in this sweet old world.

ABOUT THE AUTHOR

CHRISTIAN H. SMITH is a novelist and screenwriter living in the dark, corn-fed heart of the Midwest. *The Black Monkey* and *Bloody Bloody Bakersfield* are the first two installments in the future cult classic *Bloody Bakersfield* series. Check out christianhsmith.com for more info!

Christian is also co-writer of the upcoming feature-length horror film, *Witch Child*. http://witchchildmovie.com/

PERMUTED PRESS

needs **you** to help

SPREAD (THE) INFECTION

FOLLOW US!

f | Facebook.com/PermutedPress

🐦 | Twitter.com/PermutedPress

REVIEW US!

Wherever you buy our book, they can be reviewed! We want to know what you like!

GET INFECTED!

Sign up for our mailing list at PermutedPress.com

PERMUTED PRESS

THE ULTIMATE PREPPER'S ADVENTURE.
THE JOURNEY BEGINS HERE!

EAN 9781682611654 $9.99   EAN 9781618687371 $9.99   EAN 9781618687395 $9.99

The long-predicted Coronal Mass Ejection has finally hit the Earth, virtually destroying civilization. Nathan Owens has been prepping for a disaster like this for years, but now he's a thousand miles away from his family and his refuge. He'll have to employ all his hard-won survivalist skills to save his current community, before he begins his long journey through doomsday to get back home.

THE MORNINGSTAR STRAIN HAS BEEN LET LOOSE—IS THERE ANY WAY TO STOP IT?

An industrial accident unleashes some of the Morningstar Strain. The

EAN 9781618686497 $16.00

doctor who discovered the strain and her assistant will have to fight their way through Sprinters and Shamblers to save themselves, the vaccine, and the base. Then they discover that it wasn't an accident at all—somebody inside the facility did it on purpose. The war with the RSA and the infected is far from over.

This is the fourth book in Z.A. Recht's The Morningstar Strain series, written by Brad Munson.

PERMUTED
PRESS

WE CAN'T GUARANTEE THIS GUIDE WILL SAVE YOUR LIFE. BUT WE CAN GUARANTEE IT WILL KEEP YOU SMILING WHILE THE LIVING DEAD ARE CHOWING DOWN ON YOU.

EAN 9781618686695 $9.99

This is the only tool you need to survive the zombie apocalypse.

OK, that's not really true. But when the SHTF, you're going to want a survival guide that's not just geared toward day-to-day survival. You'll need one that addresses the essential skills for true nourishment of the human spirit. Living through the end of the world isn't worth a damn unless you can enjoy yourself in any way you want. (Except, of course, for anything having to do with abuse. We could never condone such things. At least the publisher's lawyers say we can't.)

PERMUTED
PRESS

www.ingramcontent.com/pod-product-compliance
Lightning Source LLC
Chambersburg PA
CBHW051231260626
47162CB00002B/375